HONESTLY, I LIED

Honestly, I LIED

A Novel

CHRISTOPHER WOLLENBERG

LUMINARE PRESS

WWW.LUMINAREPRESS.COM

Honestly, I Lied: A Novel
Copyright © 2021 by Christopher Wollenberg

This is a work of fiction. Unless otherwise indicated, all characters are products of the author's imagination. Any resemblance to any person living or dead is purely coincidental. But, hey, this is a novel, and it's within the realm of possibility that things that the author experienced or heard about could have snuck into the work. Any reference to real people in a historical context is meant to be an accurate representation of their situation.

Printed in the United States of America

Luminare Press
442 Charnelton St.
Eugene, OR 97401
www.luminarepress.com

LCCN: 2021916801
ISBN: 978-1-64388-803-3

For my parents, who believed that suitable conversation with their five children at the dinner table every evening should touch on politics, history, and current events.

And: For my wife, Gail, whose encouragement and persistence means everything.

CHAPTER 1

Boom!

Everything was really fuzzy right after it happened, and time certainly hasn't made things much clearer, but I will tell you this: despite what they show in countless movies, when someone gets hit flush in the face, things break, the brain goes blank, and that person does not know what the heck happened. So, when I told my friends, the assistant principal, the school security chief, the EMTS, the doctors, my parents, and who knows who else, that I didn't know who hit me, I really DID NOT KNOW who hit me. I do remember what led up to it, so I guess the list of suspects was pretty small, but I actually did not see the guy who hit me. I like to think that I would have ducked had I seen what was coming.

I was in the stairwell on the way upstairs to math class. For some reason, I had traveled a different route from English class, maybe talking to/following some girl somewhere along the way? Or at least thinking I might get to talk to some girl. I don't know. Anyway, I ended up going up this stairwell that I usually don't use. Good news for Donnie, really, really bad news for my face, especially my left cheekbone and the bone around my eye, orbital socket, as the doctors later called it. As I started up to the landing, I heard Walter and his buddies teasing Donnie. Now, I don't why Donnie was in that stairwell either; I always thought that he was usually supervised by one of the special education aides or something. I know that Down syndrome students come in all flavors, and I guess some of them can find their way around pretty well. I always thought that Donnie was pretty cool, but he did tend to get lost easily. When I first met him in a Little League program where they paired us "normal" kids with special needs kids, I had to lead him to first base and then second, and so on, after he hit the ball. Maybe after a few years in the high school, he learned his way around. Maybe he was just off course, like me, that day.

"Downie, downie. What's up Donnie downie?" One of Walter's bunch apparently thought he was hilarious. The rest seemed to agree.

"Uh. Um. I don't know. I'm going down, not up." More laughter from the bunch.

"What's up with the backpack, downie? Is that a genuine Spiderman accessory?" More laughter. "Lemme see it. Any good food in there?"

At which point I reached the landing and inserted my nose into the discussion, literally. I probably said something like, "Hey, knock it off, guys. Leave Donnie alone." Whatever I said, they were not the correct magic words. Maybe I forgot to say "please." I remember a really hard smack against my face and saw the proverbial stars before I crumpled to the floor. Blazing pain shot through my head. It felt like my face had exploded, imploded, really. All things considered, I was pretty lucky; I dropped straight to the landing rather than back down the stairs.

The other really good thing was the arrival of Craterface. I suspect he saw who hit me, but he has always claimed he was just coming up the stairs when he heard the commotion and only saw me dropping down and hearing Donnie screech. I never saw Crate myself; I learned later that he showed up, which was a very good thing for me and also for Donnie.

I heard Crate yell something, probably the same thing I said when I first got to the landing. Well, maybe a bit less polite, along the lines of "Knock it off you mother--." Like I said, it's all fuzzy.

"Don't hit him, too; he's already ugly," laughed Walter.

Crate's response was, "Yeah, won't make much difference to me." Crate has been called about every insult possible to someone with severe acne and the residual scarring, so by now he pretty much ignores it. "I just consider the source," is his usual explanation for not getting upset. Besides, he probably was more interested in getting me help and getting Donnie to stop crying than worrying about a couple punks. A bunch of other students came piling into the stairwell, so Walter and company may have figured that getting lost would be a good tactic at that point.

My face was screaming, and there was blood flowing out of my nose as well as filling my mouth. Between the swelling left eye and the pain, I couldn't see much of anything, so I just sat there and gagged and spit blood and contemplated what just happened. Not much to think about, I decided. Noise. Boom. Down. Floor. I could feel a knot starting to swell on the back of my head also. I must have slammed into the wall or the floor when I went down. There seemed to be all kinds of noise. My ears ringing, kids shouting, and Donnie wailing with a weird, high sound. I could hear a girl's voice taking charge.

"Don't move him. He may have neck or head trauma. Someone go get help. Actually, you, in the red shirt, you go downstairs and find a teacher or security. Tell them there's a student up here who's just fallen down the stairs and may have hit his head or broken his neck or something."

What was she, the nurse? Maybe she was the only student who actually paid attention in first aid part of the phys ed/health class the rest of us all sat/slept through? Anyway, I'm glad she didn't just copy the answers for the test like almost everyone else seemed to. She knew what to do. Of course, I hadn't fallen down stairs and did not have a broken neck, but she jumped to conclusions on the side of safety. I guess Crate or someone walked Donnie away because I didn't hear him screeching after a while. I was choking on blood running into the back of my mouth, and the pain kept exploding in waves; I felt like I was going to puke.

While I sat there, a number of noisy people drifted in and out of my awareness. The girl who first took charge, a security aide, the school nurse, and then another aide all had confusing conversations around my dazed being. Eventually it was decided that I needed careful transportation to the hospital. Still going on the theory that I had fallen downstairs, no doubt, and there was the obvious injury to my head. I guess that Walter's bunch didn't stick around to clarify what happened for the reports that security and the nurse would have to write. I pretty much just sat there and tried to enjoy the blurry action swirling around me while the pain in my head and face continued to intensify.

They transported me in style: backboard, neck brace, and tied down on a gurney. If I had been more alert, I'm sure the trip down the stairs would have been a minor thrill. As it was, I had to settle for the trip in the ambulance with all the attendant nausea, as I rocked and swayed as it made its way to the emergency room. You get your excitement where you can, if you can't make it to an amusement park, I guess.

On the subject of medical thrill rides, if someone offers you a chance to take an MRI ride, find out if there are other rides available. And if you do have to take the ride, try to do it while you're in a fog, because it is truly a bizarre experience. They put you on this sliding tray and shove you in a tube and you can't move. There's a lot of banging, and it seems to take forever. And then you come out, and it's strangely quiet for a moment until the normal sounds kick in. I think a CT scan is marginally better, but again, if there are other rides available...

At some point at the hospital it came out that I had in fact been punched and not simply managed to fall up/down the stairs. I think one of the EMTs with the ambulance crew had talked to me, and I must have said something. This seemed to put the doctors in quite a position. On the one hand, they really were anxious to start a plan to fix my caved in cheek bone and eye socket and relieve any pressure on my left eye. On the other hand, the head of school security and an assistant principal were pretty interested in finding out what happened.

My brain was really, really foggy; in addition to what would be diagnosed as a concussion, I had been given some minor pain killer, so I was not exactly a useful witness. Since I was a freshman and had thus far stayed under their radar, they had no way of knowing how useful I would be in getting to the bottom of this. They did, however, think they had a pretty good handle on me: they knew my brother, Francis Xavier Jonasz, who liked to go by the nom de guerre, "Frankie X." When he had been at the school, he was apparently not an ideal citizen, at least from the point of view of those whose job it was to maintain some level of order. I had heard many artfully embellished stories from my big brother when he was in the high school and I was in elementary and then middle school, so I should not have been surprised when I found myself on the receiving end of long hard looks and occasional comments from my teachers the first few weeks of school.

"Henryk Jonasz? Is Francis Jonasz your big brother?" would be the polite version of the standard question those first few months. Others seemed to be less neutral: "Any relation to Francis Jonasz?" And, decidedly not neutral: "Oh jeez. Do we have another Frankie X on our hands?" Mr. Slate, the assistant principal, was sent to talk to me at the hospital. He had previously not had occasion to talk with me, and to say the least, our first meeting was a bit strained even accounting for the haze induced by my current medical condition. My brother and he were old adversaries, and I had heard earfuls about Mr. Titus Slate for several years. The unfortunate fat distribution on his obese body had naturally led to students modifying his first name to reflect his obvious upper chest fat concentrations. His last name fitted him well; he had a reputation for being as hard as stone when it came to dealing with teenagers and their parents.

Tits, I mean, Mr. Slate, didn't waste time when he came into the examining room where they were holding me while trying to schedule surgery. "Jonasz? Henryk Jonasz? Frankie X didn't even have the courtesy to warn me about a little brother. Who hit you and why? Don't you have a black belt in something or other, like your brother? How did this happen?"

Christopher Wollenberg

I'm fine, sir, and thanks for asking. As soon as they fix my caved in face and I get over the headaches, I'm sure I'll be able to return to the school and be a responsible citizen. Not being my brother, yet, anyway, I kept those thoughts to myself. "Uh. Yes. Um?" It was almost impossible to talk, and I couldn't think of anything useful to say. So I only admitted to being Henryk Jonasz. Name, rank, and serial number routine.

Mr. Wright, the head security guy from the school, had a better bedside manner, although I never doubted that his aim was to get to the bottom of things if at all possible. "How do you feel, son? That's a nasty bang you got there. Any way you could tell us what happened?"

I really couldn't. Couldn't remember and couldn't talk anyway, so I tried to shake my head. Mistake; new bolts of pain flashed through my head despite the medication.

"Let's start with the basics, okay? Just nod your head a little bit, if you can. Yes or no will do it. Did you fall down the stairs?" He brought his face down to me, but still seemed to be barely talking above a whisper. He had said yes/no answers, but what if I wanted to ask, or get more information. I shrugged my shoulders. At least that didn't hurt. "You don't know, or you don't understand the question?" I didn't move. "Oh. Two questions, not exactly fair. Okay. We found you on the landing of the stairwell. If you think you fell down from the stairs leading to the landing, nod yes." That was better. I nodded no. I did remember that I was on the way up, and I did remember being punched, just not who did it. "Okay, this is progress. The doctors don't think there's any other damage except for your face, and there's a big bump on the back of your head where it hit the floor. Although I guess they'll wait till they read the scan results just to be sure. The girl who first called for help thought you had fallen downstairs. I ..."

Mr. Slate cut him off. "Come on, Wright, quit playing twenty questions with this guy. I bet it was a fight. Who hit you, son? Did you get any licks in?" I liked twenty questions better. At least they always have a yes/no answer. I shrugged.

"Let me try again, Mr. Slate." Mr. Wright's voice was really level, like he was trying very hard not to show any emotion. "Henryk, did someone hit you?" I nodded my head yes.

"Told you so." chortled Mr. Slate. "Just like his brother, only not as good a fighter. Been here what, less than two months, and already mixing it up with someone over something."

I think Mr. Wright felt like he had to follow the leader, even if he was an idiot. "Henryk, did you get in a fight with someone in the stairwell?"

I nodded no.

Mr. Slate was persistent, I'll give him that. Wrong. Wrong about my brother; wrong about me. But, persistent. He wasn't going to let go of his idea. "Yeah. Right. Just like your brother. Always innocent." He clapped his hands and smiled. "You know what I bet. I bet this was some sort of gang initiation thing. You know, just sucker punch someone. If you knock him out with one shot, you're in. Punch someone with brass knuckles, something like that. Is that what happened, Jonasz?"

What kind of question was that? How do I answer that yes/no? Mr. Wright stepped in. "Henryk, did someone hit you with a weapon of some kind? A club or something." I didn't think so, although you couldn't tell it by the way my face hurt. I remembered seeing the fist coming at my face at the last split second. I nodded no. "Do you know the name of the person who hit you?" No. "If I showed you some photos from our student identification file, do you think you could pick him out?" Again, no.

Mr. Slate was getting really irritated by all this. "Come on, now, Jonasz. I can see you might not know the name of someone, but why can't you pick out his photo? Every student had his photo taken for the id cards, and we have them all on a disk. It shouldn't be that hard to find this sucker." My face really hurt, my head hurt, I couldn't see out of my left eye, and I felt like throwing up. I knew it was one of Walter's buddies, but not him; I was looking at him when I started yelling about Donnie, so I didn't see who was swinging at me. I probably wouldn't have recognized any of that crowd anyway.

Mr. Wright tried a new tack. "Listen, Henryk, the kids I talked to all said there was a bunch of people on the stairwell during that class change. I know Donnie, Donald, was there. His teacher said someone brought him to class crying about his friend getting hurt. I think you are his friend, but he doesn't seem to be able to tell me what he saw."

Mr. Slate jumped in again, "Well, duh, Mr. Wright. Donnie is a retard. He's not going to be much of a witness. Who else might have been on that landing?" I was beginning to think that Walter and his bunch were the least of Donnie's worries. I thought of a much more pertinent question but couldn't ask it, "Did your people get any other names? Like the girl who tried to help me?" That would be useful, speaking on a personal level, of course.

Mr. Wright was really getting into cop-mode now. I think he also realized that neither Donnie nor I would benefit a lot from associating with Mr. Slate. "We have some names, Mr. Slate, but so far no eye witnesses to what happened. I don't think this is getting us anywhere right now. I suggest we let young Henryk here get some rest before the doctors take their shot at him." Say what? I didn't know what the doctors planned, but I didn't like the way Mr. Wright put it. "You just take it easy, Henryk. I think your folks are here. I'll check back with you in a day or so. Maybe something will turn up." I nodded yes and drifted off.

As they left, I could hear Mr. Slate hammering on Mr. Wright. "I'm telling you, Wright, this Jonasz kid may be bad news. I think he's covering for something. I didn't want to give away the farm in there, but it wouldn't surprise me if it turned out that this was some kind of drug deal gone bad. I never caught his brother, but I think they are both slickee boys. This one's not gonna get by me. I got four years to get the goods on him. If the security cameras in the stairwell worked, we'd have him nailed to the wall already. We'd know what kind of crap he was pulling, and I wouldn't have had to listen to all your Freddie Feelgood games."

Yep. Just like the insurance company ad says, I'm in good hands. With that administrator looking after me, I would be about as safe as a man wearing a hamburger suit at a dog show.

So, the doctors were going to take a shot at me? Just how bad off was I? It didn't take long to get an idea. My parents walked in together, and the look on their faces told me all I needed to know. I was a mess. I certainly had not read my medical condition off the faces of the last two people I had been talking to. I guess Mr. Wright and Mr. Slate were either used to seeing busted faces like mine, or too professional to let it show. Or, in the case of Slate, didn't care.

"Henryk!" My mother didn't waste time getting to the tears. My dad held back a bit, but from my good eye, I could see that he was tearing up also. They each grabbed one of my hands and just stood there. They didn't know what to say. I couldn't say anything. We were rescued by the doctor. He was all business. He needed permission to treat me, although he said something about starting anyway in a few minutes if no parents had shown up.

My dad said something about "Did I just see Slate walking down the hall? Was he here? Doctor, what's going on? My son's obviously seriously injured and that clown is in here before my wife and me?" My dad and Mr. Slate went back a ways. "Let's make this perfectly clear: no one talks to my son except his family and any visitors we authorize." The doctor stammered about not being aware of the visit but agreed that from now on, no one would talk with me unless authorized by the Jonasz family. But, on to more important things: saving my eye and fixing my face, dealing with my head. I have no idea of the details of the medical conversation, but soon I was being lifted onto another gurney and sailing down the halls towards a room. Another medical thrill ride lost in the fog of medication and confusion.

CHAPTER 2

Frankie the Avenger

The day after I didn't fall up the stairs, I was waking up in a hospital room. My parents were both there just sitting. My face seemed to have a lot of stuff taped to it, and there was an IV needle in the back of my left hand. "So, how do you feel? Are you okay? Any pain?" My mother looked really, really tired, but she wasn't crying. I guess this meant that I would live. She held my right hand, a bit too tightly. She's fairly tall and strong, and has reddish-brown hair, auburn, I think they call it. She always looked to me like she had stepped out of a travel brochure for Ireland, where her parents came from. But that morning no one would have chosen her to represent anything other than an exhausted, scared mother. Even her blue eyes looked dull. Her grip, though, was for real.

I didn't think I could talk, my whole face seemed swollen, and I still felt fuzzy, either from having my head rattled or the medication, but I tried. "Uh."

"Don't try to talk, son," my dad whispered from somewhere behind my mom. "Just take it easy. You really got a hard crack in the face. The doctors think you'll be as good as new in a bit, but for now, you need to chill. They kept you here because you got a severe concussion along with the broken stuff in your face. I think they're going to be able to operate later today."

"Uh." I wish I could have contributed something more intelligent to the conversation, but nothing seemed to be coming out. "Uh. I..." I moved my head in the direction of their voices. Not a good idea. That hurt. Headache and pain radiating from the left side of my face across to the other side.

"Nurse!" My mother was going into full attack-mom mode; I could tell by the tone in the one word. "Tomás, see if you can find the nurse. Henryk, you just stay still. I can tell you're in pain, and that's not necessary." I could probably make a fortune renting my mom out to hospital patients. If she's got your back, she has got your back, and you have no worries.

An hour later, happily medicated, I was more or less sitting up and taking in the world around me. Semi-private room, curtain shielding me from the bed next to me. A window with a view of a parking garage, lots of gadgets on the wall by the bed, the IV tube dangling from a support attached to the bed. My parents had stepped out for coffee or something.

"Say, champ. What's up?" Frankie charged in, blond dreadlocks bouncing. He nearly fell onto the bed in his rush to get to me. He has played around with body building; he could bench his weight in eighth grade and had only gotten bigger and stronger since then. His huge crushing form jolted me out of dozing. He seemed to have inherited his size from our mother's side of the family. My dad had a small frame and always seemed to blend into the world around him. Pretty much a description of me: light frame, curly black hair, still short. Like our mom, you couldn't miss Frankie. "You look like you hit a truck. Or the other way around." He probably learned his bedside manner from Mr. Slate. "Mom and Dad thought you wouldn't mind a visitor. Actually, I didn't give them much choice. Had classes and work all day yesterday and didn't hear about this until late last night. I came over this morning as soon as I finished my class." There was a time when he would have used any excuse to miss a class, so I guess this was a sign of something. Probably a good looking girl in the class, but maybe he actually wanted the class. Amazing what happens when you pay for stuff on your own. Ever since our dad told him he had to pay half his tuition at the community college, he started getting serious about the coursework. I had visited him in the hospital on more than one occasion, at least one of them when he actually had hit a truck, riding a friend's motorcycle, illegally, of course, so he did have an idea of what I might be feeling.

"I'm okay. I guess." My voice sounded slightly far away, like I was speaking into a hose that wrapped around the room and came back to my ear. I couldn't see out of my left eye, but that was to be expected. "The doctor came in this morning and said, 'Hmmm.' When I asked him what that meant, he said it meant that I looked pretty good and might be leaving pretty soon."

"Mom or Dad been in yet this morning?"

"I think so. What day is it? I think they stayed all night and just stepped out. They're probably tired."

"They'll be back soon, I'm sure." He studied my face, "It looks like the doctors are going to have to get in there and put stuff back where it belongs. Amazing colors, though." He had had some experience in this caved-in face business, so I appreciated his honest assessment. Frankie looked at me sort of sideways. "You know, I don't see you all the sudden turning into big-time fighter. How did you get your face in front of someone's fist?" He had a quizzical smile on his face, but he was not laughing at me, although I half expected him to. He might have been my hero when I was younger and dumber, but he never had gotten me interested in whatever martial art he was into. I didn't care for karate, Tae kwon do, kickboxing, and the rest of his list. I think he had tried about everything at one time or another, and contrary to what Mr. Slate thought, he really didn't have a black belt in anything. A few black eyes, maybe, but no official documentation of the ability to kick the stuffing out of someone other than several suspensions for fighting.

Unlike the other day, I had a pretty good idea of what happened, but I didn't necessarily want the world to know, especially the school or my parents. "You know how Dad was always going off on you about having a 'white knight syndrome'? You know, how you got into fights because you were fighting someone else's battle, or at least you claimed you were?" That sounded mean, "Thought you were, at the time. I mean." Sometimes he really was fighting on the side of good, but other times I think he was just enjoying the action at the moment and then tried to shape the story to look like he was saving someone from something. "Well, I guess I sort of did that myself. Walter Anderson and his bunch were hassling Donnie about being Down syndrome and all that, and I guess I said something about it to them.

Next thing I know is I'm on the floor and all these people are shouting and stuff. I told Slate and Wright and Mom and Dad that I had no idea what happened, but I think that's about the size of it."

Frankie pulled up a chair and sat down next to me. "Whoa, buddy. That's some serious stuff. You going all hero on me." He wasn't smiling at all. "You know who sucker punched you?"

"Honestly, no idea. One minute I was telling those idiots to knock it off and leave Donnie alone. Then, boom, and out go the lights. I don't know how you can actually do all that martial arts stuff on purpose, much less get into real fights with bare knuckles and no rules. This hurts!"

"I've pretty much knocked off that stuff, but I'm thinking now might be a good idea to pay a little visit to Walter and kick some—"

"No!" I cut him off. "I don't know who hit me. Couldn't have been Walter, I could see him when I was talking, and I did not see the shot to my face coming at me. I don't need you to go to jail for something like this. Mom and Dad don't need it either."

"Don't need what?" Dad appeared behind Frankie.

"Um. Don't need any problems from this incident." Frankie had spent a considerable portion of his life trying to keep Mom and Dad from getting too involved in his somewhat nefarious activities. So naturally, this was bait for Dad.

"And what might that mean? Francis, I thought we had an agreement. You were going to grow up and stay out of trouble, and I was going to grow old without having to worry about bailing you out or attending your funeral." Essentially, that was the agreement. Frankie could still live at our house as long as he worked and attended the community college. "So, how could this incident, as you call it, lead to more problems?"

Frankie didn't want to say anything. Neither did I. Mom came over and patted my arm. "How's it going sweetie? Are they giving you the pain medication? She looked like she was trying to avoid looking at my face, the left side, anyway." Then she did look, examined it really. "I think the swelling has gone down some. Quite colorful, though."

Dad may not have been a detective, or anything close, but he came across to Frankie and me like he was the ace of the department. "This incident. Just exactly what happened, Henryk? I have gotten some, shall we say, divergent stories from various people I talked to. That Mr. Slate went off on several tangents, all erroneous, I hope. But Mr. Wright seemed to think you somehow tangled with someone over something. Terry hasn't said anything, so I don't know what the kids at school think happened." I think Dad was seeing this as the start of another four years of parental hell as I made my combative way through high school. Never mind that I never got in trouble in middle school. Maybe he thought I was a late bloomer. Frankie started out in seventh grade, but maybe I'm a slow starter and took all the way to ninth grade to figure out how to cause him heartache. Not the case, but how to tell him that?

Mom was staring at me the way she stared at teachers and nurses and doctors who didn't obey her immediately. Great, they both thought I was Frankie Two. "Like I told, or tried to tell Slate and Wright, I don't know who hit me. And I did not mean to tangle with Walter's bunch. I didn't start any fight with anyone. I yelled at them about picking on Donnie and got sucker punched. You remember Donnie, right? He's the kid with Down syndrome that I helped way back in Little League when he was playing in the Challenger Division. He's at the school in special ed, and I see him in the halls once in a while."

Dad wasn't quitting. "No one shoved you down the stairs? You didn't try to punch anyone? You're not involved in any kind of dealings with Walter?" I guess Slate had given him a whole range of possibilities to consider, although I had no reason to think that Slate knew about Walter being in the stairwell. Dad probably guessed Walter because he had been the scourge of the neighborhood for years, starting in elementary school.

"No sir. I was going upstairs, said something to Walter's bunch, got hit, hit the floor, and here I am."

Dad turned to Frankie, who was trying to remain invisible. "So, Francis, let me guess. It has occurred to you that what Walter needs is an old-fashioned butt kicking. And it has further developed that the best person to administer this is you. Never mind that his father is a crazy neo-Nazi with a house full of guns and a bad attitude. Never mind that if you assault a minor like Walter, you will end up in jail."

Sometimes I think Frankie is just hard-wired for arguing. "Boy, Dad, you got that right. Walter should be allowed to run around causing all kinds of mayhem because his father's another hazard to society, and we've all got to roll over and back off so we don't hurt their feelings. We're going to run scared because that's the easy way out? Bernard is not the only guy in the neighborhood who owns guns, you know." I don't think Frankie actually ever won an argument in his life, at least not based on logic. And the bit about guns was scary. Frankie did own a couple handguns and practiced at a firing range fairly regularly. Mom and Dad were ready to kick him out when he brought the first one home, but he somehow persuaded them that he could control them. They are kept locked in a gun safe bolted to the floor, and each one has a trigger lock installed in addition. Also, he keeps the ammo in a separate location also in a locked and bolted gun safe. No one is going to break into the house, steal them, and go shoot up the world. With these precautions, no one in the house was under the illusion that we could grab a gun and start fending off invaders. Still, he didn't need to remind everyone that he also has guns.

I thought Dad would explode, but I guess years of crazy arguments with Frankie had taught him the value of faking calm just when the opposite would be expected. "Well, son, you've got a point. Several good points, actually. I'm not suggesting that we all 'roll over' for thugs. And I don't think anyone is 'running scared.' Running smart would be more like it. I agree that it would be wonderful if that whole family turned around, but I don't think it would be particularly helpful for you to attempt to effect a conversion using fists. Or guns."

Mom and I waited for the next round, expecting some serious fireworks, but Frankie just shrugged. "I will just say this. If Slate and Wright come to the conclusion that Walter and his bunch are involved in this, they're going to try to nail someone in that crew. And Walter's guys are going to go after young hero here if they think he ratted them out. So, here's the choice, I poke around and see if I can 'persuade' these punks to forget about that, or you let the school make a total mess of it and have that bunch mad at Henryk for the next four years or until they get arrested and carted off to juvy." I hadn't thought about that angle. I guess Frankie's had a lot of experience in this "who hit who and who's been talking" routine. "Dad, there's a saying that goes like this: 'Snitches get stitches.' Henryk's already getting stitches, and I don't think he did anything wrong. Actually, he did something right, trying to protect Donnie, but it turned out bad; that old thing about no good deed goes unpunished. You push this too far, and things could get even worse."

I think I was watching history being made. Somehow, Frankie was making sense in a sad sort of way, and winning the argument while losing it at the same time. Dad seemed to be thinking about all this.

Mom got that look again. "Well, what we're all saying is nobody does anything? Certainly, Francis, you are not, I repeat, NOT, going to 'poke around' and try to settle Walter's hash. Dad's right, you could go to jail, assuming Bernard doesn't shoot you somewhere along the line. Cat's out of the bag with Henryk and Mr. Slate and Mr. Wright, though. They are probably going to chase down Walter and at least question him, and I can see how that could lead to the problems Francis is talking about."

Actually, I don't think I had ever given a real statement to the school people about what I thought happened, just nods and stuff, so maybe if I kept my mouth shut, this would all die down. And I really, really did not know exactly who hit me. And, other than Walter and Donnie, I did not know any of the other people on the landing. I did want to get to know the girl who helped me, though.

A doctor came in and broke up the war council. He chased everyone out, even my mother, and started an examination. He put an armful of x-rays, scans, or whatever up on a viewing screen above the bed and looked back and forth between my face and these. Of course he said, "Hmmm," a lot. Universal doctor-speak so the patient knows that his case is being taken seriously. "Lot of loose parts in here, pal." Well, that was comforting. When he pried open my swollen left eye, that was not comforting, either. He shined a light in it. Added, "Hmmm," for good measure. "Looks like your eye is okay. Swelling's gone down enough. I think we ought to go in there and undo the damage. Did you say you went a quick round with Ali, or was it Tyson?" "Both. Two for one special. Not available every day. You have to get lucky."

He laughed. "Okay, definitely ready for surgery. You've still got your wits. If we keep you here too long, your brain'll turn to mush. We'll fix this up and get you out of here as soon as possible, pal. I'm going to get your parents and tell them what's up. You just rest here and think up good stories to tell the chicks at school."

I wasn't in on the conversation between my parents and the doctor, but I'm sure he got the full treatment from them. Attack-mom interrogation about the procedure and pepper-shot questions from my father. I guess the doctor and his reasoning survived because a little later I was wheeled off in a fog of sedatives, and I got yet another thrill ride, this time to surgery so they could rearrange my facial bones, presumably back to the way they were supposed to be. I'm sure it was an interesting procedure, but I missed all of it.

CHAPTER 3

Investigation

The next morning I woke up with a headache and the IV still poking out of my left hand. Mom and Dad were sitting there. So was Terry. I guess Frankie was off at work or class or figuring out how to avenge my assault. It didn't take long for me to start worrying about Terry. He's my cousin, the only child of my mother's drug-addled alcoholic screwball sister in Boston. Terry came to live with us after it became clear that his mom was doing more harm than good, and he was really losing out on life. I think she was going back into rehab again, and since the other times had always meant that Terry stayed with one of her friends for thirty or so days, maybe this time she would stay longer, and he wouldn't need to bounce around with these "friends." He was still in ninth grade even though he was sixteen. Art was his "thing," but he was smart enough to do great in all his subjects if he wanted to. If I had lived the life he had lived, I doubt that I would have made it to ninth grade at all. So far, I think that he was hanging in okay at our high school, but it was still pretty early in the year. We hadn't gotten any report cards yet, and I hadn't heard any discussion about his grades from my folks, who could be counted on to fuss about school with little or no provocation. Not that they would intentionally let me hear a conversation about someone else's business, but I would have picked up on any school problems. I think the plan was for Terry to see a psychologist now that he was living with us, but there didn't seem to be any real pressure to find one. It's not like he showed up at our door in some angry drug-crazed state. Outwardly, he seemed like a normal dude. To my knowledge he didn't use anything but his music and his crazy drawings and paintings to relieve the strain of his life; no drugs, not even cigarettes.

"Whoa, cuz, you should have used your feet instead of your face to go down those stairs." I wondered how bad I really looked. I also wondered why he thought I had fallen down some stairs. He had a quizzical look on his face, so I think he was wondering the same thing.

"Oh, sorry, Henryk," Dad jumped in. "At least one of the stories floating around is that you fell down stairs at school. Since we don't know exactly what happened, we thought it might be safer for Terry until it gets sorted out."

This got Terry's attention. "Safer for me? Is this catching? My cousin falls downstairs, and it's genetic, so I might fall ...oh." The light came on. "Hey, man, I'm really sorry. I didn't realize you got pushed. I wouldn't have joked about that. Who did you tick off? And why would that someone want to get me?" Terry did not seem too happy about this turn of events.

"It's not as bad as it sounds, Terry, but we didn't want you to be collateral damage." Mom made air quotes with her fingers. "Right now what exactly happened to Henryk is not clear, but we think he was punched in the face. Since the school hasn't gotten to the bottom of this, it makes sense to let the rumor of a dramatic fall down the stairs be the story. We've already had to warn Frankie off this, since he would be happy to hit someone, anyone, to make up for what happened to Henryk. Of course violence isn't the answer, and Frankie's desire, while admirable in a big brother, would not help a bit if he carried anything out. I, we, have never had the slightest thought that you would try that, but we don't want you caught up in this in any way at all. Since your last name is Sullivan and not Jonasz, most of the school probably doesn't even know you're Henryk's cousin." Left unsaid, but I'm sure considered by all of us, was that Terry had lived a lifetime in the middle of violence and trouble not of his own making. The last thing any of us would want would be for him to come live with us and then get thrown into some mess like the one he left in Boston. He wasn't perfect as it was. Sometimes I thought his last name should have been Sullen, since he had his moody periods where he wouldn't talk to anyone. He'd get really down and just hide out in his room, skipping meals, telling us that he was okay and "busy." Sometimes I thought it was an act because he would push my mom and dad just so far with this and then magically appear at a meal as if nothing had happened.

I think Terry read between the lines, undoubtedly a useful survival skill developed back in Boston. "Okay, Aunt Mary. You're right. My way would not be Frankie's. No offense to Frankie, but I have heard stories. Now I see why you kept me out of school today. I thought it was just so I could see Henryk. I guess yesterday was so crazy you didn't have time to figure this out. I'll just keep my head down and try to live my life. If I do hear anything that might be interesting, I'll let you know." He gazed out the window, looking back at Boston, maybe. "I'm certainly not looking for trouble." Usually, when someone says that, they already have one foot out the door and headed for trouble. I hoped that I was wrong, but I really didn't know Terry that well. He was definitely different from most of the kids at the school, but being a guitar playing artist who wore black all the time was not the sign of a maniac in our school; we had a reasonable share of such people. They hung out together in the arts wing of the school, sat together at lunch, but for the most part no one paid attention to them. It looked like they thought being ignored was a good thing as far as they were concerned.

The doctor sent me home on Sunday. I wasn't sure if it was his idea or Mom's to keep me in the hospital Saturday. After a couple days at home, I was totally ready to go back to school, but the doctor, and probably more significantly, my mother, wanted me staying out of the crowds and the general normal life of high school halls for a few extra days. I don't think anyone thought I was likely to get hit, but no one wanted my face bumped by accident. I had some kind of insert in my face and it looked normal as far as I could tell, so once the coloring went away no one would ever know that I gotten one side caved in. I still had some nasty headaches. Everyone seemed pretty sure that any side effects would disappear with time. Meanwhile, I wasn't going to be allowed to participate in gym class for the next few months, although I could still sleep through the health class part like I had done before. Sort of win-win, as far as I was concerned, as long as I got credit for the class at the end of the year. I did not want to repeat ninth grade physical education like some of the sophomores I saw in my class.

Hank finally showed up on Wednesday. Henry Aaron Jones. His father's family had this tradition of naming children after famous African-Americans. Hank drew a famous baseball player. His sister, Phillis Wheatley Jones, drew a famous poet. His dad, usually called NT by his friends, was christened Nat Turner Jones. Nat Turner was definitely not a ground-breaking baseball player or published poet. I think NT's mother wanted to send a serious message to the world when she named her son. I think that she got the idea because she was named Eleanor Rose Barbour, a play on Eleanor Roosevelt, who, while obviously not black, was considered quite a hero by the black community in the 1930's when Grams was born. Her last name, before she married a Jones, was a name of historic origins in its own right. It belonged to a prominent family of slave holders; she was a descendent of one of the plantation's slaves. She made it a point to find heroic black people for her children's names. One of NT's brothers was named Web, probably to honor W.E.B. Du Bois; another was named Booker. I wonder if they got along with each other.

"H-man. How you doing?" I hadn't heard that in a long, long time. It was something we started, to be cool, of course, back in fifth grade. He was H-man One, and I was H-man Two, since he was born an entire week before I was. It was just between the two of us. Occasionally, over the years, I'm sure we drew a funny look when we slipped and used it in public. I'm sure that if we had been an amazing basketball duo, we could have given each other the heads-up on a blind pass, "H-man! Atcha!" but that would not be either one of us, not on the court, anyway. Hank was always taller than me, by now a good six inches taller, but not particularly athletic despite his father's hopes. And I was built along the lines of my father and about as athletic as well.

In fifth grade we discovered various forms of curse words and naturally tried them out. It turned out that our parents did not approve, and after a couple of experiences involving grounding and the deprivation of video games, we decided that maybe practicing that language wasn't such a good idea. But, never ones to resist a challenge, we invented our own words. A lot of fun, actually, because we could refer to someone as a "clueless clucker" and really mean the phrase that rhymes with, one that would guarantee us the loss of video gaming. "Tish" was a handy anagram for something you don't want to step in. For complicated reasons, "tucker" became the south end of a northbound mule, and so on. "H-man" was one of the few special phrases that could be safely said in front of adults. Using the rest of our vocabulary just irritated our friends, so we tried to keep it to ourselves.

"What took you so long? I've been waiting for your afro-headed skinny self to appear for days!" I didn't mean to sound rotten, but, really, no visit in the hospital and then two days at home? What kind of a friend is that?

"I got grounded for a couple days, and you know my dad, grounded means grounded, even if your bud's in the hospital practically dying."

"Grounded? You? What did you do, get a B minus on a math test or some such crime?"

"Close. You know how my dad has my sister and me reading up on black history all the time? Says there's more to history than Harriet Tubman, Rosa Parks, and King's 'I have a dream' speech. I was supposed to be able to talk about this lady named Madam C. J. Walker at dinner the other night, and I hadn't gotten around to reading about her. Then I said something about how Phillis should be reporting on a woman, and that set my mom off. Thought I ought to be interested in all successful black Americans, not just the men. Somehow, I managed to aggravate everyone and got in trouble. If you would care to learn about Madam C. J. Walker, you are talking to the right guy. I spent considerable time researching that lady while I was grounded. Anyway, I would have been here yesterday, but a certain lady of this house threw up a stone wall complete with a crocodile infested moat to keep out invaders." This morning, though, my mother had left for a quick trip to her job's New York headquarters, thus lowering the defenses temporarily. "Besides, Ryk, you could have texted or called me. Your cell didn't get punched out too, did it?"

"Might as well have been. Mom's been really clamping down on me. She locked it up somewhere. 'Rest means rest. Doctor's orders,' she says. Actually, to tell you the truth, it's been kind of hard to read the screen on the phone; my head's a bit fuzzy I guess. Anyway, I'm glad you're here. They won't let me go back to school until next week, but maybe I'll be able to get out and around after tomorrow. I go back to the doctor, and he's going to tell my mother to let me breathe again. If you're really dying to tell me about her, I guess I could learn about that Walker lady, but if you can live with being the only expert on the subject in the room, how about telling me about what's happening at school? I've been on lockdown worse than your dad's inmates." Hank's father, in addition to being a history nut and, actually, a pretty decent guy, was a sheriff's deputy and mostly worked in the county detention building where they kept prisoners until trial if they couldn't make bail or weren't allowed to. They also kept the convicted desperadoes there if they had a short sentence, less than a year or something like that, or until they could transfer them to a state prison.

Hank glanced around the room. "Are you okay? Aren't you hurting like crazy? I thought you'd be half zonked on medication. I don't see any pills."

I tried not to smile, "Well, yes and no. And yes again, I guess. It's not too bad, now. I do get some pain pills, but my mom and dad have this thing about opioids. Frankie, such a genius, joked with me in front of them at the hospital. He said something about me getting a really big pain pill prescription from the doctor, and he could sell the extras and pay his tuition bill."

"I bet that set them off big time."

"Oh yeah. They both went off on Frankie, of course, but also on the general topic of drugs. We had to listen to the whole nine yards of drug problems. Between Dad's job and Mom's sister, they're freaked out on the subject. Bottom line is that they keep my prescription meds locked up somewhere. They left me one pill to take during the day, and I can boost it with a couple over-the-counter ibuprofen." I like to think that I could control myself, but actually, my face still hurt a lot, and I would have been happy to use more pills.

Hank looked at me, really intently. "You know, your dad called my dad the night you got hit. Dad was working the night shift, so he didn't talk to your dad until sometime the next afternoon. I wasn't invited into their conversation, but whatever happened to you seems to have shaken up all the adults. As soon as he got through talking to your dad, he jumped me. Dad told me that I was absolutely, positively not, that's NOT in capital letters, underlined, boldface, and in italics, NOT to get involved in this thing at all. He told me to say nothing to anyone since I didn't actually know anything in the first place. He also told your dad to tell you and Frankie and Terry to say as little as possible to anyone other than the authorities who are investigating. I think your father said something about having these crazy conversations with Mr. Slate and Mr. Wright." He smiled, "I do believe that my dad and your dad both think that those guys do not have a handle on this thing, and that makes them nervous."

I agreed. "Yeah. Dad and Mom don't trust authority any more than Frankie, but they are usually able to hide that from the authorities more successfully than Frankie does. And they had plenty of opportunities with Frankie and Slate going round and round all the time when he was at the high school. So, we're all going to keep our heads down and mouths shut and not talk to anyone about anything, right?" I guess I was feeling better; I was beginning to get ticked about what happened to me. "I actually do not know exactly what happened, but I would like to know a couple things." Terry had not reported anything useful to me. With a survivor's instinct, I was pretty sure that he really was going to stay away from all this. He might or might not like being told to keep his mouth shut, but that really was the smart thing for him to do. Hank, on the other hand, thought of himself as a reporter and loved the idea of investigating a juicy story.

I had the impression that someone had yelled at Walter's bunch after I got hit, and I knew that there was this girl who seemed to take charge. I filled him in on what I did know, very little, and what I wanted to know, even though I might not want to share that information with Slate, Wright, or my parents. "So, Hank, if while you are 'not getting involved in this', you happen to find out who yelled at Walter's bunch and who the girl was that helped me, that would be useful." Weird, I didn't really care who hit me, but I wanted to know about everything else.

Hank smiled, "Speaking of girls, you gave the OMG girls had a lot to talk about." There was a certain group of girls that had amused us since middle school. They always seemed to dress the same and share the same hair stylist. They started every other sentence with two exclamation marks and "Oh, My God!" Hank called them the OMG girls once, and the label stuck with us. Other students seemed to call them "Barbies."

"Actually, I did not give the OMG girls anything. All I did was get hit."

"Well, you left in an ambulance, so that makes you the star attraction. I bet a few gigabytes of chatter flew through the air the other day. I'm surprised you haven't been swamped with sympathetic girls all over you with care and concern."

"Care for gossip and concern for drama, maybe. You forget that I, unlike the great trumpet player and Madame CJ Walker expert in this room, am not a chick magnet. No one has been here or called. When I got my phone back today, there weren't any messages or missed calls. Of course, Mom's been doing a pretty good job of keeping everyone away. I haven't heard anything from school." I was right, of course. If Hank had been in my place, even his father couldn't have kept the girls away. Everyone liked him, didn't matter what color they were.

In addition to being the world's greatest trumpet student and amazing chick magnet, Hank is a pretty good student, straight A's most of the time. He was editor of the middle school newspaper, so it was natural that he start working on the high school paper, *The Rough Rider Reporter*, as soon as he got there. Most ninth graders take a while to figure out where everything is and what they want to do. Even most of the athletes take a while, since they have to start at the bottom all over, going from being star eighth graders to the young'uns on their teams in high school. Not Hank. He wasn't interested in marching in the band, but he got into a sort of "B" team jazz group, which was pretty amazing for a freshman, and he definitely was accepted on the newspaper. Of course, he got really simple assignments, like interviewing the new teachers, but at least he had a "press pass" that let him wander the school almost any time without being seriously challenged. As long as he kept up the grades, his teachers would let him out of class to catch other teachers in their planning periods or otherwise do "newspaper business."

CHAPTER 4

A Few Answers

Thursday afternoon, Hank called me as soon as he got to his house. "I've got some good stuff for you, Ryk." I started to pepper him with questions, but he cut me off. "I'm on the way over. Dad's here, probably sleeping, but if he hears me, my life expectancy will be drastically reduced. I was pretty busy NOT looking into things."

"Kind of dark in here, big guy." Hank had let himself in and come upstairs to my room.

"Yeah. Light sort of bothers me. Don't know why."

"Really?"

"Well, my eye, and my head, and all, I guess."

"You think?" He looked pretty serious. "Get banged in the head, and all kinds of things go weird, is what I hear. It's in all the papers, you know. Sports pages are full of stories." I wondered if he had been studying up on concussions. I had tried, but the computer screen seemed to be flickering like a cheap video game, and I couldn't read it very well.

"I'm pretty sure I know who hit you, Henryk

Not necessarily what I needed to know, but, "Who? And how did you figure it out?"

"Simple powers of observation and deduction, my dear Watson. I sort of hung out over near Walter and company this morning before the bell rang. Had to talk to a bunch of the OMG girls who do their gossip thing in the hall near there, but it was worth it. Whoever hit you should have had a busted up hand, right? I mean, you've got a hard head. And, there, talking smack and wearing oversized leather gloves was your man. He kept his right hand by his side, like it hurt a lot to move. I bet he has a swollen knuckle or two and figured to hide it with the gloves. He was wearing work boots and a leather jacket, so I guess he thought it would look pretty normal. Trouble is, none of the other guys he was hanging with looked like that. They were rockin' the boots but no gloves. He needed to slide on down the hall and hang with the goth bunch where his sartorial excess would let him fit in better. Nobody said these guys were geniuses."

Hank, on the other hand, probably really was a genius, or at least smarter than the average bear. "It was a bit trickier than interviewing some optimistic first year teacher, but I think I did okay. Once I knew what they looked like, I got hold of a couple yearbooks in the newspaper office and figured out what their names were." Most of these guys had been at the school for a year or two; Walter was in his third year, although he was classified as a freshman based on credits earned; the others were pretty much in the same boat. There was no way that Hank could go up and talk to any of them; his age and race made that an unlikely scenario. But, there was that group of OMG girls who happened to hang nearby, and, what a surprise, certainly one or more of them was dying to have Hank talk her up.

I was impressed. "Not bad detective work for one day. I wonder why Slate or Wright didn't think of checking hands."

"Walter's boys are not the only non-rocket scientists in the school. I've got a couple other things, too." Hank really has a future as an investigative reporter, assuming there are any newspapers left by the time he gets out of college. "Two names. Craterface and Melantha." He shoved a pile of dirty clothes off the chair by my computer desk and plopped down on it. He propped his feet up on my bed, crossed his arms and said nothing.

"Okay. I'll bite. Beg, even." Start with the girl. "Who is this Melantha? Someone I know? An OMG girl with actual information to relay?"

"Better than that. She was the girl who tried to help you after you hit the floor."

Now we were getting somewhere. "How did you find her? What's her last name? How?"

Hank cut me off. "Not so fast, cowboy. All I've got is her name. Actually, just her first name." He was pretty much laughing at me.

"My guardian angel, and all I get is her first name?"

"Actually, Craterface is the one who saved you, if anyone did, or needed to. And I did talk to him."

"Okay. So how did you find out anything? It was a random bunch of people in that stairwell. I didn't know any of them except Donnie and Walter. Do you think someone else saw the whole thing?"

"No. Well, Walter's boys, but they aren't talking of course." Hank laughed, "As my dad says, snitches get stitches, so I doubt anyone else who saw anything is likely to come forward."

"Your dad says a lot, but I guess he's right more than half the time, which puts him right up there with the gods, ahead of all the other adults we know. So you used your super powers of observation and deduction and figured it all out?"

"I should say yes to keep up my image, but actually, like a lot of investigative work, I got lucky. Like they say, persistence beats counting on luck, but don't discount luck. Anyway, some kid that I barely know in gym class told me real quietly that he heard my buddy, that's you, got hurt bad. Then he told me that he didn't see anything but that I might want to talk to Craterface. I guess he's a friend of Crate's, and Crate was sounding off to him about what happened."

"So, what did Crate do?" Craterface, known officially as Curtis Jordan, was an old line buddy from elementary school. Since Hank and I also had last names starting with J, the three of us often found ourselves standing in line together, the "J Team" in fifth grade, of course. He had the worst acne-scarred face anyone could imagine, hence the cruel nickname. And, he got it early; in fifth grade he was already a mess. He ought to have the world's biggest chip on his shoulder with a handle like that, but he went by the name so much that even his friends used it. I guess it was like black guys calling each other the "n-word," as my mother puts it. This kind of kicks the legs out from under the planned insult even if it does makes us white folks a bit nervous. When we got to middle school, he did the exact opposite of any normal teen. The first day, when a teacher called on him as Curtis, he announced, "Well, ma'am, my name is Curtis, but everyone calls me Craterface behind my back, but that's too long and too formal sounding, like a Hollywood movie villain, so please call me Crate." And it stuck. From that day on, he was Crate.

"I caught up with Crate on the way to class, and he gave me the short, probably only, version of what happened. He was coming up the stairs when you and Walter tangled. I don't think he saw you get hit, but he did see you dropping to the floor. He probably knows who hit you or could make a good guess, but I didn't ask, and he didn't volunteer. He yelled at the bad guys, like you heard when you were going down, and that's about it. He saw the girl, Melantha, starting back down to help you, so he just grabbed Donnie and hustled him out of there. I guess he has a class with Melantha or something, so he knew her name. Got anything to drink around here?"

He knew where the refrigerator was as well as I did, so I guess that was his version of, "The End." He went off in search of a soda, and I contemplated all the news. I didn't have Crate's number on speed dial or anything, but we had hung out together off and on since the elementary school years, and I definitely owed him a big thanks. My guess would be that once Walter's boys saw some blood, mine, they would want to add to the collection on the floor with more of mine. I could see those work boots coming at me from all sides. Not a nice vision at all. I tried to substitute a vision of this Melantha girl. Nothing appeared. Not an OMG girl, I was sure, but other than that? White? Black? Latina? Asian? Nerdy? Probably. She proved it by knowing what to do. Remembered what the teacher said in health class about emergency procedures and didn't opt for, "When in danger or in doubt, run around and scream and shout." So, I had two serious things to do, neither of which included talking to parents or school administrators: thank Crate, and chase down Melantha.

I had to use the bathroom, so I hopped up to head down the hall. Big mistake. I got very, very dizzy. I guess the concussion was still with me. I sat down on the bed and breathed slowly. Then I stood up, also slowly. I walked, carefully, down the hall. When I returned, Hank was on the chair, drink in hand.

I got back on the bed, "Are you going to write this up for the *Reporter*? It seems like a pretty big scoop. I know you're just a lowly freshman, but maybe if you write a really good piece, they'll run it anyway." I caught myself holding my breath.

"Right. I was thinking huge headline: 'Ninth Grader Smashed on Stairwell. Bloody Details on Page Two.' Or maybe, 'Neo-Nazi Punks Jump Caring Ninth Grader.' Or, maybe not. Actually, I was thinking I might be able to write an article or editorial on the general subject of bullying, but without mentioning any names or specific events. What you and Crate did, both of you, was pretty cool, and someone ought to say something about it. Also, what Walter and punks did was really awful, and someone ought to say something about that, too, but keeping it general can't get too specific." When Hank got really focused on something, he could be amazing.

I started breathing again. I realized that from about ten different angles, the last thing I needed was for a big deal to be made out of all this. My usual style is to lay low. Let Frankie go crazy on his big white horse as he either saves the world or gets killed in the adventure. I like to think of my approach as being the sane I-want-to-live method.

"It's like that quote on your dad's office, you know, something about 'They came for the socialists or something, and I didn't say anything because I wasn't one of them. And then they came for some other people and then the Jews, and I wasn't a Jew, so I didn't say anything, and when they came for me, there was no one left to speak for me.' Well, you and Crate spoke up, you for Donnie, Crate for you. I think someone ought to point that out to the school. "

"But no names, right? I'm not a hero, and Crate probably doesn't want anyone to know who he is either." In television and movies the hero gets a couple bumps, or maybe beat half to death, but in the end he isn't hurting, the bad guys are all gone one way or another, and he gets the girl. Maybe a whole bunch of them. I was still hurting, the bad guys were still running loose and likely to continue, and I still didn't know enough about this Melantha. "Oh, and that quote's from a guy named Pastor Martin Niemoller. I think he was caught up in the Holocaust in some way. My family's sort of Catholic, not Jewish, but my dad is pretty fixed on this Holocaust thing. He and Mom both really believe in what that poster says."

"Well. They always say stuff about one person's misfortune being someone else's opportunity. You got hurt, Donnie got scared, and I get an idea for an editorial. I'll figure out how to write it without telling anything but getting my points across. Good journalism, huh? A story without any of the five W's: who? nope; what? nope; when? nope; where? nope, why? well maybe just a little."

"If any of those W's do get into your article, everyone will figure out who the story is about, and I'll be dead for sure."

"There's another great headline: Student Who Assisted Down Student Turns up Dead a Month Later. Sub head: Police Suspect Foul Play. Sub-sub head: Administration Doesn't Suspect a Thing."

I started laughing, not really a good idea considering the state of my face.

CHAPTER 5

The Indignities Game

They say laughter's the best medicine, even if it is a little painful; I guess maybe so. Anyway, I got semi-sprung the next day. Hank had his weekly trumpet lesson, and I was allowed to ride along. I guess Mom trusted Hank's dad, Deputy Sheriff Jones, to keep me out of trouble and keep my face from an accidental bump. NT was working the night shift at the county lockup this month, so he was available to drive. Hank's mom was at work. I always liked going to Hank's trumpet lessons. Carl, his teacher, was an interesting old guy who had played in all kinds of jazz and rock groups as well as doing studio session work. He still played some gigs, but he didn't like to travel much anymore, so he was able to schedule afternoon lessons with a select group of students. Not everyone got accepted or kept by him, so it meant something that Hank was in his second year with Carl. Also the trip to Carl's was a trip in itself. The part of town where Carl still lived was getting a new look as richer people were starting to buy up houses and totally gut and rebuild them, so the street looked the same at first glance, but the houses, inside, were all new, and expensive. Also, at one end of the area, a couple of blocks were being leveled and turned into condos with stores and restaurants on the first floor. And, riding with NT was just plain interesting.

"Caught DWB. After ten minutes of checking your license and registration, and looking at all your lights, you are told to move on, but make sure you obey the speed limit." In the rearview mirror I could see NT's eyes twinkle as he smiled. "You were going maybe three miles over the speed limit, five at the most. Lose one turn."

Hank laughed. "Driving while black is only worth losing one turn. But," he paused dramatically, "if the cop that pulls you over is black also, you have to move back a space as well."

NT added, "You know, my white friends routinely drive five or ten over the speed limit; my black friends routinely drive one or two below speed limit, and that includes my cop friends."

I recalled that Hank once mentioned that even though he was over a year away from driving, NT had given him "The Talk" about how to act when stopped by the police. Both hands in plain view on the wheel, announce your moves, all that. My father apparently hadn't felt the pressure to give this to me, although considering that his job involved working on cases of wrongly convicted people, I guess I had lived with a version of the safety lecture all my life. Cooperate, to a point, but don't overshare or admit to anything. Left understood, but unsaid: don't be a person of color; a lot of his cases involved racial elements.

They both laughed. "Might be two spaces back in that case. We'll have to decide in the final editing." NT glanced at me in his mirror. "Question, young hero?"

"Actually, I was sort of wondering?" I had no idea what was going on.

Hank jumped in, "Oh, it's just a new game that Dad and I are developing. Going to put all those other board games to shame, make us millions, put Phillis and me through college, and let our folks retire. Might call it 'The Indignities Game.'"

"A board game about racism?" I may have been hit in the head, but I'm still sharp on some days. "That sounds like a big seller."

"It didn't start that way," said NT. "We were kicking around what to do with all those people Hank and Phillis have been studying, and I thought we should make up some kind of game with them. Turns out that there are all kinds of board games and card sets with black history themes. But nobody, nobody, has created a game like this." He slowed down to turn into Carl's driveway. "I wanted to call it 'Whitey's Game,' but Hank doesn't like that. Says it sounds racist or something."

"Well, duh, Dad. That's because it is." Hank laughed. "Phillis and I can't get involved in any kind of protest. Dad says it wouldn't look too good if a cop's kid got busted protesting police actions. He also claims that no matter what happened to us in an arrest, people would claim the cops either went too hard or too easy on us because of our father. And when he says no, that means NO! I guess this is a sort of compromise. We're trying something, but so far, not too dramatic or public." Later on, he would tell me that he thought Phillis would bust out in college once she was a bit out of NT's reach. I'm not sure if he'd hold out that long. Both my parents worked in civil rights organizations, but that didn't mean they wanted me on the street either, although I think both had "records" of some kind from their younger days. Hank grabbed his trumpet case, "You coming in, or what, Ryk?"

"He'll be in shortly, Hank, I want to talk to him a minute." NT killed the engine, waited until Hank was a bit up the walk, and then turned to look at me. "Some conversations are best done with no witnesses."

I could deal with my dad's occasional forays into my deeds and misdeeds, but I wasn't anxious to get into anything with NT as my interrogator. "Huh? Sir?"

"No need to 'sir' me, Henryk. You're not in trouble."

Right. I've heard that before. Not as much as Frankie, maybe, but enough to know that 'not in trouble' is code for 'in trouble,' just not the way you expected. "No, sir," I smiled, sort of.

"What'd I just say? Oh, never mind." He glared at me. "Point is, what happened to you has been a topic of conversation at our house. I've told Hank to keep his nose out of it, but I'm not so sure he will. Now Phillis is coming home with tales. She's in eleventh grade. Why would an eleventh grade girl care squat about some run-in among freshmen?"

"I'm sure I don't know." That was still pretty much the truth. We were all operating in the dark here as far as I could tell. I hoped Hank hadn't said anything to anyone.

"Well, I've heard a variety of stories; how about you tell me what you think happened. Doesn't have to be what you told the school or even your parents. Just tell me what happened."

He listened intently while I told him what I knew. I didn't tell him about Crate or Melantha other than what I think I knew before I learned what Hank had told me, since that would let him know that Hank had been looking into things. Since I really was telling the truth, it was pretty easy to tell NT all about it. "Honest, sir," I finished up, "it was all noise and bam! And my head and face hurting. I'm okay now, though."

"Good. You look pretty good. No headaches? Truth, now."

"No. Well, some, but not too much. I think the concussion is about gone. I saw the doctor this morning, and he did a bunch of tests, questions and stuff, and he told me my head seemed clear. I'm still going to be kept out of phys ed activities for a while, but I can go back to school next Monday. I guess even when the worst part is gone, a concussion still sticks around a while. It's getting kind of boring sitting at home." What I didn't tell him, or the doctor, was that I was spacing out once in a while. Video games were a mess; sometimes, I was playing like I was just learning them. When I really think about it, though, I actually had lied, but just a little. It seemed like a good idea at the time.

He looked at me, a bit intently, I thought. "What are you going to tell people at school? If this has drifted all the way up to Phillis's friends, it must be topic A in the ninth grade. Everyone's going to be bugging you, so you better have good answers. Good answers means short, simple, reasonably truthful, but no details." He looked worried. "I've dealt with this kind of thing practically all of my adult life, first in the army as a military policeman, and now at the detention center. I am not telling you to cover up anything, but I am telling you that if a lot of details get back to whoever was responsible, he might come gunning for you. Figuratively speaking, of course; I don't mean someone would shoot you. But you won't win any friends and you might influence a few enemies by opening your mouth. If the school administration wants to talk to you, of course, talk to them. But do it on the down low. Don't let anyone know you're talking to them. If they do something stupid like call you into the office publically, or if you get there and one of those guys who attacked you is sitting there, clam up." He looked pained. "I mean, remember that you don't remember because you hit your head, right? That's been your story so far, and it's a good one."

"Well," I said, "it's true. I am pretty foggy about what happened." I remembered reading something that Mark Twain said, about always telling the truth because then you only have to remember one story. Good point. Frankie's life would have been a lot easier if he had tried that approach. So far, I haven't had to be Frankie.

"I know it sounds like I don't trust the school administration, but I don't trust crazy kids even more. Like I told your dad the other day, if these guys start some sort of vendetta, you're going to get hurt even worse. If one of them gets identified legitimately by other witnesses, and you stick to your story about not actually seeing who hit you, these guys will just chalk it up to bad luck getting caught. Most of these types are idiots. They get away with stuff just enough to think they're smart, and then they do something really dumb or really bad, and get nailed. Someone ought to get nailed in this case, because this really is bad, but they just might slide on this one, get nailed next time out."

Several hundred years ago in England, they did this really dramatic way of getting people to talk: put them on a rack and start dislocating arms and legs until they told their interrogators what they wanted to hear. We're too modern to do that, maybe, but I felt like I was being racked anyway. I was being pulled in all directions at once. Tell the truth. Shade the truth. Talk. Don't talk. Tell some. Tell all. Try to remember. Don't try too hard. And it wasn't just the adults doing this to me. I was even doing it to myself. I wanted Hank to tell the story or at least comment on it, but we didn't want anyone getting hurt. Well, Walter maybe, but not me or Crate, or this Melantha. So far, I guess I had done okay. My arms were figuratively, and literally, still in their sockets, but it was beginning to get confusing.

I survived that round of questioning by NT. He started the car and said, "Well, I've got to go down the road a piece and get my mother. I dropped her off over here yesterday afternoon to stay with an old friend, and I'm supposed to pick her up and bring her back home when Hank gets through with Carl. You run on in and chill, and I'll see you in a bit."

Carl's house had definitely not undergone any sort of updating. He had lived there forever, and he liked it the way it was. A number of people had tried to buy his house in recent years, but the answer was always, "No. I could use the money, sure, but where would I move to? Besides, I couldn't face myself if I sold out and let some rich bozo come in here tear it down or change it into something crazy." He was a friend of Hank's grandmother; she had lived nearby for years, and she was always after him to move out. She once pointed out in my presence that, "White folks going to move in anyway, no point in hanging on for that to happen. You should take the money and run, Carl."

"Eleanor Rose, you know I'm not staying put for any reason like that. We got white folks here already, and most of my old neighbors have long since died or moved out. I just want to stay where I am. That's all. Not a race thing or a money thing. It's a don't-want-to-move thing. Also, I don't have a fine son like you've got who could take me in. I'm better off here for as long as I can hold out. I guess you're better off over there. You've got white folks over there, I'm sure, so I don't see your point anyhow." Hank's grandmother had only lived with his family for a few months. Maybe she hadn't noticed that most of us around her were white. Although, actually, she seemed to notice white more than anyone I knew. Of course, since I was white and most of my acquaintances were white, I guess we wouldn't notice white anyway. It took me a long time to figure out that this was an ingrained habit born of self-preservation rather than racism.

Still, though, I thought there was something there that wasn't good. A few weeks back I had complained to Hank about it.

"I wish your grandmother wouldn't refer to me as 'that white boy.'"

"Oh. You've moved up. You used to be my cracker friend. But I think my dad gave her stink-eye on that one, or said something to her."

"I don't see why she doesn't like me."

"It's not you. My dad says she's just scared to death of white folks in general. He says it's been quite an adjustment for her since she moved in with us."

"I can sort of see that. I guess it doesn't matter anyway. Just an old folks' thing maybe."

"Well, at least Grams isn't accusing you of being Jewish in addition to being white. My dad says that somehow she got the notion that Jews are the source of black folks' troubles. Maybe she's listening to that Farrakhan fellow or something. Dad even pointed out that some of the civil rights stuff was led by and or paid for by Jewish folks, so I don't know where that's coming from."

CHAPTER 6

Grams

I sat in the front room of Carl's house and thumbed through old issues of *Downbeat* and listened to the music lesson. Carl had converted half the house into a sort of studio. He had put up sound absorbing tile on the walls and ceilings in what would normally be the living room and one of the bedrooms where he did his private lessons. He had a scarred upright piano in the front room and had hung some African fiber art on the walls that added color and helped keep the sound under control. Sometimes he would get several of his students together, and he'd teach them to jam in the front room. He also had jam sessions with his friends there as well. His main instrument was the trumpet, but he could definitely make a sax talk and played a pretty cool piano. Once in a while when I came with Hank and waited, I'd get quite a concert, as he worked with him in the front room using the piano or his own instruments to help Hank.

NT and his mother came in and plopped down on the old couch along one side of the room opposite the old couch I was sitting on. "Hi, Mrs. Jones," I smiled. "Did you have a nice visit with your friend?"

She smiled back, "Yes. Thank you." She sat there and looked at me, but didn't say anything else.

NT broke the silence. "Any idea what Hank is playing in there?" We heard a trumpet, then the same riff played, somehow crisper. Carl was showing Hank something.

"No clue, Mr. Jones." I could tell that Hank played and then Carl, but I practically need a program to tell me when someone is playing the National Anthem. "No idea what the tune is." It was true; I love music, but I have to hear something almost all the way through before I can figure out what's going on.

We sat in silence a few minutes, and then Hank and Carl came in.

"Eleanor Rose, your grandson said you'd be by." Her face lit up, and she practically jumped off the couch. "How you been?" He reached out to embrace her.

Hank, his dad, and I stood around for a while as the two old friends caught up with each other. Finally, NT spoke up, "Well, Mom, I guess we better get moving. I've got to get you all back home before I go to work tonight."

In the car, with Grams in the front seat, of course, Hank started another card for this crazy game he and NT were inventing. We were passing some sort of wig shop that had a bunch of wigs in the window mounted on various colored mannequin heads. "How 'bout this, dad. All the so-called black mannequins in stores have cute little pert noses, skinny lips, and the skin's not even dark. And sometimes, in the movie theaters, they have ads that show black and white folk having fun together, buying sodas of course, and they always show very light skinned black folk. Lose one turn."

"Say what?" Grams had been looking out the window as we rolled along and saying nothing, but now she was alert and on the job. "Say what? NT what on earth is he talking about?"

Hank started to defend himself, "Well, it's just that, uh, like when you see..."

NT cut him off, "Your Grandmother might not have the same sense of irony about these things, son." His tone and his eyes reflected in the mirror told both of us in back that the subject did not need to be pursued. "Nothing, Mom, just some foolish guy stuff." He waited to turn right onto a street as a black boy and white girl, holding hands, made their way across the intersection.

Grams flipped out. "Oh, no! Look at that, NT!" She was pointing at the couple. "That boy want to die or something?"

"It's okay, mom, I saw them. They've got the right of way. They're in the crosswalk, they've got the light, and I'm paying attention. Not saying they shouldn't maybe take a peek at the traffic, but they're okay." NT looked at his watch. I'm sure he wanted to get moving, but probably figured that running over pedestrians would only delay the trip home, so he waited.

"Not that, NT. Look at them. They're holding hands!!" Grams was really getting worked up. "She's white!" I was beginning to feel a bit uncomfortable. I knew she was a bit nervous about white people in general, but this was sounding like a lot more than nervous. "That boy's going to get himself killed before sundown if goes around like that. Holding hands with a white girl!"

Ah, so it wasn't a traffic issue. Hank tried to explain, "It's okay, Grams, really. They're probably just friends is all. I'm sure nothing big will come from it. No marriage or anything like that." I guess he thought he was being funny. Didn't work.

Grams wailed, "No! They could kill him!"

NT glared at Hank through the mirror. His voice was gentle. "Mom, it's okay. They're okay. He's okay. It's not like in the old days."

This didn't seem to mollify Grams a bit. She went off on a five minute tear about Emmett Till and what happened to him. "That boy didn't do anything at all, nothing like holding a white girl's hand, and look what happened to him. I saw it, all over Life magazine. What they did to that boy. Look what happened to that kid in Florida. Just walking around, and some security guy ups and shoots him. You gonna tell me that couldn't happen to Hank?" She gave a final sob and slumped in her seat.

It was very, very quiet for several blocks. We were almost home. NT finally spoke. "The take-away here, boys, is that everyone sees the world through different lenses in their glasses. Mom has seen some tough, tough things in her life, and it kind of colors the way she sees the world. Doesn't mean she's right or wrong, just sees things differently than younger folks do."

None of us thought she was listening, she had been so still, with her eyes clenched. "NT, I'm right and you know it."

"Mom, that's ancient history. It isn't like that anymore. At least I keep hoping so." He sounded pretty doubtful, but I could tell that NT had been over this ground before. Funny thing, though, I wasn't so sure it really was just ancient history. There were plenty of Bernards and Walters running loose in the world. And some of them were police officers or school administrators and politicians.

When we got to Hank's house, his dad stopped the car at the end of the sidewalk by the driveway so Grams could get out easier than in the garage, and I hopped out to get the door for her. As I held it, I eyed Hank, and I could tell he was about to explode.

"Thank you, young man." Grams said as I helped her start up the sidewalk. "I can make it from here. It's just too hard to get out of the car when it's in the garage, can't open the door wide enough. And then there's all that, that stuff in the way." She had a point; despite being a former military man, NT was not very neat. There was always stuff piled up in the back seat, on the floor, in the garage. Maybe after years of keeping everything in its place, this was his quiet civilian rebellion. For some reason, I hopped back in the car instead of just closing the door and waiting for NT to park it. Hank could no longer contain the explosion.

"Dad! What's up with Grams? Doesn't she know it's the twenty-first century? Folks don't go around lynching blacks anymore. It's embarrassing, her talking like that in front of Ryk. It's just plain racist. No different from Walter and Bernard and their neo-Nazi bull."

"I just know you are NOT criticizing your grams! Right?" I almost never saw NT raise his voice, much less get angry.

"But..."

"But nothing. Your butt, maybe, keep this up. But nothing. Like I said in the car, Mom's seen some real tough things in her life. This makes her see the world a little different than the way you get to see it. And I emphasize that, the way YOU get to see it. You think I haven't seen some stuff, too? And read about a lot more. Here you are living where your mom and I chose to live, not where some cracker, sorry Henryk, told us we had to live. Here you are going to school with Henryk and all kinds of folks. She was lucky to get a few months of schooling each year. Shoot, I bet you don't even know why she moved up here to that neighborhood where Carl still lives."

"But..."

"But nothing. Tell you what. Since you have all this time to criticize your elders, I've got a little project for you to research. Henryk, you can help him. Do you both some good to find out about this little corner of the world you live in and the corner my mom grew up in. I'll give you one hint. She and your granddad moved us up here from Prince Edward County in the fifties. See if you can figure out why. Don't start by asking her. After you get it all figured out, you might want to ask for some of the gory details. You might see why she looks at the world the way she does. She's still scared, plain and simple. Angry, too. And another thing, don't even bring Bernard and his bunch into the conversation. There's a world of difference between what those clowns proclaim and what your grams has lived. Although, I guess, when it comes down to it, they're probably scared, too, but for reasons they invented in their pathetic little minds."

I expected another "But..." from Hank, but NT shot him that "shut-up-don't-say-a-word" look, and surprisingly, Hank snapped his mouth shut and lowered his eyes. I wasn't sure if I should feel complimented or put upon to be included in Hank's punishment research exercise. I decided that it granted me some sort of membership in the family, and therefore it was an honor.

Hank normally would have fooled around on his trumpet for an hour or so after his lesson with Carl to experiment with the points Carl made and perhaps set them into some sort of concrete. Since I would be a distraction and obviously of no musical use, I usually went home after we returned from a lesson. The general rule in the Jones household was that whatever the punishment inflicted, it was immediate. That day, we went straight to the internet.

Pretty amazing. Not lynch mob gruesome, but astounding in its own way. Apparently the good (white) citizens of Prince Edward County, Virginia, decided that the best way to avoid integrating the schools, as ordered by the US Supreme Court in 1954, was to have no schools. Thought they were pretty smart, I guess. So, in 1959 the public school system shut down. No school. For anyone. Period. For the next five years, until the courts said that this was illegal, there was no free public education. Of course, the white folks found ways to educate their children in private (all white, of course) academies. The black folks set up schools in their churches or sent their children to live with relatives in more enlightened parts of the country. Ironically, one of the original cases that led to the Supreme Court decision was started by a sixteen year-old girl named Barbara Johns who led a walkout in 1951 in Prince Edward County to protest the substandard education she and her friends were getting in the segregated schools there. NT was born in 1958 in the county, and in 1959 his parents moved the family to Northern Virginia, where they still had to live in a segregated neighborhood, but at least their children had a chance for some kind of education. Other counties and cities hadn't shut down, but they had made it pretty much impossible for black kids to get any real education. It was called "Massive Resistance" and had the blessing of the state legislature; it should have been called "Racist Persistence." Some of the school systems that did follow the law and integrate became all black as the whites pulled out leaving an underfunded skeleton school system that didn't educate anyone. By the time NT got to elementary school, there was one integrated school system, although his school was mostly black due to the segregated neighborhoods that fed into it. My version of events is somewhat shortened; I'm sure that Hank's report to the family at dinner that night covered a lot more details, and I'm sure that he and his sister would be talking to their grandmother about it in the near future.

CHAPTER 7

Interrogations

Finally, back to school. No headaches. Face looking pretty normal with maybe a tint of yellow and black, but nothing really dramatic, except for the white of my eye, which was still almost completely bright red, kind of like one of those lizards. As soon as I stepped off the bus and started up the sidewalk into the building, Mr. Wright caught up with me. "We need to have a conversation, Henryk. Now."

Yes sir, and it's nice to see you too. You're looking well, I guess you've recovered from the shock of seeing me with my face bashed in. His tone made me almost feel like I needed a lawyer, and as far as I knew, I was strictly the victim. While I was walking in the hall with Mr. Wright, someone bumped me coming from the opposite direction. I wasn't particularly looking in his direction when he ran into me, and I started an automatic, "sorry," but in a split second I realized that he was one of the fools that hung out with Walter. It wasn't an accidental bump; it was a warning shot, fired with the chief of school security right there. I had to admire his chutzpah, though. I have always appreciated what's called "chutzpah" in Yiddish. It's being really gutsy in a situation where that's

Christopher Wollenberg

probably not the best call. The traditional example involves the guy who's on trial for killing both his parents and asking the judge for mercy because he's an orphan. My brother Frankie had an abundance of this attitude, and although it often got him in trouble, it was sometimes actually a good thing, and occasionally entertaining. I'm not sure if this guy had chutzpah or was just too stupid to notice who I was walking next to. In any case, Mr. Wright seemed not to notice, so score one for the bad guys.

My most important goal in coming to school that day was to figure out how to meet my guardian angel, Melantha. However, since I had been hijacked by Mr. Wright, I adjusted my goal to getting through a conversation with him without getting into trouble. I couldn't figure out why he seemed to be treating me as the bad guy, but maybe that was his fallback position, a result of all those years as a county police officer before he retired and took a safer job with the school system. Certainly not saner, who wants to sort out petty teen problems all day, but the hours were regular, and his summers were pretty relaxed, unless summer school sessions were being held in our school.

There was no one in his office area when we entered. I remembered what NT had said about making sure that I wasn't in the same room as the bad guys, although I wasn't sure if that mattered since one of them had already seen me in school walking alongside Mr. Wright. We went into the back office, and Mr. Wright closed the door.

"You've been a difficult guy to get to talk to, Henryk." Ah. Mom's stone wall and moat, as Hank put it. "But now, now, you are on school property, and no one is running interference for you. I really need to wrap this up, so we're going to have the conversation I have been trying to have for the past few days." He didn't sound particularly angry, but I could tell he was a bit put out by my mother and dad keeping him away from me, treating him like he was the enemy. "How about you tell me the entire story as you remember it. Start from when you walked up the stairwell that Wednesday, a couple weeks back."

I did have to stop and think for a minute. I wasn't planning on lying, but I didn't want to add in any details that Hank had dug up. I didn't want to drag anyone, like Crate, into this unnecessarily. As I was telling Mr. Wright the story, the same as I first tried to explain in the hospital, but in coherent sentences instead of nods and guesses, Mr. Slate walked in. He didn't knock.

"I just heard you've got young hero Jonasz in here. 'Bout time." He pronounced my name "joan-ass" rather than "joan-ahz". It's Polish and should be "yoan-ahz," but the J throws everyone off, so we just go with "joan-ahz" never "joan-ass." I mean, really? I got this from the kids in middle school, but really, an adult? It's not like the name was new to him; he'd had four years with Frankie to get it right. Oh, and nice to see you, too, sir. I am so glad you also have recovered from seeing my face all bashed in. Did you have a nice week pulling the legs off flies? Mr. Wright looked startled at the intrusion. "Wright, did you ask him why he was in that stairwell? That was not the logical route from his previous class. Did he tell you who else was there? Did you ask him if maybe, just maybe, he owed someone some money for, uh, something, and didn't have it? We really need to clean out the rats before they sink the ship, Wright."

I couldn't decide if this was a clumsy good cop/bad cop routine, or if it was what it looked like: Tits barging in and throwing his weight around. I almost felt sorry for Mr. Wright.

"Henryk was just telling me what he remembered about the attack last week. He still maintains that he was going to class, more or less minding his business, except for saying something to Walter Anderson about picking on Donald Sampson, which got him creamed."

"Really?" Mr. Slate stared at me intently. I tried to look blank. Frankie had taught me a long time ago how to not show emotion when it's a tense situation: just keep your lips together, but drop your jaw and keep your eyes steady, look at your opponent's nose, not his eyes. That will look like you are staring them down, but it's easier to stay steady. Look for a pimple or something. Scared or nervous people tense their mouths and look around a lot everywhere. Mr. Slate threw his hands in the air. "Kids pick on kids all the time, doesn't get anyone punched in the face. I doubt Downie, Donnie, even knew, or cared, about what they were saying to him."

I could feel my blank, neutral face dissolving into anger. "Um." was all I managed before Slate cut me off.

"If I had to do something about every time some kid made fun of some other kid in this school, I wouldn't have enough time to do anything else. I'd be playing kindergarten cop all day. Downie might as well get used to it; the rest of us do." Right. I wondered what he'd say if I used his school-wide nickname to his face right now. I let that idea slip on by, however. The goal here was to escape without making my life difficult. I'm sure Frankie would have followed a different course of action, and then spent the next three days at home trying to explain to our father why calling out Mr. Slate on his hypocrisy was such a grand idea. "I'll just say this, Jonasz, you might want to consider who you mess with in this school. Don't mess with me. Don't mess with Mr. Wright here, and maybe, just maybe, you should leave the correction of fellow students to those of us entrusted with the noble calling of guiding teenagers." I couldn't decide if he had just told me that he basically was willing to let the Walters of the world rule, or if he actually thought he had a handle on things. Either way, I was beginning to see why NT didn't want me talking to the authorities, although he told me to. I didn't trust myself to say anything safe, so I just sat and tried to regain my slack-jawed poker face.

Mr. Wright slid his chair back. He seemed to be doing this in a very deliberate manner, maybe it was his way of controlling his own body language. "Well, gentlemen, if we've got an understanding here, I guess we can let Henryk go on to class. Henryk, see Mrs. Hernandez for a pass. Sorry to have held you up on your first day back." He smiled at me, but I did not see him even look at Mr. Slate.

"Oh my god! Let me see your face!" Rats, two seconds into the hall, and this.

"Oh. Hi, Bibi. It's right here. Pretty much where it's always been." How did she find me so quickly? Do the OMG girls have some kind of telepathy? Her real name is Beatrice, but by middle school she had established with everyone that she was "Bibi". I believe only her mother used her given name. Teachers did on the first day, of course, until they got blasted for it. Then she would be Bibi for the rest of the year. I tried to edge away.

"No, really, Henryk. Let me see." I wondered if she would want to take a photo to send to her gaggle of friends. "So, what really happened? I heard you fell downstairs last week. Someone thought you fainted or something and just went, poof, down the stairs."

NT had warned me about interrogations, and I guessed the wrong answers in this one could cause me as much trouble as wrong answers in the official ones. I resorted to my fallback response, figuring it worked for Wright and Slate. "Um."

"Oh, I'm so sorry, Henryk. I guess that might be embarrassing, being a guy and all that. Anyway, if you hit your head, I guess you don't remember much anyway."

"Um."

"Well, anyway, I'll tell the girls that you are fine and look, uh, okay." Story of my life, I look "okay" to girls, on my best days. "Glad you're back." Sure, you're glad I'm back because that puts an end to speculating about me and leaves room for the next drama.

"Um."

I made it through my two morning classes with only a few sideways glances from students. My English teacher said something about Frankie and unnecessary fights that I chose to ignore. I got a genuine "welcome back" from my math teacher. In fourth period my history teacher, Mr. Arnstein, also made it a point to welcome me back. He had me step into the hall for a moment. "I'm glad you're back and on the mend, Henryk. You know, I had your brother a few years back." I thought I knew where this was going, and I didn't like it, but I was wrong. "I always admired his rebellious spirit. Smart kid, but a bit impulsive. I saw him recently; he seems to be growing up. Got his act together, I think. Be sure to swing by the history office where my cubicle is to pick up the work you missed." I don't know why he mentioned Frankie, but it was nice that at least one person in the school didn't think of my brother as the devil.

CHAPTER 8

Melantha

When the lunch tone rang, I made it a point to not visit the scene of the crime such as it was, and did not use the stairway where I got hit. I found Crate in the cafeteria. Before this, I had never noticed that he ate lunch the same shift as I did on even days. We have ninety minute classes that alternate every day, so on even days, I have one set of classes and on odd days, the others. First period is every day and is only about fifty minutes long. For me, my lunch is in a different shift on even and odd days since the lunch schedule is set up to send all English classes at some set time, all Math on a different shift, and so on, balancing the load in the cafeteria. On odd days, my lunch happens at the same time as Crate's.

I sat down across from Crate, who was working on a sub from the sandwich line. I had pizza from a different line. It was typical lunchroom noisy, but I didn't want to shout. "Hey."

Crate nodded. "How you doing?" He studied my face. He has crystal blue eyes, and they seemed to be scanning me mechanically, left-right, and back again. He was allowed to look all he wanted; after all, he had saved it from being attached to a dead me. He grinned, "Not bad. Certainly no uglier than before. Looked worse the last time I saw you." His face, on the other hand, while it looked the same as it had for years, was awful. His longest acne condition on record had left a mess. He had old scars on top of old scars, and he had new eruptions scattered around. He was built, as NT would say, like a "brick outhouse." Stocky and solid. He wasn't at all tall, but no one wanted to mess with him, I'm sure.

"Doing okay. Doctor says I can't do contact stuff like PE or getting punched in the face for the next month or two, but they think I'm going to live. Thanks to you, I hear."

"Where'd you hear that?" He sat up a bit.

"Just someone. Don't worry, I haven't said anything to anyone. Far as I know, Wright and Slate don't know squat. Me. I didn't see anything. Really. I don't know who hit me, and I'm not sure I care. I know it was Walter's bunch, and I know someone stopped them from doing more damage, but I was pretty much out of it between the punch and hitting my head on the wall or the floor, so I really, really don't know much and can't tell anyone anything about anything. I'm just pretty sure that I owe you."

Crate relaxed a bit. "If you say so."

"So, since we're on the subject of my debt, let me give you a chance to add to it." Objective one accomplished: thank Crate. Now the other objective. "I don't suppose you know some girl named Melantha, or something like that? I heard she was there also, maybe did some first aid or something?"

"I wouldn't know about that. Donnie needed to get out of there. I do know a chick named Melantha, though. She's in the same class with me first period. We both usually go up that stairway on the way to our second period classes. Psycho one-oh-one."

"That's the class? Psychology?"

"No. Her." He smiled. "We've got different math classes. If I didn't know better, I would bet that she was thinking about drinking some of your blood. She's way out there. But, no, wait, she's a vegan type, not a vampire. Maybe in her next life, though."

"I'll keep that in mind. I'm going to try to see her during this life, before she goes over to the dark side."

"I'm telling you, she's out there. She's like the opposite of Donnie. Really, really smart. But, I don't know. She doesn't do much better with people than he does. He talks to everyone and smiles a lot and has no idea what people are saying half the time. She doesn't talk to people much, but when she does, I'm not sure she really knows what they're saying either. Weird."

"Actually, you could get the whole experience for yourself. She's sitting over there." Crate nodded in the direction of the far side of the cafeteria. "See if you can guess who she is."

Not too difficult. Even from the distance. Long black hair hanging limply down her back. No ties or bars. It looked like she was wearing some sort of old fashioned loose blouse or dress. Definitely not like the tight clothes most of the girls seemed to be wearing. Other key tells: sitting alone and no cell phone in her hand.

"No time like the present, ace. Go get 'er. Just remember, I warned you, so don't come crying to me. Psycho one-oh-one." Crate grinned.

I grabbed up my tray and walked over.

"Can I sit here?"

"May."

"Oh. Yeah. Right. May I sit here?" After a moment of

silence, other than the cafeteria din, I sat down across from her. No "No" means "Yes." At least in this case. She seemed to be concentrating intently on her lunch. "I wanted to thank you for helping me in the stairwell a while back, when I got, uh, hurt."

"Yes."

"My name's Henryk. Henryk Jonasz."

"Yes."

"I'm ..."

She cut me off. "Of Polish descent. Jonasz means something like dove. It's related to a Hebrew word that means dove."

My turn to sound intelligent. "Um."

"Do you know if there are Jewish people in your background?"

I still needed to sound intelligent. "Um." Funny, that got me through sticky conversations with my other interrogators, the ones in charge, but now this didn't seem to be such a good tactic. Not that I was trying to use it. I tried to find my tongue. "I don't think so. Your name is Melantha, right? Does that have deep historical roots?"

"Well. I looked up your name. Maybe you could check on mine." She almost looked at me. She might have almost been smiling. Smirking, maybe. Whatever that moment was turning into suddenly changed in a dramatic explosion of sound, and my "accident" instantly became old news.

The entire room seemed to erupt as the students all started yelling to each other. A wave of emotion flowed across the room from one corner. Students began furiously pecking away at their cell phones, stopping for a second, then hammering again.

Melantha looked panicked. She did not reach for her cell. I realized that I had automatically pulled mine out and was also glancing at it. "What's happening?" she asked.

The crying was louder now. Some of the boys were wailing or pounding the tables. I looked over at Crate. He pecked at his phone for a few seconds, and then mine vibrated. It took a moment to digest the message. Melantha still did not have her phone out.

"It's okay, Melantha." I tried to look into her eyes. She was looking wildly around the room, as if searching for an escape. The noise really was something else. Nothing like I had ever heard before, not at a football game, or in the middle school cafeteria when two groups of guys got into it. "Some kid just got killed in a wreck. I think. Maybe a senior or something. I don't know him, but I think he's a football player."

Teachers and administrators who had lunchroom duty were running around trying to calm everyone down. Students seemed to be alternating between crying and hammering at their phones. Now a name was coming out of the din. Two names. One was the starting quarterback. It appeared that two students had gone off campus during lunch and managed to wreck their car. Definitely against the rules, driving off campus during the day. Wrecking your car was not specifically prohibited in the school handbook. Mr. Wright came striding in, followed by the county police resource officer and other security staffers who weren't already in the cafeteria. I'm not sure if dealing with mass hysteria/panic is something you can really practice for, but Mr. Wright was giving it his best shot. After a few more minutes of rising chaos, he stepped out of the room so he could talk on his radio.

The school's PA system blasted out three short beeps. Everyone stopped their crying and texting and looked around. We had heard these sounds once, when the school did its first-week lock-down drill, the active shooter drill. We didn't have the slightest idea where we were supposed to go if we were in the cafeteria when a gunman entered the school, so we just stayed still. Mr. Wright immediately stood on a table and basically announced what everyone already thought they knew. Yes, a student had died in a car crash off campus, and yes, another was injured. He couldn't go into details for reasons that I lost, but we all needed to have a moment of silence for the two students and then go to our next class. Then the school's principal came on the PA system and pretty much repeated the act.

The end-of-lunch tone sounded in the middle of this moment of silence, and everyone started filing out for class, few students bothering to put their trays on the dish return carts. I took one last gasp attempt to talk to Melantha. "Can, may, I talk to you later? Where?"

"Yes. Locker 1129. It's blue-green-brown-ish."

"The locker?"

"No. The number. It's a prime number. I made them give me a prime number locker."

A bit mystifying, to say the least. "Have a good class." Lame. Very lame. "See you later." Better. "See you after last bell."

After the last class was dismissed, I found locker 1129 remarkably quickly considering that I'm new to the building, and the numbering system was designed by the same guy who numbered all the rooms in the school, someone who must have been using hallucinatory drugs as an aid to clarity and creativity.

"I'm here." Another great line.

Melantha agreed, "Yes."

I'm pretty sure that Hank would have had something intelligent to say at this point. Even Donnie would have done better than I was. I looked at the number on her locker. Beige locker, black digits on a small silver-colored plate. I know what a prime number is, of course, but I couldn't remember how to check this one. Melantha was busy putting things in a satchel of some sort. She didn't say anything more. It did seem like I need to say something. Preferably not lame, or at least not very lame.

"Your locker number? You said it was blue-green-brown?" I know that at some point guys usually compliment girls on some appearance item or another, but this was at the top of my list right now. She did look nice enough, though. No make-up, dark, almost black, eyes, delicate features, pale white skin, no jewelry.

"Yes." She looked at me with that almost a smirk again.

I 'm pretty sure that my face showed question, but she didn't seem to read this at all. "What does that mean, blue-green-brown? It's black, like all the others. Maybe the angle of the light and the silvery background makes it look that way to you?"

"No. Do you want me to explain? Or would that be too complex?"

"Explain, I'm all ears." She looked oddly at my head, and almost seemed to be counting my ears. Or looking for extras. "It's an expression. It means I'm interested in what you have to say."

"Oh." She smiled, for real. "Sorry." She looked at me, at the locker number. "Oh, yes. It's called synesthesia. Only girls of Greek descent have this magical power."

My turn to look puzzled.

"Oh. Sorry again. That was a joke, although the word is from Greek. It means that sometimes my senses overlap, so that I see numbers as colors, some letters as colors, also. So, your name, for instance, is kind of red-ish at the start. It's hard to explain."

To say the least. This girl was going to have me hitting the books, well, Google, all night. Her name. Her "magical power" or condition, if that's what it was.

She stood there and looked at me, no smirk, no smile. Sort of serious. "Actually, you're the first person I've told this to. I don't know why I did." She looked at her watch, which was analog, not digital, I noticed. "Excuse me. I've got to catch the bus."

I tried one more stab at an intelligent question: "Have you got a phone number? So I could text you. Maybe an email? Are you on Facebook or Twitter or something?"

"No, of course not. Why would I?" She looked at me as if this was the strangest question anyone ever asked her. "I must go. Bus to catch. Goodbye."

"Yeah. Bye. I've got a meeting I'm about to be late for." This I tossed at her back as she took off. I headed to the literary club meeting. It produces a small literary magazine on an irregular schedule, wherever there's enough to print, I guess. I was hoping to get something going, although I didn't know what.

CHAPTER 9

Grams II

As it turned out, I didn't see Melantha for a while. The school was a mess. The story we got Monday at lunch was pretty accurate. Two seniors, the quarterback and a girl, had gone off in his car at lunchtime and presumably planned to do any number of stupid and/or fun things that normally would not have resulted in their death. The girl, first reported as injured, had died also. Ironically, they never had the chance to do much on their little adventure because some lady who "was on medication" ran a stop sign and plowed into them. Just really, really unlucky. We spent most of Tuesday hearing about it from our teachers, one way or another. Some seemed to be using this as a lesson on behaving and following the rules, others seemed to feel terrible. I wasn't sure if I was supposed to feel bad. Actually, I sort of felt bad that I didn't feel all that bad. I mean, the kids were doing something dumb, and they weren't personal friends of mine. On the other hand it really was terrible. It was like it was the death penalty for doing one dumb thing. I think a lot of people didn't know what to feel. It certainly toned down the OMG girls. They hung around and talked, but there were no squeals coming from their clusters.

Wednesday was better, although still not normal. And, I didn't catch up with Melantha at lunch, even though I was prepared to tell her all about what her name means. I think Melantha comes from Greek and means dark flower. I wasn't going to tell her what synesthesia meant, but I did know that her definition was good, although there is more to it than just words and numbers and colors. I was pretty sure she knew it all anyway. I didn't have time to look for her at her locker after school; my mother was supposed to pick me up. I had a follow-up appointment at the doctor's office, so she took the afternoon off to drive me. Hank was sitting in the back seat when I got to it.

"Slight change of plans, sweetie. Sandra got tied up in a meeting, and NT's at some training thing this afternoon. We're going to drop Hank off at his lesson on the way to the doctor."

Except for the starvation aspect, I was fine with this. "Any food?"

"Told you, Mom J. First thing he'd say. My mom says we both have one track minds." Hank had a point; his mother, Sandra, Mama J to me, saw me often enough at their house to keep extra food on hand. When we were little, maybe three or four, I called Hank's mother, 'Mama' because that's what Hank called her, and he was calling my mother 'Mom' because that's what I called my mother. At some point the adults straightened us up on whose mother was whose, so we started using 'Mom J' and 'Mama J' as their handles. "Oh, and, Hi Henryk. Did you have a good day at school?"

"Sorry, Hank. Hi. Etcetera. So is there anything to eat here? Or do we have time to stop on the way?"

There was some food; Mom was looking after me, and I dug in.

"Hank, we also need to pick up your grandmother to take her back to your place after the lesson. We're going to swing by the doctor's office, and then go get her while you're in your lesson. Can you tell us how to get there? Or should I figure it out with my GPS?"

"No problem, Mom J." Hank gave his best smile. "That way you won't have to listen to me butcher the music." He paused, probably waiting for one of us to say something about what a great player he was, but we didn't rise to the bait. "When you leave Carl's, turn right and go down to the corner."

"Is that a right if I back into his driveway and then come out and turn right, if I'm backing out of his driveway?"

"Oh. Just park in front to drop me off and go straight. When you get to the corner, turn right. You are driving forward, right? Then go a couple blocks and turn left. You turn left where there's this big old oak tree in the front yard."

"No one likes a wise guy, Hank. So, I'm driving forward and turn right?"

"No, left at the old oak tree. You turned right to get on the street the oak tree is on."

"Okay. Got it. Left at the oak, a few blocks down from the stop sign."

"Yes. Then, another block, and Grams's friend's house is on the right. I think Ryk has been there. He should recognize it."

I had been there once or twice, but I hadn't paid much attention to it. It was one of the original houses in the area, like Carl's, and they all looked sort of the same, even though each one had any number of changes and add-ons, porches enclosed, carports, garages, out buildings, and so on.

"Got it. Look for the oak tree. You don't know the names of any of these streets by any chance, do you?"

"No ma'am."

The oak tree. "Wait," I said, "that oak tree's gone. Remember? Your dad pointed that out last time. Said he had stories and stories about that tree, but now they've gone and cut it down because they're tearing out that house and building a modern new one."

"I think I'll try my new GPS," mom said, "Sandra gave me the address. Besides, I forgot, we're going to the doctor's office first."

We dropped Hank off and drove to the doctor's office. I guess I was in pretty good shape. There were no doctor "Hmmms," just a few questions about my vision and whether or not I was still having headaches. Of course, I claimed everything was perfect. He reminded me to avoid a lot of physical activity, like getting punched, and sent me on my way. My mother was not amused by his punch comment. We somehow found our way to the house where Grams was visiting. Yet another old house was coming down in that block, too.

Hank came out of Carl's when we pulled up. With Grams safely tucked in the front seat, staring quietly out the window, and mom negotiating rush hour traffic home, Hank and I entertained ourselves in the back with the game. We should have realized mom and Grams were listening.

I started it. "Your local pro sports team has a name that is obviously a racist slur, the owner won't change it, and people seem to accept it. What's the penalty?"

"Whole community moves back two spaces. No, wait, the white community stays put, because that's what they've always done; the minority community moves back two spaces. They can't just ignore it because they aren't the ones being slammed."

"Maybe just one space. I mean, they're probably so used to racism, they don't even think about it, so it's not all their fault."

"Good point. We'll have to see what my dad says."

I had another one. "A TV station shows the photos of suspects in a violent crime. Only the black suspects are shown. They are already in custody, and the excuse is given that "No photo is available" for the two white men also arrested. One could ask why any photos are necessary, since the men have been captured. Lose one turn while they try to defend their weak excuse. It's the same with the newspapers. Ridiculous."

My mother caught my eye in her rear-view mirror. She seemed to be paying more attention to what we were doing than the road. "And what, pray tell, are you guys cooking up back there?"

"Um." My usual lead off answer to adult questions these days. "Um."

Grams surprised us. "What he means to say, Mrs. Jones"

"Please, I'm Mary."

"Oh. Boys, how about this. You're playing in the neighborhood with your friends, and a deputy sheriff, white, of course they were all white back in those days, drives up and wants to know whose dog that is yonder, running loose. You try to tell him it's yours and you'll go get it, and he says, 'Can't have no loose dogs, might bite somebody.' He pulls out his big, big gun and just shoots it. Right there in front of the children and all. Just shoots it. Dead. Lot of crying children right after that. Can't do nothing about it, though. The deputy was called Deacon because he was a big deal deacon in his church. Very respectable. How many spaces back?"

She got it. She knew what the game was. We had forgotten that NT had told us to drop the game around her.

"That really happen, Grams? To you?" Hank was really, really quiet. "That's not just an indignity; it's way more than that."

"I guess not." Grams was staring straight ahead. "I'm not sure any of your game, as you call it, is funny or ironic. I've been meaning to say something to NT."

For once, my mom didn't get too inquisitive. I was certain to be grilled on the subject at home, but that was not the time or place for lengthy discussion. "Well," she said, as brightly as possible, "it looks like the traffic is a bit lighter now, we might actually get home by dinner time." At least she didn't say, "How 'bout them Redskins?"

Grams did have one more thing to say, and it felt good, to be honest. She turned back and looked directly into my eyes. "You know, Henryk, I was thinking. I do that sometimes, now that I have time to, you know. You always call me Mrs. Jones. All those white folks I worked for all those years, none of them ever called me Mrs. anything. It was always 'Rose this and Rose that.' Except for one family where the little girl, cute as a button, couldn't say her 'R's' so she called me Bessie. I guess that was the maid before me. So, to that family, I pretty soon became 'Bessie.' I'm not sure any of the children in any of those families ever knew my last name. Now, when I hear you call me "Mrs. Jones," I start out thinking you're talking to Hank's mother, Sandra. She's Mrs. Jones. I think you all had best call me Grams, like Hank and Phillis do. Yes, that would make a lot more sense."

We did not continue the game for the rest of the drive home.

It occurred to me that I might, just might, be getting a hint of why Grams seemed so negative about white folk. That must have been back when she was growing up in Prince Edward County. Hank and I knew something about it after NT made us look it up. That was an entirely different world back then, I thought. Trouble was, maybe that world wasn't so different from what was happening now. Grams certainly didn't seem to think so.

And she might have been right.

Thursday, I was in my fifth period class, history, after we had returned from lunch when Mr. Wright came to the classroom. He called the teacher out for a second, and then she motioned for me to come out. Mr. Wright had a terrible look on his face. "Hi, Henryk. Something's come up. I need for you to get your books and come with me." It looked like I was about to be back on page one of the cyber gossip news.

Mr. Wright didn't say anything as we walked to his office. "You are Terry Sullivan's cousin? He lives with you?"

"Yes." Why would this matter?

"I had to take him home today. Actually, to the Jones's house, across the street. Until then, I didn't realize you two were related. Actually, I didn't know Terry from Adam."

"Yes. He moved down here from Boston. Family thing. Why did you have to take him home? Is he sick?"

"No. And yes, I guess." I think years of practice helped Mr. Wright maintain a neutral face in most circumstances, but he seemed really upset. More so than when he tried to talk to me after I got hurt. "He got jumped by some punks in the locker room at the end of PE this morning. I don't know why. I don't know who, and he wouldn't or couldn't say." He didn't seem to want to continue.

Now, I felt horrible. A terrible sinking in my gut, much, much worse than when I heard about the students who got killed. "Is he? Hurt?"

"Not exactly. Pride, though, big time. I think that young man has had some difficulties in his life, and this is not good."

"Um." I couldn't believe it. I was going to my automatic response to anything I thought might be interrogation. I was fighting panic about Terry, and I was beginning to get angry, too. "What happened? Exactly. And why am I here?"

"These, punks grabbed him, wrote something nasty on his back, and threw him out in the hall. No clothes except for his underwear. The clothes they threw in the shower." Mr. Wright looked pained.

I felt sick and then really, really angry. Walter. I almost said it, but forced myself to settle. "I need to go home and see him. Where is he?"

"The Jones's house. I had Mrs. Hernandez pull his emergency card and called home. Eventually, she got your mother at work. That's when we made the connection. Your mother and Mrs. Jones have your families listed as back up emergency contacts for each other, also for Terry. She had us contact the Jones family, and Mrs. Jones, senior that is, agreed that we could bring Terry over there, since she couldn't drive to pick him up. I just got back from dropping him off. I would have come to get you first, but he was a bit of a mess."

"I really, really need to get home, Mr. Wright. Can you get me out of school? Call my mom, I'm sure she'll excuse me. I can take a cab." Terrible images and questions were bouncing around in my head like a video game gone berserk.

"Already got that covered, chief. I'm driving you home myself, right now. I'm a bit concerned about your cousin." We walked to my locker. He didn't say anything more, but a lot of questions were beginning to flood my brain, none that I really wanted to ask him, but all ones that I wanted answers to. A stupid one came up as we walked: he was walking in front of me, but straight to my locker, as if he had been there before. Why did he know where it was? Had he been in it for something? I know it's technically legal for an administrator to search it without me, but I still didn't like the idea of someone being in my locker. Not that I had anything to hide; I'm not Frankie X.

As I grabbed my stuff from the locker, it crossed my mind that I didn't particularly want to be spending time with Mr. Wright. The "free" ride home might be paid for with more interrogation, more questions. As we walked through the halls towards the back of the building where Mr. Wright's car was parked, one of Walter's boys saw me and started to say something. "Hey, Broken-face boy, I...Oh." He realized that I was walking next to Mr. Wright and cut himself off.

"Who was that?" Mr. Wright must be on ready alert all the time. He turned to look back at the rapidly disappearing punk. "What did he want?"

"Um. I'm not sure." Accurate answer to both questions. I was beginning to think that Mr. Wright would decide that I was in fact an unreliable liar, since I always seemed to be telling him that I didn't know the answer to his questions. "I think he's a friend of Walter Anderson's. I don't really know him at all. Just seen him around."

"Hm." At that moment a teacher stopped Mr. Wright with some question, and my problem got pushed back for a while. I should not have said anything.

Christopher Wollenberg

Surprisingly, Mr. Wright did not bother me on the ride to the Jones's house. Just before he let me out, he did talk. "You know, Henryk, kids can be cruel." Oh great, I thought. He's going to give me the old story about learning to ignore petty cruelties, but he surprised me. "But adults, now they can really make a mess of things. We had a gay kid getting picked on a couple years back, and Slate, I mean, we, the school authorities, didn't do anything to help this guy out. So he brings an old kitchen knife to school, presumably to, quote/unquote, protect himself. But he got caught with it before he could use it. Fell out of his backpack in plain sight in class. He left school in a police car, charged with bringing a weapon on to school property. Next thing we know, he's gone and killed himself in juvenile lockup waiting for disposition of his case. Terrible, terrible situation. It could have been prevented if the adults in charge had read the signs and gotten him help instead of telling his mama that 'God doesn't like homosexuals' and letting him fend for himself." He didn't have to tell me who made the comment to the boy's mother. "That memorial plaque in the front hall that talks about we're all family and the need to respect each other developed from the incident. A bunch of students insisted we do something; I guess a lot of them realized what had been going on, but somehow the administration missed it all. We don't need any more wake up calls. We need to get ahead on these situations, instead of putting up a plaque after a kid's dead." He looked out the window, at nothing, I think, and said, "You know, I was a cop for twenty-five years, saw more than enough dead people, but the kids, man, the kids. I remember every one of them." His voice was almost cracking. He cleared his throat and recovered.

He looked at me for a moment, and then added, "You're Frankie's little brother, aren't you? Of course. I seem to remember that one of his memorable fights involved attempting to defend that kid from people who were harassing him. He knocked the hoo-ha out of a couple idiots. A noble cause for sure, but not really the best way to handle the situation." He fished into his pocket for something. "I think your cousin is in for a tough time, Henryk. I don't know his back story, but I don't think it's a good one, and now this." He handed me his card. "On the back are two numbers, Henryk. One is his assigned guidance counselor at school. It's her private cell. She asked me to make sure it was available to Terry. The other is a teen suicide hotline." He looked directly into my eyes. "If you think you need to call either one of these, do it."

That wasn't very encouraging. All the ringing in my ears and dizziness and headache from the concussion seemed to jump back into action. "I will. Thank you, Mr. Wright." I tried not to slam the car door as I hurried out of there. Grams opened the door as I got to it. Her face was terrible. She looked like she was about to cry. Or maybe had been crying. "Come in, young man. Henryk. He's in the living room."

Christopher Wollenberg

CHAPTER 10

Laundry Ticket

Terry was sitting on the couch, wearing sweatpants, a sweatshirt that didn't match, and cheap worn out sneakers, some old gym clothes, probably old lost stuff they kept in the office for various clothing emergencies that come up. He was staring blankly at the wall opposite. His face was puffy and his eyes were bloodshot.

"Hey, man." Again, the great conversationalist.

Terry stared at the wall for a few seconds. "Hey, you, too." This was a dry croak. He didn't say anything else. Stared at the wall; he hadn't looked at me yet.

Grams motioned me into the kitchen. I followed. I wanted to take Terry home, but ...

"That boy's in a world of hurting, son." Tears started floating down her face. "I've seen worse back in the day, but this is close." She sobbed. "One of my friends got, uh, attacked by some white boys when we were all around fifteen. Did terrible things to her. Dumped her off in our front yard about five in the morning." She cut herself off to wipe her eyes. "Terrible, terrible time. In the end, when nothing was done to those boys, and..." She stopped, like she was thinking back, "and you, know, the community didn't do right by her either. I mean her parents were all upset with the boys and all, but they also somehow treated her different, too, after that. The white boys treated her like she was nothing but meat, and the black folks treated her like she was tainted meat. Seemed like everyone did, the preacher, her kinfolk, everyone except me and her friends. She died a few months later. I don't know for sure if she was pregnant or not, but she missed her monthly and killed herself pretty soon after that." Grams was crying pretty steadily now. She blew her nose. "So, you got to look after your cousin. Don't let this do that to him." She nodded at the living room. "Go on, now. Take him home."

I wondered if she had somehow told some of this to Terry. When I walked in, he stood up, croaked, "Thank you, Mrs. Jones," and gave her a long hug. He followed me out the door and across the yard to our house. In my pocket, I fingered the card Mr. Wright had given me.

The thing about guys is that we will always cover up any weakness with macho garbage. I had no idea of what to say or do about what had happened, so I took the easy, macho-stupid route. "So, Terry, you think maybe you could get into some decent threads? I mean, old sweatpants don't seem like your style." I handed him a bottled water, and he took a long drink.

"I didn't know you were a fashion critic. You writing the style column for the paper? But, you know how it is. Dumbass me, I stupidly sent all my clothes out to be showered, forgetting that I didn't have other threads with me, so I had to borrow these. Got 'em from Hank. His second-best wardrobe, I think." He forced a smile.

He took another drink. My turn, but it was hard to stay light. "Seriously, you okay?"

"Yes and no. Probably mostly no, but a little yes. I hope. I need some time to think about all this. I think I'll head upstairs now."

"Anything I can do?"

"Not really." He started upstairs. I could feel Mr. Wright's card in my pocket and I could see Grams's face, hear her story. "Actually, there is one thing. I don't want you to think I'm going all weird on you. But while I was sending my clothes out to be showered, I also got this writing on my back, sort of a laundry ticket, if you know what I mean. I'd really like to get it off, and I can't reach it myself."

He turned around and lifted up the sweatshirt. I reflexively gasped, and I think he gave a little sob himself. "FAGBOY" was written across his back with a black marker. Big and bad as could be.

I had to retreat to macho-stupid again, what else could I do? "Well, if you're sure you don't need it to claim your clothes. Let me get a bottle of that remover stuff and a couple rags. Meet you in the bathroom upstairs."

It took a while, a lot of scrubbing, even with the magic removal stuff. And I'm sure it wasn't good for Terry's skin, but I got it all. He didn't say two words the entire time. Not the time for me to go into macho-mouthy, so I didn't say much either. I really wanted to ask him who did it, all the while being pretty sure I knew and not wanting to deal with that. I had had recent experience with interrogations, and didn't want to put Terry through all that right then. Mom and dad could be counted on to chime in. And who knew what Frankie X would do.

"All done. It looks kind of raw where the letters were; you probably ought to run through the shower before you get some decent clothes on. Wash any leftover chemicals off." I fell back on my other cure for any situation. "Want something to eat? I'm going downstairs."

"Clothes critic to the end, eh? And a waiter, besides. No. Thanks. I'll pass. I'm going to take a shower and then go sit and think. Or something."

When I went downstairs with the rags and bottle of remover, Terry was in his room blasting heavy metal music. I remembered what Grams said and decided that in a little while I would make up some excuse to go check on him.

At about four o'clock, I couldn't take it anymore and knocked on his door. The music was still blasting. A person could do a lot of damage to himself under the cover of loud music; I pounded. Tried the door. Duh, it wasn't locked, so I went in. Terry was at his makeshift easel painting furiously.

"I'm okay, cuz. Thanks for checking on me. You can go now. I'm kind of busy."

Mission accomplished. I wouldn't have to use the phone numbers Mr. Wright gave me. I left.

My dad got home before my mom. He heard the music, of course, and looked at me.

"He's okay." I said. "At least that's what he says. He asked me to leave him alone, but he's okay. I hope."

"Your mom called me at work and said there was some sort of problem at school. You know anything about it?"

I told him what I knew, leaving out speculation about Walter's bunch, and trying to gloss over some of the details. I didn't want to let him know how worried I was, so I didn't mention what Mr. Wright told me about the suicide of the gay student a few years back.

"What, exactly was written on his back?"

No way out of it, so I told him. My voice was shaking when I did. I thought I might cry, not exactly a macho thing.

"So, it's off his back now? And he's just up in his room painting? Busy, as he put it?" This was new territory for Dad. He'd dealt with Frankie X and his troubles, all of which he instigated, and I of course, had had my bad moments, but this was totally out of his area of expertise. Mom would clearly have to figure out what to do. She walked in the door just in time.

"Where is he? Is he okay? Why didn't you answer your phone? I've been calling all afternoon."

Ah, the phone. I had forgotten to turn it on after we left the school. "Mom, we're okay. He's okay. I guess. I forgot to turn on the phone after I left school. Sorry. I've been busy." I had to repeat the whole story to her. Apparently, Mr. Wright had left out most of the details and allowed her to think that Terry was sick or somehow had a minor problem in PE. Retelling the story did not make it any easier. My voice was cracking again when I got to some of the details. I told her what was written on Terry's back without being prompted.

To her credit, she didn't go into full mom attack mode immediately, but Dad and I knew it was coming. "I'm going to go see him. Now. Have you been up there yet, Tomás?"

Dad shook his head. "Just got in myself. Just got the full story." He looked at me quizzically. "I think. Anything left out, Henryk?"

"No, sir. You and mom know as much as I do."

Mom went upstairs. To avoid piling on, Dad stayed downstairs. I didn't like the way he looked at me. I think I was beginning to get a Frankie X complex.

The music level went down. We couldn't hear them talking, though. In a couple minutes, mom came back downstairs. "At this time, I can only report that Terry is 'busy,' as he put it, and that he would prefer to be left alone. We need to respect his wishes, at least for now. Let's eat. Henryk, I'm sending you up with some food for him in a bit. Luckily, Francis has a night class so he won't be home to put in his two bits worth for a long time."

After mom and dad threw together some dinner, I took a tray up to Terry. He thanked me, said he was busy, still painting, and turned his back to me. I returned to the kitchen.

As everyone knows, the cliché about the elephant in the room is pretty accurate. No one at dinner wanted to say anything about what happened to Terry, and everyone at dinner wanted to say something about what happened to Terry. Pretty hard to ignore. Finally, Mom broke our silence.

"Henryk, this thing they wrote on Terry's back. Are the kids at school saying this stuff about him?"

Well, they will now, I was sure. I hoped against hope that no one got a clear photo of Terry or his back, but it was a school full of phones/cameras, so good luck with that dream. "No. I don't think anyone pays any attention to him at all. He has a few friends that he hangs with, but they're pretty much out of the way. No one really cares one way or the other about them. This was just…" I started to say something about Walter's bunch, and cut myself off, "just, some crazy rednecks trying to prove they're tough guys." Which, was, actually, a pretty fair description of Walter's bunch. "As far as the gay part goes …" This time, Dad cut me off.

"I don't know if there is speculation about Terry being gay. And I don't care. I would think that would be something for Terry to announce, so our discussion of it amounts to baseless gossip. It wouldn't make any difference how anyone in this family feels about him, so it's a pretty irrelevant discussion."

Ouch. I wasn't even thinking about that. Just about what the kids might be saying, which was nothing, at least before this happened. "I forgot to bring him a drink." I grabbed a bottle of his favorite from the fridge and went upstairs before anyone had time to strategize or otherwise plan an attack on Terry's privacy. When I knocked, Terry told me to come in.

He bumped the music up a notch. Somehow, he talked under it. I could hear if I paid attention, but no one downstairs would. I handed him the drink. "Forgot this on the first trip."

"Thanks."

I had heard somewhere that if you don't talk, the other person will. I didn't look at the door, just stood there. I could see the corner of a fresh painting behind Terry, but that was it.

"What makes me maddest is, it's not true. I've got friends who are," he made air quotes with both hands, 'Fagboys,' but I'm not." He trailed off. Tears collected in his eyes. He looked straight at me. "Just because your mom's boyfriend uses an eleven year-old kid like he does your mom doesn't make you gay. It makes you a lot of things, but gay ain't one of them. I think you're probably born one way or the other, and it takes a while to figure it out. And just because the kid goes along with it, doesn't make him gay, either. He goes along with it because said boyfriend threatens his mom. And someone's got to protect his mom. The kid becomes what they call in war, collateral damage. Collateral damage from the private war his mother is having with her own demons. Spills over to her kid, sometimes." He took a long drink and stared off, maybe back to Boston. "It makes you really, really angry. Ready to fight the whole world. Maybe shoot a few people."

Ouch. This wasn't good. I didn't need a degree in psychology to notice. "But not yourself?" He knew where Frankie kept his guns and ammo, but, as far as I knew, didn't have keys.

"Oh no. I'm going to keep on fighting. At least for now. Can't let some pieces of caca or mom's boyfriend control my life."

"You ever think about seeing a shrink?" First thing that came to mind, I swear. I know that there had been talk about Terry getting professional help, but he seemed to be doing pretty well up to now.

"Been there. Done that. Couple times in Boston. Some of my schools kind of made me. I'm doing what I call art therapy on my own. Honest, you could look it up. There really is such a thing. People get degrees in it or something." He looked over at the painting he had been working on all afternoon.

It was amazing. Nerve-wracking in a way, but amazing. It was Terry's self-portrait, showing him as this totally angry, maybe even malevolent, boxer. Fists up, ready to kill with them. On a second look, maybe not malevolent, but cornered, terrified, and ready to kill. I was happy to see that he was not holding an Uzi or Glock in the painting. Just the fists. And he was alone. There was no particular target. The world, maybe? Himself?

Now it was his turn to say nothing. Forced me to talk. "Um." At my usual level of intelligence, again. "Um. Wow, Terry. You have some kind of talent. I, um, you, I mean…"

"I think what you mean to say is that you understand that I don't really want your folks, or anyone else, to know the stuff I just told you. I know they're going to bug you about what happened, and you're going to have to give them the general story, but don't get too specific, okay. And don't say anything about this painting or what I told you."

"I'm cool with it. Just don't shoot anybody. Or you. And don't lose the painting. It's something else. I'm pretty sure it truly qualifies as art." I retreated back downstairs.

On the way down I quickly scrolled through Facebook and the other social media to see if any images of Terry's attack were up. One post was all, but it was blurry and just showed a naked back with the writing on it. Terry was not identifiable in the photo, and whoever posted it must not have known who he was. You could read the word "Fagboy," though. The caption said, "Disgusting attack at Teddy Roosevelt." I didn't have time to read the hundred or so comments already up, but the first one said something like, "In these times, people still do this to other people?" and the second one seemed to echo that idea. How long would it take for someone to figure out it was Terry and post his name?

"Everything okay up there?" Dad eyed me. "The music got turned up when you went in."

I didn't have much to say, so I didn't. "Um."

"Well, is he okay?" Mom wasn't going to buy my short all-purpose answer.

I thought about the new painting. I thought about what his mom's boyfriend had done to him. I thought about my promise to keep the information to myself. I lied. "Yeah, he's okay. A bit shook up, but I guess he's had some experience in these things and knows he'll live. He wasn't hurt like I was, but ..." I didn't know what to say, didn't want to say much of anything.

"I'm not sure what to do at this point," Mom muttered. That was a shock; she always knew, or thought she knew what to do. "I do know we don't want to get Frankie involved. This would definitely put him on his white horse."

"Do you know who did this? Is the school going to do anything about it?" Dad was beginning to sound like he was about to mount his own white horse and go charging off.

I repeated the part about Mr. Wright bringing me home. "In the car on the way home, he didn't say anything about who did it. I don't know if Terry knows, or if Mr. Wright thinks he knows, but I sure don't." Dad gave me his Frankie-you-are-lying look. "Really, dad. I don't know and I don't think Terry does either. He's too new to the school to know anyone but the people he hangs with. Maybe Mr. Wright can look at security video or talk to people, or something. He really tried to find out who hit me; he talked to me a couple times and tried to find witnesses in the stairwell, but I don't think he wanted to talk to Terry today. Maybe tomorrow or sometime, I don't know."

Mom was sniffling. "I just hope this isn't some sort of vendetta against the boys from this family. I hope it's just a coincidence."

"Anyone at the school even know you and Terry are cousins?" Dad asked.

"I doubt it. Maybe a couple, but even Mr. Wright didn't make the connection until he had his secretary chasing down emergency contacts and they realized that his contacts and mine overlapped."

"Well, let's hope that tomorrow is better for everyone. And let's not tell Frankie." Mom stood up, "I'm going up there and wish him a good night and see for myself that he's at least 'okay,' as you claim."

Hank called me a bit later, and I told him the story, leaving out the part about Terry's hellish past in Boston, of course.

"There's serious stuff going on around here." Hank was back on his own soap box. "I'm going to look at the posts and see what people are saying. Like I said when you got hurt, one person's tragedy is someone else's opportunity. I am definitely writing an opinion piece on bullying for the *Reporter.*"

This could get to be a problem. "No names. Don't get too specific. Find some other examples to prove your points. I've got enough to worry about with this on top of Walter's bunch."

"Right."

CHAPTER II

More Boom-boom!

There were two surprises awaiting the staff and students at good old Teddy Roosevelt High Friday morning. The first was a particularly unwelcome surprise for the administration. The administration got a quick lesson on the power of social media within the student body.

There were hundreds of notes all over the school. Slapped on lockers, taped to windows, stuck on students; there were all kinds of paper used, all kinds of colors, but mostly yellow post-it notes were used. They all said the same thing: "#notinourschool," and, underneath, the universal "No" sign of a circle with a line diagonally across it. This sat on one word: "Fagboy."

I'm sure the instigators had good intentions, but the execution came off a bit clumsily. Security staffers began pulling the signs off lockers and other public places but left the students alone. Once the students got to their homerooms, some teachers thought it was an anti-gay sign and immediately made the students take them off. Other teachers realized the intent, but since almost no adults knew about the attack on Terry, they didn't understand what was happening either. I don't know if the principal even had time to get an email out to the teachers; the student organizers really caught them by surprise. I managed to take a couple photos of the notes all over the place to show to Terry later on. I'm sure that in many classes there were impromptu discussions about students' First Amendment rights along with speculation about what had happened, but those got stopped by the announcement that there would be an assembly in the gym to honor the two students killed in the car accident. It was to begin as soon as morning announcements were over.

We had a vocabulary test scheduled in my English class, so I was happy to have it bumped to Monday. The teacher was not so thrilled. I guess it would have been bad form to have the assembly on Friday afternoon, at the time we normally had pep rallies. Somehow, sad-sad/rah-rah would have been too much. They had postponed the Friday game, anyway. I think it was really a memorial for the star quarterback who got killed, but since it would have been rude to ignore the girl who died with him, the event was announced in both names. As we walked down the hallway to the gym, people were talking, but not loudly. I was lost in thought when I literally bumped into Melantha who was also lost in thought.

In my normal smooth manner, I apologized first. "Oops, sorry. I wasn't looking. Oh, hi, Melantha, what's up?"

She looked at me blankly for a long second. "Oh. Yes. Henryk. Cafeteria on Monday. And then my locker." I guess I looked a little surprised by this. "Oh. Sorry. It's how I remember people. Where I saw them last. Helps me make the connections." She smiled a little. "Going to this, uh, thing?"

"We have a choice?"

"In the cosmic sense? Yes. But practically speaking, probably not." We continued walking with the crowd into the gym and headed for seats in the bleachers as directed by a teacher. Melantha had to speak a bit louder. "What's this all about anyway?"

I wasn't sure, but I made my best guess. "I think it's a sort of memorial thing for the two seniors who got killed in the car accident last Monday. Remember, we were in the cafeteria when the news broke out. I think the school wants to do something, and also maybe make an impression on us. The take-away message is going to be, 'Follow the rules, don't skip class, don't leave campus during school, and don't get hit by drugged up drivers.'" I surprised myself: only nine years in public schools, and I had become cynical. We took our seats amidst the clamor and waited.

"Is this going to be religious or anything?" Melantha asked. "Can they do that?"

"I'm not exactly a constitutional lawyer, but, no, I don't think so. They'd probably have to make it voluntary if it was actually a church service." Of course "voluntary" in a school can be pretty hard to pin down. Who would not go to something like this? They'd be publically declaring themselves different, or worse, anti-God or something. At the very least, anti-football, which is almost the same in some circles.

I was saved from any more philosophical thought by Walter's bunch. "Hey. Look! It's Broken-face boy!" Great choice of seats. Three rows down from those guys.

"Oh, yeah. Red-eye guy." My adrenaline started to flow, I think. I felt jumpy, but I couldn't tell if I was scared or angry. I really didn't know what to do, so I did nothing.

Another voice, "Who's he with? Morticia?" Figures, these guys probably still watch "The Addams Family" every day after school on some children's re-run channel. I could picture them sitting around in some basement watching old TV shows when they weren't playing video death games or out trying to terrorize the neighborhood.

A different voice chimed in, "You mean Amish girl, there." He pronounced the "am" syllable to rhyme with "ham," so it took me a moment to recognize the reference. He had a point, though. Mel was wearing a long dark skirt and a billowy long-sleeved white blouse. Her long hair wasn't in a bun, and of course she wasn't wearing a bonnet, but with no makeup she did remind you of the photos of Amish girls you see once in a while.

The first voice came back. "Might be, One Punch. You want to bang her out, too?"

"I don't know. Too skinny. I might one-punch the punk, but I'd do a lot more than one shot at the chick, and I don't think she could take it." Great, now the guy had a nickname based on taking me out with one punch. "You guys would have to call me Three Punch if I got a shot at her."

"Right, OP. Three Punch. That would make you TP. Like in toilet paper." His buddies laughed.

"Guess I'll stick to OP. Like in that old TV show. You know Opie and his dad and that aunt, what's-her-name."

I really wanted to turn around and see exactly who this guy was, but…

I glanced at Melantha, who seemed totally unaware of all of this. I stared straight ahead, my hands shaking, and hoped the assembly would get started. I've heard of PTSD, who hasn't, but I never thought about it happening to me. I could almost see the fist, OP's fist, apparently, coming at my face, and I could almost feel myself knocked into oblivion all over again.

My phone vibrated, and I took a quick glance at it. Hank: "For the game: White football player and black cheerleader headed for an afternoon's delight, car crash, etc., back two spaces. Black player, white cheerleader, back a kazillion spaces. Both participants white, no crisis, no points, other than the pointless death, of course." I smiled, stress gone, for now. I replied: For once, the OMG girls have the appropriate phrase at tongue tip. Stupid and sad way to go." I think Mark Twain once claimed to be quoting a man about to be hung as saying something like, "If it weren't for the honor, I'd rather not be here." I'm sure those two seniors would have rather not been the center of attention first period on Friday.

The assembly staggered to a start with the screech of microphone feedback and then the request to stand and recite the Pledge of Allegiance. I was thinking about what would constitute "and justice for all" for Walter's bunch when the principal started.

I didn't know either victim, and I didn't think I would have an emotional stake in the assembly. I thought it would be an interesting exercise for me to observe. Some of the player's teammates came on stage and read short items expressing their loss and what a great guy he was. For once, the OMG girls were a somber lot. A couple of them were recruited to say something appropriate about their girl, although it was unclear what she really meant to them. There was none of the chaos and pain of the cafeteria the day we found out about the accident. Everyone had had time to get used to the idea of the deaths. For a lot of us there was still something there because we had never experienced the death of a contemporary. Most of us had the experience of relatives dying, but not someone our own age.

Walter's bunch really showed their colors. That is, they were their natural selves, never a good idea, but especially at a memorial service. They found a new target, the football player who died. We were far enough back in the gym that they thought no one would pay them any attention as they whispered and joked among themselves. I couldn't quite make out everything they said, but there seemed to be some comments about the activities the player and the girl were presumably planning and jokes about who got a bigger bang out of the experience. At one point one of them laughed out loud. A teacher sitting at the end of a row nearby gave them the stink eye to shut them up, and they lowered their whispering. What might have served them better, and really quieted them down would have been to look behind them. Along the top row of the bleachers was the entire JV football team.

Turns out that cracking jokes about a Down syndrome student like Donald, or Muslims, or even attacking an anonymous freshman or two is a reasonably safe hobby. Cracking funny about football players and their dear departed leader, not so safe. At least, not in front of said players. It also turns out that when a bunch of guys are already upset, hitting something, or someone, might make them feel just a little bit better.

When they dismissed us from the assembly, Melantha and I were just stepping off the bleachers on to the gym floor when the players exploded on Walter's bunch. I turned around to see some players shoving at the crew, others just yelling about the insults. Someone took a swing at Walter, who was standing one step lower than the player. The fist caught him in the side of his face and he toppled backward and sat down to keep from falling down. At the same time, one of his boys went flying down the bleacher seats on his back, either hit or shoved by a player. The boy stopped in a heap at the bottom next to where we were standing and didn't move.

Melantha stared at the kid for a second or so and then went into her rescue mode, the one she must have remembered from health class. "Don't move him. He may have neck or head trauma. Someone go get help. Actually, you, in the red shirt, you go find a teacher or security. Tell them there's a student here who's just fallen down the bleachers and may have hit his head or broken his neck or something."

In a bizarre flashback, it seemed like a rote repetition of what she said when I went down. I looked around and saw no one in a red shirt, which I thought was strange, but it didn't matter because all kinds of teachers and security people were rushing over. Walkie-talkies barked, and the adults started moving the students away. The players and Walter's bunch quit their beefing and left also.

Melantha looked stunned and started to reach for the kid, but I grabbed her arm to hustle her out of the gym. I couldn't see any advantage to sticking around. More questions and so on.

"You're not supposed to leave the victim until qualified assistance arrives or the scene has become too dangerous for you." She was half resisting my pull towards the exit. "Are those people qualified?"

"As qualified as any around here. They have radios and can call for the nurse and ambulance if they need to." I didn't add the obvious, that the scene had become dangerous for us, although not in the traditional textbook sense of possible physical harm to us.

She looked pretty dubious but followed me on out. We nearly ran into Mr. Slate as we turned the corner. He was holding his radio next to his ear.

"Jonasz!" Still pronounced wrong. "What are you doing?"

Honesty, as we all know, is always the best policy. "Leaving, sir."

"Not so fast. Did you see what happened in there?"

My fallback answer, "Um."

"Not good enough. You, and the girl, Mr. Wright's office. What's your name, girl?"

"Melantha." She did not look at him. She looked at me, and I shrugged.

"Melantha what? Come on, I don't have time for games."

Melantha looked at me again, confused. "Melantha what? Oh, my last name. I am Melantha Raptis." Oh, I thought. I don't think I actually knew, either. I guess I had a new piece of the puzzle to figure out. I was sure, if she ever talked to me again, she would expect me to know where her name came from.

Mr. Slate grimaced a moment. "Weird." And then to his radio, "On the way."

"Where's Mr. Wright's office?" Melantha looked very confused. "I'm supposed to go to my trigonometry class right now. We always have an interesting challenge problem to start the class. I don't want to miss it."

"I don't think we really have to go right now. They're kind of busy. If Mr. Wright really wants us, he can find us. That was just Slate sounding, well, something. Just go ahead to your second period class. I am." Wow. I actually got several coherent sentences out without sounding too stupid. Couldn't last, though. "Wait." Melantha stopped and turned around.

"Something wrong? I really want to get to trig."

"Trig? You're taking trig? I thought you were in ninth like me. How can you be in trig?"

"It's the next class after the algebra and geometry courses. Isn't that what everyone does?"

Couldn't argue with that logic. "Um. So you already finished two algebras and geometry before you got to ninth grade?"

"So it would appear. I did take one in summer school, so that pushed me ahead, too. I'm going to be late. Or not. I hope."

I hurried to class trying to figure out if I had even heard of anyone who had earned three credits of high school math before even starting high school.

I got called down to Mr. Wright's office just after I got settled into my seat in fourth period, Spanish class. Not good. I didn't care one way or the other about missing the class, but lunch period would be during this time, and I didn't want to miss lunch. Melantha had lunch at the same time. She was probably in fourth year Latin or something.

When I got to Mr. Wright's office, Walter was there. I guess they took Walter to the nurse's office to put ice on his bruises and then brought him up to Mr. Wright's office to explain what transpired. I looked at Walter, and he at me. I didn't say anything, didn't nod; I worked on my poker face. Walter did about the same, although I think if he had tried to talk, it would have been painful. I've had some experience in these matters, and he didn't look too comfortable; his face was puffy, and he held an ice bag on the left side of his face. I was having a very difficult time trying to work up any sympathy. I wasn't sure why I was in the office. Had Mr. Wright finally figured out that Walter was involved in my injury, or was I there because of the dustup in the gym? Mr. Wright came out of his office.

"Mr. Jonasz," he pronounced it almost correctly. "I need to talk to you. In my office, please. Mrs. Hernandez, did you track down that girl Mr. Slate mentioned? Melantha something?"

"Raptis. I called the classroom, sir. Her teacher said she was there and would send her as soon as she finished a short quiz or something."

Mr. Slate walked in as she finished. "Mrs. Hernandez, send an office aide to retrieve miss, what was her name? Call the classroom and tell the teacher that the girl is to come when we call, not at her convenience.

I went into Mr. Wright's office still working on my poker face and thinking about what not to say. Mr. Slate charged in behind me and practically slammed the door.

"Why is it that you always seem to be right where there's trouble, young Jonasz?" Very kind of him to ask after my health, I thought. I didn't answer. I thought about what Frankie X might have said. He would have pointed out that Mr. Slate always seemed to be around trouble, also. Both just lucky, eh?

Mr. Wright spoke up. "We got a chance to look at some video of the gym this morning. Seems like you were only sitting a few rows in front of the guys that got into it. You know anything about what happened? One teacher thought that some words were exchanged, but she didn't know what they boys were saying. She said it seemed like the whole JV team just went crazy all at once. You have any idea what might have precipitated the brawl?"

"Um." I couldn't see any real point to ratting out Walter and company. I mean, it wasn't going to help me personally.

And, I figured, looking at Walter's face, that he had pretty much gotten the point. Sort of instant education, provided for free by angry peers. "I think, um, that Walter and the players had a disagreement that, uh, escalated into fisticuffs." That sounded almost like the six o'clock news. Lame. But, accurate.

"We got that much figured out on our own, Jonasz." Slate chimed in. I didn't correct his pronunciation. "What happened up there? What were they talking about? It sure wasn't the weather. Something got the boys fired up. Did you see anyone swing first?" I probably did, but I didn't want to get into specifics.

Mrs. Hernandez knocked and then entered with Melantha in tow. Melantha looked at me and arched her eyebrows and nodded her head back and forth a split second, the universal questioning look.

"Miss, uh, what's your name?"

"Melantha Raptis. I really needed to finish that quiz before I left class." She stared at Slate and then Mr. Wright. "Am I under arrest?"

Where did that come from? It set both men back for a second.

Mr. Wright jumped in before Slate could cause more damage. "Goodness, no, Miss Raptis. Melantha. We just were hoping that you and Henryk here could shed some light on why those boys suddenly erupted in a brawl in the stands behind you. Mr. Slate recalled seeing Henryk and you in the vicinity of the fight. So, could you tell us what you saw or heard just before the fireworks?"

"Fireworks?" Her turn to be set back a step. She looked at him like he had pigs flying out of his mouth.

"You know. The yelling and shoving and fighting. What did they say to each other to get all that ruckus going? A teacher said she thought they were arguing or something before the fire-, the fighting broke out."

"Oh. They had a lot to say. At first, just the boys that got hit." She didn't know Walter's name, but she was right; it wasn't so much a fight as a beat down. The JV guys weren't fighting, they were hitting, and Walter's bunch, standing lower in the bleachers, wasn't really fighting; they were just getting hit, or trying to avoid being hit.

Melantha paused, not for dramatic effect, but to collect her thoughts. "'Hey. Look! It's breakfast boy! Oh, yeah. Red-eye guy. Who's he with? Mortician?'"

Amazing. Audio playback. Except that she thought that "Broken-face boy" was "breakfast boy," and she heard "Morticia" as "mortician." She continued to repeat exactly what they said about us. It was just a stream of sentences, no identification of who said each one. "'Might be, One Punch. You want to bang her out, too?'

'I don't know. Too skinny. I might one-punch the punk, but I'd do a lot more than one shot at the chick, and I don't think she could take it. You guys would have to call me Three Punch if I got a shot at her.

'Right, OP. Three Punch. That would make you TP. Like in toilet paper.'

'Guess I'll stick to OP. Like in that old TV show. You know Opie and his dad and that aunt, what's-her-name.'"

My adrenaline started to pump up again, even though they weren't in the room saying it, and Melantha was repeating it all in a flat monotone with no inflection or emotion.

Melantha looked at me and then Mr. Wright, and then me again. "I don't know why they would be talking about a mortician. And I don't know what they meant by 'bang her out.' And 'one shot at the chick.'" Melantha didn't seem at all upset by this reportage. She could have been quoting stock market prices. "Then those boys started saying things about the boy and girl that died in that accident. 'That boy sure got a big hit Monday. Worse than in a game. Bet he was going to bang with that girl. Wonder what she was doing for him when they got banged. Yeah, that's it, when they got banged.' They laughed a lot, although I don't see what was so funny. I don't know who said what, but they were going back and forth and thought they were pretty funny. I don't know why." Melantha glanced at me, and I shrugged. "They said some other things, too. 'Look at that picture of the pretty boy quarterback. Bet he doesn't look so pretty now. Yeah. Closed casket funeral for him. Bet he looks even worse than Crate. I don't know. If he dies in his sleep, people'll still beg to have a closed casket.' I don't know why they started talking about Crate like that." She looked at Mr. Wright. "Then a teacher, I think, looked mean at them, and that made them quiet down, and I couldn't hear what they said. Then, after the assembly ended, and we were going out, they all started yelling at each other. I couldn't understand what they were saying, but it was very loud. And then the boys at the top started hitting and shoving the boys on the lower level, just above where we had been sitting. Someone got knocked down to the bottom of the seats. Is he okay?"

I moved around as if to stand up, and she glanced at me. I tried to shake no to her. Slate and Wright had already heard more than enough. I wondered if they would be a bit curious about why they called me "Broken face boy" and who the "One Punch, OP," was that she mentioned in her recitation.

"So, Jonasz, is that about the size of it? Your short bus girl have the story right?" Slate did his best imitation of a penetrating stare at me. My girl? Um. "Short bus girl?" Now he's telling us that he thinks Melantha is disabled in some way because she has total recall of some comments? And, it's okay to insult her this way? All in all, though, this was not the ideal time for Melantha's total recall to kick in. "And you didn't think all this was germane to the conversation we've been trying to have with you?" Slate was really, really, beginning to irritate me. "Who would you be trying to protect here? And why?"

Good question, actually. Easy answer, though. Me. "Um. Well, you see…" Mr. Wright cut me off.

"Okay, Henryk. We'll get back to you later. I think we have a pretty good picture of what happened in the bleachers today. I'm beginning to think I have an idea of a couple other incidents as well, but that's for another time. Mr. Slate, we need to deal with young Walter Anderson out there along with the rest of this mess. Melantha, Henryk, see Mrs. Hernandez for passes. Have her send you to lunch and then class if you've missed your regular lunch time." He called out to Mrs. Hernandez, "Please send in Walter. I'd like to hear his version of events."

I just hoped Walter wouldn't blame me for all the information they had, but he probably would. Ironically, it really was my fault. If Melantha hadn't been dragged into this when they caught up with me, Slate and Wright wouldn't have gotten such a clear picture. Who knew that she would be the audio recording the surveillance cameras didn't provide?

CHAPTER 12

Silence is Golden

Melantha and I were standing at Mrs. Hernandez's desk while she wrote the passes. Walter had already gone into Mr. Wright's office when Walter's father, Bernard Anderson, stormed in just behind us. Mrs. Hernandez was smiling at us when she saw Bernard. The smile disappeared. Melantha grabbed her pass and practically ran for the door. I brilliantly stayed put, stupidly holding the pass and waiting for the show.

I've seen Bernard Anderson driving down the street wearing his full Nazi costume, and that is definitely a terrifying vision, but his normal, work-a-day self is just as intimidating. Especially for poor Mrs. Hernandez. She must have been new this year, because I'm sure that Walter and his father had been in the security office previous years, and other secretaries would have had to face him. He was about six and a half feet tall, wearing heavy boots, dirty black denim pants, and a denim jacket. He owns a small masonry company, so in the middle of the day this would have been his normal appearance. But 250 or 300 pounds of angry bear in your office can be a bit unsettling. Bernard had definitely been in the office before. He charged directly over to Mr. Wright's closed office door and jerked it open. I could see Walter sitting in a chair holding an ice pack to his face and looking sort of pathetic. He jumped to his feet when his father burst in. The door slammed shut and the noise started. Out of the corned of my eye I could see Mrs. Hernandez on the walkie-talkie calling for other security people.

The look on Slate's face when Bernard charged in was probably worth the price of admission, but all I got was the audio feed. I could hear Bernard's yelling and Slate's voice and even Mr. Wright's, so it had to be pretty intense in there. This seemed like high entertainment, so I hung back a moment, even though Melantha was waving at me to leave with her. It quieted down some, and I couldn't make out what was been said. Presumably, either Mr. Wright or Slate was giving Bernard the general story. I don't know if they told him all the details Melantha had provided, but it was obvious that Walter had gotten punched out, and I guess that was enough for Bernard. I heard him yell, "You let some punk nigger knock you down. He only hit you once, and you didn't take him out!" I wonder if it occurred to Bernard that Mr. Wright, although not a punk, was clearly in the other category of subhuman he mentioned. I also wondered what Mr. Wright thought about this. The next sound was Walter getting hit by his father. Just one very loud crack. I wondered if that's what it sounded like when I caught that punch in the stairwell. Two security aides came rushing into the office and pulled the door open. I could see Bernard standing over Walter, who was sitting on the floor. "You either fight to the finish, or you start over with me, and I finish it!" Bernard glared at the security guards, almost daring them to stop him. He looked briefly at the other two men, glared at Walter again, and turned, and stormed back out. Walter yelled at his father as he left. It sounded like, "I'll kill you some day! You know that, right!" I think he waited until his father was far enough away to miss the threat. Once again I was in the middle of a crime scene, or at least close enough for it to cost me time, so I nodded to Mrs. Hernandez and hustled down the hall to lunch.

I ran into Hank in the hallway and quickly told him about the morning's events. I could see the wheels turning as he composed yet another story for the *Reporter*. "Hey, I've got a lesson with Carl this afternoon. How about you ride along and fill me in on the details. Dad's picking me, us, up at the usual place right after the last bell." I caught up with Melantha at lunch, before we went to our fourth period classes, or what was left of them.

I tried to tell her what happened after she left, but she …

"Henryk, I am so lost right now. I feel like we just had an earthquake. First, those awful boys saying all that about you and then about that football player and that girl and Crate and then the fight and then Mr. What's-his-name giving you and me all that trouble when we didn't do anything and then that crazy big man running into the office!" Her hands were actually shaking. I don't think there was a lesson in health class to deal with this kind of excitement, no rote response recommended. "I probably don't want to know what happened after that man got into the office. I don't want to spend more time with those other men trying to explain things. I don't think they listen much. Especially the assistant principal."

Oh. She had a point. I was probably going to be back in the hot seat again with Slate and Wright after me, and she didn't need that. "Well, it was a lovely service," I muttered lamely, and tried to smile.

Melantha looked at me like now I had pigs flying out of my mouth. "Hunh?"

"Never mind. A joke. What a mess." We ate quickly and didn't say much.

"I'm going to class. I've missed too much already today." I couldn't tell if she was angry with me or just stressed over how her day had gone so far. I almost said, "See you sixth period in Wright's office," but it resisted another lame attempt at humor.

I was right, of course. About ten minutes into sixth period, the call for me to report to Mr. Wright's office came through to the teacher. I hope that the fourth and sixth period teachers had not dealt with Frankie, because this getting called out to the security office certainly could add to their idea of me as a mini Frankie. Twice in one day. A couple of the other students from fourth period were there, and they couldn't resist commenting. Frankie would have left with a grin and considerable swagger. I slunk out.

Mr. Wright was in the office alone. He did not smile or stand when I came in.

"Have a seat, Mr. Jonasz."

Mr. Jonasz? Not Henryk? A command to sit? What was my new crime?

"A couple of questions: One. What did you actually see in the office this morning, when Mr. Anderson joined us?"

Somehow, I thought my fallback, um, would not suffice. Still, old habits die hard, "Um. Actually, nothing, sir." Good try. Semi-honesty is always the best policy, right?

"Nothing nothing, or maybe something, but mostly nothing?"

"Well, I did see Mr. Anderson come flying in, and I did see him go flying back out after a couple minutes."

"And, in between? Did you happen to hear anything? See anything else?"

"Um."

"Henryk. Here's the deal. We didn't call the police in after the little set-to in my office. At least not yet. Mr. Slate and I need to talk with the principal and a social worker first. So, if you saw, or think you saw anything, it might be best if you keep it to yourself until we can sort this mess out. Have you talked to anyone about what happened, or what you may think you saw or heard?"

Clearly, now was the time for a straight out lie. "Oh, no, sir. I went to lunch and then right to sixth period." I did not want Melantha or Hank dragged into this. I was hoping that he had forgotten the second question he promised me. No such luck.

"Second question. Let me put this as, uh, gently as I can. After hearing what Miss Raptis reported about what was said by Walter Anderson and his buddies, do you think it is possible that one of them was the guy who hit you in the stairwell a few weeks back? It seemed like there were some early comments that indicated something along that line. Do you know any of these guys? Have you had other run-ins with them?" Technically, that was more than one question, but who was I to point that out?

"Um." And, "Well, yes. Maybe. The hitter part. Walter lives near me, and I've known about him since elementary school, and tried to stay away from him and his father all my life. Mostly, no problems. They were giving Donnie a bad time, and I said something. But I don't know who actually hit me. I know it wasn't Walter. I was looking directly at him, and he was too far away up the stairs. At the assembly, when they said that stuff, I didn't want to turn around and look at him. Maybe because I was a bit scared, didn't want to look like I wanted to start something." Ouch. I just realized that I had pretty much told the truth. Not usually a good policy, but there I was. NT would have been mad at me for getting conned into giving up information, but the cop in him would have appreciated Mr. Wright's successful attack.

"Interesting. I thought I heard something about 'One Punch' in that remarkable little rendition of the events by your, uh, lady friend. Thought I might get close to the bottom of your attack sooner or later. Well, in any case, what we need now is for you to go on about your business. Stay away from Walter and his band of fools. If I were you, I would just lay low and wait for it all to blow over. Maybe sometime in the future whoever hit you will get identified by the usual means; one of his buddies rats him out to avoid some other problem. Or maybe, one day when I have lots and lots of spare time, I'll try to figure out who 'One Punch' is. You never know. Henryk, have a good rest of your day." I think his smile was genuine. "And, Henryk, try, really try, to stay away from possible crime scenes. Mrs. Hernandez will give you yet another pass back to class."

Excellent advice, about staying away from crime scenes. But, was I in the middle of another one, covering up a witnessed assault by a father on his minor child? I was glad Hank invited me to ride along to Carl's; I really needed to talk to NT.

CHAPTER 13

Dismal History Lesson

NT picked us up as promised. Hank got in the front seat, I got in back. "How was your day, boys?"

"Funny you should ask, Dad," Hank volunteered. "Mine was pretty routine, considering that we had an assembly about those two seniors who got killed last Monday. Ryk's was a lot more interesting. He always gets in on the fun stuff."

"Do tell. Henryk? You weren't attacked again, were you?" He adjusted the rearview mirror so he could see my face. I could see his face, too, of course. How can someone interrogate you by mirror?

"Oh no, sir." He frowned. I forgot, I'm not supposed to call him "sir." Unless I'm in trouble, probably. "Walter's bunch got themselves attacked."

"By the entire football team," chortled Hank. "I wish I had been there. I heard some stuff in the hall, but…"

NT smiled a little. "And how did you end up involved? You friends with some of the team?"

"Oh no. Nothing like that. It had nothing to do with me. I just happened to be nearby when it all took place." I looked directly at NT's reflection. He looked like maybe he didn't totally believe me. I wasn't so sure I really wanted to talk about it after all. Hank didn't give me any choice, though.

"Yeah. He was there for that, but then he was also in the office when Walter's father kicked his butt. I would have paid to see that show, too."

"Whoa! What happened?" NT wasn't smiling; he frowned in the mirror at me. "Why did Walter's father attack him?"

With as little detail as possible I retold the story. I left Bernard's racial comment out of the tale. "So that's about it," I finished. "Kind of a strange day, but better that Walter gets hit, twice, than me even once. Not my problem." I looked at Hank. "Unless some newspaper reporter decides to write about it."

Hank looked back at me. "Now, why would I want to write about some punk getting what's coming to him? I could title the article, 'What goes around, comes around.'"

I was beginning to panic. "Hank. Not good. I was the only student in there. You write a story, and everyone who knows I was there will figure I'm the source. I'd have the administration and Walter on my case. You might as well write my obituary at the same time."

"Oh, I doubt that. Probably just a story about a student with a tendency to end up in the hospital." Easy for Hank to joke. It wasn't his face about to get kicked in. Again. "You're right, though. Maybe this is one story that doesn't get told."

"Good thinking, Hank. Anything that happens may be news, but that doesn't make it news that needs to get out to the public." NT looked at me in the mirror, his face blank.

He checked the traffic, signaled, and changed lanes. "Game time, boys. I thought of this while I was watching the game on TV last night. You are a famous black athlete and get slammed by a black sports commentator for not "acting black enough" because you don't sound like you're from the "hood" when you talk, and/or you're dating/married to a white woman. Go back two spaces." He laughed. "Really. It happened a few weeks ago. Story got, funnier/sadder, though. The commentator was caught up in the game he didn't even know he was in. He should have, though. He got fired by his network. Oops. Guess he had to move back a few spaces, too."

"That's got all kinds of layers of problems, doesn't it? Can't even tell who's most wrong in that situation. Maybe everybody." Hank looked back at me. "Like I texted you this morning. Black athlete has all kinds of ways to lose points."

"I thought both the kids that got killed were white." NT made the last turn onto Carl's street. "Their photos were in the paper. Nice lookin' kids."

"Yeah, dad. I was just sayin' that if the boy was black and girl was white, it would have been an even bigger mess. Everyone still just as dead, but a bigger mess."

"So you don't think the trouble Walter started was racial?"

"No. Not really. He was just running his mouth and—"

NT cut me off. "And his alligator mouth overloaded his canary butt."

"That's about the size of it. The JV players that jumped him were white and black, with a couple Hispanics and Asians thrown in for good luck. It was a team thing."

"That's good. Tough for the coach though. I'm sure half of him wants to congratulate the boys for standing up for their teammate, and the other half of him wants to point out that you can't go around assaulting people just because they have big mouths." NT pulled up to Carl's. "Come to think of it, isn't the security chief, Mr. Wright, one of the football coaches?"

Hank opened the door and reached back for his trumpet. "Yes. I think he helps with the JV linemen or something. Don't look at me like that, Dad. I know a little about football. I got sent out to cover one of their practices and interview some players for a story we were working on. Gotta run."

"Sure. Good lesson, son. Henryk, stick by for a second, would you." I was hoping to talk to him without Hank around, so, no problem. "You don't look happy, young man ...?"

"No, sir. I mean, no. It's this Walter thing. I'm, um, I'm okay with him getting his butt kicked and all. Couldn't happen to a more deserving guy, far as I'm concerned, but this thing with his father..."

"Yeah. I picked up on that, too." NT was sitting sideways so he could look at me directly, instead of through the mirror. "You're sure that his father hit him. Right there in the office, in front of two administrators?"

"No doubt. I didn't see it, but I heard the yelling, and heard the smack on Walter's face, and then when the other security staff opened the door and ran in, I saw Walter on the floor holding his face with Bernard yelling at him about not losing fights." Again, I left out the racial stuff. Everyone knew what Bernard was, so no need to repeat the nasty stuff. "It's funny, part of me was kind of happy to see Walter get smacked around, especially by the football team; he really did have it coming. But part of me is disgusted because I liked it. All in all, though, I'm not really at all happy about what his father did."

"You know, your mom and dad are showing up in you right now, Henryk. That sounds like something they would say. You might turn out to be a decent human being."

Left unsaid: Unlike Frankie X, who would have been all over the place on Walter's double beating. "I guess I don't see why Bernard wasn't arrested. Right there in the office. There were two adult witnesses. If some kid in the hall just upped and pounded someone in front of Wright and Slate, he would have been arrested as soon as they could locate the school resource officer."

NT nodded at me, "You'd kind of expect that."

"The main thing is, and don't tell Hank this. Mr. Wright called me back down to the office and practically told me to lie about it." NT's eyebrows went up in question. "Actually, what he told me to do was not talk about it to anyone. This was after I had already told Hank in the hall. And now I'm telling you. It feels like he's afraid of Mr. Anderson or covering up for some other reason. He said something about Slate and him talking with the principal first."

"Well. Much as I would love to have Mr. Anderson as a guest at my fine hotel, there may be more to this than you've thought of. What would happen to Walter if his old man got busted, especially for hitting him?"

I hadn't even thought about that. Walter's a repeat ninth grader, sure, but he's still probably only 17, technically a minor. "I don't know. He lives only with his dad. Foster home?"

"He's pretty old for that. And with no mother in known existence, they'd have to find a relative to take him in. Might be hard, considering the kind of gentleman he is. I can't imagine anyone with a lick of sense voluntarily taking him. Can't put him in juvenile detention unless he's a danger to society. Being in danger doesn't count. Didn't something like this happen way back in elementary school?"

"Yes," said. "One of the kids noticed that Walter was walking really funny one day, and we all got to talking about it. Pretty soon Walter heard our discussion, and he lit into one of the boys. Started hammering on him, but he did it right in front of a teacher, who grabbed him immediately and held on to him until another teacher came to help out. Walter was crying and swearing. Eventually, it got out that his father had really pounded his rear for some reason. Probably left some serious marks along with leaving him limping. We never found out exactly what happened to Mr. Anderson, but Walter kept on living with him, and we all learned to not talk about Walter. At least not where he could hear us. Seems like we've all been scared of the Andersons for years. The kids don't mess with Walter, and it looks like the adults don't mess with Bernard."

"Oh, child protective services probably has a fat file on him and his son. Trouble is, there's only so much the law can do. And when the kid makes it all the way to 17, well… I guess everyone hopes he just moves out, joins the army or something as soon as he's old enough. I've seen kids that were sixteen or seventeen who just leave, start living with friends. You know, a few weeks at one friend's house, then on to another. You'd be surprised at the number of homeless kids at your high school right now. They are living completely under the radar. But, there's a big difference from Walter: They're pretty good kids, so their friends' parents don't make a fuss, don't mind helping them out. Pretty hard to imagine anyone other than some of his crew putting up with him for any length of time." He opened the car door. "Well, I'm not sure what happens next. I guess you keep quiet for now, and we'll remind Hank not to breathe a word about this. Let me know if something new, or dangerous, develops."

We waited in Carl's front room for fifteen minutes or so, me checking the phone for messages and surfing the social sites, NT reading a back issue of *Downbeat*. The music, as always, was amazing. I can't sing or play any kind of instrument, and these guys could make music that won't quit.

When Hank came out, we piled back into NT's car and started over to pick up Hank's grandmother. Hank and I sat in the back. "Continuing the game," I said bravely, "A local sports team has had a racist name for maybe eighty years and doesn't want to change it. Half the community supports the tradition, because, after all, it's tradition. Half the community sees the point being made by the complaining ethnic group and is all for a new name."

Hank laughed. "I wonder what team that could be, Dad? But, Ryk, who moves back spaces, and how many?"

"I haven't worked that out, yet. Everyone, maybe, for putting up with the name for so long without making any real fuss?"

NT glared at me in the mirror. Time to let it drop. Not often that anything I ever say irritates an adult, other than my parents, of course. But I think this did. And I wasn't particularly trying to. I had been thinking about what game he had probably been watching when he heard the sportscaster make a fool of himself. Well, duh, he did have that team's bumper stickers on both ends of his car, and he always wore the team sweatshirt when he watched their games. In silence, we arrived at the house where Grams was.

"Hello, Henryk. How are you today?" Grams grinned at me as she climbed in the front seat. "Flo and I made some cookies this morning while we were gabbing. Don't suppose you'd like a couple?"

"Yes. Thank you, Mrs. Jones. I mean, Grams" She grinned again.

Hank made an exaggerated cough, "Hi, Grams. This is Hank, your grandson, here. And yes, he'd like a cookie or two, also. Please."

"Hi, Hank. I know who you are. Here's the bag of cookies. Don't you two eat them all; save room for dinner, and maybe even a few for your sister. Want one, NT, before these poor starving boys inhale them?"

NT stuck a hand over the seat and Hank put two cookies in his hand. "So, mom, how is Miss Florence? Any hot gossip from the old 'hood?"

"Just the usual stuff, who's moving out, whose grandchildren are doing what. It's interesting, what these young folks are doing. Used to be all I ever heard about was the kids going off to the army, like you did, NT, or maybe getting a job of some kind. Now, some of them are heading to college. Still hear stories about kids gone bad, probably ending up where you work, but on the other side of the bars. But, most, they seem to be trying to make something of themselves."

I hadn't thought about that. In my neighborhood and in my family it was not news if someone was headed for college. It was news if they didn't.

"That going off to college stuff got me to thinking about some old, old stories about colleges and things that Flo and I were talking about. Might be part of your game somehow."

NT, had expressly forbidden us from mentioning the indignities game in front of Grams, and now we had her coming up with an idea in front of him. His face stayed hard in the mirror.

"NT, you might remember this a little bit from when you were young, probably remember it better than your brothers since you're the oldest. When we went south, to visit relatives in South Carolina, we couldn't just stop for the night at any old place; we had to go to a motel that black people, called us colored or Negro back then, could stay in. We had this little book, a green one, with the names of places where we could eat and stay. Flo and I were talking about that and visiting college kids and all. NT's daddy, my Jonesy, worked as a groundskeeper for a local motel like that, and I was a maid there for a while, before we moved up here, of course." Grams paused for a moment. "You know, I think that's mostly all behind us, but there's still plenty of other things that sort of set you on edge."

I could see that NT was really hoping that this little venture into history by Grams wasn't going to get too gruesome, but it did, in many ways.

"Here's a tough one, boys. You know what lynching is?"

I nodded, and Hank said, "Yes, ma'am."

"Well, they had one in my county, back when I was little. My parents kept me away from it all, of course, but I heard all about it from my cousins who snuck over to watch. I couldn't sleep for weeks for worrying. Now, I'm talking about the stuff you see in movies and TV shows, ropes and mutilating and burning and all that. But we all knew that other people just got killed; some white guy has a grudge or wants some black man's property and, bang, just like that, the black man gets it. And nothing was done about it." I was thinking, no wonder she named her first born after Nat Turner. I wondered if she was more shocked or proud, or both, to have NT end up being a career policeman. I thought she was finished, and I'm sure NT was hoping she was, but she was just getting started.

"Your family learns that your great grandfather died of syphilis given to him as a part of an old experiment on the treatment of the disease. This experiment was run by a well-known black college with government money. Flo was telling me about how they gave these men the disease, and then gave some of the men a drug to maybe cure the disease, but others, including, I guess, her uncle, or someone, got one of those fake pills that didn't do any good. No why on earth would they give a sick man fake medicine?"

Hank jumped in, "It's called a placebo, Grams. When they test medicines that they don't actually know will work, they give some people the experimental medicine, and others get the placebo, the fake. If only the people who got the real medicine were cured, then you know the medicine worked." He looked at his dad, "Is that a true story, Dad? Did that really happen?"

Before NT could answer, Grams jumped in. "'Course it did, Hank. Flo told me all about it. Her uncle was one of the patients. They gave him the syphilis and then didn't give him the real medicine. All her family knows about it. Terrible, terrible thing."

"There's another story too, that fits your game. Charles Drew was a great doctor, went to college and all that. He figured out how to do that thing where they put someone else's blood in you when you've lost too much, like in an accident or an operation."

"Transfusion," I said.

"Yes, that's what it's called. He was really famous and respected, all over, by whites and blacks. Everyone. Well, up North, anyhow. One day he was going to a medical conference somewhere, Kentucky or Tennessee, I think, and he got in a car accident. The local hospitals wouldn't treat him because he was black and he ended up dying from loss of blood."

Hank, again, "That true, Dad?"

Grams's face tightened. "What's this, 'That true?' business? I told you, didn't I. Everyone, well, anyone over fifty, knows the story. Flo and I can remember it plain as day. Happened way back in the forties or fifties, I believe. I'm not sure how you figure out what spaces to move back or turns to lose, but I'm sure you can do it." She didn't say another word for the rest of the trip.

After she got out of the car, before NT put it in the garage, he said to us, low-voiced, "Boys, one of those stories is mostly true, but one isn't. Challenge: which one? Challenge number two: find out more information about both incidents. I'm talking about the syphilis story and the Charles Drew story. No question about the murders, and, obviously, no official records to look at. Maybe someday one of you guys will research all those murders that were covered up all over the South. Hank, since you're so willing to challenge your Grams in front of people, you can fill us in at dinner tonight. I'll be interested to see how you explain the inaccurate story with Grams sitting there. Henryk, you'll just be another step ahead in your education."

As it turned out, we found out that NT was right and wrong about the contributions Grams made to the "Game," as we had started calling it. In the 1930's researchers, working with doctors at Tuskegee Institute identified around 400 locals with syphilis and then followed them for life, until they died, either from the untreated disease or other causes. They were told that they would be treated and got free medical care for whatever life they had. In fact, they were not given any treatments at all, even after penicillin was found to be pretty effective. The researchers wanted to learn about what the disease did to people. About 200 men who did not have the disease were also included in the study to see how their health developed. In 1972 someone blew the whistle, snitched, you could say, and the whole program came to a crashing halt. I think that years later a few million dollars was paid out by the government to either the men themselves or their surviving families. No one was actually intentionally infected, they just were intentionally not treated. We also found out that in general, when drug companies do studies to get a new drug approved, they find people to test, but they don't pay attention to whether or not the race of the patient makes a difference in the effectiveness of the medication. So sometimes a drug that works well with one race is not so effective in another, but the doctors don't know this and prescribe according to the pharmacy company guide.

The Charles Drew death story was mostly ironic and sad, but not actually southern evil. He really was very important in the development of the entire blood bank system. Basically, he was the father of the modern blood bank system. He did die from a car crash in the South, in North Carolina. He was taken directly to the nearest hospital for treatment, but he died anyway. At least one of the people in the car with him was also a doctor and felt that Dr. Drew was so badly injured in the accident that he was certain to die.

I'm sure Hank had an interesting time trying to explain to his grandmother why he was checking up on her stories plus explaining that she didn't have her facts lined up. Probably a good exercise for a journalist, but I was glad it wasn't me.

CHAPTER 14

Enlightenment

The weekend had been weird. Terry had not gone to school on Friday. No one said anything. He just didn't come downstairs Friday morning. We all would have been shocked if he had gone to school. We just gave him space. Saturday and Sunday, he came down like nothing had happened, ate something for breakfast, and went back upstairs to his room. Back down a couple times for food or drinks, and back up to his room. He played his normal eclectic collection of tunes at his normal volume, loud, but not obnoxiously so. He came down for dinner, but didn't say much. I tried knocking at his door a couple times, and I'm sure Mom and Dad did, too, but the response seemed to be some variation of, "I'm okay. Thanks." No screaming to leave him alone. Monday morning, he came down to breakfast, ready for school like any other normal day.

As I gathered my stuff for school, Dad caught my arm. "Just for today, maybe, I think I ought to drive you two to the school. Can't tell what's going on, and the bus would be an easy place for trouble to develop." I didn't argue, and neither did Terry, so Dad drove us. I think we both felt a little baby-stupid, getting a ride to avoid bullies, but it did make sense.

Terry was quiet on the trip. When we got out of the car, he said, "Thanks, Uncle Tomás. Catch you later, cuz" and walked off to his locker. I turned to head towards mine and practically ran into Mr. Slate. I think he realized just a moment too late that my dad was there; he couldn't get away. Dad popped out of the car and called.

"Good morning, Mr. Slate. Got a minute?"

I stopped walking and turned to watch. Mr. Slate looked around, but there didn't seem to be any pressing emergency to rescue him. "Uh. Sure. Sir?" All those conversations with Dad about Frankie, and he still didn't know his name, although I sure he recognized him.

"Mr. Jonasz. I'm Henryk's father. Terry Sullivan's uncle. Could we chat for a minute?" Somehow, Dad kept his voice totally even; he did not betray the slightest irritation at Slate. Frankie would have been proud of the perfectly neutral demeanor. I'm sure that Frankie had learned this technique from observing Dad, although he probably wouldn't admit it.

"Oh, yes. Of course. Let's go into my office." I started towards my locker, but he snagged me. "You, too, Henryk. Maybe we can get a couple things straightened out." I wasn't aware of anything that needed to be "straightened out," but I didn't seem to have much choice, so I followed along behind Mr. Slate.

"Let me park the car. Be there in a minute." Dad sounded cheerful, way too cheerful. "I believe I can find your office."

Mr. Slate went into his office and sat behind his desk. He didn't invite me in, so I stood awkwardly at the door waiting for my dad to appear. There were probably six other students in there, some waiting quietly, some chattering away as if sitting in the assistant principal's was part of the normal day. One morose looking girl sat there with her mother, who fidgeted with her purse and frowned. When Dad got there, we both stood awkwardly for a few more minutes. Finally, Mr. Slate motioned us inside. "Have a seat, Mr. Jonasz, both of you." He pronounced our name correctly, but he couldn't seem to remember my first name. He indicated the two chairs across the desk from him, so we sat.

But then, I guess as a power play, left the room and appeared to be consulting quietly with Mrs. Hernandez. I looked around his office. There were no photos. Not a single one. Either he had no family, not even a dog, or was embarrassed by the lot. Or, most likely, he didn't want anyone to think he had a human side; might wreck his image. Dad and I sat there looking at the assortment of diplomas and certificates on the wall and the administration manuals parked on bookcases. He returned and sat back behind his desk. He didn't say anything, just raised his eyebrows in question.

"So, Mr. Slate," my dad began quietly, "any idea about what's going on?"

"Going on? In what way, sir?" Slate looked at him blankly.

"In the way that first my son gets assaulted and severely injured in the hallway, and then my nephew gets attacked and humiliated in class."

"The locker room, actually." I think Slate thought he scored a point.

"The locker room is a free-fire zone? Not under supervision by the phys-ed teacher?"

Point not gained. "Oh. Uh. Well, I meant, oh never mind."

"So, as I just asked, any idea what is going on?" Dad leaned forward just a little and looked over his glasses at

Slate. "Should my wife and I feel that our kids are safe in your school? Should we believe that there is adult supervision and that students who attack other students will be dealt with in an appropriate manner?"

Now Slate leaned in, "We are looking into the incidents, but there may be more to these things than you know. Some details that maybe you aren't aware of."

"Such as?"

"Well, in the case of, uh, your nephew, uh?"

"Terry, Terry Sullivan." I can only keep quiet for so long, after all.

"Yes, Sullivan. That's right. There may have been some provocation in his incident."

"What do you think he did to provoke some kids to strip him and write a homophobic slur on his back?" Dad's voice had just developed an edge to it. He wasn't faking cool any more. "And what's this 'incident' thing? These were attacks. Both events. Not just some little incident. How did Terry provoke this attack? What would the justification be?"

Slate went off on an entirely unexpected tack. "You know, Mr. Jonasz," he pronounced our last name correctly again, "the Bible has some relevant passages that might shed some light on Terry's incident."

Dad just stared at him. I've seldom seen him at a loss for words, but this one stopped him. "Bible passages?" he finally managed to say. "Such as?"

"Romans. Chapter 1. Leviticus 18, also." Slate sat back, as if he had just scored the decisive point. Nothing left for Dad to do but slink out of the office. "I don't want to try to quote them, because I might leave out a word or two, but they both seem applicable here, given your nephew's, uh, lifestyle. If a boy has a little sugar in his blood, as they say, you know, switch hitting, well it can lead to unfortunate situations."

Mr. Slate could be excused for being ignorant on one point. It probably never occurred to him that Dad would know the Bible well enough to understand exactly what he was getting at. I certainly didn't. Both NT and Dad would have said, "Look it up," and I would, as soon as I got home. In all likelihood no one told Slate that way, way back in Dad's early, and he would jokingly say, misspent, youth, he considered going to the seminary and becoming a priest; he had devoted quite a bit of effort to studying the Bible. However, that was then, and this was now. I thought Dad would explode. He gripped the arms of his chair and grimaced.

"Mr. Slate, I know exactly what you are getting at. And the leap of your logic is more than amazing. Even Francis in his most convoluted arguments wouldn't have made that kind of jump. Justifying an attack on a boy because of a perceived sexual orientation is astounding on its own, but citing the Bible as the reason is just plain nuts. I don't know which is more dangerous to society, a secular human-ist like me quoting (or misquoting) the Bible or a, quote, unquote, Christian using it to prop up his personal phobias and hang-ups, but here goes. "Love thy neighbor. Can't cite chapter and verse, but it has a nice ring to it." Dad stared directly into Slate's eyes and held the gaze. Among the stu-dents this was a time-honored means of provoking a fight. "I don't suppose you have the relevant passage to cover the attack on my son? Maybe a convoluted interpretation of the parable of the Good Samaritan?" (Another thing for me to look up.) Dad was on a roll. "I guess it goes like this: my son got what was coming to him because he stopped to help Donnie when he was being harassed by some as-yet-unidentified thugs, and in your understanding of the story, someone should get the tar beat out of him for helping a fellow human in trouble."

Before Slate could respond, Dad stood up. He looked at me with just the faintest hint of something on his face. "Mr. Slate, I imagine you have important matters to consider, and I know Henryk is dying to get to class." He smiled, "Oops, probably the wrong word to use around here, let's say, anxious, to get to class, so maybe we should table this discussion for now. Perhaps we can explore these issue at some future time. Thank you so much for giving us your views on these events. It's been most enlightening." Mr. Slate tried to get up, but Dad waved him down. "No. That's okay, don't get up. I assume the secretary can give Henryk the pass he needs?" And we marched out of the office. To me, Dad muttered, "Seemed a little late to show courtesy, didn't it. Most enlightening meeting, I must say. See you at home. Have a good one. Try to find some more enlightenment in your classes."

At my locker, I found a note stuffed in my locker. It seemed to be inviting me to partake in more medical experiences of my own. "Snichez get stichez." I looked around, and shoved it in my pocket. I didn't know if I were being watched or not, and I wanted to appear totally cool and unconcerned. Inside, not so much. But, if Terry could walk into the school as if nothing had happened, I guess I could get a little piece of paper and act that way, too.

I ran into Melantha in the hall, but she seemed particularly uninterested in Friday's excitement. "Hi, Melantha, how's it going? You okay after Friday?"

"Henryk. Right. Hi. Friday's gone. It can stay gone, too. Can't talk now. I have class." She glared at me like I had done something wrong and hustled down the hallway. I was going to ask if she got a note, too, but I didn't have the chance.

I ran into Terry in the hall later, on the way to third period. I was on the way to science class; he was headed to the gym area for PE. Where he was jumped on Thursday. I nodded at him; he nodded back but didn't say anything. I couldn't believe it. I would have been a total wreck, especially going back to PE. I could not have even walked into that class. My knees were shaking just thinking about it, but if he was feeling anything, it wasn't showing on his face. Maybe he had had so many horrific things happen to him that this was how he dealt with it all. Just blot it out and keep on keeping on.

Terry had this cool poster in his room. It was one of those old Zap Comix hippie posters of a crazed looking man with big feet way out in front of him and the phrase, "Keep on Truckin" printed across the top. Terry had added a stylized "Keep on Keepin' On" across the bottom. Maybe getting stripped and thrown into the hallway was a minor setback in the minefield that was his life. For a split second I thought about Columbine and all those other schools where some kid was picked on and then got his revenge in a big way with a gun. But, no, I didn't think that was Terry's style; at least I hoped it wasn't. I wanted to ask him if he had gotten a note like mine, but that wasn't the time. I even thought about following him to the gym area, but what could I do? I had to hope that Mr. Wright or someone had talked to the PE teachers and the security staff and would have someone in the locker room. I could barely concentrate in third or fifth period class. I kept expecting Mr. Wright to come get me again, but nothing happened.

Strangely enough, there was no talk at all of what happened to Terry, which was strange since there had been the big notes event Friday. I could only assume that other "exciting" replacement events had occurred over the weekend. No one said anything about the little dust up in the gym on Friday, either. That was also amazing, since most of the students were still around when it happened.

Hank caught up with me at lunch.

"Everything cool today, Ryk?" He sat across from me and looked at my face. There were other students there, but I felt like he was about to interview me. Get the last words of a student before he once again is hauled off to the hospital?

"Nothing exciting, so far." He didn't say anything, just looked at me. I think he had acquired his dad's method of interrogation without realizing it. Sooner or later, you just felt like you had to say something, to fill the dead air. "Dad drove Terry and me to school today. Far as I know, Terry hasn't had any problems. Neither have I." I had decided not to mention the note. I certainly couldn't talk about the meeting with Slate, not at school anyway. So far, I was doing pretty well. He just looked at me, waiting. It finally made me mad; why was he pushing me? Time to lie. "Sorry. I haven't even seen Wright or Slate today. No Walter or crew, either. You'll have to go find some OMG girl to liven up your day." I really did want it to be a normal day, so I buried the meeting and the note in my mind and, like Terry, kept on keeping on.

And, it was a successful Monday at school. No one bothered me. Terry and I took the bus home as usual, didn't talk to anyone; we just enjoyed the peace of the noisy bus.

At home Terry retreated to his room and I to mine. I checked the social networks I was, sort of, wired into, just to see if anything horrible had popped up and was happy to see that there was nothing new on the attack on Terry last Thursday other than a few photos of all the students with the yellow notes taped to their clothes. There wasn't anything at all about the mess in the gym on Friday. I didn't expect to see anything about what happened in the office, since as far as I could tell, I was the only student other than Walter who knew what happened.

At dinner things got a bit livelier. Frankie was there, no class and finished with work for the day. This was good, to a degree, because it limited what Mom and Dad could bug Terry and me about since they didn't want Frankie to know about the attack. Still, nothing can completely stop a mom attack.

"Got a call from Mr. Wright, this morning, Henryk," Mom's opening salvo. "He said he was just making a courtesy call to see how you're doing. I got the impression that he hadn't seen you around lately. He wanted to make sure that your face was healing properly, I guess." I bet he also asked about Terry, but she couldn't say anything about that with Frankie there.

Without thinking, I said, "Actually, I saw him Friday." Oops. How does she do that?

"Oh. And?"

"Um." I wasn't going to add any more if possible.

"And was he checking on your medical progress?" Dad was piling on. Not fair.

Frankie was beginning to take an interest, "If it had been Slate calling, he would have been hoping for bad news."

"No. Actually, he called me in because I saw Walter and his buddies get jumped." I was hoping that I could do a little damage control by getting only part of the story out before they decided that making a call to Mr. Wright might be instructive. "It wasn't much. Walter and friends were saying stuff about the dead football player, and some football players took offense. Teachers and security broke it up really quickly. I happened to be in the gym near where it all happened." That wasn't enough information. I ended up telling a limited version of the whole story, leaving out Melantha's contribution to Mr. Wright's interrogation. I glossed over most of the comments Walter's crew made, and didn't mention what I witnessed in the office or the threatening note I got.

"Oh. Maybe Mr. Wright wanted to make sure that your trip to the office didn't lead to repercussions."

"Or, concussions!" laughed Frankie.

"That was not funny," Dad muttered. "Has Walter been leaving you alone?"

I was kind of mad at Frankie for his comment and didn't think before I answered. "Pretty much. He called me a 'Jew boy' in the hall the other day. I don't know where that came from. I guess his father has him thinking everyone who might possibly be a problem for him is Jewish. I, personally, am trying to not be a problem for him, not a Jewish one or any other kind. Probably a bit late for me to become a Jewish one in any case."

"Not as late as you think, since you are, in fact, of Jewish descent." Dad grinned. How long had he been sitting on this information? Fourteen years, in my case. Frankie stared at him. So, I guess, twenty years. Terry perked up. Mom just sat there trying to show a neutral face, but it looked like she was fighting back a smile.

CHAPTER 15

A Little More History

"Like all family histories, boys, it's a bit complicated."
Dad had our undivided attention. "A couple generations back, in Poland, being a Jew was, as I'm sure
you know, a bit difficult in some areas. Hellacious might
be a more accurate description. There were these attacks
on them, called pogroms. At some point, your great-great
grandfather must have converted to Catholic, probably just
to stay alive. No one I know actually knows what happened.
In any case when your grandfather came here, he had this
long Polish name that he could barely spell in Polish, much
less English, so at Ellis Island he got his last name listed as
Jonusz, which means dove or Jonah, which is a Jewish name
from the Old Testament. But, being the poor spellers or
sloppy writers everyone connected with this story was, he
ended up being Jonasz. So, even though all of my family in
the USA and going back a generation or so in Poland has
been officially Catholic, Walter and his father are technically
right, at least on your father's side of the family. Frankie,

Francis Xavier, to be precise, has a pretty straightforward Catholic name. Henryk Kerry has his Polish grandfather's first name and an Irish middle name, from County Kerry. He grinned and toasted us with his water glass, "Jew boy! Boys. Mazeltov!" I was glad I hadn't mentioned that actually Walter called me a "fag Jew boy." I also had a private grin for myself when I reflected on Hank's comment about Grams not trusting white folks, but at least not calling me Jewish to boot. Last laugh for me, I guess. I'd have to decide whether or not to tell Hank about this development.

Terry joined in, "Actually, Uncle Tomás, I believe the Jewish lineage is traced through the mother. I'm Irish on both sides, so I'm pure Mick. But I guess we can think of my cousins as Mick-ish." Actually, since his last name was Sullivan, the same as his mother's, I don't know if the exact identity of his father, Irish or otherwise, was clear.

Dad looked at Mom and laughed again. "Mary, now would be the time to tell us you're not Irish through and through. Maybe 'Jirish?'—Jewish-Irish?"

Mom managed a brief smile. "No such story, guys. Sorry. My side of the family is as Irish as can be, County Kerry Sullivans and O'Briens and what-have-you, all the way up the line. Irish Catholics, although a few of us have lapsed considerably." She went back into her interrogation again, "So, have Walter and company been harassing you at school? I thought that was all finished in elementary school. Wasn't he a couple grades ahead of you at one point? And I thought the incident in the stairwell was a one-time thing. Is he making a habit of going after you?"

Incident? Same word Slate used. Something that puts me in the hospital is more than an incident. I determined not to let this get big, though. "Um. No. We are more or less in the same grade now, ninth, because he isn't getting enough credits to move on." The only reason I knew he was in ninth grade was because he was at the ninth grade assembly that the school had early in the year. By my calculation, he had heard the welcoming speeches, and threats about behavior, from Mr. Slate and others at least twice before I got there. "And, no, he's still the same old Walter, but he's not harassing me." Frankie was staring hard at me during this performance, but I don't think Mom or Dad noticed. Terry did, though.

"Walter's had a difficult life," Dad said. "That doesn't mean we cut him any slack, but just the same. With that crazy neo-Nazi Bernard for a father, a true thug if there ever was one, it's a wonder that Walter isn't locked up by now. Whoever hit you should be locked up, but I don't think any of those boys are talking. I bet they're all from goofy homes."

"Actually," Terry said softly, "I'm from a pretty goofy home, and I'm hanging in there without attacking people." Couldn't argue with that, so no one said anything. Frankie stared at Terry now. Terry forced a smile and a fake cheerful expression, "Well, I guess some of us are just naturally better equipped to deal with the world. If you'll excuse me, I need to hit the books. I missed a bit last week and have some catching up to do."

Frankie looked at me and nodded quickly toward Terry's departure. I wanted to follow Terry upstairs, and I didn't want Frankie asking me anything about Terry's missing school. "I probably ought to get to work also. Frankie, since you're here tonight, you can clean up the dinner dishes, right?" I would hear about that later, I was sure, but I needed a chance to figure out how to not say anything to anyone whenever someone started pressuring me.

After he finished cleaning up the dinner dishes, Frankie came upstairs and stuck his head into my room. "Got a minute, bro?" Ah, hip-talk-friendly. The interrogation couldn't be far behind. "Maybe you and I and Terry could sort a couple things out?"

What could I do? I nodded and we crossed the hall to Terry's room and knocked. The music was not too loud. Terry let us in and turned up the music a decibel or two. I don't think he was surprised to see us there.

"You boys better never, ever, I mean ever, get into a poker game. I was watching you two when Mom and Dad were poking around. I guess they bought the playing-dumb act and half-way answers, but I don't. What's going on? There was a lot more not said than was said at dinner tonight. It was all over your faces. All over the way you sat there. You okay, Terry? You don't look okay. You, too, Henryk. You don't look so okay either. Did something happen last week that I missed?"

I looked at Terry, and he looked at the floor. "Terry?" He slowly nodded his head, yes, so I continued. "Frankie, if I tell you what's been going on, you've got to promise two things."

Terry kept his head down, Frankie had the beginning of a grin on his face, happy, I guess, that he had gotten me talking. He got serious again. "Most likely. What's the deal?"

"One, you do not tell Mom and Dad any of this. None. Nada. Not a word."

"Okay. Been there, done that before. Far as I can tell, you never ratted me out when I was, uh, maybe getting into trouble."

"Two. You have got to promise not to try to get involved with getting revenge on anyone. I hate to sound like I agree with any adults, but if you go after these guys, you'll end up in worse trouble than you've ever been in, and nothing will be any better for Terry and me. Except we'll lose a brother to the legal system."

No smiling at all now. "Sounds serious. I'll promise that, too. Although it may be hard to keep."

So I filled in Frankie. The attack on Terry, the complete story of what happened in the office, including Bernard hitting Walter. I even told him about Mr. Wright's little conversation about keeping quiet. I didn't tell him about the note. I didn't want to worry Terry or add fuel to Frankie's indignation pyre.

I expected Frankie to explode. He didn't. I didn't know what to expect from Terry, although, true to form, he did his best to keep up a calm appearance. He didn't know about my further entanglements with Walter, either.

"Wow. I figured you were hiding a bit at dinner, but you two had a major load packed away. Especially you, Henryk." He looked around the room. "Don't tell me I just promised to stay out of this. I mean, really, did I just --? No. I didn't. Tell you what, boys, I'm going to get this stuff stopped for once and for all. I'm not having that little rat and his jackass father push us around anymore. Just because those two clowns have an attitude towards the world doesn't mean that we have to be at the receiving end of it. Let them go bug someone else."

Terry raised a hand, almost like in class. "Uh, Frankie? Did you hear a word your brother said to you? If you go after them, you're going to get hurt a lot worse than me or Henryk. Either they'll shoot you or you'll end up locked up."

"Oh, I'm not going to do anything to get myself locked up. I'm just going to have a friendly conversation with them.

Actually, I think I'll just talk to Bernard. He's going to have to get his boy into line before something bad happens. I know that if I say anything to Walter, he'll say something, and after I kick his butt, I'll be in jail. School guys are too chicken to deal with those people, and technically, the police really don't have any reason to bust anyone. Nothing's provable. But I know, and you know, and the Andersons know what's going on, and they've got to know that it's got to stop. Now. No one's harassing my family." Before I had time to say anything, Frankie stomped out the door. I pulled it shut behind him.

"That went well, didn't it?" Terry almost smiled. "I guess it's good that someone wants to deal with this. But I'm not so sure that Frankie's the best choice for the job."

"Probably the worst. He'll get himself into big-time trouble and not do anything useful for us." I was really worried and didn't see an easy solution. I sure couldn't tell my folks, not after I had just finished glossing over a lot of stuff at dinner. Besides, what could they do? Frankie was an adult. He had a perfect record of not listening to their pleas to stay out of trouble in the past. About all they could do would be to threaten to cut off college money or kick him out.

"Maybe he's just blowing a lot of hot air. Putting on a show for his baby bro and cuz?"

"I could hope so, but that's never been his style before. I think the best we can hope for is that he doesn't go off tonight to set things right. By tomorrow he might figure out that he's more likely to put his butt in a sling than do anybody any good."

"You just can't talk to anybody, can you? Adults, they get all legalistic and start talking about technicalities, or they just go right to hysterical and it gets even worse."

Terry was pacing back in forth, almost frantic. "Then, when everything calms down, and they start talking to you about what happened, they act like they don't believe half of what you say, make you tell the same story over and over, like they want to catch you in a lie or something. Most want to not believe you because they hate to think they let it go on." At some point I realized that he wasn't talking about this particular set of events, but about what had happened to him in the Boston. I was pretty sure that I didn't want to know what happened, but what a lot of baggage, as they say.

I continued with his thoughts, "And then, we've got Frankie who's happy to believe everything and cut straight to the chase. Did you notice that he didn't even ask one question when I was telling him about your Thursday and my Friday. He just got pumped up and ready to go kick some butt. Mom and dad would have interrupted ten times to clarify some little detail."

Terry nodded his head, "Yeah. And the police or social workers would have been all over anything you said that might be open to interpretation. Would have asked you if you were just imagining that Wright was trying to shut you down." I think Terry had been there, done that, on more than one occasion.

"Well, the only thing I can hope for now is that Frankie is, after all, the master of big mouth. Maybe he really is just blowing a lot of hot air." For the first time since I walked into the room, I actually looked around and focused on things. "What is that?" I was staring at this bizarre painting.

"Oh. I've been busy these last few days. You know. I, uh." Terry drifted off to a corner of the room by a window and stared out.

The painting seemed to be a Nazi swastika slowly melting away, sort of like those Dali clock faces. The symbol seemed to be turning into a pool of blood. There appeared to be various ghosts hovering around; some looked vaguely like Terry, others like generic teenagers, boys and girls; some of the figures seemed to be both male and female. All sorts of races/ethnic groups seemed to be included. Some seemed to have that "Scream" face by Munch that we see all the time. Others had expressions of vindication. There were little stars of David and pink triangles scattered around. It looked like there was the hint of a rainbow rising up in the background. I'm sure it could be picked apart by an "art critic," and I'm sure that a psychologist would have had a field day with it, but it blew me away.

"No one can accuse you of painting cutesy kittens and puppies, eh, Terry?" My usual smooth tongue, again. I really didn't know what to say.

"Oh, I guess if the right girl asked, I could do a puppy. Don't know about kittens, though." His gaze crossed the room and I followed it. I'm not sure if he really meant to get my attention, but that's what happened.

Leaning against the wall was what I think of as his "Anger" self-portrait that he did that Thursday after he was attacked. Yeah, this guy was definitely not a kitten or puppy painter. "Not sure you're ready for employment in the greeting card industry, either."

"Not quite." He actually smiled. "By the way, were you going to tell me about the yellow notes all over the school Friday?" Oh, rats. I had completely forgotten about them. I should have told him sometime over the weekend, at least before we went to school.

"Sorry, Ter. I should have. You would have loved it. Spontaneous performance art or something. Ticked off the administration, coming on top of the dead students and all that."

Terry was still smiling. "No problem. I saw something about on social media, and my friends at school filled me in." He looked at his painting, "I don't know what happens next, but, well, it's been great, cuz." He practically shoved me out the door.

What worried me was exactly that: what happens next. Mom and Dad were both scheduled to go out of town on separate business trips and wouldn't be back until sometime Friday. Terry and I would be okay, probably order in food and goof off, but mostly, business as usual. What we did not need, however, was Frankie to choose to get on his high horse and go work things out with Bernard and Walter. I didn't even know how to find a bail bondsman, but probably Terry could help with that when the time came.

CHAPTER 16

A Question of Terms

"**N**igger! Nig-" NT broke off, glancing at me and Terry. NT was practically screaming. I'd occasionally seen him get worked up about something, but this was way over the top.

Terry and I were at Hank's for dinner. Mom and Dad had both needed to go out of town on separate business trips, and although we were still staying at home, his folks had volunteered to feed us dinner. Frankie was at work, and it spared us one order-in pizza dinner, so we were happy to be at the Jones's.

NT's rant was all Hank's fault. He happened to comment that some of the kids in his English class were laughing about the use of the word, "Negro" in *To Kill a Mockingbird*, which the class was reading at the time. "Some of the kids thought that was really outrageous, but the teacher said that actually, when the book was written in the 1950's, using "Negro," and when written, using a capital N, was the most polite way to refer to people of African descent. Likewise as the story is set in the 1930's, using "Negro" would be the proper and correct usage. The white trash characters in the book use the n-word." He glanced at me. I wondered if he was holding back because I was there, or if, like my family, we always said "the n-word" rather the real word.

I used the word "nigger" once. Once. I was six, maybe seven. We were in a restaurant, probably in DC or Arlington, and I had been watching some black people eating at a table near us. This was a chance to show off my newly acquired vocabulary, the beneficial result of going to school. I said something like, "Oh, that nigger boy over there is eating the same thing I am."

My mother's eyes clouded, tears rolled. "Oh, my," she said to my dad. "We have to move. I can't have my son learning that word, that attitude."

Dad had a sad look on his face, too. "Where? Helsinki? If we just moved to New York, I don't think we'd hear that perjorative, but we'd still have to deal with the attitude."

Mom just sat there crying.

I didn't use that word again. Looking back, though, I wonder what kind of idiot I was, since my best friend, Hank, who had lived across the street from me since we were born, was black. I guess I didn't actually know the word was meant to be a major slam and represented an entire history of hatred.

There were some other interesting run-ins with the n-word. In middle school there was white guy, Jake I think, who basically grew up in a neighborhood with black kids who used the n-word freely with each other. He didn't even realize that it could be used as an insult until he was joking with a new black student. He said something like, "Hey, n-word, what's up with that Bulls hat?" and the guy was all set to kill him before Jake's friends tackled him and cooled things down. And it wasn't because the kid was sporting a Chicago hat, either.

Phillis kicked in with her own classroom experiences of the n-word. "Dad, you really can't get away from it. We're reading *Huckleberry Finn* in my AP English class, and one of the main characters is Nigger Jim, and the n-word is all over the place. The teacher told us that some people were having a fit about using that book in school, but we needed to realize that although Twain was a racist by today's standards, he was one hundred percent against slavery and the mistreatment of blacks."

Actually, this is what set NT off. "What's up with these books? What's up with the school even allowing them to be in the building?"

Terry and I looked at each other and tried to be invisible.

Hank gave it another shot, "But, dad, if you read the book, my book anyway, it makes sense." He made air quotes, "In the book, the 'good' white folks always say 'Negro' ever so respectfully; although, ironically, many of them are just as racist as the redneck white trash. They just talk more politely."

NT was still livid, "No! We didn't go through all the civil rights stuff and integrating the schools and all that just to have the teachers throwing this garbage in our kids' faces." I don't believe I had ever seen Hank or Phillis challenge their father like this before. "You can't sit there and tell me that this is education. It's practically telling the white kids, all the kids, that that word is okay." He glared at Hank, "How many times have I jumped you about your friends saying, 'nigga this and nigga that?' Like they think they are so hip and fake ghetto and all, using that word? I hear it all the time from the inmates at the jail, and it makes me sick. We worked way too hard to get that out of the vocabulary, and now it's coming back on us. Too many rap songs fall into that trap. And the school is just promoting it by using these books."

Mama J hadn't said a thing, and Grams just sat there as well. Terry and I continued to wish we were wearing functioning invisibility cloaks. Phillis and Hank looked at each other and shrugged. "Dad, have you actually read either one of those books?" Phillis did not sound overly confident. "I mean, they have a lot to say, most of it good. I read *Mockingbird* in ninth grade, too. I bet some of the kids in my class learned more about what it was like for black folk in the South from that book than anything they heard in history class. It was real. *Huckleberry* seems to be real, too."

I don't think NT had actually read either book. "Well, maybe you better just educate me, young missy. Tomorrow night I want a copy of each book here at the table. Get your teacher to give you an extra copy, go to the library, buy 'em; I don't care. We'll see what there is to see."

Grams spoke up, "Good idea, NT. I'd like to see what the fuss is all about also. Sounds like Phillis might have a point. Hank, too. If these books really do tell it like it was for us folk back in the day, that might not be such a bad thing. Phillis, see if you can find large print copies, would you? My eyes aren't what they used to be."

Mama J tried to change the subject. "Say, what about the Redskins? Season going to be okay with the new coach?"

Hank and I laughed at the same time. NT glared. All three of us remembered the conversation we had about racist team names in the car the other day, but I guess we had a slightly different take on the subject.

"What? What's so funny?"

"It's kind of complicated, mom." Hank jumped in.

Grams took over. "Actually, Sandra, it's, well, different. These guys have this crazy game, the Ironies Game, I think they call it. They try to come up with different ways the good folks in this country manage to make a mess of race things, especially for us folks, although we've heard about other things too."

Mama J threw a questioning glance at Hank and then NT. Phillis sat up and leaned forward. Terry tried to keep the invisibility cloak tight.

Grams continued, "Here's one for you boys. In this fair state it was illegal for black folks and white folks to marry each other. They thought they needed to keep the race pure; the white race, of course. They had some long name for this crime, but what it came down to was, if a black and white got married, they got arrested and thrown in jail. Now, this is where it fits your ironies game, NT. The couple that got this law changed by getting married, getting arrested, and then going to the Supreme Court, was named Loving. Yes indeed. The Lovings loved each other in Virginia and got married and went to jail."

Phillis smiled. "I think I heard something about that in my government class."

"This was a long time ago, right Grams? Like right after the Civil War? Ancient history, right?" Hank had quit eating to listen.

"Ancient history to you, maybe, being so young and all, but actually, I think the case was finally decided in 1967. That's nine years after your dad was born, children. Not so ancient."

Phillis jumped in, excited. "That's where I heard about it! The Supreme Court had that gay marriage case, Obergefell something, a while back and said the Loving decision was one of the precedents that would let the court rule the way it did."

"Really? They went to jail because they got married? And it took the US Supreme Court to get them out? Wow." Hank looked puzzled. "I don't know where that fits in the game. How many spaces back? And who gets the penalty?"

NT laughed. "Mom, we've been calling the game, 'Indignities,' but I think maybe you've got something there. Ironies. That certainly fits. We'll have to take it into consideration."

"You might notice, son, that when I think about your little game, I don't tend to see things as funny as you boys do. This wasn't funny, except for the name of the people involved."

Hank's mom looked at me. "So, Henryk, how do the Redskins fit into this game? What was so funny?"

"Oh, I just was thinking out loud the other day, about how everyone hates racism and all, but they still like that team name. I guess Grams is right, it's more of an irony, except for the people who actually don't want to be called that word. For them, it would classify it as an indignity." Now I was standing up to NT, and I didn't look at his face when I said this. Hank looked at me, Phillis, too. "I guess we have to balance between tradition and what's right. I don't know where to draw the line." I was on a roll. I'd probably never be allowed in NT's car again, much less his house. Oh well, in for a dime, in for the dollar, my dad always says. "I'm sure some white folks in Virginia thought they were just keeping a good old tradition going, like they did with segregation, but maybe there comes a time…" I don't seem to know when to stop. I was right, but…

Phillis came to my rescue. "Good point, Henryk. We talked about this in class the other day, and it spilled over into lunch. We were arguing, sort of, at the table, and I said that considering the large number of black players on the team, they ought to change the name to the Washington, uh, n-words. Just as racist, but more accurate. For some reason, not everyone at the table thought that was a good idea." She giggled. "Well, I thought it was funny. And at first, no one laughed. The white kids just sat there like they wanted to slide under the table. The black kids kind of groaned. But then one of the kids, a white one, I think, said, no, they should name the team the DC Kikes, since it's owned by a Jewish man. Next thing, everyone is coming up with outrageous racist team names. You know, there's at least one racist term for about every nationality. And who knows what they say in other parts of the country where there's a different mix. When we went back to government class, the teacher thought we'd gone crazy with all the," she made air quotes, "inappropriate words we were throwing around. Pretty good teacher, though. He managed to steer the conversation into a discussion about the names of all the high schools around here that are named after Civil War generals, from the South, of course. That's another can of worms that's getting opened, firing up a lot of people around here."

Hank really, really could have kept his mouth shut. I had aggravated his father enough, and Phillis had shifted the heat to herself, so why say anything? "Well, speaking of ironies for the game. Try this: you're named after a former great black athlete instead of a leading intellectual or artist, like James Baldwin or Langston Hughes or Gordon Parks. Or even Thurgood Marshall. Go back one square?" It was totally quiet at the table. I wanted to get under the invisibility cloak with Terry. NT just gripped his fork tightly, said nothing. Hank took a sharp intake of breath. "Aw, come on, Dad, I was only kidding."

But I know he wasn't. He once said about the same thing to me. "Why'd they go and name me after a baseball player? It's not like naming me after an athlete would make me an athlete. I should have been named Louis Armstrong Jones. I'm better at trumpet than any sport."

"How about Denyce Graves?" Phillis tried to break the tension. "There's an outstanding artist. She can seriously sing, one of the best opera singers in the world. Kids could call you, DG Jones. Good name for a rapper, like, dig your grave jones, or any kind of writer or musician." No one laughed. Her mom and dad glared at her, now. She was on a roll, too. "Well, actually, Hank, if you think about it, you do share a name with a famous musician who did a lot of black music. Elvis Aaron Presley. You're Hank Aaron Jones. And everyone knows that Elvis practically stole his music and style from the black musicians he saw down where he grew up and lived." She giggled again, "Hank Elvis Aaron Jones. I'm sure when you're eighteen, you can legally change your name." She grinned at her dad and added, "Yeah, Dad? Mom? Why'd you stick me with Phillis Wheatley Jones? No one spells Phillis that way anymore. You could have named me Toni Morrison Jones. A lot more up to date, to say nothing of a few literature prizes, and Toni's easier to spell."

Terry and I exchanged glances and with telepathy decided that we had a lot of homework to do. We excused ourselves as gracefully as possible and headed back across the street to our house.

There were only three text exchanges with Hank that night, none of them complimentary towards me, mostly calling me out for cowardly behavior in the face of fire, bailing on him. In other words, I had left him to deal with his father on his own.

I guess he was still ticked; at the bus stop he got to the bus just as it arrived, so we didn't talk. And he managed to find a girl to occupy his time at lunch. He had newspaper stuff right after school, and I didn't see him that afternoon either.

As it turned out, we didn't have to order in for dinner Wednesday night, either. There wasn't an invitation from the Jones, probably not to be expected in my immediate future, so no surprise. But Frankie had a good surprise for us. Mathilde, Tildy to her friends. She was a French girl he had met at the community college. She once told me that since every American she met either butchered or Americanized her given name, she decided to get it over with and introduce herself as Tildy. Besides, it seemed like Americans preferred nicknames anyway. She spoke reasonably clear English, was beautiful, and seemed to keep Frankie in line. He left us a note Wednesday morning, telling us not to accept any dinner invitations. He and Tildy would throw something together.

And did they ever. I know it's stereotyping, but this particular French girl could cook. When we got home from school, Tildy was banging around in the kitchen. Mom likes to be an experimental cook, so Tildy could find what she needed in the way of spices and pots and such; she didn't look like she needed any more help than what Frankie was providing, so I grabbed a snack and headed upstairs.

Terry was up in his room, tunes on. I knocked and walked in.

"Out." Terry didn't look up from his easel. He was working on a new project. This was a pencil drawing. There were sketches of various handguns and rifles roughed out on a big sheet of paper. He was working intently on the details of one of the pistols. It looked like a nine millimeter semi-automatic, although I'm no expert. "The door. It's still open. You can use it to leave. Now." He was trying to sound commanding, but there was a tremor there. His tone was more panic than command.

"What's up, Terry?" I took a step in and closed the door behind me. "I know that's not another attempt at greeting card art. So, what's up?"

"Two days. I got two whole days of normal before they started up again."

"Walter's bunch?"

He nodded. "Yep. Got a note handed to me in the hall today."

My turn, "Snitches get stitches? Misspelled and with a z at the end instead of an s?"

He put down his pencil. "How'd you know?"

"Got that note on Monday. I didn't see any big advantage to mentioning it to my parents or Frankie, so I sort of forgot about it."

"Someone just handed it to you in the hall, like with me? Did they say anything?"

"It was stuffed in my locker. You?"

"Someone bumped me from behind in the hall, said something like, 'Hello, fag boy, got a message for you.' And then handed me the note. I put it in my pocket and read it later."

"Well," I said with my best false professor's voice, "what we have to decide is, do these benighted gentlemen need a lesson in using spell check, or in cool? Do you think using the z was intentional or just a further manifestation of basic ignorance?"

"Might not be an either/or situation. Might be a both. Uncool ignorance." Terry actually smiled a bit. "I'm beginning to think that putting Walter out of his ignorant misery would be a good deed."

I was not at all happy about the direction this was going. "Getting him out of our misery would certainly be a good deed, but after we spent all that time trying to convince Frankie to leave it alone, wouldn't we look kind of stupid doing something stupid?" I couldn't avoid looking hard at his gun sketches. "Those look pretty good. I didn't know you were into that stuff."

Terry grimaced, "There's a lot you don't know. One of my mom's boyfriends was a big gun nut. For a while, there were probably six or seven of them sitting around the house. I went out shooting with him sometimes. Bonding time and all that. We always practiced with human form targets, not those bullseye types. Believe it or not, I actually got pretty good at hitting what I aimed for."

"You're not thinking about substituting Walter for one of those practice targets, are you?"

"Oh, I've thought about it, but, hey, like you've said to Frankie, there's some down side to that plan. Jail and all that." He went back to his detail work, "Still, a guy can dream, can't he?"

Being a bit short on smart replies, I went with lame. "Well, I guess you're okay. Frankie's girl is cooking tonight, going to be good. I'll call you when dinner's ready."

"Yes, mother. And I'll remember to wash my hands, too, even if you don't remind me."

Dinner was indeed amazing. It was only chicken, but whatever Tildy did with sauce and some fresh vegetables made it a whole lot more than "only chicken." Dinner started out peacefully. Without Mom and Dad there to interrogate us, it looked like Terry and I were going to be able to keep our missives from Walter under wraps. I tried to keep the conversation far away from school by questioning Tildy on everything and anything I could think of regarding France. You would have thought I was a total French nut. Terry helped out with a lot of music and art questions, had she been to the Louvre and Musée d'Orsay? And so on.

Didn't work. Apparently Frankie inherited our parents' suspicious nature. Or maybe, he had used that tactic on more than one occasion to divert our parents when he was up to something in school. Out of the blue, practically interrupting Tildy's glowing report on a rock concert she attended in Paris, he jumped in, "So, Terry, how's it going at school? Those idiots that were hassling you find a new target this week? You know, sort of a victim of the week club?"

Terry was so caught by surprise by the question that he wasn't able to get his face into neutral. He's way better at the poker face routine than I am, but he's not a pro, especially when ambushed. He stuttered, not much, but just a bit. And he frowned, just a little. "Oh. Okay, I guess. I try not to pay too much attention to those guys."

"I'm sure. But the real question was, are they paying attention to you?" Frankie looked at me. He looked at Terry. I guess the best answer would have been a quick one. But he could tell that we were thinking about what to say. And if you look like you have to think before answering a question, you look like you're lying, or at least thinking about lying. "Okay, let's try again fellows. Are those guys leaving you alone or not?"

Tildy seemed to be in on the story. I don't think Frankie had particularly planned to quiz us at dinner. It's not like he and Tildy plotted this out, but once he started, she played her part. She studied us while we danced around for answers. He could ask her later what she thought of our performance if he needed to.

I took a shot at an answer. "Yes and no."

"And? What's the yes part?"

"They let it be known that they would deeply appreciate it if we would refrain from consulting with the authorities regarding their recent misbehavior, and, if need be, their future misbehavior." I tried to look as relaxed as possible.

"I bet. Didn't punch either of you, I guess? A little more subtle than that?"

We both shook our heads, no. "We're okay, Frankie. Really." I looked at Terry for confirmation, and he nodded, although not enthusiastically. "We're not interested in getting them into trouble; they just wanted to be sure that was our attitude. You know how those types are, always running scared." I thought I was spinning it pretty well.

"Not scared enough." Frankie was genuinely angry. "Maybe I ought to go over to Bernard's right now and get this straightened out." Yeah, I thought, go over to that house full of guns and maniacs at night. That would certainly have a happy ending. "Tildy, that was an amazing meal. I've got to go take care of something, do you mind if you and these guys clean up?"

I'm not sure Tildy had ever seen Frankie fired up. He was probably on his best behavior around her, but she reacted to this attitude perfectly. "Oh, my dear Frankie, I'm sure Terry and Henryk can handle clean-up without me. Why don't I just ride along with you when you go visit this gentleman?" Was she serious? Did she even know what Frankie was considering? "You see, Frankie, dear, I'm sure the two of us could be much more, how do you say it, persuasive than just you by yourself. How could it be possible that he wouldn't listen to reason with me there by your side?" Did she know exactly what Frankie was thinking? Maybe she was going as backup carrying one of Frankie's guns? Frankie had probably taken her out to the firing range a few times. This was headed towards being the shootout at the OK Corral. Not a pretty picture. Tildy smiled ever so sweetly and looked directly into Frankie's eyes. "Maybe if we stay here instead, they can clean up the kitchen and we find something else to do together." If she looked at me like that, I would have done about anything. It worked on Frankie, too.

They disappeared upstairs, and we didn't see either one of them before we left for school.

CHAPTER 17

A Death

As we got off the bus, I nudged Terry. "Just for grins, how about checking in around lunch? Keep on keepin' on, right?"

Terry nodded. He usually was the master of that concept, as far as I could tell, but he had seemed pretty tense on the way to school.

Hank caught me in the hall on the way to second period. "I've got a session with Carl this afternoon. Dad's driving me. He mentioned at breakfast that maybe you'd like to ride along."

I stared at him. "Really?"

"For real, man. He brought it up, not me." Hank shrugged. "I don't know what's up, but…"

If NT wanted me in his car, then I figured I wanted to be in his car, even if I didn't know it. "Okay. Meet you in the regular place. I'll tell Terry so he doesn't worry when I'm not on the bus."

"Worry?" Hank hadn't heard about Terry's new problem with the crew.

"Nothing. Just that since my parents won't be back until sometime tomorrow, we sort of keep track of each other. He's fine. I'm fine."

"Did I miss something?" Reporter's instinct kicking in. Again.

"Nothing exciting. I just feel like I ought to keep an eye out for him. After all, he's my cousin, and he's had a complicated life."

I guess Hank bought it. He nodded and headed off to his class.

"Hello, young hero." NT gave me his usual greeting; there was nothing special in his tone. Just his usual hello. "School go okay today?" Interrogation or innocent question?

"Yes. Pretty normal. Nice to be normal. Boring, but boring is not as bad as people say."

NT laughed. "People don't always appreciate the value of routine, boring days until they've had a string of exciting ones. Kind of the story of police work. Ninety percent routine and boring, ten percent exciting bordering on terror sometimes."

"Well, I've had my days of excitement. I'll take this any time." We were working our way into traffic. "Um, NT?"

"Yes?"

"I just wanted to apologize for the other night."

"For what?"

"I maybe got a little carried away at dinner, talking about the team name and all that. I didn't mean to come across as disrespectful to you."

"Dis--?" He looked at me in the mirror, his eyes seemed to be laughing. "Oh, no. That wasn't disrespectful. That was logical. What you said. You've got a pretty good point there. It's just taken this old fan a while for it to sink in. It probably looked like you were picking on me, all three of you young ones, Tuesday night, but you weren't. All three of you were trying to use your God-given brains to make a point. Can't argue with that. I haven't read those two books yet, but I will, and I'll think about what you all were saying when I do."

Hank let out an audible sigh. I suspect he'd been tiptoeing around his dad for the last two days. "Yeah, and Dad, I, uh, kind of got carried away with what I said, too." I know he was positive that he was right about the name thing, but he didn't want it to become a wedge between them.

"Right." He paused while he negotiated a turn. "For what it's worth, Hank Aaron is not just some athlete. He's a class act. You wouldn't believe what he went through when he was getting close to breaking Babe Ruth's homerun record. He was doing something revolutionary, the next logical step after Jackie Robinson got in the game, and both of them stayed cool, didn't let the racist world rattle them. I don't like the name Jackie, so you missed out on being Jackie Robinson Jones." He finished the turn. "The game: I was thinking about this the other day when I was reading the paper. Three or four dudes get popped for some heinous crime that the media just has to report on, newspapers and TV both, and somehow, even though there's white and black guys in this little bunch of thugs, only the black mug shots get published. Now, if these guys are already in custody, why do we need to see their ugly faces? And if we do, why is it we only need to see the black faces? Who goes back? The hoodlums are already back by a bunch. Is there a place in the game for the media to go back a step or two? Same thing with black victims of crimes. Somehow the media finds it necessary to dig into their allegedly criminal background even though that has nothing to do with their sad situation."

"That's a good question, Dad. I think Ryk said something about it the other day in his mom's car. Maybe we need to have some sort of community pot so that when indignities are created by a specific group like the pro team or the media, they could get thrown into. We could call it the toilet bowl. Then, if the individual player won something good, he could get bonus points by pulling one of the toilet bowl cards out and discarding it."

"That is, uh. Complicated, son. But, there might be an idea in there that might work."

I didn't want to mention it, but it seemed like so far, everyone in the game was only losing turns or moving backwards. Of course, that might be the point.

We got to Carl's, and, what a surprise, NT held me back a minute while Hank went in for his lesson. "Henryk, really, how's it going? Nice riff on boring, but I don't know that I completely buy the story. Try again?"

My mouth went dry, and of course I went to my standard approach to adult questions. "Um."

"I thought so. Um, nothing. Something else has happened? Those idiots still causing trouble for you and Terry?

I have got to come up with a better answer. "Um" has become my tell, like in poker; when I say it, people assume I am lying or at least covering up, hiding something, like aces, or, in my case, eight high. "Well, not too much. Nothing we can't handle. They just sent Terry and me invitations, on engraved paper, of course, inviting us to not talk to anyone in charge. The gist of it was that Terry and I might have serious medical needs if we talk. They seem to think that we might know something that would interest the school administration. Actually, we don't have anything to add, but I guess they are a bit nervous."

"Guilt will do that. Did you follow my suggestion to keep your mouth shut with everyone?"

"I haven't talked to anyone at school. Somehow Frankie

pried it out of me. I'm kind of worried about that, though. I don't want him to do anything. But, really, NT, there's not a problem. They want us to keep our mouths shut. We want to keep our mouths shut, so everyone's on the same page."

"For now, Henryk. What happens if, rather, when, one of them does something else stupid and gets caught? Are they going to blame you right from the get-go? Carry out whatever threat they conveyed with their message?"

I hadn't thought about that. He was right.

"It's kind of sad, but I spend so much time around these clowns I automatically start thinking like them. Thinking might be giving them too much credit, but you know what I mean. It's kind of the downside of my profession. I usually see how the bad side of almost anyone can come out in stressful times, like when they're under arrest. I try not to look at the world this way, but it creeps in. Of course, it's also kept me alive through any number of exciting situations. Do you have a plan here?"

"Not really. Terry and I are going to try to keep our heads down and stay away from them." If he was worried, maybe I should be worried, too?

"That's probably the best you can do now. I know we're all hoping Frankie is too busy to get involved. Well, I have a couple errands to run. You go on into Carl's and hang out. I'll be back for both of you in a bit."

At Carl's I read magazines and listened to everything from tentative attempts at some new technique to bars and bars of amazing music, both from Carl's demonstrations and from Hank's instrument. They finished and came out to the front room. Carl glanced at his watch.

"Next guy's a bit late." Then, out of the blue, "Hank, I ever tell you why your Grams won't marry me?"

Hank had a smacked-in-the-face look. "No. Why should she? She was married to Granddaddy forever."

Carl smiled, "Oh, no, not while she was married to Jonesy. Afterwards. After he passed on, I waited a proper time and started seeing her. Was going pretty good, but there was a snag. A serious snag."

He had Hank's fullest attention, mine, too. Carl looked like he wanted to back out of this whole conversation, but he started it, so it was up to him to quit.

"Yeah. She's a straight shooter, you know. Calls it like she sees it. And there was one thing about me she didn't like to see. Smack." We both looked at him blankly. "You know. Horse. Heroin." I don't think we looked so blank now. "Oh, it's not a problem. Hasn't been for a long, long time. But, well, way back it was. I guess she was afraid I'd go back. I won't. Nasty stuff. Terrible."

We were not clear about why he was telling us all this, and I guess it showed. Hank swallowed hard. "It's okay, Carl. That's all history."

"Ancient history. I promise. But to your Grams, once a junkie, always a junkie."

"But you're, you're--"

"Practically perfect, I know. That's now. That's not thirty years ago. But that's not why I'm telling you this now. When's your dad coming back, Hank?"

"Pretty soon, I guess." I said. "He's running a couple of errands."

"Okay. I'll get to the point. It's not about your Grams, that I'm telling you all this, Hank. I read the paper. I see where smack has made a comeback. All kinds of folks using now. Not just black boys in the ghetto and jazz musicians." He did smile a little when he said this. "There's all kinds of stories about good kids, kids like you guys trying this and trying that and getting into heroin. Their moms and dads are using, maybe started out with a prescription or something, and now they're hooked. All kinds of people."

We still didn't know where this was going.

"And, yeah, I know NT and your parents and teachers and everyone is preaching no drugs, but I'm adding my two bits worth. Been there, done that, so maybe you'll listen to me. Pot's probably no big deal. I'd do some now if I wasn't trying to stay one hundred percent clean one hundred percent of the time. But, if you get your pot from some dude who might have some pills or smack or something, don't listen to him. Stick to pot. Stay away from alcohol as much as you can, too."

As far as I knew, Hank had never messed with pot or anything else, and I knew that I hadn't, so this was a weird conversation.

"Don't feel like you have to share this with your dad, Hank. He might have a different take on pot, being a sheriff's deputy and all." He looked hopefully at the door, willing NT or the next student to appear. "I've had a pretty good life despite losing a chunk to smack, but I didn't get, and I'm not going to get, Eleanor Rose. Ever. And you don't want to live with regrets. Ah, I hear NT out there. You guys scoot. See you next week."

We were out the door and headed to the car. We exchanged glances, but didn't say anything.

"Hey, guys. How's it going?" NT looked at us in the mirror as we piled in.

I guess Carl's little drug lecture was on Hank's mind. "Hey, dad. Here's one for the game. You get busted for selling maybe two hits of crack cocaine and while you're sitting in court there's a guy who's gotten busted for selling a couple hits of cocaine powder. Judge has to give you about ten times the sentence the guy selling coke gets. Move back, a lot of spaces."

NT stared in the mirror. "What brought that on? You in trouble? One of your friends?"

"Oh, no, Dad. I was just thinking about something I read in the paper the other day."

NT laughed. "And something Carl told you. I guess he told you about his nefarious past?"

"Yeah. I didn't know."

"Well, he's clean now. Been clean, far as I know, for a long time. I wouldn't be bringing you over there if I thought he was a problem. He's a good man." I wondered if he knew of Carl's interest in becoming his stepdad. "The federal government is working on that sentencing disparity you're talking about. I doubt Virginia will, until they figure out how much it costs keeping these clowns in jail forever. Of course, if they ever really fix the sentencing and quit putting all these dudes in jail, I'll be out of a job. Which, on balance, would be worth it."

We played around with a few other ideas for the game and reached the top of the neighborhood. As we turned in, we saw a slew of police cars parked in front of Walter's house. There were officers stringing crime scene tape around it. The flashing blue strobe lights were blinding. NT pulled over when he saw a police officer he knew. They chatted for a minute, and then NT pulled back out.

"Bad situation back there, boys. Bernard Anderson was just found dead in his house."

"What happened? How did he die? When? Who found him? Who did it?" Hank and I had all the questions in the world. And NT didn't answer one. Not even a hint. Funny how we assumed he was killed by someone. What do we know? But we doubted that there would be that many cop cars, marked and plain, at the scene of a natural death. If NT knew anything, he wasn't talking. He reverted to pure cop and clammed up on us. When we got to the Jones's house, I said my goodbyes and went over to my house. I had a terrible feeling that I did not want to know the answer to the whodunit question.

CHAPTER 18

Whodunit?

Frankie? Terry? Walter?

Most definitely Walter. It had to be. Only this morning I had heard a couple of guys riding him in the hall between classes. "Hey, tough guy, I heard your old man, or was it your old lady, kicked your butt the other day. Right in front of Slate, I heard. Wow, still smacking you like you was six or something. Wow." Walter didn't say anything, and I don't think he saw me, but I wasn't happy. What if he thought I told someone about what happened in Wright's office on Friday? His new hate buddy kept it up, laughing with some friends. "Yeah, one of your tough guy buds told me you were all upset, practically crying, I bet, 'cause your old man smacked you around." Well, that was good to hear. Sounded like his own crew ratted him out. He probably was complaining about it Friday, and like all juicy gossip, it couldn't be contained. The important thing, though, was that I wasn't going to be blamed for blabbing.

No one was at the house. It was about five-thirty, maybe a little later. Terry should have been there. Frankie was probably at work, or in class, or maybe hanging out with Tildy. I thought I should feel pretty good about Bernard's death. The world could always get by with one less evil person, but I was surprised to find out that I felt something, but it wasn't glee. Part of my problem may have been that a huge part of my mind was thinking that Frankie or Terry might be involved.

While I was running various murder scenarios through my head, starring first Frankie, then Terry, and then Walter, Terry came in. He was carrying his guitar case. He waved vaguely at me as he headed upstairs.

"Where've you been?" Boy, I sounded just like my dad there.

"Out." Terry giggled. "But now. I'm in."

I was way too young to start acting like my dad and mother. "Okay, Ter. Pizza for dinner tonight? I don't see any signs of more super Tildy food. Don't know where Frankie is."

"Sounds good. The usual ones, plus extra cheese, spicy sauce? Text me when it gets here." He went upstairs. I heard the music, loud, before he closed his door.

I ordered the pizza online and started pulling out napkins, paper plates, and some sodas. I was mechanically setting the table when I realized that the clothes washer was running. I also heard the shower running. This seemed like a lot of cleaning up for one afternoon.

When Frankie was around thirteen, he started to kick about our parents invading his privacy and making unreasonable demands, like we keep our rooms halfway clean and neat. At that time I didn't see what all the fuss was about, but I became an ally in his fight. In the end, the compromise was that they could "invade" our privacy as far as using the computer and cell phones went. They promised they would not check into our various online activities without our being present, but they also promised that they would look, and they would not warn ahead of time. Frankie tried in vain to argue that an old civil liberties guy like our dad and a peace-loving radical like our mom should know better than trample on the sacred rights of an American citizen, but their argument prevailed: yes, we were indeed citizens, but first we were their children, and they wouldn't abdicate their parental responsibilities. The other half of the deal was the "CYOR" rule. As long as we complied with the "clean your own room" rule, including doing our own laundry, with training, of course, they would stay out of our rooms unless invited in. It should be noted that somehow either Dad or Mom found an excuse to be invited in nearly every day, but it was a pretty benign check-up. When Terry moved in, he was more than happy to agree to these terms. So now, just after Terry comes home, just after a neighbor has been killed, Terry is washing his clothes. I hadn't thought to check him out for blood or other signs of mayhem when we discussed the pizza. Not the world's best detective, I guess.

The pizza guy hit the doorbell, I got the pizzas and texted Terry to come down. He plunked down into his usual seat and tore into the pizza like he hadn't eaten all day. I ate a couple pieces and watched. "You're washing clothes, Ter?"

"Yeah. Just realized that I was running short on stuff. Now's as good a time as any. Did you need to use the machine?" He took a long, slow breath, like he was trying to calm himself down. "Also, I spilled a coke on my jeans." Now that he mentioned it, I could see that the clothes he was wearing were different from what he had on when he came home. His eyes looked pretty red. I hadn't noticed them when he came through the kitchen the first time.

"So, school okay today? No Walter and company?" I was

trying to figure out how my parents usually managed to find out where I had been. "Bus ride peaceful?"

"The usual." Now he was eating almost too slowly. "No excitement. Some students are idiots, some just plain fools; some teachers are morons, some aren't quite that smart, but no one said or did anything to remember. Didn't see Walter or his bunch all day, so that was good."

"Did you have your guitar at school today?"

He looked at me, a question almost on the surface. "No. Stopped by after I got off the bus this afternoon. Why?"

"Um. I was, uh, surprised to see you come in with it so late."

"Yeah. I figured you and Hank were off with NT doing the thing with Carl, so I did a little music, too. I caught up with some friends in this guy's basement, and we jammed for a while. Went pretty good, except I spilled the coke." Well, that was mostly good. He was hanging out with alibi witnesses. Frankie came busting in.

"Yo, boys, what's up?" His blond dreds were dancing all over. He was carrying his pistol case. "Had a blast with Tildy at the shooting range. That girl's a natural. Steadiest shooter I've ever known. Hey! Pizza? Hope you saved some for me. Be down in a sec." He went upstairs.

I wondered if either of them knew about Bernard. I wondered how they could have missed all the cops up the street, and then, worse, I began to wonder why they chose not to mention it.

Frankie bounced back in, sat down, and started to grab at a slice of pizza. There was a knock on the door, followed by the doorbell, followed by another knock.

Frankie jumped up. "I've got it." He went to the front door, I heard some low conversation, and then Frankie called back, "Hey, guys. I've got to step outside with these fine gentlemen. Do not, I repeat, do not, eat all the pizza while I'm outside."

Terry and I looked at each other for a split second and bolted to the door as it closed. We watched through a living room window. Outside, we could see two police officers talking to Frankie. He nodded, apparently in agreement, and walked down to the patrol car parked in the driveway behind his car. He got in the back, as did one of the two officers.

Terry spoke first. "What's going on? What'd he do, you think?" Was he playing dumb, or did he really not know about Bernard? "They didn't cuff him. They didn't search him. And a cop got in back with him. That's a funny way to arrest someone."

It was kind of funny that Terry would calmly assume that Frankie was being arrested. Terry seemed to know a lot more about police practices than me. I wondered if he had a record of his own, or had he just seen some action in his mother's neighborhood, maybe seen a couple of her boyfriends taken away?

"Do you know about Bernard?" I decided that my go-around-the-block approach to detective work wasn't working, so I took the direct route.

Terry looked blankly at me. "Who?"

"Walter's father. You know, the big guy with the swastikas and all that. Guns"

"Oh, him. I guess I knew he was Walter's family, but I didn't know his name." His still-bloodshot eyes were steady as he looked at me. "So what's this Bernard got to do with the cops being here tonight?" I know he'd heard of Bernard. I'm sure Frankie or Dad had mentioned him when we were all talking about our problems with Walter and crew. Terry seemed to have gone on automatic pilot: act cool and collected no matter what came up. I gave up.

"You didn't know about Bernard being found dead at his house this afternoon?"

"Ah. That explains the cop cars I saw when I came home. I was over a few blocks and didn't walk by Walter's house, but I saw a couple cop cars cruising when I came home. I didn't see any need for me to, uh, become involved at that particular time, so I just came home. So, really, Bernard's dead? Anyone know how he died? Struck by lightning maybe?"

It was beginning to look like Terry didn't know anything about Bernard's death, and, most importantly, didn't have anything to do with it. Still, if he really did know where Walter lived and knew who Bernard was, he could have gone over there to "clear things up." And Frankie only came in with one pistol case, so that meant his other one was still at the house when he got home from school. And you certainly could carry a handgun in a guitar case with little difficulty. And no one in his right mind would approach Bernard or Walter at that house unless pretty well armed.

Terry ate yet another slice of pizza and headed back upstairs. "Well, I've got to shift that laundry over to the dryer, maybe hit the books a little. Pound on my door when you find out what Frankie's up to. Hope he's not in trouble."

"Probably just a witness or something." I said it, but I didn't believe it. Well, maybe a witness, but a lot more, too. I stalled around the kitchen, cleaning up. There wasn't much, but I made a big production of straightening up and putting away things that we had left lying around. My parents would be home the next day, Friday evening, and we didn't need to leave a complete mess in the kitchen.

I texted Hank and told him there were cops at our house to see Frankie and see if his dad was around. Hank texted right back to say, sorry, his dad had to go into work early for some reason. Then, he texted again, and said that he was pretty sure that his dad would tell Frankie not to talk. Actually, what the text said was, "tell ur fool bro to shut up."

Good advice, but Frankie was already out of reach from our legal advice.

Frankie finally came in, almost an hour after he left with the police. "Starving! Food! What a bunch of idiots!" He picked up a slice of pizza. "Ugh. Cold." He ate it anyway, but he threw a few more slices in the microwave while he ate the cold one. He opened a bottle of beer and sat down. "What are you staring at, little Bro? We're at home. Dad won't care if I drink his beer. Want one?"

I shook my head no and sat down, too. I had boatload of questions for him, but after I didn't get anything out of Terry with questions, I thought I'd try the silent approach. Make him talk to fill the dead air. It worked.

"So, I bet you would like to know what those fine officers and I talked about. It wasn't about the Redskins, I can tell you that." I was beginning to enjoy this. The longer I didn't ask him anything, the more he wanted to talk.

"Well?" I smiled.

"Well, it appears old Bernard went and got himself shot, like I figured."

"Figured?"

"Yeah. When I was driving home tonight, going past their house, I stopped and asked one of the neighbors what happened. They were all standing around like it was the greatest show in the world. I wasn't paying much attention to who was in the crowd, and I said something like, 'So, which one of you shot Bernard? Did you all draw straws, winner got to shoot him?'" Frankie grinned. "Not smart. I guess I just assumed that Bernard had been shot. No particular reason, but it made sense, what with all the cops around. I sure didn't think heart attack. The cops had not actually told anyone how he died. I guess there was a detective standing there. Dumb me, didn't even see him. But he sure heard me. That's why the po-po came to our house so quickly. He must have just followed me back to my car and checked the tags on his computer. Didn't have too much trouble finding me, did he."

"Okay. I get it. They think you shot Bernard because you said he got shot and no one else knew it." This did not seem very funny to me. But Frankie was laughing now.

"Oh, they don't think I shot Bernard, they hope I did. That way, they solve their case in like, fifteen minutes. Look like geniuses. Only thing is, I didn't do it. Still, they took their best shot. Asked me a mess of questions, where I've been all day, do I own any guns, where are they, all that kind of stuff. So I guess old Bernard really was shot, since they asked me about guns. Of course, there's about twenty guns right there in the house, so you wouldn't have to bring one with you to shoot him. Just borrow one of his. I pointed that out to the cops. They were not impressed. They even tried to get me to give them fingerprints. While I was sitting in the patrol car talking to this one detective, another one handed me a can of coke. Some goodwill gesture. I drank it, but I also smudged my fingers on the can so they won't get any good prints. I don't know why they bothered, though, they should have my prints on file from some of that juvy stuff I did back in the day. Also, they could have used a cleaner can. It was sort of sticky, like another drink had spilled on it."

I could tell Frankie was trying to put on a good show for me. Tough guy, been questioned by the police and all that, and still standing. But, I could see his hands were trembling, even now, hours later. He had a white-knuckle grip on a bottle of beer he was holding.

"First of all, I didn't do it. Second, I should have. Third, I wish I had. But, I didn't do it. End of story."

"Nazi creep got what he deserved," I agreed.

"Yeah."

And, no matter what Frankie hoped, it would not be the end of the story. Nowhere near the end.

He headed off to his room. "Oh, uh, little bro, if I were you, I would keep our cousin away from the po-po tonight. He's not fit to talk with anyone in authority right now."

"Why?" I've got to be the densest kid on the planet. "You think he had something to do with Bernard's death?"

"Don't know about that, but I do think he has been smoking non-tobacco substances, and that might not go over too good with the cops. Also, that would also make tonight a particularly bad time to explain anything. I can tell you from personal experience that the time to chat with the police is not when your brain is only working part time."

Well, duh. That would explain a lot about Terry tonight. Cleaning his clothes to get the smell out. Shower for the same reason. Eyes. Eating like crazy. I gave myself an F minus for observational powers. Make that an F plus. I did notice that Frankie said something about being the last person to see Bernard alive today. What was that about? As far as I knew, they had no reason to ever talk with each other. Especially on the day that Bernard got himself killed.

With a number of rather disturbing possibilities poking me, I went up to check on Terry.

Now that I knew that I should be looking, I could see the signs. The room, despite Terry's rush to wash clothes, did have a faint sweet odor to it. And, although he was a long time away from his friends, his eyes were still a bit weird.

"So, Henryk, did friend Frankie X the Ferocious bump off Bernard the Barrio Butthead? The neighborhood Nazi? Was he hauled off to the hoosegow? Jammed in jail? Slammed in the slammer? Pounded into prison?" I started to answer, and he giggled and held his hand up. "No, wait, I'm on a roll here. Do the mini-minded minders of the law think they have their dastardly deed doer? Have the county constables corralled their culprit?" He stopped to take a breath and giggled.

I jumped in before he could start up again. "Sorry to disappoint you, Terry, but they only questioned Frankie."

Terry looked genuinely disappointed. "Oh." He looked down at his feet. "I was kind of hoping he did it." That sounded weird, and he knew it. "I mean, I don't want him to do it and get in trouble, but if someone was going to get revenge for me, Frankie riding his white horse like your dad says would be my choice." He paused for a few seconds. I didn't know what to say. "So, what I mean, is, I'm glad Frankie's okay and all that. But, you know, no one's ever really tried to help me, other than your folks, and, uh..." He trailed off. Frankie was right. We did not want this guy talking to the police tonight. He was not making much sense, although I think I knew what he meant. Somehow, I didn't think my folks would see shooting Bernard as a particularly good action on Frankie's part, no matter how much it might have improved the world.

"Well," I finally said. "It's been a strange day, and I'm ready to call it quits. Should be interesting in school tomorrow. I wonder what they do when one of their student's parents gets murdered? Can't exactly hold a sending off ceremony like they did for the football player. Besides which, probably Slate and Wright are smiling even now. I don't think they had much fun dealing with Bernard." Terry nodded, he seemed half asleep already, so I left.

CHAPTER 19

Everybody's Talking

ank and I talked quietly on the bus. He was pretty excited, from a reporter's point of view, of course. "Think about it, Ryk," he said with a grin, "how many high school reporters get to cover a real-life murder right in their own neighborhood?"

"Poor choice of words, Hank." I tried not to smile.

Friday was indeed interesting. The local TV news programs had led with Bernard's murder; all that was reported was that a delivery driver found him around 4:00, and that he had been shot. Although most students probably had not been glued to their TVs watching news programs Thursday night, thanks to the cellphone gossip cloud, nearly everyone knew about Walter's father being found dead. The hallways were buzzing with speculation. The rumors about the cause were pretty amazing. It seemed that quite a few students had some knowledge of Bernard's neo-Nazi persona. That really helped with the rumor mill. Everyone had a theory about why he was killed. Killed by a secret Jewish organization? Killed by a rival white supremacist group? Killed by his own group in a power struggle? Killed by a black revenge group? Killed by some as-yet unidentified middle-eastern terrorist group? Some kind of gun deal gone bad? The cops themselves? By Walter? Who of course was not in school.

I ran into Melantha on the way to class. She dragged me into a corner of the hall.

"Terry Sullivan's your cousin, right?" She was looking very intently into my eyes. She never did this. Usually, her vision seemed fixed on something somewhere else.

"Yes. Why? I thought you knew."

"Maybe. Just making sure. I'm in a music class with him. My brother, Phil, also plays the guitar, and we were at his friend's house yesterday. I went along, just to get out of the house, maybe; I don't know. There was a bunch of guys in his basement, playing, or at least trying to play, music with their guitars. Terry was talking about Boston, I guess." Her eyes went far away. "How long you guys been putting up with Walter? All your life I bet. In Boston, over in Southie, where I come from, that didn't happen. He would have got the message to leave everyone alone. Loud and clear. In about second grade. Either he runs things his way, or, more likely, his ass is grass. We all get together and kick it for him. We don't put up with ten, twelve years of this stuff he's been handing out to you guys like candy." She looked at me blankly. Before I could say anything, she started off. "I've got to get to class. See you later." And that was it. Just like in Wright's office when she repeated almost exactly what Walter's bunch said in the bleachers that morning. Monotone, could have been reading the ingredients label on a can of beans or something.

That had me rethinking Terry as Suspect Number One all over again. He could have had time to stop off to deal with the Andersons before coming home. I didn't really know the timing of the death, just the guesses I heard. The chances are that no one could say for certain when Terry left that basement. The guys he was hanging with might remember what he said, although that was not likely. Pot smokers are not the most reliable of witnesses. Even if they did remember Terry's little speech, they wouldn't be sure if they heard it or imagined it. In any case, they wouldn't want to draw attention to themselves and their afternoon's activities. It occurred to me that Melantha could become a major hazard to Terry's freedom. What if she repeated her performance in front of someone else, especially an adult?

We only crossed paths at lunch on days with an even schedule, during fourth period, and I didn't know her odd day schedule well enough to track her down, so I'd have to hope for the best and try to catch her at her locker at the end of the day.

In first period the principal did make an attempt at acknowledging Bernard's death. He made a special announcement that did its best to gloss over the murder aspect of this event. He did not even say Bernard's name. He simply said that a parent of one of our students had died and that it would be an excellent idea if we all respected the family's privacy and show support for the student when he returns to school. I wanted to add a bit more to his little speech, but, alas, he didn't consult me before giving it. I wanted to add, "And, please, faculty, and this includes you, Mr. Slate, no, that means, NO public celebration; keep that on the down low." But, chicken me, I didn't even add it to the class conversation that erupted when the principal finished.

The teacher, who apparently had never even heard of the Andersons and therefore had no particular interest in the events, eventually got us back on task with the appeal of studying another tale of murder, with sex and drugs thrown in for good measure, *Romeo and Juliet.*

Most students would probably welcome a break from class, but I did not. Mr. Slate had me summoned to his office in the middle of third period. Up to this point I had always dealt first with Mr. Wright, and then Slate would barge in and make a mess of things, so I wasn't happy about starting a new round with him alone. Mrs. Hernandez greeted me like an old friend, which was nice enough, I guess, but who wants to be that cozy with anyone in that office?

"Mr. Jonasz," still mispronounced, "good of you to come down on short notice." He smiled like he had said something funny and pointed to a chair. "Sit. We have some unfinished business." He was sitting behind his desk. There were stacks of file folders and papers. Still no photos. I looked around at the various framed cer-tificates on the wall, some proclaiming graduation from colleges or universities, others indicating various other accomplishments. It seemed that they were indicating successful completion of different programs; one was probably for a secret government torturing course, also known as "enhanced interrogation techniques." "Mr. Wright is on professional leave today, so that it makes it just you and me." He waited for me to squirm and start getting nervous. I focused on calm, slack jaw, eyes on the bridge of his nose. Easy, slow breathing. He stared at me, still smiling.

"Yes sir?" Rats, I shouldn't have said anything. I should have waited him out. Score one point for him.

"Yep. Frankie junior, you and me." He leaned forward. "I have been thinking about your little set-to with those guys in the stairwell a few weeks ago. And I have a theory. Mr. Wright doesn't like it, but I do, so I want to run it past you, see what you think."

Well, this was good news, at least he didn't seem to have Terry in mind. "Okay, Mr. Slate." Probably not a good idea to reply with a sarcastic comment about needing a shovel to handle the bull he was about to hand out, so I resisted. Frankie would not have been able to contain himself. I have noticed that "Don't be like Frankie" was becoming a sad mantra for me.

"Yes indeed. I think that actually you and that bunch that hangs with Walter Anderson, he of the late and dear departed father, are in cahoots. Do you know what that means, Jonasz?"

I started to answer. Of course I knew, but why did he think I was in some sort of conspiracy with Walter? This was one weird day, and getting weirder.

"Yep. Those guys and you have any number of little side deals going on around here. Little pot, some pills, maybe a weapon or two, and you, YOU, forgot to do the one thing that is supposed to happen in these deals. YOU forgot to get Walter's share of whatever to Walter on time. That little love tap in the stairwell was a reminder that there is a price for doing business around here."

More than weird, completely into another realm of existence. Not a realm that I, or probably even Frankie, ever lived in. My efforts to stay calm were beginning to evaporate. I needed my fallback reply. "Um."

"Um, nothing, Jonasz. Here's the deal, long and short of it. Walter and his bunch have been a pain in the butt here for a couple years, and I don't see that changing. What has changed is that Walter's father, that massive pile of, well, whatever, isn't going to come charging in here to interfere. So what you are going to do is help me trap this little rat and nail his tail to the wall. I'll be honest. Right now Mr. Wright and I don't have anything specific on you, but you know, and I know, that will change if you keep working with Walter, or if you actually are operating on your own. So, you help me set the trap for Walter and company, and we won't find you doing anything. And, being at least one IQ point smarter than your brother Frankie, you will be smart enough to stay out of trouble the old fashioned way: don't do illegal stuff. You help us and then quit. You walk away from the short life of crime and become a model citizen."

Wow. Didn't see that one coming. I had spent my whole life trying to stay away from criminal behavior of any kind and Walter in any case. "Um?" What could I say? I didn't have the foggiest notion how to go about launching a criminal enterprise to trap Walter, and I had no interest in learning. It also occurred to me that Slate might actually be trying to set me up. He never got Frankie, but now he'd take a shot at the little brother, before I got hip and figured out how to avoid his trap. I wondered if he ever tried this with Frankie. "Um."

"Not good enough, Jonasz. I, we, need your full cooperation here. You know, I have an alternative to getting you to voluntarily help me." He flashed his really, really aggravating crocodile smile, "I could bring Walter's boys in here with you, and we could all have a nice sit down, a pow-wow so to speak, and iron out all your differences. I'm sure that would make your life very interesting. Who knows, another love tap or two might show up in your life."

No amount of practice in faking calm could help me now. I was totally panicked, and I know it showed on my face, my whole body language. I had a friend in elementary school who was a bit different from the rest of us allegedly "normal" people. His response when stressed by either other students or adults, was to throw up. I never figured out if that was an actual strategy, or it just happened, but it was effective. By the end of third grade, none of the students bothered him. And the teachers seemed to give him his distance also. I wondered how I could make myself throw up, preferably all over Slate's desk full of folders. The problem was that I had barely had any breakfast, just a piece of toast. A nice plate of left over lasagna would have been perfect for the job, but, no luck. I was about to start another "um" response when Slate's walkie-talkie barked. A shrill voice was saying something, possibly including the phrase "Code one", and Mr. Slate jumped up from his desk.

"Got to run, Jonasz. Duty calls. Nice talking to you. Get a pass back to class." His back was to me as he rushed out the door, "We'll finish this conversation later."

I have no idea what scientific gems were imparted during the rest of class. Couldn't focus on the grand historic concepts that were covered in fifth period, either. I pride myself in not getting into trouble, and when I do, usually I think I stay pretty cool. Not Frankie X cool, but cool enough. But this, this really had me frantic. The break in fifth for lunch is the third shift; it couldn't come soon enough. I found Hank as quickly as possible.

"Dude, you look shook!" Hank laughed. "Are you mourning Bernard? Or just missing Walter? No one knows where he is, you know. Just disappeared."

"How do you know all that already?"

"Sources. I've got my sources." He smiled again, "Well, like all good reporters, I also get lucky sometimes. I overheard one of the security aides talking on his radio. I guess the police were having them go through the school to look for Walter. In case he just showed up."

I could almost smile also. "Yeah. That would be Walter. The guy who skips so much that he never passes, shows up at school the day after his father dies. He's not smart enough or dumb enough to hide in plain sight. If they want to find him, they need to search the houses of all his crew. He's in someone's basement, most likely." I couldn't keep up the pretense, though. "Anyway, it's not my problem. I've got an interesting problem, or two, or three of my own." I dropped my voice and leaned across the table. I had to hope no one was paying attention.

"Melantha, already? And?" He was almost laughing.

"I wish. Listen, this is just between you and me. Not your dad, not your mom, and none of our friends. Not Melantha, either. And, of course, no one in charge of anything here at the school."

Smile was gone. "Serious stuff, huh? What's up?"

I outlined my crazy conversation with Slate. "What am I supposed to do now? You know the whole story. I have stayed away from Walter all my life, best as I could. There's no way I could trap him into anything. Never mind that he's not even here to trap."

"Offhand, I'd say that you keep up the good work. Distance between you and that bunch is always a good idea. I hate to say it, but you might want to talk to either my dad or your parents. I don't think a school administrator can do this. Got to be all kinds of laws about this. Or there should be." He threw some food in his mouth. "Man! What a day for this reporter. Murder case in the morning, and now this. And this, I can't do anything with. Can't write a word."

"Don't even think about it." All I really needed to make my life complete would be a story in the *Reporter*. There would be two stories, that one followed shortly by my obituary.

"Don't worry. I'm not sure what I can say about the murder at this point, but I know I can't and won't say or write anything about Slate's insane plan. Although, that would make a great headline, "Slate Sane?" You said there were a couple of problems?"

"Yeah. The murder thing. I've got two highly motivated people in my family who also had means and opportunity yesterday afternoon."

"Let me guess. Terry? How? When? Frankie? Yeah, I can see that. But he's too smart to do something that dumb, isn't he?"

"I think they are both too smart to do something that dumb. But, they're both pretty upset with Walter and company, and either one of them could have tried to say something to Walter or his father, and then things got out of hand somehow." I briefly outlined the timeline as far as Terry and Frankie were concerned. "The problem is, they both have holes in their stories. Terry could have come and gone ten times and his buds might have not figured it out. Frankie, well, I don't know. He has a good cover story, but he could have tweaked the times a little to fit what he needs."

"I'm having a hard time seeing Terry walking up to Bernard's house and blowing him away. That guy was gun nut. And he probably thought everyone was after him, so he would have answered the door with a gun handy. Hard to get the drop on someone like that."

"Everyone probably was after him, or at least enough that he'd be careful. Still, you never know. If he saw Terry at the door, he wouldn't think anything of it. I don't think he knew Terry or what happened, courtesy of his son, so Terry could have surprised him." I wasn't really eating, just pushing food around. "You know, I really don't know Terry that well. He's had a lot of bad, bad things happen to him these past few years. And he's seen a lot of bad dudes. He may have learned a thing or two. I know he can handle a gun; he told me. One of my aunt's boyfriends showed him. Sounded like he was actually good at it."

Our lunch period was almost up, and we'd gotten nothing figured out. Hank took a bite of his salad and stared at me. "You know, Ryk, you might be borrowing trouble, as my grandmother says. Terry was in school all day, right? So if Bernard was killed some time before two or two-thirty yesterday, Terry couldn't have done it." He chewed a bit and added, "But, I guess that doesn't eliminate Frankie. If he wasn't in class or at work all day, he would have had the time. But, I still don't think he'd do it; he's not that kind of dude." He picked up his tray. "I hope."

I know Hank was trying to be helpful along with hopeful, but for some reason, I thought that Bernard had died late enough for Terry to have been at his house that afternoon. It certainly seemed like the police had only been at the house for a short while when we drove up. They were still stringing yellow tape, and there wasn't any kind of crime scene van or coroner's van parked there yet. Of course, there could have been a long time between when Bernard was killed and the delivery guy finding his body. I wondered if I could find out more from Melantha.

Not so likely, as it turned out.

I saw her at the end of the day at her prime number locker. "Hey, Mel. Got a minute?"

She didn't look at me, kept her head down, digging things out of her locker, putting other things back in.

"Hi, Mel. Got a minute?"

She didn't look at me, but muttered, just enough for me to hear, "Who?"

"It's me, Henryk. I wanted to –"

"I know it's you, Henryk. I just wondered who you thought you were talking to."

"You, silly. Mel."

"There's a Melantha here, but no one I know named Mel. Is that someone else you know?"

I could feel my face heating up. Okaaay. "Melantha it is. Can I start over?"

"May."

"May. Melantha, do you have a minute? Or can, may, I walk with you to the buses?"

Now, she looked at me. "Sure. I guess. What do you need?"

"It's about Terry. Yesterday. Do you have any idea when he came over to your friend's house with his guitar and when he left?"

"They were down in the basement. We all were, and someone lit a cigarette. Steve, he's my brother's friend, told him to take it outside so his parents wouldn't smell it. The dog came in when he went out, so I went upstairs with the dog. Steve asked me to feed him, said he eats at 3:30, and I noticed it showed 3:33 on the microwave when Terry came to the door while I was putting the food out."

"Could Terry have left and come back later on?"

"Maybe. But I don't think so. I was up and down a couple more times, and he was always there. Except they kept going outside to smoke that cigarette, maybe two cigarettes, I don't know." She frowned at me. "Why are you asking me all this? Is Terry okay?"

I couldn't really tell her what I was worried about, and I couldn't tell her not to talk to anyone. "Um. Terry said he lost his capo or something, and we were trying to figure out where he might have lost it." That was lame, but what could I say. And I said 'um" again. I left her at the bus hoping a lot of things. Hoped that no one would decide to talk to her because I was seen talking to her. Hoped that she would buy the lost capo explanation. Hoped that she wasn't the curious type.

I got on my bus, half expecting to see Walter there grinning like an idiot, but he wasn't, of course, and the ride home was peaceful.

CHAPTER 20

Playing With Guns

There was an unmarked police car sitting in front of my house when I walked up from the bus stop. There appeared to be a detective sitting in it. I walked up to the front door and let myself in. I was not surprised when seconds after I closed the door there was a knock. I think I was expecting one of those hard pounding knocks that we see on TV shows, but this was normal.

"Yes?" I was working hard on my "calm" mode, but I didn't know how long I could hold it if I had to talk.

"Hello, son. I'm detective Watson from the county police department." He flashed his credentials wallet at me. He had a gold colored badge on his belt. "I wonder if I could talk with Francis Jonasz. He does live here, doesn't he?" As if he didn't know. I wondered if he was one of the detectives Frankie talked to last night.

"He does live here. He's my brother, but I don't think he's here now. His car is gone, and he works and takes classes at the community college. I don't know when he'll be back." I was trying to follow what I called "Frankie's rule:" don't tell anyone in authority any more than necessary. Ever. For all I knew, Frankie and Tildy were off playing in one fashion or another. Not my business, or the cop's.

"Well, could you maybe call your brother and find out where he is?" He looked at me, still trying to maintain cool. "We talked last night, and he was most helpful. He's not in trouble. Not now. I just need to clear up a couple things."

Lies I am not inclined to believe: "This won't hurt." "We appreciate your suggestion." "You are not in trouble." So, Frankie was in trouble. I didn't want to add to it, so I let the officer in and rummaged around my phone for Frankie's number, stalling and hoping something brilliant would come to mind.

Frankie relieved me of the worry. He wasn't paying any attention when he drove up to the house a few minutes later, before I could call. He parked right behind the cop car and trotted up to the house as if nothing could possibly be wrong. He opened the front door and froze.

Got to admire my big brother. He recovered amazingly quickly. "Oh, hi, Detective, uh, Watson, is it? How's it going?"

"It's going, Mr. Jonasz, it's going." Detective Watson was really good at showing calm. Nothing in his voice or the way he stood showed anything of intense interest. He could have been talking about the weather. "I don't suppose you have a little time to talk with me, do you? I have a couple questions to follow up on our conversation of last night."

"Sure. I've got to be at work in an hour, but I can talk a bit. How can I help?" Frankie was already moving into the living room. "You need a drink, ice water or something?" Pretty good, I thought, Frankie was trying to take over his own interrogation. Keep it on his territory and make it seem like he was the host, not the target. He looked at me.

"I'll get you both some water and leave you alone," I said. "I've got some homework to deal with." I went into the kitchen and got the ice waters. When I got back into the living room, Frankie was sitting in what we all thought of as "Dad's chair." The detective was sitting across from him on the sofa with a notepad in hand. I really, really wanted to watch this, the pro and the fairly accomplished amateur going at it, but I couldn't figure out how to stay, so I went back to the kitchen, grabbed a snack, and went upstairs. A few minutes later I heard Terry come in. He yelled a quick "Hi" to Frankie and scooted up the stairs. Didn't stop for a snack. I'm sure he knew what was going on and didn't want any part of the conversation.

Terry did not turn up the music today. I knocked quietly on his door and went in. "You thinking what I'm thinking?" we both said at the same time.

"He's not here to arrest him, you know." Terry tried to smile.

"I guess you're the expert, huh?"

"I've never been arrested if that's what you mean. But I've seen it done enough. They would have sent out a couple uniforms, some kind of back up." He looked grim. "But, that said, it is generally not a good thing when a homicide detective wants to talk to you about a homicide. Better to be talked *to* than to be talked *about*, as the victim, I suppose, but still not good. Do you think he had anything to do with Bernard's death?"

I was trying to decide if Terry was fishing for ideas because he knew exactly who killed Bernard, or if he was totally in the clear and really worried about Frankie. I didn't want to repeat what I said to Hank, about he and Frankie both having motive, means, and opportunity, so I skated. "Actually, I really don't think he did. But I'm not sure that the cops believe that. I wonder what he said last night that made them come back over here today and start again?"

We heard the sound of Frankie tramping upstairs and we listened as he clumped back down a few minutes later. We heard voices downstairs in the hallway and front door open and shut. Terry paused as we listened, and then, "Yeah. Hopefully, it's just the cops making sure they cover everything. Frankie's probably got a good explanation for where he was whenever Bernard got killed, and there's probably witnesses and all that, so he'll be okay. Your parents getting home soon?"

"Any minute, I would guess. They're coming from different places, but dad's plane and mom's train were supposed to get in sometime this afternoon."

Luckily, Detective Watson had left the house by the time my parents got home. He may not have needed back-up cops to talk to Frankie, but he would have wanted a swat team if he had run into my parents. I wasn't sure if they were madder at Frankie for talking to the police, or the police for talking with him.

"What!" Mom was in full attack mode, but it wasn't clear who the target was. We had all sat down to dinner, Thai take-out since we had no way to plan dinner, no Tildy to cook it, and Mom and Dad were pretty tired from travel. Part way through dinner we mentioned Bernard's death. We got through that okay, although Mom's first take on it was, "Poor Walter. What a life. What's going to happen to him now?" Dad just shook his head sadly. He had as strong a dislike of the Anderson family as anyone, but I think he agreed with Mom in principle. The fireworks came when it developed that the police had a big interest in Frankie's whereabouts Thursday afternoon. "Why on earth would they be interested in you, Francis?"

Give him credit, Frankie was back to his old self, trying

to bluff his way through. "Oh, no particular reason. I drove by when the cops were first setting up their perimeter, and they were kind of checking out everyone who was on the sidewalk or otherwise hanging around."

Dad shot a glance at Mom and his eyes narrowed. "And their interest in you was confined to taking down your name?" I guess he knew Frankie better than I realized. He had spent the last twenty years trying to figure him out. I hadn't seen any tells from Frankie, but Dad had almost instantly decided that part of the story was missing. "There was a card from a Detective Watson sitting on the table in the front hall. Was he in here, or did you carry the card in with you yesterday?" He looked at Terry and me, "You guys know anything about this? This detective gentleman?"

Neither Terry nor I was about to rat out Frankie, but our silence probably told him enough. "Well? Did you guys have to talk the police also?" He waited expectantly.

"No, Dad." Pretty close the truth. I did let Watson into the house to wait for Frankie, but I didn't actually have a conversation with him.

Terry chimed in, "No, Uncle Tomás. Never met the man."

Mom set her fork down loudly. "But he was here? In the house? Talking to Francis?" This seemed to be directed at me, but I shrugged and looked at Frankie. "Oh, it was just follow-up stuff, you know. Nothing interesting." Frankie did his best relaxed look. "I guess they're just going over stuff. Nothing here for them. I don't know when it happened, but I wasn't here. I drove by, like I said, when they were setting up the perimeter, so I really couldn't tell them much. I think they were hoping for someone in the neighborhood to remember a strange car or someone unusual walking around." He didn't mention Detective Watson's long conversation with him just before they got home. As far as they knew, Frankie's sole conversation had taken place Thursday evening, and Frankie seemed content to leave it that way.

We got through the rest of dinner, mostly hearing all about Mom's various misadventures with train and taxi travel to and from New York, nothing dramatic. Dad was pretty tired from traveling, and he surprised Terry and me by not interrogating us about any doings with Walter over the week. We were not about to bring it up ourselves. Mom headed to the office she and Dad share at the back of the house, and Dad went upstairs to head for bed. Terry and I cleaned up what dishes there were and went upstairs ourselves.

I stopped at Terry's room when he motioned me in. "So, cuz, has Frankie been a bad boy? In a good sort of way, of course." I couldn't tell if he wandered if I knew more, or was trying to figure out what his own situation might be. Before I could say anything, Frankie walked in carrying three opened bottles of beer.

"Gentleman, I owe you. Want one?" He proffered the beer towards us. We shook him off. I'm sure my parents knew that Frankie was occasionally drinking a beer or two from Dad's stash and probably didn't care, but with Terry at 16 and me at not quite 15 would probably be seen in a different light. "You guys did good down there. I don't want you to ever feel like you have to lie for me, but I appreciate the, uh, limited information you volunteered."

Terry smiled, "So, really, why was the defective detective here today? I thought you took care of all that last night."

Frankie looked sheepish. "I'm getting to that. "I was at the gun range, like you know. And Tildy was there with me. And we fired off a lot of rounds, maybe three boxes, four actually. So, when the cops talked to me in the back seat of their squad car last night, and they handed me a soda, I thought they were trying to get fingerprints, which like I said, was dumb because they've already got them." If anything, he looked even more sheepish. "Turns out I was the idiot. They didn't want my prints, they wanted to see if I had fired a gun recently. They had something on the can, I thought it felt weird maybe even sticky, and that must have gotten gunshot residue off my hands. It's called the GSR test, and it can tell them if someone has fired a gun recently."

"Is that even legal?" I was channeling my dad. "That's like illegal search and seizure or something, isn't it?"

"I don't know. Don't want to find out, either. The trouble was that I sort of neglected to mention I was at the gun range all afternoon when I talked to them yesterday, so they had a pretty good reason to come see me today after the GSR test came back positive. Didn't know they could even do it that fast."

"So why didn't you just tell them where you were yesterday afternoon. You could have told them last night when they first talked to you. Did you today?"

"Pretty much had to. Otherwise, they might have busted me for murder. Obviously, Bernard got shot." He looked at me morosely. "They took both my guns. Tildy and I only had one at the range, but I figured I better turn them both over since I told them I had two."

Terry started channeling my dad now. "What!" Maybe my mom, too. He was practically yelling. "Without a warrant? Haven't you learned anything? Did you at least get a receipt with the serial numbers and all?"

Frankie was startled. "I guess you're the expert, huh? No worries, mate. Those guns have never shot anything but targets. Bernard had a ton of guns in his house, and all his friends and enemies had them, too. So the cops have lots of choices. I figured I'd get them off my back a lot quicker if I let them test them. They better take care of them."

Someone else, specifically Terry, could have used the gun that did not go to the range to free the world from Bernard. That would explain why he was so upset with Frankie for turning over the guns.

"Well, you've got Tildy for an alibi witness," Terry pointed out.

"Well, yes and no. Mostly no." If anything, Frankie looked even worse. "Tildy was there with me, all right. We were there from around 1:30 until, what, 4:30 or 5:00 or something. I signed in when I paid, just like always, so the cops can check it out if they want to. Plus, there's video cameras all over the place, so I'm on about six different feeds. So is Tildy. And that's the problem."

I couldn't see that. "How's that? She's legal. She's a responsible person, maybe more than you, Frankie. The cops talk to her, see you guys on the video feeds, and you're home free."

"I don't want the cops to talk to her." He glared at each of us. "Remember, you don't say anything to anyone about tonight, right?"

Terry and I looked at each other, nodded to Frankie.

"She's here legally, or at least was. But, to stay here she was supposed to be a full-time student at the college."

"And?"

"And she had to drop a class; I'm not sure it was even her fault. I think it got cancelled. Something about the professor leaving or getting sick or something. She just figured she could spend a little more time at work and not worry about it. Take the class another time." He shook his head. "I guess she didn't focus on the student visa thing. She should have made them give her another class. It probably wouldn't matter unless someone starts asking questions. And the cops, they do like to ask questions. And then there's the work thing."

"She's a chef, a cook, anyway. How's that a problem? Is that a cover for some nefarious activity? Is she trafficking in truffles? Is she foisting fake foie gras? Is she filching fillets? Is she curdling her cream sauces? Is French cooking now verboten?" Terry laughed. "Seriously?"

Frankie groaned, "Tildy's here on a student visa; she's not supposed to work. They love her there, pay her cash, so there's no paper trail."

"No taxes either." I was beginning to think like Dad. "That does make it a bit sticky. What is she going to do?"

"Nothing for now. If the cops start asking too many questions and want to talk to her, I guess she'll split." He looked heartbroken.

"Maybe they'll just check the sign-in log at the gun range. That would be okay, wouldn't it?"

"Yeah. It's not like the range operator wants to know exactly who's there. They just want a name and their payment. They know me there, so probably that's all it will take. They tell the cops that I was there, show that I paid, and that's it."

"Unless they want to be sure you were there the whole time." Terry seemed to have a pretty firm grasp on cop-think. I did wonder what his life in Boston involved. "They might ask for the surveillance videos to see if you came in and then left, and then came back."

"Well, I didn't. We didn't." Frankie glared at Terry. "I told you exactly like it was. I didn't have anything to do with Bernard's passage to hell, sorry to say. And I was at the range all afternoon with Tildy. I didn't even stop at her apartment to, uh, talk, when I dropped her off on the way home. My time is good. I just don't want them looking at us on video. I don't want Tildy involved."

"Aren't the guys at the range going to tell them about Tildy anyway?" I was beginning to think, protect Tildy, and not worry about Frankie. He seemed okay.

"Who knows?"

Terry didn't laugh this time. "Oh, they'll mention her if they saw her. She's beautiful. Doesn't look like your average gun nut. No insult intended, but you know what I mean. Not your typical pistol-packin' momma. And, if they heard her talk, they'd remember the accent." Terry did his best imitation of a redneck, "She sounded like one of them foreign things, might be ay-rab or something." He frowned, "Have they seen her before?"

"Well, she's been there with me other times, although I don't know if always been the same guy checking us in. So, yeah, I can see how this isn't so good."

Boy was this so not good. Tildy in trouble, maybe. And now, maybe, Terry is back on the suspect list; it seemed like Frankie was off the hook, unless after they did the tests, it turned out that he really owned the killer weapon.

CHAPTER 21

Night Mission

aturday morning Hank had to go to the big shopping mall to play in a jazz concert. The high school jazz band that Hank played with was one of several high school groups appearing each weekend. Probably win-win for everyone. The students got practice performing in public, and the mall owners looked good because they were supporting the local schools. To say nothing of getting a few students and their parents into the mall on a Saturday morning with the possibility that they might spend a few dollars there.

Walter was there, too, as I discovered, although not to enjoy a jazz band or spend money, of course. Actually, he discovered me. I was standing along the edge of the courtyard where the band was performing when he nudged me in the back. I turned to look at him, and he hissed, "Don't say anything. Meet me over there." He nodded towards a children's apparel store. Actually, a pretty good choice, we'd look like a couple guys waiting for their moms buying stuff inside. He backed off. I waited until the group finished the tune and drifted over to the front of the store.

I always thought that line in so many stories about someone's heart pounding was an exaggeration, but it seemed real to me. He didn't look at me. I hoped Slate wasn't around to see this. "You got my message?" Walter sort of growled and whispered at the same time.

"I guess." What else could I say? I didn't really know what message he was talking about.

"Well, keep on not talking. To anyone. My crew thinks they saw you with Slate. You get buddy-buddy with him, and, well, you know."

Boy, did I know. I could easily imagine his response if he knew what Slate wanted me to do. "Won't happen, Walter. Really. Not a chance. He's been after me ever since he figured out Frankie is my brother. I'm not Frankie. I don't see anything. Don't know anything. Live and let live, that's me"

"Yeah. The live part sounds pretty good, doesn't it." He glanced at me. "If anyone asks, you did not see me here, right?"

"Right."

"Well, I've got shopping to do. Can't really go back home to get clothes and stuff. Cops have the house all sealed up." He did look a bit rough, now that I thought about it, worse than usual. His hair was stringy and dirty, not that he ever had spent money on an actual haircut, but it was usually trimmed long and reasonably even around the edges. He had splotchy patches of whiskers; it looked like he had occasionally tried to shave, but with a dull razor in bad light. He gave off the definite odor of someone who could use a decent shower. He probably slept in his clothes. "I might be able to sneak in there in a few days. Don't guess you'd wanna help me shop, would you?"

"No."

"Didn't think so. My buddy Thirsty will be along in a few."
He looked around. Was One Punch somewhere nearby, too?
Was he going to have One Punch hit me again? Not good.
"You wouldn't know what to do anyway. We got a system. I'll
be the sharpest dude in the mall in about an hour." I didn't
feel it necessary to contradict him with a mention of his
face and smell. I saw his buddy coming along with a few
different shopping bags dangling from an arm. "Remember,
you haven't seen me. But," and he paused a beat, "I might
be seeing you."

He walked away, and headed into a sports clothing
store. Thirsty followed him a few minutes later. The clerks
would not connect the two of them. They wouldn't look
too obvious to anyone monitoring security feeds around
the mall, either.

So, he was still in the area. Must have been staying
with friends like I guessed. He definitely had been living in
someone's basement or the back of a van for the past week.
I vaguely thought about how he planned to "shop" and
get away with it, but he and his friends had probably been
doing it for years. I also got to thinking about his house.
I wondered what it looked like in there after the cops got
through with it.

I went back to watching the concert. Ten or fifteen minutes later I got another nudge in the back. "The restroom.
Five minutes. The one by the food court." Walter definitely
watched too many movies. I expected him to mention a
song for me to whistle (which I couldn't have done anyway)
and which stall to find him in. I looked around; he was
walking calmly away, wearing different clothes already.
Hank and I had come with his mother, and I guess she
had had enough music and was doing some shopping; she

wasn't around. In proper spy/thriller fashion, I walked the opposite way from the food court and circled back around to the restroom.

In one part of my brain I was thinking, "You fool, you fool, you fool! What are you doing with this clown?" But another part of my brain was visualizing a kid who crossed Walter in middle school when I was in sixth and he in eighth grade. Walter just pounded and pounded on his face, right there in the front hall as we headed to the buses. That kid was screaming and bleeding like crazy. That image plus my recent experience with One Punch pushed me directly into that restroom.

Walter walked in a minute or two later. He looked into the stalls before talking. "Here's what I need, Jonasz. Here's what you're gonna do." I was trying to keep my no-worries look on my face, but this was crazy. Right out of a late night rerun movie. "You're gonna sneak into my house for me. Tonight. I can't get near the place, the cops and all. I don't want them to get a chance to question me. I need money. There's money in there. My old man always kept a big stash. Said you never knew when you might have to leave town in a hurry, and besides, the government's always after everyone."

I looked at him, blankly, I hoped. Didn't say anything.

"Hey. Jonasz? You listening? We don't have much time here. Someone might come in."

I just looked at him. I thought about what Slate said about me being "in cahoots" with Walter, and now it looked I was. I couldn't just walk out; he was blocking the door.

"My crew is still at school, remember? One Punch can find you and maybe take two punches this time, right? Maybe a bunch. He also knows about your girl, Morticia or whatever. I don't guess she'd want a round with OP either." He grinned. His teeth looked like they hadn't been brushed in a month. I resisted the temptation to tell him I would pick up a toothbrush while I was in his house. "So, we got that straight. I get some money, you keep your good looks. Pretty nice deal, if you ask me." What could I say? He had me with the mention of One Punch. He quickly explained where I could find a key to his house and where the money was stashed. "That big rock is still at the end of your driveway, right? Just put the money in a black plastic bag and stick it down in the back so it doesn't show. I'll get it sometime tonight. Make sure it's there before the newspaper delivery goes through the neighborhood. Now, go into a stall for a couple minutes so you don't come out with me on the mall cameras."

In the stall, I had time to think. Mostly what I thought about was that maybe I had somehow slipped down the rabbit hole from *Alice in Wonderland* or otherwise gone crazy. I thought about dealing with One Punch, and decided that Walter's demands were something I could live with. After all, if he had killed his father, I didn't want to help him start on the path to being a serial killer by being his next victim. I also kind of wondered how much money we were talking about. Did Walter know? And, why would Walter assume that I wouldn't skim a little for myself before making the delivery? Ah, One Punch. Walter probably thought I was either too honest or too smart/scared to steal from him.

On the way home from the concert Hank was jazzed up by the experience. "Amazing. We played some set pieces, and then we basically jammed, like Carl's been showing me. First one of us, then another. Smooth as can be. Riffing on the same tune but in different ways." He rattled on and on, and I let him. For different reasons, we were not interested in talking about the indignities game. He was too wound up over the performance, and I was mired in worrying about Walter's demand. Obviously, I didn't tell him about my conversation with Walter. When he calmed down, we chattered aimlessly with his mother about the concert or the mall or something until we got home. I practically jumped out of the car when we pulled up. "Thanks for taking me along, Mama J. Text me after lunch, Hank."

I don't know how Walter thought I could just waltz out the door at night to go break into his house without my parents noticing, but I guess he had a lot of experience in zero parental supervision and assumed everyone came and went like that. However, with the exception of the arrival of Melantha, things worked out, due to luck, though, not brilliant planning.

My parents had some big function to go to, a major dress-up, big-money fund raiser for a worthy cause. They would be leaving at six and wouldn't be back home until one or two. Everyone, without consulting them of course, made plans for a great Saturday night. Frankie announced that he would pick up Tildy after she worked some banquet her boss was catering, and they would disappear into the night somewhere. Terry told me that he and his guitar-playing friends would be taking over the basement for an extended jam. We didn't discuss the possibility of non-tobacco smoking products being consumed, although I did remind him of the house rules about smoking inside. My dad, for all his alleged virtues, did occasionally have a cigar out back on a nice day, but I'm sure that we all agreed that we didn't want smoke of any kind in the house, so it really wasn't an issue. I filled in Hank on my dilemma, and we decided that two criminals out at night was better than one and made plans to meet in the back around eight. Since it was fall, it would be dark enough then, but not too cold. We'd wear black, like all good operatives and carry some sort of flashlights. Walter had told me how to approach his house without being noticed; a neighbor on one side had his garage there and no windows. Walter's back door was shielded by a carport and some bushes.

In all the spy movies, the hero always has this beautiful girl who sometimes helps and sometimes hinders him. I got Melantha. She showed up with Terry's guitar bunch. I was still clearing the table after dinner, and Terry answered the door. I heard the usual, "Hey, bro" "'Sup?" and "Man" and then, "Hello, Terry. Is Henryk present? Here?" Melantha's voice. Definitely. But?

I walked into the front hall drying my hands. She was dressed, as usual, in a longish flowered skirt and wearing a dark shawl sort of thing. "Henryk said we should get together some time besides at school. Since my brother Phil was coming over here with his guitar, I thought now would be a good time." I stood there, pretty much stunned, I guess. Not smacked-in-the-face-by-One-Punch stunned, but stunned. Terry turned to me grinning.

"You dog!"

Melantha stared at him, "Dog? You have a dog? Henryk?"

"It's okay, Melantha. Don't pay attention to Terry. He's just talking. Come on back to the kitchen." We retreated back while Terry and friends moved their guitars downstairs. "Have a chair while I finish up these dishes." And figure out what was going on. I knew that getting a big bump on the head, now several weeks past, was supposed to cause memory problems, but somehow I didn't think that I had invited Melantha over. Certainly not tonight.

Hank tapped on the back door and let himself in. He saw Melantha and stood still. "Hey, Ryk. Ready to, uh?" I could read the question on his face.

"Oh. Hank. This is Melantha. Melantha, this is Hank. I'm not sure if you've met before."

Hank found his voice, and his killer smile "Hi, Melantha. I might have seen you around. How you doing?"

"Very well, thank you." Her voice seemed flat somehow. "And you?"

No one said anything. I could hear Terry and his friends teasing each other as they went downstairs. Hank shifted his weight from one foot to the other and stared at me. Melantha stood there with a blank look on her face.

Hank caught my eye and mouth "That's Melantha?!" He had told me some time back that his sister had been raving at dinner about this "total nut job" freshman in her trig class who couldn't answer a simple question without a complicated explication of the mathematics involved. Hank was now making the connection.

"So, Melantha?" I started. "You're here. Tonight."

She brightened up a bit. "Yes. Remember, last week some time you said that we should get together outside of school. I decided to come over here with my brother. He's one of Terry's friends. You know. I told you about him and me being at Stevie's house Thursday."

I think Hank was laughing at me, but he managed to keep a straight face. He's probably used to girls showing up at his house unannounced, but this was new to me. For that matter, I only remember one time when Melantha even started a conversation with me. She would talk when I caught up with her, but she had never gone out of the way to talk to me, except when she reported Terry's monologue about how to deal with bullies. "Okay, Melantha. I see." Was this an improvement over "um" as a stall tactic? "Well, it's like this…" Still stalling. "Hank and I have this, um, errand to run tonight. We're supposed to go pick something up for someone. We won't be gone long." Hank and I were already dressed in black. On the back porch I had stashed a flashlight and even found a light mounted on a headband to bring along, just in case, so we were ready to go, once we solved the Melantha problem.

"No problem. I'll just go along with you. Where?"

Hank caught my eye and shrugged. What could we do? "Sure, Melantha. But there's a couple things you ought to know before we take off." I filled her in as we walked down the street. It was several blocks to Walter's house, the walk extended by needing to approach it from a specific direction on his street so we wouldn't be seen. We had plenty of time to explain, and, luckily, she didn't seem interested in the details. So we left out whose house it was and why we had to do this at night, now.

We stopped on the sidewalk between street lights. I looked at Hank and then at her. He smiled nervously, and she spoke up, whispering, "Okay, Henryk. This is what we're doing. We are going to this house, you get the hidden key, we go in, you find the hidden money, get it, and we leave. Then we go back to your house and talk about things." She stopped walking for a second. "Oh, and we have to be quiet and not tell anyone what we did. I don't know why."

She made it seem so simple. No James Bond stuff at all. In and out and back home. A cakewalk, as they say. I mean, what could go wrong? Three kids breaking into a house where a murder was committed, stealing the dead man's money, and then giving it to his fugitive son who probably made him dead in the first place? No problem.

Actually, it really was pretty simple. There was no police car parked anywhere. We had no trouble staying in the shadow by the neighbor's garage and working our way around to the back door. The key was where Walter said it would be, and we could easily duck under the strand of yellow "Police Line. Do not cross" ribbon stretched across the porch.

"Wait a second." Melantha whispered. She stood totally still, so we did to. Did she hear anything? "I just want to look." We did not need to be standing out there where someone could accidently wander by and see us or hear us, but we waited. She stared intently at the back porch, the windows, the door, and the stairs. "Okay. I've got it." Whatever that meant.

Once inside, we moved away from the door and windows and flipped on the flashlight and headlamp. The stench was horrible; decaying animal and mold. There was a large chunk of carpet cut out of the ragged rug in the front room, probably where Bernard ended up. There was a large brown stain centered on the bare spot but extending on to the remaining rug. There was dried blood scattered in various places, on the walls and on some broken furniture. It looked like Bernard Anderson had not died easily. We couldn't resist looking around. It was strange: creepy weird because there had been a dead body in there just a few days back, but also scary weird because there was all this Nazi stuff, flags and banners with slogans on the walls. SS lightning bolts, iron crosses, and swastikas decorated these things. Hank and I thought we knew all about Bernard's obsession with Nazism, but we had no idea of how far he had gone with it. I also had no idea of the kinds of stuff these people could buy to feed their craziness. In addition to the flags on the wall, the tables and shelves had a mishmash of items scattered around. There were hats, belt buckles, pendants, pins, badges, shot glasses, and coffee mugs with things like, "100% Politically Incorrect!" and "Hitler Was Right!" and "100% White and 100% Proud!" and "2nd Amendment." This last one had an automatic weapon showing. There were almost as many similar Confederate flag things, too. There were several gun racks scattered throughout the house; no guns. The police had either picked the locks or forced each of them and taken all the guns. They even got into a gun safe in one of the rooms and left it open and empty. It looked like the police had opened up every cupboard and closet, but they hadn't really messed anything up. They had looked at but not gone through everything. There was fingerprint dust everywhere. There was a note to Walter along with Detective Watson's card on a table in the kitchen. Of course, it suggested to Walter that he call the police and help clear things up. The whole house stunk of dirty toilets and mold, which appeared to be slowly taking over the entire house, in a slow-motion horror film style. Melantha stopped and seemed to study the contents of each room we walked or looked into. She'd put her arm on Hank or me to hold us back before letting us get closer.

"Enough of this, guys," I realized that we were getting off track. "We need to get out of here. Let's take care of business and split."

Walter's instructions were good: top shelf in Bernard's office, big blue book with the words "Building Code" in the title. As I pulled out the book, a stack of loose file cards tumbled down me. Mel picked them up and handed them to Hank.

"Whoa!" He said this way too loudly. "What's up with this?" Each card had a name, some had addresses or identifiers of some kind; and there were some other notations also. Hank's last name was there, with an N written down. Mr. Wright's also had a large N on it. On the Jonasz card was a J. There were other cards with the names of teachers from elementary school on up, probably ones Walter had tangled with, as well as cards identifying various policemen, and social workers. Some had racial notes, such as W or N, others just indicated the connection to Bernard. There were lots of names I didn't know, probably people Bernard worked with, either employees or customers of his masonry business. We restacked the cards and put them back on the shelf. It was a surprise to find them; presumably, the cops would have liked to look at that collection. They would have loved the book, too. This book was not your everyday building code. It was hollowed out, and inside there was a fistful of money. Some hundreds, lot of good that would do Walter, but also fifties and twenties. Great planning; we forgot to bring a bag or something to hold the money. We stuffed it all in our pockets and left by the same route we used entering. Door locked, key back in place, we started to leave.

"Wait a second." Again, Melantha. She stood where she had before and surveyed the scene like she had on the way in. "Something's wrong. Something's different." Hank and I looked at each other with raised eyebrows. "Got it." She started back towards the door. "A piece of white was right here." She pointed to a spot between the door and the frame, close to the bottom. "Where is it?"

Hank whispered, "I don't know. Why does it matter?"

"I don't know. But it was here when we came in, and it's not now." She sounded almost panicky. "Give me the key. No, wait, you do it. Open the door, carefully. Now shine the light down there around the floor." I did as told, and we all saw what she was looking for. There was a white card, one of Detective Watson's cards lying on the floor. It was bent, as if a door had closed on it.

Hank almost spoke out loud. "Melantha, you're a genius. We both missed it. Never even thought about it." Detective Watson had used a simple way to figure out if someone entered the house, at least through the door. I was sure there would be a card wedged in the front door as well, but we didn't have time to check. He probably wanted to know if Walter ever returned.

"You don't suppose the police had any cameras set up in there, do you?" I whispered. "We never thought about that either."

"I didn't see any," said Melantha, "but then, I don't know what they would look like."

"You know, a spy cam." Hank said, "People use them all the time, to check on their babies, watch their dogs, probably to check on their teenagers. They can just use their phones to see what there is to see."

"I don't know," said Melantha. "I still don't know what we would have seen. I didn't seen any Nikons or TV cameras on tripods."

"Could be anything. Look like a clock or an electric socket, but it would probably just be a little thing with a lens sitting on a table or taped to the wall."

"Well, it's too late now," I said. "We can't do anything about it. At least we don't look like Walter, and the cops probably don't know who we are."

We carefully put the card back in the door frame with the crease in the same place and what Melantha said was the right height and closed the door on it. We eased through the shadows and were back at my house by nine thirty.

I grabbed a black trash bag from under the kitchen counter and we hustled upstairs to my room. We did not need to run into Terry or his friends. We counted the money, I don't know why, and wrapped it up in the trash bag. There was just under $4,000, but a lot was in hundreds, which might be a problem for Walter to spend, although he probably had some nefarious contacts who, for a small percentage, would solve his problem.

At the end of the driveway there was this huge boulder, a big honking chunk of limestone that, for some reason, my mother and father decided was awesome. They bought it somewhere in West Virginia and had it trucked to our house, probably when I was around four or five. I remember that Hank and I liked watching the unloading process. Over the years the bushes they surrounded it with had grown, so it made a good place to stash something. We stuck the bag of money down where Walter expected to find it and went back inside.

CHAPTER 22

Games

We grabbed some cokes and chips and went up to my room. Melantha looked at the chips and coke like they were alien beings, but she took a few sips and ate a couple bites while Hank and I inhaled the snacks. This criminal business really made a guy hungry. I absolutely had no idea what to do or say. We sure weren't going to talk about our little raid on Walter's house. Hank probably felt like a fifth wheel and wanted to leave, but I guess he realized I was hopeless, so he stayed.

Hank was usually pretty smooth with girls, or at least thought he was, but Melantha threw him off. She didn't say anything, which was normal. Hank looked at me. I looked at him, expectantly, I'm sure. He gave up and broke the sound of chewing the chips. "So, Melantha, did you just move here this year? Or are you one of those students who got shifted over to Roosevelt in the boundary change?" Good question. Now that he mentioned it, we should have seen her around in middle school. I thought her bus went to one of the areas that fed our middle school, but maybe it was part of the boundary adjustment that riled everyone up when we were in eighth grade, and she had been in the neighboring middle school.

"I went to a different middle school." She kept her eyes on the can of soda.

She didn't seemed to want to elaborate, so Hank tried another direction. "How do you like our school?"

"It's okay. I guess. I'm not so sure about some of the administration, but the teachers seem nice enough."

"She's been introduced to Mr. Slate," I pointed out.

Hank laughed. "Lucky you."

"Lucky?" Mel frowned and look at me. "Why does he say I'm lucky?"

"It's just the way Hank talks, sometimes. He's not a big fan of Slate either."

"Big fan?"

"Doesn't like him. Thinks he's mean."

"Yes." She got that faraway look and her voice went flatter than usual, "Jonasz! What are you doing? Not so fast. Did you see what happened in there? Not good enough. You, and the girl, Mr. Wright's office. What's your name, girl?" She even mispronounced my name the way Slate always does.

I told Hank, "That was in the hall, after the big brawl, when Slate saw us leaving."

Mel continued as if I hadn't said anything. "So, Jonasz, is that about the size of it? Your short bus girl have the story right?" She grimaced with the memory and continued to quote Slate word for word. "And you didn't think all this was germane to the conversation we've been trying to have with you? Who would you be trying to protect here? And why?"

Hank definitely was trying to figure this audio playback thing out. I reminded him. "We were in the office, later that day."

Mel sat there, saying nothing more. She sipped at her drink.

"That sounds like the Slate we all know and love," laughed Hank. "Mr. Nice guy all the way."

"Love him? Who?" Mel looked blankly at me.

"It's nothing, just a joke. Hank sometimes says things."

"Yes," he agreed, although he didn't know what he was agreeing with.

"Do you play video games?" I asked Melantha. It seemed like a new direction in the conversation might be helpful.

Before she could answer, Hank jumped in with some comment about his new found favorite, which he then proceeded to explain in excruciating detail before anyone could stop him. This was so unlike the Hank that I saw with girls, that all I could do was gape at him. He was going a mile a minute, and, honestly, not making much sense. Melantha and I let him rave on for a few minutes. I guess he was trying to steer us away from anything so serious as school and Slate and Walter, but it was crazy. Eventually, he slowed down.

Melantha had that, "Are you really from Earth?" look on her face.

"Well, my brother and his friends play. A lot. They have never interested me."

He handed her a control set. "Here, I'll introduce you to the, uh, twenty-first century." Before she could protest, he started a game up. He had chosen the simplest game possible, and he was off on a second blast of energy explaining the controls and the game. He handed me the other controller. "I'll help you get the hang of it; Ryk can be our opponent."

"Hang of it?" Melantha seemed as confused by Hank's phrase as by the game itself.

"Nothing, Melantha. Just another way Hank says things."

To my surprise, she really tried to play the game. We fussed with it for an hour or so, almost acting like normal people, if you didn't count her constant questions and comments along the line of, "That's impossible! No one does that," as the game's characters performed their usual supernatural feats. Luckily, Hank had not chosen a particularly bloody game, but it still had outrageous violence, which drew a number of "Oh, no's" from Melantha.

Hank and I were getting bored with what amounted to a "baby game," and he popped the game card out and started to insert a new one. He began another rave about why this was such a great game when Melantha brought him up short. "Do you ever feel like you're different?" He stopped and looked at her. "I mean, when you really, really know all about something that no one else does, and you can't stop explaining it in complete detail?"

"Um? Different?" Hank was tongue tied for the first time in years. "I don't know." He put the game stuff down. "Different? How" I wondered if this was heading to a race question.

Melantha looked at me, then back to Hank. "Well sometimes, especially in my classes, I feel like I'm operating in a different plane of the universe. The other students don't get me. At all. And part of it, I think, is that I sometimes explain too much." Her voice drifted off. "Sort of like how you've been telling me about these video games."

"Oh," said Hank; he looked downcast, "TMI."

Melantha looked blankly at him, then me. "Too much information," I explained. "Usually, we use that to mean too much personal information, but I guess it applies here, or in class. Too much information for the brain to absorb."

"Oh. Yes." Melantha smiled. "That happens to me all the time. If a teacher asks about who the president was during a certain period of time, somehow I end up telling the class all about the man's presidency, a lot more than his name."

Hank said, "Yeah, in elementary school and even middle school, the kids called me the 'Black Brainiac' and got on my case every time I answered a question in class. I probably did do a lot of TMI, but looking back, they were still wrong. Jealous, too."

Hank had sometimes complained about this to me. His dad had told him to ignore the ignoramuses, and his mother told him to be thankful he had brains and could use them. I think it was case of a kid actually listening to his parents. I never saw him back down.

Hank made a production of looking at a clock and said, "Oh boy, Ryk. Getting late. Got to go."

It was, and my parents would be home eventually. "Yeah. We better knock off. I ought to tell Terry, too. You know, we didn't exactly tell the rents what tonight looked like, so we ought to clear everyone out."

Melantha agreed, "I'll get Phil and we'll go."

Hank stepped in front of her and tried to look into her eyes for a moment. "Melantha, you know what we mean about not telling anyone what we did, right? Don't tell anyone anything. Not your brother, not some girlfriend, and for sure, no adults."

"Oh yes, Hank. I understand. We don't talk."

He grinned, "Pinky swear?" and held up his baby finger.

Melantha looked blank. "Uh?"

"You know, we all swear to keep our mouths shut," I put in.

"Well, I don't swear. And what does this have to do with baby fingers?" She seemed to think Hank and I were completely nuts.

"It just means --" Hank started, but she cut him off.

"Something, I'm sure." She smiled vaguely at him. "Well,

I won't talk about this. I've got to go. Thanks for the adventure. Nice to meet you."

Hank let himself out the door, and Melantha grabbed my arm. She let go quickly. "Henryk. You, uh, know how you keep trying to call me 'Mel?' I was listening to Hank call you Ryk, and I think I like that. It's, uh, friendly. Or something. I think you should call me Mel, if you want to. Just you, though, no one else." She frowned a little, "I'll have to think about whether or not I should call you 'Ryk.' That might be just for Hank." This little speech pretty much finished her for the night, I think. She turned towards the basement door.

I was beginning to wonder if providing Melantha Raptis with "adventure" was such a good idea. I walked her down to the basement to collect Phil, and we listened to the guys jam for a few minutes before she left. She seemed to be following the music with all her senses, bobbing her head, tapping her feet, watching the fingers pick and move across the frets.

CHAPTER 23

Night Mission II

I went to school Monday with several very important goals: don't run into Slate, don't run into anyone from Walter's crew, and maybe, just have a normal day. Didn't seem like too much to ask, and I made it all the way to lunch, third shift in fourth period, with Melantha.

I sat down across from her. "Hi, Melantha. How's it going?"

"Mel, remember? Hello, Henryk. Life is very interesting." Her voice did not sound as flat as it usually does.

"Yes?"

"Yes. Life here, especially since I met you, has been very interesting."

"Okay." Where was she going with this? "I'll bite. What's happening?"

"Bite?" She looked at my mouth. "Oh. Never mind. I got this in the hall." She held up a piece of folded paper. "Someone bumped me from behind and called me Morticia, and when I turned around, he handed me this. It is addressed to you." She handed me the paper.

Scrawled on it was one sentence: "Call this number" and a telephone number. School paper is pretty common, but somehow this note reminded me of the threat I got in my locker a week ago. I was pretty sure Walter was summoning me.

"Did you read it?"

Melantha looked shocked, "Of course not. It's addressed to you. What does it say?"

"It's a phone number someone wants me to call."

Now, she looked directly at my face, and she seemed to be speaking very carefully. "The guy called me Morticia." She pronounced each syllable of the name distinctly. "Do you think it was one of those guys from the gym that Friday, the assembly?" Her face reddened. This was a different Melantha. "Are you going to call?"

Definitely one of Walter's boys. And I did have to think about calling. The penalty for not calling was probably a go-around with One Punch. The penalty for calling was probably something illegal or stupid. This seemed like the classic "stuck between a rock and a hard place." I wondered if this is how Frankie got started. "Yep. Might be someone telling me that I won the lottery." I did my best no worries smile, but it wasn't working. I could barely eat lunch. Melantha glared at me and didn't say anything for a long time.

"This isn't funny, you know." I realized that she really wasn't eating either. "I walk around this school feeling frightened all the time anyway just because there's a tremendous number of people present, and sometimes it seems like just a jumble of sound blasting me, and now. Now, there's some, some, demented boys calling me a name I still don't understand. I mean, I looked it up, and it's sort of a real name, but it's related to death, and almost no one is named it anywhere except on some old TV show. And besides that, we get caught in some kind of disturbance, and we get chastised by an assistant principal who is very rude to us, and we end up one night going out on some kind of secret adventure and go into someone else's house where there's a police investigation, and, and. I just don't know, Henryk." Her dark eyes seemed even darker, but there were tears there, too. That was also the longest she had ever spoken except when reciting what other people said. And she was just getting started.

I probably needed to look at it from her point of view. For Frankie, this whole mess would have all been business as usual, water off a duck's back. For me, a bit unnerving, maybe, but still okay, except for the broken face part, of course. But for Melantha, this duck was drowning in the water. Not good.

The tears were flowing now. "Saturday night, I almost felt, what? Normal? I mean, we hung out with your friend Hank and had snacks and talked and stuff. After our adventure to that house. That wasn't normal, I guess, but it was interesting. Fun." She wiped at her face and continued, "I was thinking Sunday, all day, about how you're going to call me Mel. Mel, just you, not Hank or anyone else, of course, but then this happens. I feel scared, Henryk. Scared. And I don't like being scared, and I'm already scared enough just being in this big school. And these boys who for some reason want to hurt you want to bother me, too. I think. And then there's that assistant principal. Mr. Slate, is it? Does he hate everybody? Or just the students at this school? You got hurt really badly for no good reason, and now they want you to call them? So you can get hurt again? Or not. Maybe? I like rational. I am used to being logical and rational, or at least what I think is rational. And my Sunday was not rational or logical. I spent most of the time thinking about you, and that has never happened in my life. Thinking that much about one other person. And I think I've got things under control, and my mind starts up all over again when I get this note. I have never been this confused in my life. And so scared."

One thing about high school lunch periods, they're too short to solve any of the world's problems. I realized why so many kids skip school after lunch; they need to deal with things that, at that moment, seem more important than school. Part of me wanted to go around the table and just hold on to Mel until she was okay, and part of me just wanted to run. The bell signaling the end of lunch rang, and I took the chicken road out. "Well, Melantha, Mel, I don't know what to say. Maybe we can figure some of this out after school."

She nodded and wiped her face. "Yes. I've got to get back to Latin class." She snatched up her tray and purse and dashed off.

I looked at the note with the number, debated whether to ditch the last half hour of Spanish, just to get time to think. But, not being particularly good at cutting class, not knowing where to hide, and all that, and since I didn't want to get into any trouble that would bring me to Slate's attention, I went to class. Not that I absorbed any Spanish, but my body was there. I decided to call Walter whenever I got the chance. Not calling him seemed a bigger risk, although I sure didn't want any more "assignments" like the last one.

I got another assignment like the last one. No surprise there.

I called between classes, and his instructions were short and precise. He needed to leave town, and had decided that the best way was in his father's truck. He told me where a set of keys was hidden, along with a set of different tags, and probably some more cash. "It'll be easy, Jonasz. Just like last time. You go down in the basement to where I'm telling you and find my dad's stash. He has everything so the government can't find him. Couldn't find. Someone sure did. Anyway, this will be the last time. You put the stuff where you did last time by your house, and I'll come get it, put the plates on truck, and be out of here. You'll never see me again." I wanted to ask him to take One Punch along with him, but I resisted. He gave me until Wednesday night. I would call and leave a message, and he would come by some time after midnight to pick up the stuff.

I couldn't wait to tell Mel, about this new development. She would be thrilled, I was sure. So would Hank. I wondered if they had a witness protection program for kids. Sixth period was PE, and we were now out of a set of health class lessons and back in the gym where I couldn't participate due to my head, so I had plenty of time to sit and worry.

I ran into Hank on the way to Mel's locker and begged off on riding to Carl's for a trumpet lesson. He was excited and wanted to fill Carl in on his first public jazz jam session in the mall. "Well, I guess if a lady calls," he smiled. "Catch you later. Don't get into trouble."

Yeah, right. He's thinking girl trouble, and I'm thinking trouble-trouble. "No chance of that, Hank. You know me, Mr. Clean!" I hoped I sounded normal. "Text me when you get home. Got a couple things to run by you."

Mel was getting her things when I got to her locker. "Hey, Melantha. How's it going?"

"Mel." She kept her head down on her things. "Better, I guess. I've been thinking about all this too much, and it was hard to concentrate in class." Welcome to my world. "Did you call that number?"

"Yes." I didn't want to look at her. I was afraid she'd be angry. Or disappointed. Or scared.

"I thought you would. If it's those guys, you probably can't just ignore it. What was it about?"

As we walked her to the bus, I filled her in. I still didn't tell her Walter's name, but she knew it had something to do with the same bunch as before. She didn't say anything until we got to her bus. "Here's my house phone number. Call me if you want some help going over there." She handed me a folded piece of paper and jumped on the bus. The note was printed with perfectly printed block letters and numbers: "Mel(antha) Raptis. 703.555.7890." She must have spent half her sixth period class creating it.

When I got around to checking my cell phone, I found two messages from my parents. Both of them had late meetings, so dinner was either pizza delivered or whatever Terry and I could scrounge up. Talk about being tempted by Fate! What I really needed was someone to lock me up before I could get into any serious trouble. Witness protection equals idiot protection?

When Hank texted, I called immediately. "Hank. It just keeps getting better and better. Tonight I am going back over to that house to aid and abet Walter's criminal behavior." I told him about Walter's brilliant plan to take his dad's truck complete with fake plates, and drive off into the sunset.

Hank just laughed. "Another made-for-TV movie getaway. Look at it this way, Ryk. If you can get him out of town, your problems are over."

"That sounds like another famous lie, but I'm willing to take the chance."

"That's the spirit. You might try to get him to call off his boys while you're at it, though. They are too dumb to do anything without him, but they might get antsy with him gone. And he owes you big time. Changing the subject, how are you and Melantha doing?"

"Hard to tell."

"That's good."

"Really?"

"Sure, any time a girl has you not knowing if you're coming or going, or if she's coming or going, you're getting into her and she's getting into you. It always works that way. It's when you think that you know what's going on that you're in trouble." We should have been on FaceTime. I bet he was grinning like a fool when said it. We agreed to meet up at the big rock at the end of my driveway at 8:30. He could tell his parents he was going to hang out at my house for a while. We decided that I had to call Mel and let her know what we were going to do. She was probably going to hang up on me, and that would be that, unless she started reciting our recent history to someone, but we were afraid that if I didn't call her, she would really be upset and be more of a problem. Basically, it seemed like a lose-lose situation no matter what.

Frankie wasn't home, and after dinner, I told Terry I needed to go to Hank's, and out the door I went. We met at the rock. We were really getting good at this. Black clothes, bag to carry things, flashlights including the headband lamp, and Hank even thought to bring along some dark cloth to throw over the cameras if there were any. Of course Mel had to go along. We swung by her house and met her at the corner. I don't what story she told her mother to get out, but there she was. Black clothes, too.

At the back door of Walter's house, we waited while Mel looked it over. We could see what she saw, too. "The card is different. It's not where we left it Saturday night." A very small part of it was sticking out of the door jam, but quite a bit above the handle, instead of low down.

"Cameras?" we almost said in unison. Hank whispered, "That cop's been back. Remember. We all shine our lights bright just as we open the door. If he has a camera facing the door, we might be able to put a white spot on it until we can cover the lens. It could be on the floor, on a table, or taped to the ceiling. Melantha, you aim low; Ryk, put the head lamp and the flashlight on the middle, and I'll go high. Soon as we find it, I'll try to get next to it with the cloth while you keep it blinded."

"Sounds like a plan," I said. "What if there's more? In the hall or something? We have to get down to the basement this time."

"You look all over as quickly as you can," suggested Mel. "With the headlamp on you might blind any other ones if you see them. I'll keep my light on the one Hank's covering and then we can all look."

To our slight surprise, it went right. There was a camera. It was sitting on a chair opposite the back door. Easy to cover. We didn't see any others on the way up the hall, although we could see one on a chair facing the front door. We left that one alone. Mel still made us stop at the start of each part of the house so she could look for anything different. We didn't want to take too much time, partly because we didn't know if the camera system would send some sort of alert to Watson, and partly because the stench in the house was unbelievable.

"Wait a minute. Wasn't there an old war relic right there?

A Nazi arm band?" She pointed at a corner of a table in the hallway. "I'm sure there was. Where did it go?"

Hank and I shrugged. "If you say so, Melantha," I said. "Does it matter?"

"Details always matter."

I was afraid she wouldn't move on until the mystery was solved. "Well, maybe Detective Watson grabbed a little souvenir for himself when he came over yesterday to check on things." I really hoped that wasn't what happened, but it was enough to mollify Mel.

"Maybe. Nothing else is missing, so it wasn't some other people in here. They would have stolen a whole lot of this stuff."

We went downstairs. Carefully. "No booby traps, are there?" asked Hank?

"Doubt it. Until last week, Bernard lived here, and Walter used to, too. Besides, the cops probably searched the whole house, and they would have tripped them then. We're looking for a bookshelf next to a wall, near a video game setup."

The basement was part storage mess, part man cave. There were old banners and posters leaning up against one wall. There was a lot more white supremacist garbage around, and on one side was a tired old couch and a couple of chairs. There were two different video game boxes sitting on the floor and a decent-sized screen mounted on the wall opposite. Next to it there was a bookcase with a collection of smaller neo items on the shelves.

"Walter said to pull the bookcase like opening a door. There's some sort of secret space back in there." We carefully eased the bookcase out of the way and could see the cutout in the drywall behind it. There was a small screw sticking out for a handle, and we eased this little door open also.

Hank forgot to whisper, "No way!" he exclaimed.

"Sh! Wait a second. Let me look." Mel was all business. She stared at the collection. She probably didn't even know what she was looking at. Guns, serious weapons. It looked like there were a couple .50 caliber machine guns and maybe a rocket launcher lying down there. There were also all kinds of other guns back there, too. Assault rifles, pistols, and whatever. Boxes of ammunition. We weren't there for an inventory.

"Where's the stuff Walter wants?" Hank whispered.

There was a box that had "GO NOW" scrawled across the top. We opened it. Jackpot. Keys to the truck, a set of license plates and paperwork to make them look legal. There were even two worn-looking driver's licenses with Walter and Bernard's photos on them, but different names. They were the old style, the kind that the government said were too easy to forge and therefore haven't been issued for several years, so they probably wouldn't work with most cops, but I guess it was the best Bernard could get. There were several maps, one for North Carolina, one for Georgia, and one for Idaho. I didn't open them of course, but I could see that there were some black marker circles showing through the paper, probably marking specific places that Bernard thought he could run to. And, of course, more cash. A mix of old twenties, fifties, and hundreds. There was a duffel bag hanging on a hook. We glanced inside; it seemed to have clothes, probably for Bernard and Walter, but they weren't important. We needed to leave as soon as possible. And we couldn't have hidden anything bigger than the plates and cash by the boulder anyway.

We carefully closed up the hiding place and went upstairs. I shined my lights on the camera placement while

Hank pulled off the blackout cloth, and we backed out of the house, taking time to put the card back where we found it. There were no police outside, so apparently the camera's temporary blackout hadn't been noticed. Hank's best guess was that Detective Watson had the cameras set up so he could check them with his phone, but he would have needed to be checking at the exact time we were messing with it to realize there was a problem. .The other one was still working, so he might have thought it was just a little glitch when the back door camera blinked for fifteen minutes or so. If he was recording, we hoped he wouldn't see anything useful to identify us when he checked.

We worked our way back to my house by way of Mel's. It was quite a long ways to go, and I couldn't see much of her house when we got there.

Mel smiled at me and Hank. "Another adventure, guys. I know, don't talk about it. Ever. What was that phrase you taught me the other night? Oh yes. Lips sealed. My lips are sealed." She walked off to her front door.

"That was indeed an adventure, wasn't it, Ryk?" Hank stopped between two street lights. "Can you believe this reporter has yet another amazing story that he can't tell? I must be the unluckiest reporter alive."

I had been thinking as we walked. "Yeah. What are we going to do? Walter sure didn't know what was in that hidey hole. Obviously he knew his dad had some stuff stashed. He knew about the truck plates and money, but he would have said something about the guns if he knew."

"Yeah. I can't believe he sat there with his buds for years playing video games and watching TV and never looked inside that room. I mean, his dad was probably out all the time. He would have had plenty of opportunity."

"Unless the weapons collection was a new addition. Maybe his father got them after Walter basically ran away from home." I was pretty sure that Walter had not gone home after that day in the office when his father knocked him down.

"And that would explain what happened to Bernard." Hank was in full reporter mode now. "He gets the arsenal, and other bad guys want them, so he gets offed because he won't give them up."

We started walking again. I wanted to get home and dump the stuff before we ran into any problems. "Only trouble with that theory is that the house wasn't tossed. When we went in, it looked like that police had searched for murder clues, but even they didn't tear the place apart. Anyone who thought Bernard had a prize collection of fire-power would have torn the place apart. Also, they wouldn't have just shot him. They would have tortured him to get the information."

"Maybe they got interrupted. Maybe they ran through the house thinking they would find a big pile somewhere and just gave up."

"Could be," I agreed. "Or maybe they ran out of time. We still don't know when Bernard was killed. They might have thought Walter would be coming in the door after school."

"Actually, what we don't know is a lot more than what we do know." Hank stopped walking and looked at his hands as if he held a notebook of details. "We don't know when he was killed. We don't know how, other than shot, maybe by a gun like your brother has. We don't even know if the delivery man was for real, or just a story the police put out."

We were at the boulder by my driveway. Since we had brought along a couple black trash bags to carry stuff in, we figured we could just leave everything wrapped up and stuff it down in the bushes. I couldn't wait to call Walter and tell him to get it all. "Last question, Hank. What do we do? Shouldn't we call Detective Watson and tell him about the weapons stash?"

"Absolutely. Let's call him right now. We can tell him we broke into the house not once, but twice, we disabled his camera, that we're helping Walter, and, we found a small arsenal." Hank should have been smiling. He wasn't. "Oh, and by the way, Mr. Watson, you're a crappy detective. You missed a big, big clue. Oh yeah, we, you, definitely should call him."

"Yes. But somehow, we ought to tell him. How about your dad?"

"Sure. Dad, we just did all this stuff, but it's cool because we found this illegal stash. Why don't you tell your dad. He's the one with the lawyer connections, which I am pretty sure you'll need if the cops get a hold of you. If my dad finds out we did all this, I won't just need a lawyer; I'll need a complete medical team."

"Can't we just call it in anonymously?"

"Well, we aren't in this for the hero stuff. We're just trying to keep you from meeting One Punch again, so that might work. But, I don't know. If we call from any of our phones, they might be able to figure out who called. I don't think there's a dedicated tip line set up for this case, so any call would have to go directly to the police station."

We had finished wrapping everything up and stashing it, so we decided to split up for the night.

CHAPTER 24

Phone Snitch

As I walked in, the house line was ringing. I know, it seems lame to have a land line, but my folks were old school and didn't fully trust the cell system, and they needed to be able to fax things. Besides, there was the entertainment you just didn't get as often from cells: constant solicitation calls.

Caller ID showed up as an out-of-state number I didn't recognize, so I didn't answer. The number ended in something like 6500. Just for the sake of experiment, and maybe harassment, I dialed the number. I expected a busy signal, but instead I just got no answer, even after twenty or so rings. Obviously, the soliciting company didn't have an operator standing by for incoming calls. That's when it hit me. I called Hank.

"Hank, there's a phone in the newspaper office, right?"

"I'm not calling from there. It would still get traced."

"No. That's the point. It goes out through the main switchboard. When we get calls from the school, either robo-calls about school parent meetings or weather, the caller ID just shows the main switchboard number. It doesn't show the specific number called from. I just checked in our house phone call log on the phone system we have. No one ever clears it. I went back and found a call from the school office. I think it was when Terry got attacked. It was the school's main number, not the actual number from Mrs. Hernandez's desk or whatever. You can call from your newspaper's office, just don't let anyone see you. Make it short and sweet. You know, 'Detective Watson, look in the basement behind the bookcase.' And hang up. If anyone sees you on the phone, fake a couple more sentences and a loud thank you. Do it in the middle of the day so there's lots of phone traffic in and out."

Hank wasn't happy. "Well, maybe. But we should do a dry run first. Let me call your house from that phone, and you see if you're right. It's my rear end if you're wrong."

I agreed with him, but, "That sounds reasonable, but what if some of Bernard's crazy neos get there first and get all those guns?"

"Probably a good argument for phoning right now. From your house, or your cell, not mine. We do not need to get my dad tangled up in this in any way. Gotta run. Call me if you do anything crazy tonight."

I had one more idea, "Wait a second. What about using a cell phone and hitting star 67? Doesn't that block your phone number from caller ID?"

"Sure, I think so, for us mere mortals. You want to bet the cops don't have a way around that? If I were the government, I'd make sure that I could trace every single call possible."

He was probably right. I wasn't going to chance it. Maybe by morning, we would come up with a better plan. I called Walter. "I've got your stuff behind the limestone boulder, like you said."

Walter was perplexed, "Hunh? Where?"

"You know, that big rock by my driveway."

"Oh, yeah. Thanks Jonasz. I'll get it tonight."

I wondered whose cell phone he was carrying. Surely not one of the ones in his father's business account. The police would have been checking on any of those. I considered asking him to call off his boys, but mostly I just wanted him gone, so I kept it simple. "Good luck, Walter. See you around."

"Yeah."

Tuesday morning I did not have a better idea. Other than the possibility that Hank would get in trouble, I still liked my telephone idea. I had Detective Watson's number written down and in my pocket to give to Hank. At the bus stop, Hank shook his head and wouldn't take it. "If you want to do this so bad without a test run first, count me out. If it turns out they can trace the call directly to the newspaper office, it'll surely come back to bite me. Find another phone."

Actually, it wasn't too difficult. There are phones all over the place, once you start to look for them. Teacher work areas, the clinic, all the secretaries for the different offices. On the way to science class, I just ducked into an empty office, punched in 9 and Watson's number. As soon as someone picked up, I spat out my message. "Tell Watson to go back to the Anderson murder house and look in the basement behind the wall behind the bookcase. It's very urgent. Tell him to look at the file cards on the desk upstairs, too." I pushed down the button and continued talking, louder than before. "I know, Jennifer, I should have called, but my phone is down. I'll call later, bye." I hung up the phone and walked out. If any teacher saw or heard me, it would probably be noticed as just another guy in trouble with his girlfriend, trying to weasel his way out with lame excuses. I hurried on to class, hoping that Watson would act quickly. If there were people who knew about the weapons, they weren't going to wait forever.

At lunch, Hank found me. "Well?"

"All done." Hopefully, everything was done, and we could get back to a normal life. "You are off the hook."

"What did you do?" He was happy to hear this.

I briefly told him.

"Did you mention Walter's plan?"

"Oh no. I don't want anyone connecting the caller with Walter. Could lead to me. Besides, if Walter got picked up, Walter would assume that I did him in. Which would lead to him doing me in. And that's not on my list of things to do this year. Remember, Slate has this idea that I am some sort of criminal associate of Walter's, so the farther Walter gets from here, the better off I'm going to be."

"True. And it's not like we actually care if Walter killed his pops or not." The reporter's eye started to gleam, "But. Don't you think it would be cool if we helped solve the murder? What a story that would be."

"Yes. You could just leap from here to the New York Times, straight out of ninth grade. We're talking dead Henryk here, and you're thinking Pulitzer Prize or something. Tell you what, Hank, keep dreaming. I just don't want you to be writing my obituary. The *Reporter* already has had to do two of them this year. I don't think they'll say anything about Bernard, but I don't want to be another feature item."

He laughed. "Yeah. I guess I can wait on the Pulitzer if it means keeping you alive for a few more years. See you after school."

"Might not be on the bus. I'm going to catch up with Melantha and make sure everything's okay. She's been kind of upset with all this stuff that's been happening."

"Good luck."

I found Mel at her locker after school. "Melantha, Mel, how's it going?"

"Okay, I guess," her usual flat tone.

"I was wondering, I, um," not at my smoothest, but I hung in there. "I was wondering if maybe I could ride home on your bus today, maybe walk you to your house."

"My bus? That doesn't go to your neighborhood."

"No, but it's not that much of a walk from your house to mine. You've done it, when you came over to my house with Phil. Hank and I did it the other night." I looked at her, expecting her to connect the dots. "You, um, seemed to want to talk yesterday, and we couldn't. And then all that stuff last night happened, and um." I trailed off.

She grabbed her stuff, "Sure. Let's get going. The bus doesn't wait forever, and I usually, always, sit on the right side, so I like to get in line early."

When we got off the bus, I had no idea what I thought would happen. No idea if Mel would even talk. "Mel?"

"Yes?"

"We couldn't talk very long yesterday at lunch. And it was noisy. And we had to get to class." I thought maybe she would go into her audio recording recitation of the conversation, but she started a new thread on her own.

"Yes. No. I don't know. What to say. Or talk about."

"Scared?"

"Yes. People, almost all people scare me. I don't know why. And as I said yesterday, there are things going on that add to my fear." Even though she had a backpack, she carried it in front of her chest and had wrapped her arms around it so tightly I thought she'd cut off her own breathing.

I again wanted to put my arms around her but I thought that would probably send her over the edge. I walked next to her, resisting the temptation to say something brilliant/comforting (or stupid squared to the nth degree.)

"You know, Ryk, you're about the only person I ever talk to, other than my mother and Phil. And the teachers when I have to." She called me Ryk. That was nice. "Do you know why I don't talk to people very much?"

I really didn't think that I should relay Crate's short analysis to her, "Psych one-oh-one," he had told me. That is, crazy. I would guess that all the kids who were in class with her would agree with that diagnosis, and obviously Slate thought she was from another world, and he wasn't adult enough to hide his thoughts. "Um, no."

"I'm an Aspie." She said this almost like it was extraordinarily amazing, like announcing that she was a mermaid or something.

"Aspie?"

"Yes. It means I have some Asperger's syndrome traits." She stopped and turned toward me and actually looked at my face. "Sometimes, it's spelled a-s-p-y, and sometimes a-s-p-i-e." I think this was meant to clarify things. It didn't. "Oh, sorry, that's probably like what Hank said the other day, TMI."

"No, go on. Aspie. Asperger's. I think I've heard of it, but…"

She launched into a full-scale speech about her condition. What I got from it was that in her case, it wasn't debilitating like it is for some people. I didn't want to stop her, and I knew that I'd have to look it up on the internet when I got home. It seemed that it had been pretty debilitating, but she was working through it as best she could. She was almost enthusiastic in telling me about it. We got to her house. "So you see, Ryk. That's why I don't talk. Much. To people. I'm always afraid I'll misspeak and make things worse. But, for some reason, I can talk to you. My big brother has been trying to help, taking me around with him sometimes, but, I don't know. We're here."

I had been to her house that one night Hank and I walked her home after our second trip to Walter's house, but I really didn't see the house. In daylight, it was amazing. I realized that I had ridden past it over the years and noticed it, but never really focused on it. There were all kinds of things, sculptures, I guess you'd call them, scattered around the yard. There were various glass and rusted steel assemblies mounted on blocks; some were recognizable as animals, but others seemed to be free form. Large and small glass balls were suspended from tree limbs, sometimes with glittery chains, in other places with plain rope. There were a number of items affixed to the house itself, old farm implements like rakes and crosscut saws.

While I was pausing to take it all in, Mel's mother came out. I could see where Mel got her fashion sense. He mother had on a long dark skirt with the outlines of flowers sewn on it, and a lighter blue blouse, also with flowers. She, like Mel, had long dark hair tied back. "Melantha! You're home. Good." She waited with an expectant expression on her face. "Melantha?"

"Oh. Yes. Mom, this is, uh." She looked at me and back at her mother.

"Go on, sweetie, you can do it." Her mother looked like she was trying to practice neutral face and not let Mel know she was getting frustrated.

Mel recovered, "Mom, this is Ryk. I met him at school."

"And?"

"Oh. Yes. Ryk, this is my mother, Ms. Elena Raptis."

"Very nice, Melantha. Well done. Ryk, it's nice to meet you. And have you met my son, Philo?" She pronounced it "fee-lo."

Talk about lessons in manners. I had been standing there gawking at the house like an idiot. "Philo? Oh, Phil, yes. Um, nice to meet you, too, Ms. Raptis."

We talked for a minute or two, really about nothing, but I could sense that Mel was getting more and more nervous, and her mother was a bit uncomfortable, too. "Well, I have a lot of work to get after, so I'd best be going. See you around school, Mel. Nice meeting you, Ms. Raptis." And I left.

CHAPTER 25

Warrant?

When I got home from Mel's, I checked behind the boulder. I had been so worried about figuring out how to make the phone call that I completely forgot to check in the morning on the way to the bus. The package was gone. I was off the hook, forever, I hoped. Life was going to become normal.

And, actually, all the way to bedtime, it was. At dinner neither Terry nor I had any major or minor trauma to report. Frankie was out, but might be coming home later. Mom and Dad seemed back on their routines. It was all good.

At 3:30 a.m., not so good.

I don't know who heard the doorbell first, but I met my dad in the hall. He was throwing on a robe; I was just wearing a pair of old basketball shorts and a tee shirt. He motioned me to stay back. For some reason I had grabbed my phone, so I waved it at him. He smiled and nodded. He went down to the door, and I stopped part way down the stairs. I logged on, keyed the phone function, and waited. The voice at the door was quiet, and I couldn't quite understand what my dad was being asked.

The answer from my dad, however, was clear. "No. Not without a warrant. And I don't see a warrant."

The police? For Frankie? I was considering calling Frankie, since I figured he was at Tildy's, when he appeared at the top of the stairs. His blond dreads were flopping around his face, and he looked confused. I held my hand up and mouthed "cops" at him.

My father's voice dropped down a little. "Okay. I'll see what I can do." He turned to me. "It's about Walter Anderson. For some insane reason, the police seem to think he might be here."

Had they identified me on camera after all? I shrugged at my father. "I don't know anything about Walter." I did my best neutral face. "Why would I?"

He had turned back to the policeman at the door. Now his voice was at a conversational level, and I couldn't make out what he was saying. He turned back to me. "Henryk, go wake up Terry and knock on my bedroom door, wake up Mom. Ask them both to come down here. Tell them there are police officers at the door. Good morning, Francis."

I woke up Terry, and, since his bedroom was on the back side of the house, I peeked outside. There were a couple of uniformed police officers standing on the path to the basement door. When I came back down, I could see the officers at the door. Here were no flashing lights, just two squad cars parked on the street. Dad still had not let them in. No warrant, means no warrant, and no warrant means no entry.

Dad made a great show of lining us up in front of him in the hall where the officers could see his performance. "Boys, Mary, here's the deal. The police are sweeping a number of houses to find Walter Anderson. They seem to think that he's hiding out with one of his friends, so they are hitting a bunch of houses at the same time. We're not the only ones getting an early morning wake-up call. By any chance does anyone here know where Walter is? I assume he's not here, but we're going to look in a minute. We are going to look, not the police. They don't have a warrant, but they do have a reasonable request."

My mom shook her head. She did not look happy. "As far as I know, Walter hasn't been near this house in what, eight, ten years."

"That would be my guess, also, sweetheart, but, just to be sure, would you check the basement and then the boys' rooms, please. We'll just stay right here and relax."

Terry, Frankie, and I exchanged glances but didn't say anything. I had not told either one of them about my trips to Walter's house and the help I'd given him. This did not seem like a good time to bring it up, so I just stood there and tried not to fidget too much.

Dad let us stand there for a while. He looked at us. He looked at the officers, still standing by the front door, but still not invited in. "Boys?" He looked at me intently. He didn't know Terry well enough to know how he'd react to the silent stare interrogation method, and he knew Frankie well enough to know that it wouldn't work at all.

I was trying not to say anything when Mom saved me. "No Walter downstairs. Oh, Tomás, let the poor officers come in. They can stand inside by the door. No need for them to stand out in the cold." She headed upstairs and called back. "Frankie, okay if I go in your room. No Tildy? Or at least decent?"

Frankie's face collapsed. Busted. "No, Mom, no Tildy, no problem," Frankie finally managed to choke out. Terry and I just stood there grinning. Moms. Who knows what they know?

Dad interrupted our entertainment. "So, Henryk?" He started the silent interrogation again, remembered he had already tried that, and then took the direct route. "Henryk, would you by any chance know where Walter is?"

"No idea, Dad. Like I said at dinner the other night, he's probably hanging out with a friend, but that wouldn't be here." I gestured at my face, "Actually, I kind of like to keep this as far from Walter and his friends as possible. We don't mix too well, you know."

Mom came downstairs, glanced at Frankie and me and gave Terry a long look. "Tomás, officers, I think we can safely say that Walter Anderson is not in this house. I've looked everywhere. No sign."

Dad held the door while the officers left, and then he locked it. He was holding a card on of them had handed him. "Detective Watson. Hmm."

"Well, that was weird," Frankie turned to go upstairs. Terry and I started up behind him.

Mom and Dad spoke almost in unison, "Just a minute, guys." They looked at each other, puzzled. Dad spoke, and Mom nodded her head, "There's a couple things we need to clear up."

We paraded into the living room and collapsed in the furniture. Mom started. "Terry."

He sat up.

"Terry, you would not have been a happy camper if a police officer had walked through your room. It wasn't going to happen, not in this house, not without a warrant. But," and for a moment, I thought she was about to smile, "but, you do know that smoking does leave a calling card, don't you." She waved at Terry to stop his reply. "All kinds of smoke leave a smell. It gets in clothes, curtains, everything. That's any kind of smoke, from a campfire to a cigarette to a non-tobacco smoking substance, whether it be for medicinal or recreational purposes. Doesn't matter, the smell is still there." Terry looked at his hands and didn't say anything. "Now, I'm not saying you're smoking in your room. The curtains are fine, but there is this, uh, peculiar odor. I've noticed it occasionally when you've walked by me, and I haven't wanted to say anything. But tonight's little interaction with the constabulary kind of wakes me up."

Dad picked up, "What she is saying, Terence, is that we are pretty sure you don't need any legal hassles in your life. I know we don't. So, please."

"Be smart," my mother finished.

"'Nuff said?"

"Yes, Uncle Tomás." Terry looked up. I understand." I think he was half expecting to be thrown out of the house. I wondered who was up next.

"Henryk."

"Yes, Dad?"

"Do you have any idea why the police thought that we might be harboring young Walter?"

I really didn't know, but I took a stab at it. "Mr. Slate?"

"Mr. Slate? What on earth does he have to do with this?" My mother jumped in with Dad's question.

Busted. But just a little. My only crime, really, I hoped, was not telling them about Slate's insane threat a few days ago. Anyway, confessing to that omission was considerably less than confessing to my recent night-time forays to help Walter, so I told them about my conversation with Slate on Friday. To say the least, they were astounded. Naturally, they wanted to call him right then and raise the roof, and more, but we were interrupted by the doorbell.

Mom answered the door, and before Dad could object, invited the visitor in.

Detective Watson stood just inside the door; he had his detective's shield in his hand. He looked, as my grandmother, on my mother's side, used to say, "Like the cat that swallowed the canary;" only this canary seemed to have a bitter taste to it. "Mr. Jonasz?" He came close to pronouncing it correctly.

Dad was really, really not in the mood. "As I'm sure you already know. And?"

"Mr. and Mrs. Jonasz, I am really sorry we had to disturb you tonight, but we felt it was necessary. I wanted to stop by your house to personally apologize. I'm the detective in charge of the Anderson murder case, and we've had a difficult time finding possible witnesses." He seemed to be looking at me and Frankie. "Walter Anderson in particular. There has been some activity at his house recently at night, and we got a bit concerned. There's been another development, too, that made me think we better move faster rather than slower."

"And what would make you think that this would be a place for the Anderson boy to hide? Do you know what he has done to us? Specifically to my son and nephew?"

"No. Is there something I should know?" Detective Watson looked uncomfortable.

Oh great, I thought. Dad, the legal beagle, was about to volunteer information to the police, maybe even a motive for one of us to kill Bernard. I guess he realized it, too, because he adopted a much calmer voice. Turned on the cool like Frankie would. "Nothing to worry about now. Ancient history. I guess you got our name from someone at the school?"

"Yes sir. Something like that. We hit six different houses tonight." He smiled, "And it worked, too. Young desperado Walter Anderson is now in custody. He was hanging out in a friend's basement. The parents claim they didn't even realize it. You know, I still can't decide if those folks are lying or are just lost. The house was chaos. That kid could have been hiding down there for the last couple weeks without them knowing it. I was with the uniforms at that address. They let us come in and check out the basement without a peep. As soon as I got down the stairs, I could smell that someone was living down there. Living there without benefit of a shower, laundry service, or maid service. All his stuff was crammed under this old couch that I guess he was sleeping on. There was a bunch of miscellaneous things thrown on top of it, so it looked just like the rest of the room. The kid was hiding behind an old cabinet, an armoire, I think they call it. For the record, he was less than pleased to be found, but he came along without a big fuss. I'm heading over to the station to talk with him now.

My father's civil rights voice burst out without thinking, "He's a juvenile, you know. Are you charging him? You said he was in custody."

Detective Watson frowned. "We are just talking. If anything develops, I think we can afford him his due process and rights." He went on the offensive. "Oh, hi there Francis. How you doing? I'll get those two guns back to you sometime soon. They're in the clear." I noticed that he did not say Frankie was in the clear, just those two guns.

Score one for the police. Dad was completely stopped. He didn't know what to say. He just stood there looking from Frankie to the officer.

"Well, Mr. and Mrs. Jonasz, I better get going. It's been a long night, and I've some serious work ahead. Again, sorry to disturb you folks tonight." He was an artist, shifting from hard-nosed cop to Officer Friendly in a nanosecond. He looked really pleased with himself. I almost wished I hadn't phoned in the tip about the weapons stash we found at Bernard's house. I wondered if the other development he referred to meant that he had indeed investigated the Anderson basement.

CHAPTER 26

The Right to Remain...

D ad didn't give me, or any of us, a lot of time to contemplate the intricacies of murder investigations or the wheels of justice. "What guns?" he thundered at Frankie when the door was once again closed and locked.

"Dad, you know about the guns. I've had them forever."

"Oh, I know about the guns. Locked upstairs in two separate places, with trigger locks, and ammo kept separate. What I don't know about is how Detective Watson seems to have them in his possession. At least, I assume we're talking about the same two guns, and not some more that I am unaware of." My mother slumped in a chair, and Terry and I sat down on the couch. This could take all night.

"Okay, Dad, I can explain." And, to his credit, he did. Frankie actually told the whole story, straight up. He explained how the gunshot residue on his hands from the trip to the range with Tildy led the police to take an interest in his guns. He did not mention Tildy's student visa issue. Dad didn't interrupt. Neither did Mom.

"So, that's it?" You've lived here all your life, sat at the table all those nights we talked about my research work with the legal rights group, and none of it, at least very little of it, sunk in? You never heard of any our clients being busted by the cops who are in a hurry to close a case and either make amazingly stupid guesses and screw up their procedures or even create evidence to fit their theory?" He sat down. He looked tired. "Do you have any idea how many zillions of hours the lawyers at the group spend trying to untangle bogus evidence claims? We have an excellent police force in this county, but that doesn't mean they don't make mistakes. They want to solve this case as much as any, even if most of them can't stand what Anderson stood for. And you, you handed them a chance to make their life easier. Could have been their ticket to a promotion and yours to prison."

I thought it was interesting that Dad was more concerned about Frankie's failure to learn anything than the fact that Frankie obviously failed to mention that entire conversation with Watson last Friday afternoon. The one where he gave up the guns.

"Did I let them search the house tonight?" He glared at each of us. "No. And I didn't think we had anything to hide. Terry, maybe I need to know more?" He almost smiled. "But the general idea of warrants and all those legal niceties is that they force the police to have reasonable grounds to invade a house. They didn't think they did, or they would have found a judge to agree. Since they didn't think they had reasonable grounds to search, neither did I."

I was beginning to think I was also a fool. After all, I did let Detective Watson stand inside the house while we discussed Frankie's whereabouts on Friday, the day he got the guns from him.

Dad started up again. "Remember what I always say about writing it down? Yeah. Everything, every time. Document, document, document. Francis, please tell me you at least wrote down the names of the cops you talked to Thursday and made a note about what Detective Watson said on Friday. Please tell me you at least got a receipt for the guns you so willingly parted with. That's a receipt with the officer's name and the serial numbers on the guns." He crossed his arms and glowered at Frankie. "Have you not learned anything sitting here all these years?"

Frankie didn't say anything, no defense, not even some variation of his usual flippant retorts. Terry continued to study his hands and stayed silent. I figured we had all had enough truth outing for one night, so I got up off the couch and edged towards the stairs. Mom put a hand on my arm.

"Henryk?"

"Um?" What could I say? Where was this going?

"Walter's mother is completely out of the picture, right?"

This was easy enough. "Yes. I think she left back when he was in elementary school. Around first grade."

"So, Dad has a point. What happens to Walter now that his father is gone, too? Who looks after him now?"

I couldn't resist, "Assuming he doesn't get locked up for murdering his father, you mean?"

"Really, Henryk!"

Dad couldn't resist, either. "Well, Mary, it is within the realm of possibility. Walter is not exactly a model citizen."

"Tomás, you said it yourself to the detective, you asked about his rights."

"Well, that was stupid on my part, Mary. I just antagonized the cop although I certainly didn't mean to. In theory, though, I do care about his rights, same as anyone else's."

Frankie jumped in, "But in practice, the kid's a piece of __" he glanced at Mom, "work, and after all the trouble he's caused our family, it's, uh—"

"Pretty hard to feel sympathetic," Dad finished, "but your mom's right. Ever the worst of the worst have rights. And who's to say Walter did anything besides panic and run? What will probably happen is that the court will appoint a guardian ad litem to look after his affairs until he's eighteen, unless, of course, they charge him, in which case he'll get a public defender."

Dad had not heard Walter shout something like, "Someday I'll kill you!" as Bernard stormed out of the office that day after he knocked Walter on his keister. I wondered if Slate or Wright had shared that tidbit with Detective Watson. Probably not, since they seemed to want to hide that entire transaction with Bernard.

Frankie looked at Terry and me. "Uh, Dad?"

"Yes?"

"You said something to Watson about stuff Walter has done to your son and nephew. What did he do to Terry? Did I miss something?" This was good; he knew what happened, and he knew our parents had kept it from him, so here he was, jerking their chain, to be cute or something.

I guess Terry was feeling appreciative towards my parents; they hadn't given him any real grief about the pot. He jumped in and covered for everyone. "It was nothing, Frankie. Those tough guys," he made air quotes with his hands, "hassled me a little bit. Nothing I couldn't handle. Mostly just aggravation. Uncle Tomás and Aunt Mary didn't want to make a big deal about it." He flashed a pretty good smile, "No worries, mate."

"It's almost 5:30, gentlemen. Too late to go back to bed. What do you say to a real family breakfast?" Mom smiled, "My treat. I know, we haven't done this in a month of Sundays. Maybe since right after Terry joined us?"

"Sounds like a plan, Mary. Henryk, why don't you stay down here and help your mom. The rest of us can hit the showers. You can take second shift, after the water heater recovers."

As we were eating, pretty quietly since we were all a bit dazed by our early start to the day, Dad casually dropped a small bombshell of his own.

"Henryk, do you remember when we had that little visit with Mr. Slate a week ago?"

"Yes?" I wondered where this was going. I tried to remember if I had said anything that could be checked on and found untrue. It's really difficult to lie; you constantly have to remember what you said, and where and when, so you could back your story if the subject got revisited.

"Remember I said that the visit was most enlightening?" I nodded. "Well, as I said, it was. Very enlightening. I'm sure you noticed all the diplomas and certificates on the walls? In the past, when I had the pleasure of being in that office, it was over some misdeeds, alleged misdeeds, by your brother. I was usually so upset with him and Mr. Slate that I could only focus on the problem at hand. But when I was in there with you, while I wasn't happy with Mr. Slate, I wasn't at my wit's end, either, so while Mr. Slate had us standing there pretending to look through important papers just to show off who was in charge, I was looking at the things in the frames. And I was thinking about how a guy could have all those degrees and certificates and yet be as inhumane and basically evil as he is. And then I actually focused on one of the degrees, and I could have sworn that one of his degrees was from a known diploma mill."

"Diploma mill?" I didn't know what he was talking about.

"Fake degree company," Frankie chimed in. "Maybe a post box in Florida. You write away and send them some cash and get this fancy looking diploma." He made air quotes.

"Something like that. In this case, the diploma was from uh, I can't call it an institution of higher learning, but what purported to be such an establishment. Our legal group sued a bunch of them awhile back because they were taking huge chunks of money from unsuspecting students, helping them get expensive loans, all that, but not delivering any real education. The students would get a few online so-called classes each semester, do almost nothing, and then get college credit. They seemed to target minorities." He made the air quotes now. "I thought one of the diplomas looked familiar, so I went back to our files. Sure enough, they lost their academic accreditation, and the government wouldn't let their students get government-backed student loans to take classes, and we got some money for our clients."

Terry brightened, "So, Uncle Tomás, what you're saying is that Mr. Slate has a fake degree?"

"Can't say that for sure, but he seems to be displaying a Master's of Educational Administration credential from a fraudulent institution." Dad took a drink of coffee. "I'm not sure what all this means, but it is an interesting development. And, most likely he acquired this sheepskin a long time ago, before the institution got exposed. He might have thought it was legitimate, but anyone with brains would know you were buying a degree when you did almost zero work and got all those credits. And a diploma."

The ride to school with Hank was going to be interesting.

CHAPTER 27

A Growing Game

"I can't believe it! Scooped again!" Those were Hank's first words after I told him what about the night's excitement. I didn't tell him about Slate's diploma; that was a story for another ride.

"Not really, Hank." I had to laugh. "There's no story here. At least nothing that you could possible write about for the *Reporter*. And don't act so hurt. What was I supposed to do? Call you at three in the morning and tell you to get your sorry self over to my house to watch, what? Nothing. Cops came. Dad wouldn't let them come in and search. No warrant. Mom searched the house for them. No Walter, of course. Then Detective Watson shows up, and I think I am really in trouble, but it's only to say he's got Walter. So, end of story. End of no story, I mean."

"Why did he come to your house? He couldn't have gone to all the houses you said they checked last night. He had to get on with interrogating killer Walter. So why stop by your house?"

"I don't know. Might be Frankie's still on his list, and he wanted to see what Frankie would do or say. Shake him up a bit. Of course, he shook up Mom and Dad, since they didn't know anything about Frankie giving the cops his guns."

"Was he trying to get a look at you? Did he maybe see something in the videos? If Slate gave him your name, and he probably did, Watson might have wanted to see if there was any chance that he could link you to the night-time activity he talked about. He probably knows the tip came from a phone in the school's phone system, but that wouldn't lead him to you or your house. Was he trying to shake you up?"

"Well, if he is, it's beginning to work. When I left the house this morning, I thought I just had an entertaining story to tell you. But now you've got me worried. This can go bad in a lot of ways. If Slate's got him thinking that I am a partner with Walter, then I'm in way too deep. Do you think they'll get anything out of Walter? Got anything, I mean, last night, talking to him?"

Hank chuckled. "The king of 'snitches get stitches?' rat someone out? Probably not.

Remember, he's highly motivated to say nothing. If he did kill Bernard, which I sort of doubt, he's not going to say squat. And if he figures he can get away from them pretty soon, he's not going to mention the money or his plans for the truck. I bet he's still thinking he can just disappear. Do you think they might search the house where they found him hiding?"

"My dad would say they'd have to get a warrant. Of course, we're not talking about legal eagles here. The family might just let the cops search their house to get them out of their hair."

"Or, the family might poke around and find the money themselves." Hank clapped his hands. "That would be something else. I can just see it. They find this stash of money, and call the cops. Not."

"The important thing is that they lose interest in my brother. And me, for that matter. It would nice if Walter's bunch would lose interest in me, too."

But that wasn't to happen. They trapped me in a restroom just before fourth period. "Broken-face boy! How ya doin'?" It was One Punch. Thirsty and a couple others were standing behind him.

"Hangin' in there. What's up?"

"The cops got Walter last night. You know anything about that?"

"We got woke up around three last night. Cops at the front door; cops at the back door. Parents pretty pissed off. Cops seemed to think I had Walter stashed in my basement or something."

"Why would they think that?" Thirsty sounded genuinely puzzled.

"Beats me. I didn't have anything useful. They searched. They left." I decided a little humor would help. "None of you guys ratted me out, did you? You know what they say about snitches."

They actually laughed. Maybe I would live, live long enough to find out if I could make it as a stand-up comedian? "You got guts, I'll give you that," said Thirsty. "But somehow, I can't see you giving us stitches."

"Well, no. I don't think so either. But I would like to know why the cops were at my door last night."

One of the guys in the back piped up, "Yeah. Well, they hit all our houses at three. Found Walter at--" An elbow shut him up.

"Look, guys. I have zero, nada, none, and no interest in getting Walter or you guys into any trouble. I don't know anything about anything. I hope they turn Walter loose, and he gets on with his life. I'm sorry his father got killed, but that's not my concern."

"Old man got what was coming to him." Thirsty spoke up again. "No loss."

It was nice that we all agreed on something. I think I read somewhere that the secret to successful negotiation is to find common ground. My interest was getting out of there without damage; theirs was making sure I wasn't going to be a problem. "So, guys, if we all agree, I keep on keeping my mouth shut and stay away from the cops …"

"And you keep your good looks. Well, could-be-uglier looks." One Punch thought he was funny, so did the others. "Get out of here, punk, 'fore we change our minds."

I looked at Thirsty before moving. One Punch may be the biggest and have the mouth, but I thought Thirsty was really the king for now. He nodded towards the door, and I left. I nearly ran into Crate as I turned the corner.

"Hey, Crate. What's up?"

"Nothing too exciting, I guess?" He seemed to be almost asking me.

"Everything's cool. Smooth and cool as usual."

I caught up with Mel at lunch during fourth period and related the night's activities to her. I did not tell her about the restroom conference.

"Strange. Why would the police think Walter would be at your house?" She was eating some foul-smelling concoction out of a plastic container. She was using chopsticks. "It wasn't random, of course, but why would they think you of all people would help Walter?"

"Other than the fact that we helped him twice in two nights?"

She looked startled. "They know about that?"

"Oh no. I just meant that I did in fact help him, but as far as I know, only you and Hank know about it. Maybe one of his boys, but I don't think so." I hadn't told her about Slate's insane theory from last Friday, so I filled her in. "So, my guess is that the cops got all these names from the school, and mine was in the mix. Thanks to Slate, I'm sure."

"Can he do that? Just invent things and put the police on you like that?"

"I guess."

"Can't you do anything about it?"

"Who am I going to talk to?"

"Mr. Wright seems like an okay human."

"Maybe. But what can he do? I think I'll just sit tight and see what happens."

"You said something about maybe that detective wanted to see you or your brother." She took another bite of the weird stuff. "You know, it might not help if the detective saw you and Hank and me together. He might have some video of the three of us when we first got to the house before we blinded his camera. We were pretty well covered, but if he saw the three of us walking together, he might make a connection. Maybe the visual of our sizes or the way we walk or something."

"You sure you weren't a professional criminal in a previous life? I never even thought about that." I wasn't sure Detective Watson was that observant, but maybe that was a gift he had, like Mel's remembering every detail of a room. She would have made a great spy. Or not.

"Previous life? You believe in all that stuff?" Her tone suggested that I had just said the earth was obviously flat.

"No, no. A joke. You know, like, um, never mind. Still, you're right, we don't need anyone to even think we know anything. I hope it'll all blow over in a couple days."

"Blow over?" Again, the puzzle tone.

I started to say, "You know," but obviously, she didn't. "Go away. Like the wind blows things away. I hope the police get to the bottom of all this and--"

She interrupted, "Bottom?"

"And figure out what happened to Bernard." I had to quit using idioms and clichés with her, or I'd be explaining every other sentence to her.

It became her turn to confuse me. She started explaining some complicated mathematical problem her class was tangling with, and I just let her rave on. It was kind of relaxing, or entertaining, or something, to listen to someone that dedicated to something I had no knowledge of and even less interest in. I didn't feel the need to interrupt her for clarification; I just let her words wash over me and didn't even think about my criminal behavior for the rest of lunch.

CHAPTER 28

Adjustments

Hank caught me in the hall on the way to PE. "Ryk, my dad just texted me. He's taking me to Carl's today, and he thought maybe you would like, no make that: he expects you to ride along."

More interrogation? "So, I am commanded to ride along."

Hank grinned, "Whatever. See you this afternoon at the pick-up lot."

While we waited for his dad, I told Hank what my dad had figured out about Slate's diploma.

"For real? He has a fake administration diploma? That probably means he can't be an assistant principal. You sure about all this?"

"Dad seemed pretty sure that the company that issued the diploma was a degree mill, you know, a business that sold credentials."

"This might be something I could write about." The investigative reporter wheels were definitely spinning. "Of course, I can't just write this up without proof. I'd have to get copies of the diploma, all of them actually. And then – Oh, there's my dad."

"Don't say anything to anyone about this, Hank."

"What, and blow up my own story? You make sure you don't tell anyone else. You think your dad'll make a stink about this?"

"I doubt it. I almost felt like he was handing me the story to pass on to you. He's got a lot going on right now." NT's car stopped in front of us and we hopped in.

Hank started the game as soon as we got in the car. "Your teacher tells you to read a Langston Hughes poem out loud over again and 'try to sound more like an African American this time.'" Go back a step.

That got NT's attention. "Please tell me that did NOT happen to you. Today. In this school."

"Oh, no, dad. I just saw something about it happening somewhere else and thought it fitted the game. It really happened. This teacher had all her kids reading poems in class, and she had some black kid read a Langston Hughes poem, but she wanted him to make it sound more like a poor black from Harlem, from the thirties. Like anyone knows what that's supposed to sound like."

I wasn't sure that NT actually knew who Langston Hughes was, but he hung in there. "So, this teacher, white, I assume, she got fired?"

"No. I don't think so. Not yet, anyway. I'm not sure she should be." Hank's tone told me that he wished he had not mentioned this.

It seemed like I was always explaining something to someone. "Yeah, since Hughes wrote poems about Harlem folk in dialect, she may have just meant that the poem was supposed to sound like that." NT gave me a funny look in his mirror. "It was still pretty stupid of her to put the kid on the spot, so, yeah, move back a step. Or lose a turn."

He focused on the road for a moment, and then said, "You know. There's sort of the opposite of that, too. Sandra speaks really clear, standard English. Has all her life. On more than one occasion she has had some, cracker, I mean white guy, tell her that she doesn't sound black. I mean, sure, I have some southern in me. I was raised right here. But she was raised in the North by educated parents, both teachers. So she's got pretty good English."

Hank cut in, "So, you're speaking textbook correct English and some dude basically says you are either a fake 'Negro,'" he made air quotes, "or you are out of your, or rather his, league. Back a space or?" He trailed off, shaking his head. I know that this had happened to him on more than one occasion. In elementary and middle school, Hank did not have an easy life. He caught a lot of grief because he speaks more or less standard English, certainly not a deep southern or black dialect, and some kids thought he was showing off. Also, he was called "Home Run," not so much because he was named after Hank Aaron, but because he avoided fights and didn't want to prove himself fighting; he would just go home when things got out of hand.

"Okay, then. More not-so-ancient history, or at least from someplace else." NT was ready to move on, too. "Police try to arrest you for B & E in your own house when a neighbor calls in a "suspicious person" hanging around your house, trying to break in at two AM. The cops refuse to believe you live there. Then, when you write a newspaper article about your experience, everyone accuses you of "playing the race card" to get attention." He laughed. "Really. It happened up in Connecticut or somewhere. This guy was a full professor at some university, and he locked himself out of his house. When he tried to get in through a window, the neighbors called the cops, and it went big. The first lesson of the story is, cops should not bust people who are professors and know how to write newspaper articles. The bigger lesson is, don't be black and point out the obvious because someone will claim you're just playing up race. Who loses a turn here?" He drummed his fingers on the wheel for a moment. "Of course, I guess another big lesson might be neighbors should know each other, talk to each other. All those folks should have known each other before it came to that."

"I have one that sort or fits, maybe," I said. I was a bit nervous, since the last contribution I made thoroughly ticked off NT when it attacked his precious football team. Hank gave me a hard look, and I avoided looking at NT's eyes in his rearview mirror. "This is also not-so-ancient history. We have family friend whose last name is Archibald. But I just found out that his father was actually named Archibald Goldstein, but his friends or his boss advised him that to get ahead in their business he would have to change his name, so he became Gary Archibald. Not so Jewish."

"Really?" NT snorted a half laugh, "White folks do that?

"What's that supposed to mean, Dad?" Hank jumped in.

NT stuttered, "I mean, uh, well, it seems funny. I guess we all know what names sound Jewish and all, but we never pay it no mind. White folks are either good folks or bad folks in my book. I've never really paid much attention to which ones were Jewish or anything else for that matter.

Hank shook me off as I started to reply. "It's like this, Dad, maybe they left it out of your history classes, but there's been a whole bunch of white folks that got the short end of the stick, like black folks, here in the good ol' US of A." I was beginning to feel bad; once again I was setting up a fight between Hank and NT. It probably would have helped if Hank would let me fight my own battles, but I also think he liked battling with his father, especially when he thought he could win. Hank was warming up to the topic. "There's been all kinds of religious wars since the 1600's. All about white folks warring on white folks. Connecticut and Rhode Island were carved out of Massachusetts to keep the good folk of one brand of religion from hassling the good folk of another brand. Being Irish and Catholic in the US was not cool in the 1800's. And don't even think about being Polish or Slavic of any sort and expecting fair treatment in the early 1900's. Italians didn't do so great, either. Of course, they also went after all the races, Indians, and Asians, and Latinos, and, obviously, black folk. But, Ryk's right. Jewish people were getting the shaft at least into the 1950's. They had quota systems for Jews in some of the big-name private colleges and universities. Kept themselves pure by keeping out blacks and Jews. Or at least keeping their numbers down. And a lot of places, including New York City, had what they called redlining, where they would try to make sure that no Jews or black folk bought or rented houses and apartments in certain sections of the city."

I noticed that he did not point out that his grandmother, Grams, had occasionally ranted about Jews. One time, probably when we were in seventh grade, he said, "You know. I just don't get it. Grams is all about her church and her pastor, and she makes me go to church with her some days. Today, her loving pastor basically accused the entire Jewish race of everything evil he could think of. I mean, really, this is a black guy preaching hate. I know there's a group of people who think that Jews are bad and all because they killed Christ, although that was really the Romans who should be blamed, and there's a whole history of crazy accusations about Jews and children's blood, but I can't see how this fits in a modern church."

NT drove silently for a while, then he sort of laughed, "Kind of complicates the game, when you think about it. It's not just 'whitey's game' dancing black folk around. It's more like everyone trying to get over on some other group."

When we got to Carl's, I already knew the drill. I sat in the car without being told and waited for Hank to start up the walk to the house. I stared out the window and tried not to worry.

"So, I understand that there was some excitement at your house last night?" He had been on shift at the jail, or I'm sure he would have noticed the commotion outside his house, even though the police had kept their lights off and been as quiet as possible.

"Yes sir. A bit."

"And?"

"And, the police came looking for Walter Anderson. They didn't find him, of course."

"I thought they did." He looked at me like he thought I was lying.

"Oh, yes. They found him. Not at our house, I mean. He was hanging out in some friend's basement." I wondered how he found out Walter had been caught.

"Yes. I know. In their raids last night, the officers found an eighteen year-old with an outstanding warrant, probably a lucky accident. For them, not him. The cop that brought him over to check him in at our hotel told me about their big night. He said something about even raiding a house in my neighborhood, and I figured out that he was talking about your house." He smiled. "Great party. One of the best kind. They got their guy. Got a bonus fish. No one got hurt. Very peaceful."

I thought about how peaceful it was for us, having the cops show up at three in the morning. Still, he had a point. It had gone well. No body count. No real excitement.

"It gets even better, Henryk. I had to call my old friend Detective Watson to ask him something about the kid his men brought in, make sure he was supposed to be in the adult lock-up. It gets complicated if they are wanted on a juvenile warrant but have magically turned into adults while on the run. Anyway, he happened to mention that they had gone back to look into Anderson's house during the day and found some hidden guns. Not just plain guns, but war weapons. He wasn't too specific. He did say, though, that he was tipped off by someone about where to look. I think finding that stash is what made him decide to step up the hunt for Walter. If that kid knew about those guns and had plans for his crew using them, some really bad stuff could have gone down."

NT was definitely studying my face. I was definitely working on blank-face. I didn't want to say anything. He hadn't accused me of anything, but I thought silence might make him think I was hiding something, which, of course, I was. A lot of things. "Wow. More guns? Everyone knew Bernard had a bunch of guns. Wouldn't the police have taken them all out when they started their investigation?"

"I guess this was a secret stash or something that they didn't see in the first go-around." Still studying me. "Any idea why on earth they would think they should check out your house for Walter?"

I told him about Slate's crazy theory about Walter and me being some kind of business together. Telling it made it easier to get my voice and body language back to normal.

"What, does he think you're like your brother Frankie?" He sort of coughed. "I don't mean that Frankie is really a criminal, but…"

"I know. He had his moments. But, yeah, Slate's mentioned him more than once."

"The sins of the father, well, the brother in this case, visited upon the young'ns. Cute."

NT sill did not look convinced that I was totally innocent in this mess. Something about my voice or face? "Okay, Henryk. Let's assume that what you're telling me is accurate. Just in case, though, I better point out something to you. There's a crime called 'accessory.' It means that if a dude helps another dude break the law, or covers for him, or something along that line, he can be charged as an accessory. You mostly see it when a girlfriend covers for her boyfriend, or dudes cover for their buddy, and usually in serious cases where the commonwealth's attorney and the detectives got jerked around by witnesses. So, if it turns out that Walter committed a serious crime, like improving the world by offing his old man, anyone, friends, or otherwise, who have information about it and don't tell the police or are covering for him could be charged as accessories. Accessory after the fact is the charge, I think." I believe that NT's face was telling me that I had better not fall into this category of criminal.

"Yes, sir. I understand. No problem here." He gave me a dark look, either because he wasn't convinced that I was totally innocent or because I forgot and called him, "sir."

"Good. Oh, and Henryk, that stuff you said about your family friend having to change his name. All that's true? Even nowadays? They still hate Jews, some of 'em? I mean, besides the obvious haters like the KKK and the Aryan Brotherhood and the Bernard Andersons of the world.

There are a bunch of them, I know, but how many is that, really?"

"Weird, I know. But it's true. I think there are still chunks of America that basically hate Jews, or at least don't want 'em around. I don't know how many, but we're a big country, around 350 million, so even a small part of a percent could be a few hundred thousand. Now, you know that this guy's name change happened back in the fifties I think, but. –"

"Still not that long ago. I guess it's like segregation. It's ancient history to kids your age, but I remember it clear as day, and of course, my mom lived it every waking minute of her life back then." He smiled. "Anyway, thanks for the history lesson. Let's go see what Carl and his young prodigy are up to."

On the way back home, I opened a different can of worms, but one that wasn't insulting. "You know, I've been thinking about the game."

"Yeah?" Hank's tone was defensive. I was messing with his baby here. "In what way?"

I plowed on, "Don't worry. Nothing bad. I was just noticing that it seems like no matter what anyone does, whatever happens, someone loses a turn. No one ever goes forward."

NT laughed, "That'd be the point, young hero. No matter what happens, black folks seem to lose a turn or go backwards."

"Oh, I see that, but?"

"He's got a point, Dad." Hank was moving his finger in the air, along an imaginary route on a game board. "It's roll the dice, pull a card, maybe, and something bad happens. Where are the tokens actually going? Do they ever actually move forward? What's the goal?"

"Uh? Live, maybe? Winner is the one who gets to the finish line alive." NT seemed to think it was clear.

"Some board games," I started, "have different pots of things, maybe things that are community property for a while, or are used for some sort of rescue mission. Or a bank of some sort that can players can get help from. Some of the things we've talked about seem to be community problems, need some sort of community punishment instead of an individual getting nailed. Like the thing about the news media managing to publish photos of black suspects but not their white accomplices. Or photos of black folks that have already been arrested, so there's no need for a general lookout photo."

"Also, there's no reward system. If someone, or the community pot gets burned by an action, there ought to be the opposite, where someone, or the community pot, gets a bonus for doing something right." Hank was starting to get into this, too. I relaxed a little. Maybe I wasn't coming up with a new way to insult.

"How about KK's?" NT said. "You, know. Ku Kluxers. When it's a society thing, a little KK guy goes into the bucket. Individual situations move people forward and back, but your news media example puts a certain number of KK figures in the bucket."

"What would be the opposite?" I asked. "For when the community response is the right one? How about an MLK's? For Martin--"

"We know who MLK is," Hank said. "That might work. And he is the opposite of the KK."

NT interjected, "I don't suppose we could go with a simple X, could we?"

"For Malcom?" Hank asked. "Might be confusing, and

besides he had his days, especially his early ones, where he was not necessarily on the side of good."

NT smiled at the mirror, "Just a thought. Seeing as how Nat Turner is already taken."

"Actually," I said, "this could work. You roll the dice, and sometimes you just go forward a few squares, and nothing good or bad happens. But sometimes you hit a space and have to draw a card with good or bad things happening on it."

"Yeah, and then you move back or forward, depending."

NT was warming up to this now. "So, like when a black kid gets killed by, uh." I think he was going to say white cop, but hated to. "Killed by a white vigilante, and there are as many white protesters as black protesters, that would put a MLK into the pot."

Hank wondered, "But who would redeem the MLK? Or how?"

The rest of the trip home was devoted to trying to figure out how to decide whether an event would be considered an individual setback or a communal setback. We also didn't figure out how to apply the communal setbacks in the pot.

CHAPTER 29

Poor Walter

O ddly enough, no one was very lively at dinner. Getting up at three in the morning kind of slows a person down by the end of the day. Still, Dad was pretty fired up.

"Got a call from Detective Watson today. Some interesting developments in our big case." My stomach barely had the energy to sink; I just tried extra hard to maintain calm face. Even that was tiring. Had Watson figured something out that involved me? The phone tip? Walter's getaway stash? The little matter of Mel and Hank and me breaking and entering not once, but twice? Or, none of the above, new drama instead. "It seems the Andersons are both dumber and smarter than we would have imagined. Well, the remaining Anderson, anyway. Detective Watson told me that Walter wants me to be his lawyer, to represent him."

This got everyone's attention.

Mom was the first to erupt, "Tomás did you tell Watson that you're not a lawyer?"

"Of course. Actually, he knew it from our conversation the other night. It probably came up when I was explaining why I wouldn't let anyone search without a warrant. Anyway, Watson thought it was hilarious that Walter wanted me, especially considering that he had the general idea that the Andersons and the Jonaszes were not exactly on friendly terms. He doesn't know the whole history, of course, but enough to know that we should be the last people Walter would go to for help. Watson said, and I quote, 'Mr. Jonasz, now don't be offended, but I've got to tell you what young Walter Anderson said to me today while I was trying to interrogate him. He told me that he knew a Jew lawyer who could spring him. And then he named you. It seems that along with all the other racist crap that his father fed him, he was led him to believe that all Jews are smart lawyers.'" Dad laughed. "Yeah. I can just imagine Bernard ranting about the Jews controlling the world, or maybe a Jewish lawyer defending some black guy, and poor Walter jumped to the brilliant conclusion that all Jews are lawyers and are smart, besides." He paused for timing and smiled, "Not that I'm disagreeing with the part about Jews being smart, you understand."

Nobody was tired now. Everyone started talking over each other.

Terry got the first clear question in, "So, Uncle Tomás, does Walter need a lawyer? Does that mean they think he did it, killed his old man?"

"To his credit, Watson did not tip his hand on that point. I don't know. I didn't have the impression that Walter was being charged, at least not now. I'm not sure why Watson called me. Maybe he was trying to figure out what to do with Walter and hoped that he had misread the animosity between the Anderson and the Jonasz families, and that we could be useful."

My turn to get a question in, "What's to figure out? Walter had the big three you always hear about in murder cases: motivation, means, and opportunity."

"It's not that simple, Henryk. If they really don't have anything on Walter, and they're not going to charge him, they still have this juvenile with no folks."

"Technically a juvenile. He's got to be close to eighteen. And," Frankie pointed out, "the cops don't want him to just disappear. He might be a witness, assuming he didn't do the deed himself."

"Yeah, he could know something, be a witness." My big contribution.

"So what happens?" Mom still somehow seemed to be thinking about Walter as a poor orphan instead of a bully who deserved anything he got. "Where does he go to live now? He can't live by himself, especially in that house where his father was killed."

"This is not something I've really researched much, but my guess would be that if the police decide they can't hold him, they'll get some county social services department involved, and they'll go to court and get some lucky lawyer appointed guardian ad litem for him. And they'll try to find a foster home or maybe some kind of group home for him, until he's eighteen, of course. Then he's on his own."

"How terrible." Mom started up again, but Frankie cut her off.

"Terrible for the lawyer stuck with the pro bono case with a mini Nazi for a client. Terrible for whoever gets stuck with him." He snorted, "Maybe the family that hid him for the last week or so will take him back. That would be smart."

I added my two bits' worth, "Remember, Mom, Walter is the wonderful kid who secretly fed peanut butter to an allergic kid in elementary school to see what would happen. And stuff did happen. Anaphylactic shock, ambulance, and all that. Very exciting. Kid didn't die. Not much happened to Walter. He skated. As usual. Maybe Walter fed lead bullets to his dad instead of peanut butter."

Dad jumped on me. "You said something about motivation? What would that be? Other than the fact that Bernard was a lousy father. Do you know something specific?"

Oops. "Remember, I told you about Bernard smacking Walter after the big mess in the gym after the memorial assembly?" Really big oops. I forgot; I had not told anyone except for Hank. I just opened up a can of worms for no good reason; the old problem of remembering what you told to who when you're trying to either lie outright or just shade or hide the truth. Everyone stared at me, waiting expectantly. I took a long drink and grabbed a big breath. "Okay. It was like this." And I tried to tell the story of Walter and Bernard in Slate's office; I didn't think I left anything out.

Dad let me finish. "So, the gist of it is that Bernard hit Walter, at least once, in front of Slate and Wright? And why is this motivation for murder? I always thought Bernard was regularly abusive, so why this time does it lead to murder?"

I had left out one little detail. 'Walter actually yelled something at his father about killing him some day. I couldn't hear the exact words, but that's what I heard."

"And you don't think that's material to Detective Watson's investigation?"

"Maybe, but Slate and Wright were in the office, they heard it, too; they could have told Watson." I didn't think it was fair to blame me. It wasn't like Watson had ever questioned me about Walter's relationship with his father.

"You're saying that the two administrators heard that

also?" Dad sounded incredulous.

"They were in the same office. I was in the front area, by the secretary's desk getting a pass."

Frankie came to my defense. "Dad, that's two adults who didn't do anything about this thing when it happened. They were probably covering their butts. So I don't see how you can make it sound like Henryk did something wrong."

I decided to make a full confession. "There's something else that I forgot."

"Oh, no." This was my mother. She sounded weary.

"Not that much. Mr. Wright called me in later that day and asked me not to talk to anyone about what I saw, or rather, thought I heard. Said he needed to check with the principal and maybe a social worker." I looked at the ceiling to avoid anyone's eyes. "I forgot all about it until now. There's been a lot going on."

"I'll say." Dad looked grim. "What a mess. No wonder cops burn out. Even the good guys, that's us, usually, get the stories a bit mixed up or leave things out or get the timing all wrong. I've spent the better part of twenty-five years chasing down bad police work, but sometimes I guess it's also a case of bad luck and confusing stories."

Frankie took one more shot at a legal solution. "Couldn't they just hold Walter as a material witness? You know, when a dude knows what happened and won't talk, so they force him to testify."

"That only works if they know for sure that Walter knows something. He may not know anything at all about this. If he wasn't home and didn't see anything to report, then they can't make him talk. They have to convince a judge to order him held, and they can't do that if they don't have any useful evidence."

"Unless he helped the killer," I said, parading my new-found knowledge. "If Walter is helping the killer, that would be accessory after the fact, and they could bust him for that."

"All that may be true," Dad pointed out, "and I'm sure the police are looking into all those possibilities. Bottom line, though, seems to be that they have no clue about the murderer and no evidence to suggest Walter is involved, so they really can't hold him. But I'm sure they don't want to lose track of him, either."

"Well. I hope they lock his ass up in jail, and he gets it every night," this was Terry's first contribution to the conversation, and it was a show stopper.

We all just stared at him. I believe Mom almost sobbed.

"Whoa, T-man!" Frankie laughed, "Where'd that come from? I thought you said he just hassled you a little bit."

Terry stared straight at Frankie's eyes, but didn't say anything for a moment. "Like I said, nothing I can't handle. I just think it's about time he got what's been coming to him for years. Let the big bully boy be on the receiving end of things for a change." Terry didn't look at Mom or Dad, but got up from his chair. "Sorry guys, but I'm beat. I need to excuse myself." And he left.

No one said anything after he left, although I'm sure mom wanted to point out that Walter had been getting some form of abuse for years. Even Frankie held off on any comment he might have wanted to spout. He and I took care of cleaning up the kitchen; we didn't really talk, either.

Before I went to bed I tapped on Terry's door. "Okay, man?"

"Keepin' on, cuz, keepin' on."

I decided that was proof enough that he was okay and collapsed in bed.

CHAPTER 30

Medical Emergency

The next morning Terry and I walked to the bus stop together.

"Your parents okay?" He looked straight ahead as he talked.

"They'll live. One of the few times when anyone's actually shut Mom down. I know you didn't mean to, of course."

"Your parents have been terrific to me. I was just up to here about poor Walter this and poor Walter that."

"No worries. I just don't want Frankie to get any more involved. I don't want him, or you, or me of course, getting hurt by Walter and this mess."

"It'll pass. Just drama."

"Keep on keepin'?"

"That's what I do best." He threw this over his shoulder as he walked over to one of his friends at the bus stop.

Hank, of course, jumped me immediately. "So, any more excitement last night? Another police raid? A meteor strike? Anything I can write up?"

"Well, other than my dad adopting Walter as a third son in an emergency hearing before a judge at midnight, and Frankie getting accepted for training at the police academy, no, nothing happened."

"What!" He stopped walking and turned to face me. I grinned. "Oh, you're kidding. Duh. Obviously." He glared at me. "So, that means you are covering for something. Give. What really happened last night?"

I filled him in on the conversation at dinner. I left out Terry's comment. The bus arrived at school, and I could begin my ever-failing quest to stay out of trouble with the authorities.

I'm not sure how I got through the entire morning at school without any trauma and drama, but I did. I ran into Mel in the hall and even that went smoothly. She surprised me, "You know, Ryk, I kind of liked it Tuesday when you came by my house. My mother liked it, too. She told me that it was nice that I was talking to other people outside the family." I thought she was going to ask me to ride with her again. "So, I was wondering if maybe I could ride the bus into your neighborhood, and maybe we could, uh …"

"Hang out," I finished for her.

"Yes. That's it."

"Sounds like a plan. A good plan. I'll meet you by the buses after school." This was new to me, too, but I liked it. I'm sure I learned a lot in my last period class, but I don't remember what it was.

Mel, Terry, and I walked to my house from the bus stop. We let ourselves in, and I grabbed some snacks while Terry went upstairs and grabbed his acoustic guitars. Although Terry's mother had been pretty much a basket case as long as I've known her, she did occasionally do right by him. He had two used acoustic guitars and a reasonable electric, although the amp was pathetic.

We sat on the front porch, Terry and Mel jamming – who knew? I knew they were in a music class together, but I didn't realize she could play. I just sat and ate.

Grams waved at us from across the street, on their porch. Except that it wasn't a wave; it was more of an arm movement. Maybe not even that. Terry was looking in her direction while he was playing. He stopped suddenly.

"What was that?"

"What was what?" Mel stopped also. "I wasn't off key. Wrong chord?"

"Hank's grandmother, Grams. Look at her." Terry started to stand up. He waved.

She didn't exactly wave back. It was like her right arm had an invisible rope holding it to her waist. She tried waving with the other arm, but it seemed really awkward.

We all looked. Terry jumped up. "Grams!" he shouted. "Grams!" We hurried across the street. Grams was now leaning against the wall of the house and, as we got closer, we could see that her face was somehow different from usual.

We charged up the steps to the porch.

"FAST!" said Mel. We rushed to Grams. She said it again. "You know, F-A-S-T."

Terry looked at me, then back at Grams.

"Face," said Mel. One side of Grams's face was slack and unmoving.

"Arms" said Mel.

"Grams, can you move your arm?" Terry almost shouted at her. She flinched and shook her head, no.

"Speech. Can you tell us your name?" said Mel?

Grams tried to move her mouth, but then she just shook her head.

"Time to call 911," said Terry and Mel in unison.

Mel sounded like that time in the gym, "You, in the red shirt, I mean, Ryk, you call. You know the address. Tell them that you think this lady is having a stroke. Be sure to stay on the line as long as the dispatcher needs you." I was not wearing a red shirt, but I got the message and yanked out my cell. "Terry, help her sit down where it's safe. I'll put my jacket around her to keep her warm. What time is it, Ryk? The hospital is going to ask us."

I had a sudden foggy memory of Mel shouting commands in the stairwell when I got hit. She seemed to go on automatic pilot and took over. She sent me down to the street to wait for the ambulance.

When the ambulance got there, the EMTs took charge, and we just waited. Terry went inside and found her purse. He stood there holding it when one of the EMTs started questioning us.

"Are any of you related to the patient?"

Mel and I said, "No." Terry kept quiet.

I explained that Grams's son, NT Jones, was off with his son at a dental appointment and that Mrs. Jones was at work.

"Well, can you kids contact them? I gather you've got their numbers and all? Let them know what seems to have happened and what hospital we're taking her to." He turned to get into the ambulance.

Terry followed him.

"Son?"

"I think I should go with her. She'll feel better. Not being alone."

The EMT looked at Terry, in all his reddish-blonde self and said with obvious astonishment, "You are her grandson?" Although Grams was not particularly dark, she was as clearly African American as Terry was not.

"Practically family. She's very important to me, and me to her. We're, uh." Terry's voice cracked, and it sounded like he was about to cry. "It would be better for her if I stay with her as long as possible. 'Til her son gets to the hospital. He's a sheriff's deputy."

I'm not sure why he threw in the deputy part, but somewhere between Terry's tone and his mild fabrication, he won the debate. "Get in, time's a wasting," the EMT gestured to the passenger seat. "Buckle up. Hang on to that purse."

Mel and I stood there and watched as the ambulance pulled away. I tried not to cry. I'm not sure what Mel was thinking.

"Well," I finally said, "I better start phoning." We walked back over to my house. Mel had said nothing. While I called, she stood there silently. I was able to reach NT and Mrs. Jones on the first attempts and explained what I knew, which wasn't much. I told NT that Terry had gone to the hospital with Grams, but I didn't go into any details of what happened on their front porch. I'd tell Hank when I got the chance, and let him fill his parents in. Mel and I put the guitars back in Terry's room, and I wrote a quick note to my parents, and then Mel and I started to walk to her house.

"You okay?" I broke the silence when we had walked a half block or so.

"Yes. Why wouldn't I be?"

"Well, that was pretty tense back there."

"I guess." Her voice was flat, like it was when I first tried to talk to her.

Something had been bugging me for a long time, and it came out, although I tried to be careful. "You seemed to know just what to do when we saw Grams."

"Yes. We studied it in our health class. We covered all the first aid information in health class."

"Yes, but you really, really nailed it. Like you had the textbook page in front of you."

She stopped walking at looked at me. "Well, I did." I must have looked confused. "You know what I mean. I could see it. I just went down the page and did what it said to do." She held her hands out as if she had a book in them, and then started walking again.

"I'm pretty sure I read that stuff in my health class, too. But I couldn't possibly have been that accurate in repeating it all. Especially considering that it was Grams, and I was worried about her." I didn't want it to sound like she didn't care about Grams, but she didn't hear it that way.

"Oh. Well, the book says to remain calm. Remain calm and go through the steps that are listed."

"Is that what happened in the gym that day when one of Walter's buddies got knocked down the bleachers?"

"Yes."

"So, something happens, and you just flip to the correct page, in your head, just like that?" I snapped my fingers.

"I guess. But I don't seem to search for the page I need. It just shows up in front of my eyes, almost, and I do what it says." She smiled, well, almost. "Isn't that what happens for everyone?"

"Um. No. Actually, um." I didn't want to make her feel weird, but what could I say? "I don't think most students would react the way you did. Maybe a trained emergency first responder, but not most of us."

"Well, as my mother always tells my brother and me, it's our differences that make us interesting."

I'll say. I was beginning to get an idea about her. "So, is this a gift or --?"

She stopped again. "I used to think it was a curse. My mother has spent a lot of time trying to convince me it's a gift, and sometimes I've agreed with her, but other times, I was sure it was a curse." We were almost at her house. "The problem has been to get all those pages under control. If you remember everything all the time, it gets jumbled. When I was younger, I couldn't keep anything sorted out, so I guess I didn't make sense to people. My brother calls it my 'pinball mind,' like the ball in a pinball machine ricocheting all over. That's probably why they sent me to that other school. Now, though, I can control my memory system. Most of the time, anyway. Also, I try not to talk in class. Once I get going, I can't always stop, and then everyone gets nervous. My TMI problem. My brother says I have to watch out for that particular curse, along with all the others, I guess."

"I always thought a photographic memory would be great. Just look at your school stuff or whatever and remember everything when you needed it."

"Photographic memory?" Mel was looking at me with that look again.

"People call it that when they mean someone who can remember things easily, like the person was taking a photograph with her mind." I was beginning to see how this might not be so great after all.

"Well, I guess," she said doubtfully. "It can get confusing."

"Sure. I can see that. It would be like you had this armful of photos about things and dropped them. So they'd be all jumbled together and not make as much sense."

"Exactly. But now, most of the time, I can keep things organized and can find what I need when I need it. Most of the time. But, I sometimes pull too much information out, more than I need at the time. That gets confusing." We got to her house, and her mother came out to greet us. "Don't say anything to my mother about this, okay?" I nodded my head in agreement, although I wasn't sure what part I wasn't supposed to tell her mother about; I decided everything was off limits.

"Hi, Henryk. Hi, Melantha. How are you two today?" She looked like she did the other day, except that her hair wasn't tied back. I couldn't help but think of Morticia, like Walter's boys did with Mel. I needed to kick that image out of my mind. "How was school today, Melantha?"

"It was fine, mother. Same as always. Pretty normal day." She really kept her tone set at neutral. I tried this often, but seldom succeeded. I realized that she was the opposite; she had to remind herself to put inflection into her speech. I thought about Grams. Mel had probably helped save someone's life today, and you'd never know it. Her mother would probably never know it.

Her mother knew when she was shut down, so she tried me. "Henryk, did you have a pretty normal day, also?" She made air quotes as she spoke.

"Um. Yes, ma'am. Nothing exciting." Sent a very important person off to the hospital in an ambulance, but other than that, routine. Nervousness got the better of me, and I started talking, faster than usual, making stuff up as I sailed on. "Had a big math test today, and the English teacher assigned a lot of reading, but other than that, the same old same old." My mother would have picked up on my faked casual tone and started intense grilling, but Mel's mom was either an amateur or didn't think she needed to pursue this. I caught Mel's eye, which clearly said, "Shut up." And I stopped.

"Well, that's good. Calm days are sometimes nice." Mel's mom smiled sweetly at me and looked back down the road behind me. I took the hint.

"Well, I'd best be going. My mom's got an early dinner planned. Nice to see you again, Ms. Raptis."

"Nice to see you, too, Henryk. Come again some other time."

On the way home I started thinking about Grams and how Mel and Terry just jumped in like they had been dealing with things like that all their lives. Terry probably had seen more than his share of medical drama, but I didn't think Mel had been around people enough to develop any instincts for emergencies. I thought I might have a handle on why twice I had heard something about "you in the red shirt" being sent off to get help. I was willing to bet that the specific phrase would be in the health book in the chapter on emergencies. I didn't have a handle on Mel, of course, but at least I was beginning to understand her world a little bit better. I was wondering what it would be like to remember practically everything you read or heard or saw. Depending on how you filed the information away, you could really suffer from a brain overload.

My contemplation was rudely interrupted by Walter's bunch. I nearly walked into One Punch. "Whoa, Broken-face boy! Watch where you're going!"

It took a second for the situation to register with me. "Huh? Um? Oh, you guys. What's up?" I hoped they were not there to deliver another message from Walter. Even more, I hoped they weren't planning on rearranging my facial anatomy.

"Nothing, ugly. Just out, same as you." I remembered Thirsty from the bathroom. I thought I recognized a couple others, but it was getting dark, so I wasn't sure. "I don't guess you might have a couple dollars to lend us, would you?"

I hoped they weren't referring to the cash I got out of Walter's house. I didn't think he would have mentioned it to them, but it crossed my mind that he had, and that they thought I was holding out on him. "Not really. Maybe a five or something."

"Well," someone in the dark said, "that's not very much, but it's a start."

I guess the good news was that they were just shaking me down, mugging me, rather than accusing me of theft. The bad news, of course, was that they were shaking me down, mugging me. I didn't appreciate it a bit, and I found myself getting the shakes like I did that day in gym when they were hassling me. Everything on that stairwell was coming back in one big flash of panic. I was scared. Seriously scared.

Before I had time to dig into my pockets or even visualize a new trip to the hospital, a savior arrived. Not Crate this time. Walter.

"Hey, Jonasz, what's up?" Walter said this in the casual tone of someone who sees me every day. "Boys, how's it going?"

"Walter!" They all jumped on him with hugs (manly, of course) and pounding on his back. The totally useless random thought occurred to me that he didn't have a nickname. Here he was the king of this major criminal organization, and he didn't have a dramatic handle. I got over those thoughts in a hurry. He looked terrible. His hair was scragglier than ever, and his clothes seemed to be out of a grab bag; they didn't fit, and he had on a stained grayish jacket and faded yellow hoodie.

"You're out! When? Where?" the questions flew at him.

"Couldn't hold me any longer." Walter grinned. "I didn't do anything, so they couldn't keep me."

"So where are you staying?" Thirsty took the lead. "I mean, you can't go home; it's a mess over there."

"Going back to Snap's. Where I was hiding before. Only now it's going to be legal. His parents must have figured that if they didn't know I was there for a while, I could move back into their basement, and it still wouldn't matter to them." He didn't say anything about the getaway stuff I got for him, but he seemed pretty happy about things. I doubted that Snap knew anything about the big stash and the plan.

"So what about this turkey?" One of the boys in the dark spoke up. I was the turkey he was referring to.

Walter didn't hesitate, "No problem, Buzz. He's cool. Leave him alone."

A strange humming sound came from the dark.

"No noise, Buzz. I told you, he's cool." The humming stopped. I guessed that Buzz was so named because he started humming when he was nervous or challenged.

"Yeah, like Walter said, knock it off." This from the other figure in the shadows. I could make out his enormous ears, even though he had long scraggly hair hanging over them.

"Who're you telling what to do, Dumbo?" Buzz sneered at the guy I assume was identified by his ears. I wisely resisted the urge to point out to these guys that they had to have about the dumbest "bad guy" nicknames in the universe.

"All y'all knock it off. We've got places to go and things to do. And none of them involve Jonasz, here. Beat it, man."

I nodded at Walter, and at Thirsty, and backed off as smoothly as my shaking legs would let me.

CHAPTER 31

Good News

By the time I got home it was pretty dark. Terry wasn't home yet, and my parents pulled in as I was unlocking the door.

"Hey, sweetie. Are you just getting in from school? Big project or something?" Mom was her usual self: greeting and interrogating me at the same time. I was glad I hadn't texted the afternoon's excitement to her. The grilling would have been thorough and intense.

"Just stopped by over at a friend's house." I needed a few minutes to collect myself. Grams and then the almost-mugging hadn't done anything good for my brain. "Hey, Dad, how's it going?"

"Fine, fine." We all walked into the house, switched on lights, and then another question. "Where's Terry? Isn't he usually home by now?"

I snatched the note I had left on the kitchen table, buying some more time. "Most of the time. Let me text him, find out what's up." I pulled out my phone and punched away, silent.

They headed upstairs, and so did I. The text tone came as I walked into my room.

"Grams ok mostly small stroke home soon hank also"

Well, that news helped. To say the least. Maybe she would be okay.

Naturally, NT and Mrs. Jones would be staying at the hospital for a while, so it made sense to send Hank and Terry home by cab to our house.

"Mom, Dad, long story, but the short of it is that Hank is eating dinner with us tonight. He and Terry are on the way." I yelled this through their closed bedroom door and hustled downstairs.

Terry and Hank pulled up a few minutes later. I wanted to get the story from them before I told my parents. "So," I looked at Hank first. "What's the story? Terry texted. She's okay?"

"Pretty much, I guess. The doctors have to run about a zillion tests and all that." Hank obviously didn't know about the heroic response by Mel and Terry. "She's going to be in intensive care for at least a day or two, but they think they caught it super early."

Terry added more, sounding animated, although the strain came through in his voice, "They said that since we caught it so early, they could give her some drug to dissolve the clot. Remember when Mel said to pay attention to the time? Seems like that was really useful to the docs." Terry was animated, although his voice shook.

"Docs?" Mom came downstairs at the end of Terry's comment. "Who? What? Where?"

Hank had questions, too. "Mel?

"Mom, it's kind of complicated. I'll tell you all about it at dinner. Do you need any help?" I figured that once I started in on the story, we'd never get dinner. Everything would come to a complete stop while she interrogated us.

Besides, I didn't want to have to tell it twice, once to her, and then Dad.

"No, thanks. I got a lot of it started this morning. Just set the table. Place for Hank, too, of course. I don't think Frankie will be here." I thought there'd be questions about Hank being there, but it happened often enough that she didn't think much about it, I guess. Hank's mother was often late, and NT's schedule was not his own, even though he was supposed to be working the night shift. Terry and Hank disappeared upstairs, leaving me with the table. They would do the dishes.

"So," Mom started when we'd all sat down, "what was today's big adventure?" She was smiling. You said something about doctors, but I don't see any evidence of major damage. Thank goodness."

"It's Grams." Hank and Terry both spoke at once, voices cracking. "They think she's had a stroke," Hank finished and clenched his teeth to maintain control.

Mom set her fork down and grimaced, "Where? When?"

Terry looked like he was about to cry, Hank just clenched tighter, so I tried. "This afternoon. Terry and Mel and I were on the front porch when she sort of waved us over." I had to stop to get my breathing under control. "It was awful."

"And what did you do?" Dad was looking at Hank and Terry but asking me.

"We went over there, and, and Mel and Terry were amazing!" It had finally hit me how fantastic they really were. "Just awesome. Like textbook perfect." I looked at Hank. "You have no idea how amazing." I went on to explain about Mel and Terry going through the procedure for strokes like they had been practicing it every day. I even mentioned that they remembered to get the time so they could tell the doctors.

Christopher Wollenberg

"So," said Dad, "what you're saying is that Mrs. Jones is the luckiest unlucky person on the block? Having what appears to be a stroke is never a good idea, but if you're going to have one, do it with a couple of smart teenagers who know what to do."

"Exactly," I agreed. "I mean, I was in health class, too. And I remember all that FAST stuff, but that was just in the book, and on the test, of course. But they could do it. And no panic, no problem."

Hank's eyes were running now. "You guys saved my Grams, didn't you? Terry, you didn't tell me that part. When I saw you at the hospital, you just said you went with her in the ambulance so she wouldn't be alone."

Terry nodded. "Yeah. Something like that. Melantha was the real hero, though. She just walked us through it like she was reading from the book. Henryk and I just followed along and did what she told us to do."

Mom hadn't interrupted me once in my recitation; she almost seemed at a loss for words, but she recovered. "So, you guys saw Mrs. Jones having trouble and went over there to help? And then you did a 'fast' thing?" She made air quotes. "What was that?"

Terry jumped in, giving me a chance to eat. "You know, FAST. For when you think the victim might be having a stroke."

"No, Terence. I don't know. That's why I was asking."

Dad looked a bit confused, too. Although he was better at hiding his ignorance. I think that's probably a useful skill for him in dealing with legal problems at work, to say nothing of Frankie.

Terry went on to explain the FAST process.

"And they teach this in school now? As a part of the

health curriculum?" Mom sounded impressed. "Do you know about it?" she asked me.

"Of course, but Mel and Terry worked it like a couple of pros. That's all I'm saying. Terry realized she was having a problem, immediately thought stroke, I guess, and we charged over there."

Dad started up again, "So, what's the deal? The bottom line?"

Hank was happy to talk. He had been looking at his telephone for part of all this. "Dad just texted. She's doing pretty well. They think she'll be able to go to a rehab center in a few days. She can already walk better, so I guess it was a really small stroke."

We ate in silence for a while. Dad broke it.

"You just never know, do you? Cruising along, pretty normal life, and then bam, something happens, a stroke, an accident, anything. And your whole life gets turned upside down." He looked at me. "What happened to you was pretty shocking, but you're over it, mostly, I guess. And our life is back to normal. But your grandmother, Hank, and your family; this can really change things in a hurry."

"Yes sir, I know. Hopefully, it's not too bad, and she'll be okay."

Terry spoke up. "She's a tough old lady. Been through a lot, a whole lot, in her life. I don't think this is going to knock her down, not by a long shot."

Hank looked pleased. "Ryk, remember when I said something about one person's disaster being a reporter's big chance?"

Oh, oh. "Yeah? And?"

"Well, here's a story I finally get to actually write. Two stories, maybe. Kids save someone's life by using what they learned in the classroom. Tough old lady, uh, don't tell Grams I called her that. Tough old lady overcomes a stroke." He sat back and smiled.

Of course, Mom pounced immediately. "Hank, what do you mean by actually write? Are there stories that you're keeping from us? Things we ought to know about?" Her eyes narrowed as she stared at him.

"Oh. No, Mom J. I just, uh, meant, that." He finished fast, "that here was a feel-good story with only good things happening, other than the stroke part, of course." He made it a point to concentrate on eating his dinner. He did not mention that he was also thinking about writing a story about Slate's unusual diplomas. So that would be three stories to launch him on the road to fame and a Pulitzer.

Terry took a shot at distraction, "So, Uncle Tomás, anything exciting in the world of unconstitutional law enforcement?"

Surprisingly, it worked. Usually an abrupt veer from the conversation like this by Frankie or me would have provoked Mom or Dad to come at us harder with questions. Maybe they were ready for a break from drama, too. "The usual. The police couldn't get their story straight, all the witnesses changed their stories, the district attorneys got lost, and some dude, who by the way is probably guilty of something, gets to sit in prison until we sort it out. We only do appeals on egregious cases, so our miscreant does a lot of hard time before we come to his rescue." He suddenly looked particularly tired to me. "And sometimes, like this week, our guy, or gal, dies in custody before that happens."

I think Terry was sorry he brought the subject up. "Wow, that's tough."

"Yeah. Well, other cases go the right way all the way to the end, so I guess that helps us keep trying."

"Keepin' on keepin' on, eh, Uncle T?"

Dad smiled, "Like the man says."

The phone rang; it was NT saying that he was back home and that Hank could come home, too. We all interpreted that as Hank should go home immediately, so he took off, "Thank you for having me tonight, Mom J." He jumped up. "Ryk, I'll see you sometime tomorrow, once I know what's up," he threw at me as he left.

Terry and I did the dishes. He's usually pretty quiet, but I could see he had something to tell me, but not in the kitchen where we might be overheard, so we retreated to his room with its covering sound system to talk.

"You're shook up with the Grams thing," I opened. "I mean, it's pretty scary, but—"

"But yes." Terry looked even more shook than before. "She's something else, you know. Really something else." He paused to steady his voice. "Remember that time when I, uh, was, uh?"

"Yes. And Mr. Wright took you over to Hank's house, to Grams as it turned out."

"Yes. Well, we talked. A lot. I was pretty pissed off, ready to do bodily harm to any number of people, including myself, maybe, but we talked. And we talked. She told me some things you wouldn't believe. And I guess I told her some things you wouldn't believe, either. At least things you don't want to believe." Terry looked around the room, stopping on the back side of the sketch he did that day. It was leaning against the wall, facing it.

"So, you, um?"

"Yeah. No one person turns anyone or anything around

in one conversation. But sometimes, it helps. She told me that when she first saw me, all she could think of was these white kids that hurt her friend, way back in the forties or something. She said that I looked just like one of the boys. Said if my hair was cut in a butch, whatever that is, I'd be the spittin' image of this dude. And he was one bad dude, I can tell you."

I knew what he was talking about, and what happened to Grams's friend, but I didn't know how much Terry knew. He didn't know how much I knew, so we talked around it. "And so? She hated you on sight, I guess?"

"Not quite, but wasn't pleased to see me at her door, I can tell you that. I guess she hadn't really noticed that I'd been living here since August." He laughed. "Probably all white boys look alike, at least from the distance, maybe without glasses on, too."

"But she let you in, and?"

"And I guess she could see past my white self, and thought I was in a mess. Which I was. And we talked. And talked." Terry stopped abruptly.

"So that's why you wanted to go with her to the hospital today?"

"Yep. She needed me like I needed her that day."

"You and Mel. You guys were amazing. I think you probably saved her life."

"Yeah. There's something else. You're not the only one who goes off on secret missions." He raised his hand at my shocked expression. "Don't worry, your secret love life with Mel is safe with me."

Good, he didn't know about the trips on Walter's behalf. He just thought I was being cool with a girl. "And you don't think I know about your non-tobacco smoking habit after school? I've seen you come in with your guitar pretty late a lot of days, you know."

"You would be shocked, shocked I say, to learn that I was up to no good, but not the way you think. Grams."

"Say, what?"

"Yep. I went over to thank her a couple days later, and we got to talking. She'd seen me carrying the guitar up the street one day and asked about it. Next thing you know, I'm over there every couple of days playing for her." I was probably looking at Terry like he was the biggest liar in the world. I could not imagine Grams wanting to hear the music I usually heard him play. "Oh, not my stuff. Her stuff. Mostly old gospel tunes and such. Kind of country-churchy stuff, I guess. I found some of it online and tried to figure it out. And of course she can help me with the timing and phrasing. Pretty cool, actually."

"And she told you stories? About her life?"

"Yeah. Tough old bird, I can tell you that. Folks down where she grew up were mean. White folks, I mean. They, her folks, couldn't do squat without worrying about some crazy cracker messing with them. Her word, not mine."

"And you told her your stories, too?"

"Not so much. Too fresh for me. But she got the picture. Enough to know not to ask for details." Terry started rummaging through his backpack, a sign that he had probably talked enough for the night.

"Well, Terry, it's been a strange day. Think I'll knock off." When I left, he was still fiddling with his backpack.

I didn't see Hank much on Saturday or Sunday. He and his parents spent most of the time at the hospital with Grams. I tried to wangle a visit by Terry and me, but they said immediate relatives only. Terry's artistry with the

EMTs was one thing, but he wasn't going to get a free pass from NT nearly as easily, so we didn't push it. Hank texted nothing but good news all weekend; it seemed that Grams really was not too critical and would be in a rehabilitation center relatively quickly. And then, possibly for only a few days before coming home to get better.

CHAPTER 32

Secret Mission

At the bus stop, Hank came over to Terry and me. "Good morning, gentlemen."

"Top of the morning to you, sir." Terry replied. "What do you know? How's Grams?"

"Pretty good, I guess. But, weird. She can't talk right. It's like her body's almost all okay, but her mouth and brain aren't connected."

"Can she write notes?" I looked at his eyes, but he kept glancing at Terry.

"No, so I guess it's more than her mouth. She gestures for stuff. You know like water." He made a drinking motion with his hand. "Or she points to the bathroom."

Terry asked, "She can walk?"

"Yes, but someone holds on to her just to be sure. The doctors and nurses all seem to think she's a miracle lady."

"But she can't communicate?"

"Not with words, no." He looked at Terry. "She keeps doing this air guitar thing." Hank strummed a few air guitar chords. "She looks at me and plays the guitar. Why do you suppose she does that? It makes no sense."

Terry looked blankly at Hank. I don't think he wanted

to say anything, so I answered. "Maybe she wants Terry to come play for her?"

Hank's was confused. "Play?"

Terry shifted a bit. "Yeah, well. I sort of played my guitar for her once in a while the last couple weeks. You know, gospel and old country tunes, not my stuff." He grinned.

We spent the next few minutes waiting for the bus filling Hank in on Terry's musical conversations with Grams.

As the bus pulled up, Hank looked at Terry, "Hey, thanks, man. For coming over. With your guitar. I guess it meant a lot to her. I'll have to tell my parents."

On the bus, Hank sat next to me and immediately jumped me on a new subject. "Ryk, you've got to help me. You owe me, you know, after going to the Anderson house. Twice."

"Yeah? With what?" I couldn't imagine.

"Remember you told me about Slate's diplomas being bogus?"

"I said they might be funny. At least one of them. Why?"

"You know that's my big story, but I need to get copies. So I can investigate each college he claims to have gotten a degree from. That's where you come in."

"Me? Hank, you're the reporter. You get 'em."

"What am I going to do, waltz into Slate's office and take pictures? I think he'd notice that, dense as he may be." Hank laughed. "You, on the other hand, are practically his best friend. You could get in there easily."

"No. No way!" But then I had a small flash; Hank was right, almost. "Wait! You know what, you're right. Not me, though. Melantha."

"Melantha? How's she going to take pictures better than you?"

"She doesn't have to, remember? If I can get her in there, and I can distract Slate long enough, she can look at each diploma and remember enough details for you to do your research." This plan was looking genius to me. "I'll give him some crazy story about why we're in his office, and he'll buy it."

"And you'll do all this today?"

"No time like the present. All I have to do is find Melantha and talk her into it."

"That seems easy enough. Not!"

"Well, I didn't say it was a perfect plan." I tapped him on the shoulder. "But, it'll have to do. I'll make it work. Anything to keep you from writing about bullying and me." I wouldn't see Mel at lunch since it was an odd day, so I'd have to catch her in the hall.

My first period English class wasn't too far from Melantha's first period history class, so I put myself in her hall as soon as I got off the bus. The crowd in the hall was the usual: half the students were barely awake, and the other half were noisy, bouncing around like they'd drained an entire Starbucks dry. Mel did not look happy. Crowds were really not her thing.

"Hi, Mel. You okay?" I didn't mean to sound like she wasn't, but, honestly, she wasn't.

"Oh. Ryk. Too much this morning. Just too much." She shifted her backpack and looked at her watch. "Class in a few minutes. Five. I've got to go." She started down the hall.

"Want another adventure, instead?" I couldn't think of anything better.

"Adventure? Now? We've got to go to class."

"This would get you some peace and quiet for a few minutes. No trouble, either. Just peace and quiet."

Mel stopped. "You're sure? What kind of adventure?"

"I need to get into Mr. Slate's office. I need you with me."

"Who? Oh, him. Why do you need me? What do you mean you need to get into his office? I thought you were trying to not see him as much as possible."

"Well, yes, mostly. But I need, actually Hank needs, to see the diplomas on Slate's wall. We think they're fishy."

"Fishy?"

"You know," but of course she didn't, "you know, suspicious. Maybe not what they say they are. Fake even. Hank's working on a story about them."

"And why do I have to go into that man's office?"

"Because you can look at them and remember all the important details. With your photographic memory."

"Photo--? Oh yes. Details. I guess I do remember all the details of things. Can't you just go in and do it yourself?"

"I'd need a camera. I might be able to get in there and maybe take a photo or two, but he'd notice, and then I'd be dead. You can go in and just look around and try to remember the important details." My voice kept dropping down like I didn't believe in the scheme myself. I needed to be more Frankie X. I tried to sound confident. Be confident. "It'll work. We can get past Mrs. Hernandez easily; it's always busy in that office first thing Monday mornings. We go in, you look at each diploma; we leave. If Slate actually gets there after watching the cafeteria or buses or whatever, I'll gaslight him. Tell him some story about how he told me on Friday to come see him and bring you along. He won't remember if he said anything to me or not."

"Gaslight?" I wasn't going to win her over with confusion. Mel did not like confusion.

"Oh. Sorry. It means tell him he said something a few days ago when I know he didn't, but he can't be sure. Get into his head a little."

Rats; did it again. "Get into his head?" Mel was rapidly retreating from my plan, and who could blame her. It did sound pretty weird.

"Um. Confuse him. Just enough for you to look at the diplomas. Look, if nothing else it'll be peaceful in there. And Mrs. Hernandez can give us a pass to class. In and out. All we'll miss is the Pledge and morning announcements." I think the Pledge comment did it. Mel's mother was not a fan of the Pledge of Allegiance as a forced participation but didn't want Mel singled out by trying to get her dispensation to sit, like some religious groups did.

"Okay." She still sounded doubtful. "What do I look for? Look at?"

"Can you just try to remember the main details on each diploma? Of course Slate's name will be on each one, but the exact name of the institution, the location, and the issue date would be really important. You won't be able to read the names of the college presidents who signed the diplomas, but you might see some printed names. It seems like a lot, but there're probably only a few diplomas from colleges or universities. I think he has other certificates on the wall, but they don't mean anything." Hank and I had spent a few minutes on the bus hashing this out in case I really got into the office. He had gone online and figured out what most diplomas showed. He also found out that the fake institutions had names that were amazingly similar to real institutions, so you had to pay attention to the details. Mel's uber-strength was details. "Come on, Mel. You'll be perfect. It'll be a different kind of challenge."

"And I don't have enough challenges now? In my everyday life?" She actually smiled, though. "Yeah. It'll be interesting. Like sneaking into that house and finding all those guns. Who knows what we'll find."

We were almost close enough to her classroom to be spotted by her teacher; we turned around and headed to Slate's office.

As I predicted, it was not peaceful in the outer office, and the chaos in there made it easier to get into Slate's office. One student was holding an ice pack to his face; I wondered if he had run into One Punch. Three students were standing along one wall and cracking on each other, really stupid insults as far as I could tell, but they were laughing loudly. I waved at Mrs. Hernandez, and we walked confidently in. "Mr. Slate told me to meet him here first thing this morning." She barely nodded at us. She was trying to get a guy and a girl to quit yelling at each other, and they were being egged on by a couple other guys. I suspected she was not having a good Monday morning. It was indeed quiet in Slate's office. I worked on the details of my story in case I needed one while Mel studied the diplomas. There were a lot of certificates and diplomas on the walls. Some were actual college-style diplomas, and others seemed to be certificates of appreciation or at least participation. Half of them looked like the things we got at the end of summer activities camps and baseball seasons. They had nice frames. I snapped photos of the walls as fast as I could. Just as I put my phone away, Slate came storming in.

"Jonasz, what are you doing in here?" No surprise, he did not pronounce my name correctly. He focused on Mel who appeared to be studying the wall. "And what is she, what's-her-name, doing here?"

I was sure that my face was perfect; I had my most sincere look. "Don't you remember, Mr. Slate? On Friday, in the hall, near the cafeteria, I think. You told me to see you first thing today. Something about Anderson? I don't know. And you said to bring along that girl. I assumed you meant her." I pointed to Mel. I didn't want to repeat her name, didn't want him to remember it."

He frowned for a moment. "Oh. Well, things have changed. They found Anderson."

I hoped that Mel was finishing the last wall. I realized that we had not worked out a signal to let me know she was through, so I didn't know if I needed to stall for more time. "Yes. I heard. I guess he was at a friend's house. Not mine, obviously." I couldn't resist the little dig. He had probably sent the cops to my house, and I wanted him to know that I knew. "Is he coming back to school?"

"Well of course. We wouldn't keep a scholar like that from his education, would we?" He sat down heavily on his chair. "He's supposed to check in with me this morning when, if, he gets here. Tell you what, Jonasz. You go on back to class and take what's-her-name with you. I can't imagine why I'd want to talk with you, but it's been a pleasure, I'm sure. Now, get out of here while I deal with those two squabbling lovebirds out there. First thing off the bus. Jeez! They had all weekend to argue. Why'd they bring it here? Got kids getting punched out, kids coming to school when they were supposed to stay home on suspension, all kinds of fun."

It was like Slate and Mrs. Hernandez were playing a bizarre game of Whack-a-mole. First one student started yelling, then another; then back to the first one; then another one. For a split second, no, make that a nanosecond, I almost felt sorry for him, but I got over that feeling easily enough.

Christopher Wollenberg

Mel was looking at the door, so I grabbed her arm and headed to Mrs. Hernandez for a pass. The "lovebirds" were still squawking, and all the other guys were shouting louder; Mrs. Hernandez looked like she was ready for her morning coffee break already. I did feel sorry for her. Why she continued to work for Slate in that office was beyond me. Unless, of course, she needed the job; maybe she needed to eat and had bills and all that adult stuff. At least there was no chance of monster Bernard Anderson charging in and hitting someone.

Passes in hand, we hustled down the hall. Mel spoke first. "There were a lot of certificates on the walls. I've got to sort them out in my head and write it all down. I can do it in class this period. Then, I'll pass it on to you on the way to PE next period."

Wow, she came up with a plan. And she was considering doing something other than paying attention to her teacher. "That would be great, Mel. I can see Hank at lunch and show him what we got." I looked at her. She seemed really happy. "That was fun, huh?"

"Yes. Actually. Do you think there might be something in those diplomas?"

I was afraid the wheels were turning a little too much. I didn't want her to start her own investigation. "Hard to say. But I think Hank can use the information. Let's not tell anyone what we did, okay? Could be a problem."

"Ryk! It's not like I talk to a lot of people. Anyone, really. But no, nothing to my mom or brother, either. Thanks for the Monday morning adventure! It seems like we're always having adventures. The brawl in the gym. The trips to that house. The stroke with Hank's grandmother. This thing." She smiled and hurried off to her history class. It seemed weird that she thought of those as equal adventures, but what do I know?

CHAPTER 33

Intrepid Reporters

At lunch, Hank was beyond happy. Mel's list was truly impressive. She had eight different sets of details. Some of the "diplomas" really were just certificates of attendance for conferences or something, but there were four definite degree proclamations. She had managed to get all the needed stuff, names of institutions, degrees given, and dates. My photos weren't particularly great, but I sent them to Hank's phone. At home he could blow them up on his computer and maybe find more information. At least he would know which wall to check out if he needed to go back in.

"So your dad says some of these may be not be the real deal?"

"That's what I understood," I agreed. "I would guess that this Virginia college diploma is real, his Bachelor's. But all these Master's degrees will take some digging. They all seem to be from other states. He could have really earned them; they could be fakes of real institutions, or they could be diplomas from fake institutions."

"Yeah. That's kind of what I gathered from poking around online." He took a couple quick bites of lunch, "So, ask me about Grams."

"I was getting to that. Business first. How's Grams?"

"Good of you to ask. She's getting transferred to a rehab facility today. That means she basically is doing great. My dad texted a while ago with the news." He added unhappily, "It means no lesson with Carl today, and I won't get over to see her either." He brightened up, "But tomorrow, we're all going over. You, me, and your crazy guitar-playing cousin, with his axe, of course. I wonder if she would like to hear me doing gospel on the trumpet?"

"Let's not risk shocking her. Your version might be a bit too jazzy for her. To say nothing of what the rehab people might think. I can see the headlines now, the New-Time Old-Time guitar-trumpet jazz ensemble gets the boot from the rehab center."

"Point. But be sure to tell Terry that he is invited, make that ordered for medical reasons, to join us tomorrow." The tone ending lunch sounded, and we hustled off to class.

My trip back to class had a small detour in it. Walter tapped me on the shoulder as I passed a restroom. He didn't have to say anything; he just nodded.

There were other guys in there, so I wasn't too worried. Besides, I thought we had a truce going. "Jonasz."

My throat still got tight, despite my confidence. "Um?"

"Yeah. Just wanted to say, uh, well, thanks." His voice had dropped to just above a whisper. "About the stuff. You know, from the house."

What could I say? I wasn't going to ask him if he planned to take off with the truck and money. I was really, really hoping that neither Slate nor Wright would wander in. "No prob, Walter. Hope it works out." I was also hoping he wasn't about to "request" another favor.

"Well, I don't know yet. We'll see. I'm staying at Snap's house for now." He looked at me silently for a moment. "You're a stand-up guy, you know that, Jonasz? See you around."

I used the urinal, thankful that I hadn't lost it all when he first caught up with me. In the hall, I ran into Crate.

"Hey, Crate? What's up?"

"Hey, Henryk. I was on the way to lunch and saw you go in there with your buddy. Everything okay?"

I occurred to me that this was not the first time I had run into Crate after an encounter with Walter in a restroom. "Complete accident, huh? You just happened to be here?"

His face reddened, which made his acne stand out more than usual. "Busted, I guess. Guilty as suspected."

"You have been following me? Why?"

"Not exactly following you, but, let's say, keeping an eye out."

"My own guardian angel?"

"Something like that. I have to. It's the rule."

"Rule?"

"Sure, you know, karma and all that. When you save someone's life, you're responsible for them. Forever, I guess." He looked down at his feet. "I didn't make that up. Everyone knows it."

I was pretty sure that I had read somewhere that this was a complete made-for-TV concept, from some old Kung Fu show or movie or something, but I didn't want to argue. I'm not the right person to be arguing theology or ethics with anyone, even if I have my own sense of what's right and wrong. Anyway, it's a nice concept even if it's not a real rule.

"Okay, Crate. I appreciate it and all that, but there must be some way to release you from your obligation. I mean, you can't go around with me for the next eighty years making sure I don't die."

"I haven't figured that part out yet. You sure you're okay? Walter's not being a problem?"

"No. It's all good now. I think he feels bad about that dude hitting me. Nothing more." I hoped my lie-to-adults face would work with Crate.

"Well, okay, then." He smiled and brushed his hands together, pretended to adjust his magic cape and mask. "If everything's good here on this planet, I guess I'll go off and be a super hero in another galaxy."

I swung by Mel's locker at the end of the day, but by the time I got there, she had already left, so I headed for the bus. As I passed her bus, I saw that she was already seated alone in her favorite spot, head down, so I went on to my own bus. Hank and Terry were just ahead of me, Hank telling Terry about his command appearance with Grams Tuesday afternoon. "I'll check on a few of her favorites online when I get home, make sure I know them all the way through. Usually she has to help me. Which would be the point, I guess." Terry told Hank as he headed to the back to sit with his friends.

Hank plopped down on a seat and motioned me over. "We have a lot of work to do today, my investigative partner."

"We? I thought this was your story?"

"Woodward and Bernstein, partner, Woodward and Bernstein."

"Um?"

"You know, the reporters. The two *Washington Post* guys who busted Nixon. Way back in the dark ages or something."

"And?"

"And that was ancient history maybe, but I'm, we, are on to something pretty big here. We've got lying, cheating, fraud, all kinds of good stuff. Slate's days are seriously numbered."

"And my part is?

"I'm going to write the article for the *Reporter* this afternoon, and you are going to help me fact check online, and maybe even with editing."

"And who gets the byline and the Pulitzer?"

"Well, me, of course; you're not technically a reporter for the paper. This isn't poetry or fiction, like the literary magazine you allegedly write for."

He had a point. I almost never went to the literary magazine meetings, and I had not actually turned in anything in to the sponsor. I wasn't even sure what the name of the literary magazine was. "Okay," I agreed, "but you're feeding me. I don't believe in starving authors. Or assistants, for that matter."

Once we got to work on the article, it turned out to be pretty easy. There were three questionable diplomas on Slate's wall. Two were from companies that, as far as we could tell from our-online research, had changed their names several times. They apparently actually required their "students" to submit some type of written work for each "class" they were credited with taking, but it was pretty murky. We couldn't tell what work someone really had to do to complete the requirements, but we were pretty sure that we could have earned a "Master's in Something Impressive" (take your pick) in a few weeks if we spent a few thousand dollars. The other "diploma" seemed to be a complete fabrication. It appeared that Slate had simply sent his name (spelled correctly as it was to appear on the sheepskin) and some money to a printing company which then sent back a very nice "diploma" suitable for framing and display. Only the degree from the small Virginia college seemed to be legitimate.

I don't know about Hank, but I could hardly sleep that night thinking about the uproar we were about to cause.

CHAPTER 34

Uproar

The "uproar" was not quite the one that I expected. I found myself caught up in Hank's drama with the story. Hank told me that as soon as he got off the bus he went directly to the student editor of the *Reporter* with his copy of the story. He swore the editor to secrecy before he handed it over and waited for him to read it. While he waited, I think Hank was already writing his acceptance speech for the student journalism award he was sure to receive. I don't know if he was thinking a state honor or a national one, but I'm pretty sure he was expecting big doings. He may have already had his suit picked out.

The senior apparently also had learned a thing or two about masking emotions. All he said was, "Interesting." And he agreed to take it to the *Reporter's* teacher sponsor. Hank told me that he reminded the editor that he still had to original story on his computer at home. He was afraid that the editor would hijack the hot story. In fact, Hank had even gone to the trouble of photographing the first page with that day's copy of the *Washington Post* with the date showing to prove that he had the original article.

Mel and I sat together at lunch.

"Ryk."

"Mel."

"Is Hank's story progressing?"

"As far as I know, Mel. We worked half the night on it last night. It's really hot. Your help made all the difference. We've got all the ducks in a row. Going to be a big blow up when it gets out."

"Hot? Ducks? Blow up?" Rats, I'd done it again. I just turned on the fog machine, stringing clichés together like that.

"I mean, it's going great. We have lots of information; Hank's story is well organized. Clear as a, uh, very clear. The story will be the biggest one this year. Maybe any year."

Crate sat down next to us. I had to change the subject; I didn't want Mel to say anything. "Crate, you know Melantha, right?"

"Yes. History class. She's our resident expert. Ask her anything."

"Or don't." Mel smiled. I thought she'd be offended, but I guess she was learning to live with her "curse" as she put it. "Crate? Curtis Jordan, C three, or four, usually three."

I looked at Crate and shrugged. He shrugged also, and rolled his eyes. I remembered that he once described Mel as crazy. I think he called her "Psycho one-oh-one."

Mel seemed not to notice our exchange. "It's how I keep track of who people are. Curtis usually sits in the row I call C in the third or fourth seat. Second once in a while; never in the first seat."

I didn't want this to go on too long, however. "So, Crate, you find a new outlet for our hero?"

He grinned, "Yep. Very cute blond. All I need to do is save her from something."

"Besides yourself, you mean."

"Save? Blond?" Mel sounded a bit confused.

"Long story, Mel. Nothing exciting. Crate is just searching for an outlet for his super powers. Make that a victim for his super powers. He can't remember if he's supposed to be a guardian angel, or guarding an angel. Looks like he's going for option two."

"Well, Ryk, that certainly explains it." I thought she'd was offended by this, too, but she seemed to be blowing it off, not that I would ever use that phrase with her. She ate her strange food, with chopsticks, and didn't say anything more. Crate ate and looked at me grinning stupidly.

By sixth period, the sponsor's planning period, Hank was in her office explaining how he developed the story. About ten minutes into the period, I was called out of PE (still sitting on the sidelines in regular clothes to avoid concussive contact) and was sent to the sponsor's office. It was really more of a storeroom; any newspaper layout activities would have to be done in the teacher's regular classroom down the hall. The teacher had a small desk piled high with folders. There were several metal filing cabinets with more folders stacked on top, and there were some shelves attached to the wall packed full of back copies of the *Reporter*. On the opposite side there was a portable bulletin board with various story ideas thumbtacked to it. They probably had to wheel it down to her classroom for newspaper meetings. There were two old student desks crammed into the little floor space left.

Hank is not a particularly good liar; he's not related to Frankie by blood, of course, and despite all those years of being around him, he still had not learned anything through osmosis, so concocting stories does not come naturally to him. Admittedly, living with a cop as a father would have quickly curtailed any urge to invent explanations. Apparently, in the process of telling his fictional and complicated story about how he acquired the few ragged photos of Slate's diplomas, my name came up. Hank managed to leave Mel out of his recitation, but the damage was done, and there I was.

Ms. Wells seemed pleasant enough. At about five feet even, she made me feel tall.

Hank introduced me to her. "Henryk, this is Ms. Wells, not the ought-to-be famous and very dead Ida B. Wells, but a journalist in any case. Ms. Wells, this is Henryk, the guy I told you about, who's been helping me." He did not mention my last name. By now, he had learned that my surname often brought up mentions of Frankie, and that was not always helpful.

Ms. Wells looked at Hank like he had lost his mind. "Ida B?"

"Oh," said Hank, "in my family we, that is my sister and I, have to do research on important black Americans not named Martin Luther King. My sister, Phillis, did a report on Ida B. Wells at dinner the other night. She's named after Phillis Wheatley. If you had been born in my family, you would have been Ida Bwells Jones or something. My dad was named Nat Turner Jones by his mother." I couldn't tell if Hank was deliberately trying to bewilder Ms. Wells or was just nervous.

"Okaaay," Ms. Wells dragged it out. "So how about we get back on the subject at hand, and you explain how you came to these astounding conclusions about Mr. Slate and his diplomas." She smiled politely at me. "Nice to meet you, Henryk. I'm sure you wonder why I called you in since you are not part of the newspaper staff. However, I got the definite impression that you helped with this story in several ways, and I felt that it was incumbent upon me as an educator to enlighten you as well as Hank on the subtleties of honest newspaper reporting."

Ms. Wells indicated that I should sit in the student desk next to Hank. She sat at her desk. I sat, wondering why this made me more nervous than a visit with Mr. Slate or Mr. Wright.

"So, you guys got this hunch, somehow, that Mr. Slate's diplomas were not kosher?"

"Yes ma'am." At least Hank didn't drag my father's observations into the story.

I covered, just to be sure. "Yes ma'am. I was in his office." Ms. Wells looked darkly at me. I wondered if she knew Frankie. "Oh. Not in trouble. As a victim. I got attacked by some student in a random gang thing or something." Even when I didn't have to, I found myself adjusting the actual story. "So, I was sitting there and Slate, Mr. Slate, had to take a call. I was sort of looking around at all the certificates and diplomas on the walls, and I thought one of them came from one of those out-of-state companies that was in the newspaper a while back. Something about student loans or fraud or something."

"I see." For a second, I thought that settled it. "So, being good reporters, your pursued the story, right?"

Hank's confidence was back, "Oh, yes, ma'am. I researched every diploma Mr. Slate had on the wall."

"And?"

"And, like it says there in my story, three of them are a bit fishy. Totally fraudulent, in fact."

"And being a good reporter, you checked multiple

sources? You can document the alleged frauds. Government cease and desist orders, copies of any settlements between the government and the institutions, court findings, all those sorts of things? Your 'proof' isn't just based on some random internet 'information'?" She signaled air quotes around the key words.

Hank was suddenly looking very uncomfortable. I found myself sweating as well.

"And, of course, you talked with Mr. Slate, asked him for his side of the story? And I wonder, did he talk to you? I don't recall any direct quotes from him in your story. Nor do I remember seeing anything about his refusing to talk to you."

More sweat now.

"And, just to be absolutely sure that Mr. Slate used these diplomas in a fraudulent way, you asked for an interview with the school system's human resources department. They wouldn't talk with you of course, but you have it on record in your notes that you attempted to contact the department. Somewhere in your story you can show that these allegedly fraudulent diplomas were used by Mr. Slate to get his job, get his state required endorsement to be a teacher and then an assistant principal?" Ms. Wells sat back in her chair and waited.

I'm pretty sure that by now Hank was no longer writing his acceptance speech for the journalism award. I was trying to decide if we were actually in trouble. I couldn't determine the crime here, but it sure seemed like trouble.

Hank surprised me. Maybe he had picked up something from Frankie after all. He flashed his best smile, got up from his desk, and picked up the copy of the story from Ms. Wells's desk. "So, Ms. Wells, what you're saying is that

I have a bit more work to do on this story before we can publish it." He turned towards the door.

"Sit. Down. Mr. Jones."

Hank sat. I stayed put.

"Do either one of you guys know what a tabloid newspaper is?"

"Sure, Ms. Wells. Those are the ones that publish sensational stuff that sells papers, violence, sex, scandal, all that, but they're usually a bit short on the facts." Hank's tone showed that he was still maintaining his big bold attitude.

"And, they cannot document their claims." Her fake sweet smile and tone were appropriate for talking to a third grader who just got caught in a farcical story. "And, it should be noted, they get sued. A lot." She leaned back again and let that sink in.

Hank wasn't ready to admit defeat, "But, if what the paper says is true, where's the lawsuit?"

"That goes back to documentation. Proof, as it were. Which, I believe, you can recognize is not a strong point in your story." She stood up. For a short lady, she seemed pretty tall at the moment. "And, I will point out to you that this high school is an educational institution. I am trying to teach you, Hank, and you, Henryk, what good journalism is. Not how to sell papers. I also think that we should be fair to Mr. Slate, even if, uh, some people are less than enamored with his administrative and personal style. Ms. Kathleen Wells is not going to preside over a student newspaper that tries to hang someone unfairly. Period. Facts, gentlemen. Supporting facts. All the details, in black and white. No doubts."

Ms. Wells stood there waiting for us to, well, something. She didn't seem to have more to say, and we certainly couldn't think of anything that would help. Hank looked at me, and I him. It was time to cut our losses. We both stood up. Hank didn't try his best smile this time. "Sorry, Ms. Wells. I guess I got pretty excited about the story. The facts in the story." He wasn't giving up. "But, I can see that there's more to the story. I'll try to find the answers to your concerns." That was pretty diplomatic, and it almost worked.

"Well." Ms. Wells held out her hand for Hank's copy of the story. "We'll see." He handed it to her.

"Nice to meet you, Ms. Wells," I stammered out as we backed out of the room.

In the hall on the way to our lockers, Hank was quiet. Before we split, he said, "I wonder what's going on? You think she's covering for Slate?"

"Honestly, Hank? Didn't you hear a word she said?" I had to admit to myself that the thought had occurred to me also, but I was pretty sure that she was not a fan of Slate. "She actually did have a point about getting all the facts lined up. All the background supporting stuff she talked about. And, she didn't say we couldn't hang Slate, just that we couldn't do it unfairly."

He was not going to give this up. "Well, maybe. But I think we, student writers that is, have got rights, too. She can't just censor us because she doesn't like the truth."

"I don't think that's what she said. I think she said we needed to have better proof. Absolute proof. Especially the fraud part. I think we should talk to my dad tonight. See what he says." I headed to my locker.

"Don't forget my dad's picking us up, along with Terry, to go see Grams."

"Right. We'll be at the usual pick-up spot. See you."

CHAPTER 35

Terry S., Therapist

Terry and I, and his guitar, sat in the back. Hank started work on the game immediately. "Lose one turn while your mother sits down on park bench to calm herself after someone starts a complaint to her with the phrase, "You people...""

NT looked startled in the mirror, "That happen to you, Hank. And your mom? When?"

Hank looked at him, "Uh, yes and no. It was a long time ago. I was in maybe fourth grade. We had been shopping somewhere, and we were pulling out of the parking spot when this older white dude slams on his brakes, screeches his tires, all that, and starts yelling at Mom about not paying attention when she's driving. I mean, really. She was slowly backing out of a space, and this guy's in a big hurry I guess, and he almost hits her with his car."

"But he didn't, right?" I asked. NT was not looking happy. Terry looked puzzled.

"No, of course not. But he threw a fit. And he either said the phrase 'you people' or otherwise made it clear to Mom that her 'Negro-ness' was the cause of all this." Hank made air quotes and tried to laugh as he said this. "Lose a turn or go back one space."

NT relaxed a little. "You know, I think that happens to us a lot. So much that Sandra didn't even bother to mention it to me." He was looking in his rearview mirror at Terry and me. "By the time she got home, she'd probably gotten over it, sort of, and gone on to more important things. But it obviously hurts, and it made an impression on our young trumpet playing friend up here. So much that he remembers it years later."

Terry got a word in, "Lose a turn? Move back one space?"

"Oh, sorry, Terry. It's a game my dad and I, and I guess Ryk, are working on. The working title is Indignities, but some people think it should be Ironies, and now I'm beginning to think it ought to be Injuries." Hank read Terry's confusion and explained the game some more, pointing out other examples we had come up with on our trips to Carl's.

"Okay, so it would be sort of like when your white friends call you a 'wigger' because they think you're acting black or something and have black friends." Terry had caught on.

"Yeah," I said, "that would qualify."

"And the flip side of that coin," NT pointed out. "Calling a black dude an 'Uncle Tom' or plain old 'Tom' because someone thinks he's too close to the white folks."

"Or 'acting too white' by studying hard and getting good grades." Hank clearly had to deal with this issue. "Either way, back a space," Hank and I said practically in unison.

"How about what Phillis told us at dinner last night, Dad?"

"About her government teacher? The old history books? That would be a place where somebody puts MLK's in the pot, like we talked about the other day."

I had no idea what they were talking about. "History books? Earning MLK's?"

"Okay. Last night Phillis told us that her AP government teacher was ranting in class about how they teach history in American schools. He was telling the class that most history classes, and state exams, seem to be trivial pursuit efforts rather than getting at why things happen, and he said the history books themselves were inaccurate. He told them that when he went to school the American history book they used kind of glossed over slavery, made it seem like the slaves were unpaid servants, but not really that bad off."

NT added, "Yeah. I think that's about what we had in the books when I was in school."

"Well, what set the teacher off was that at least one text-book that's being used right now in some school systems is more or less saying the same thing. He said that in any case, nearly every single textbook in the U.S. is basically white history with sidebars mentioning the contributions of other races. Things like thousands of lynchings and race riots that killed hundreds of black folk never get mentioned at all. My sister couldn't believe it."

"So, MLK's?" Terry was still questioning.

"Sure, because the teacher's being a good guy and trying to stop, or at least complain about mistreatment. Positive points for positive attempts." Hank continued, "KK's, negative points, for the school administration that bought the books with the racist history."

"So, cuz, if the player gets slammed by something, like DWB, he moves back a step or two. But if he's helped by a community effort, say a mass protest by whites and blacks together, then MLK points go into a common pot."

"Or, if straights and gays protest together, that would earn MLK's, right?"

I think NT realized that the game was getting away from him, expanding into more concerns than he and Hank had originally been looking at. "Yeah, something like that, Terry. We haven't worked it all out yet. We're just playing with the ideas right now." He turned into the rehabilitation center parking lot. "Let's go see how my mother's doing today. Terry, grab your guitar. Boys, I think there's a limit on the number of visitors in the room at once, so Hank and I will go in first, then Henryk and Terry. I don't know how long we're going to be, so you might want to bring along some school work for while you're waiting." He held up a paperback book, "I've got my new friend Huckleberry here to entertain me while I wait."

Terry looked at me with a question, but I cut it off. "Tell you about it some other time, Terry. It's kind of a complicated story."

Terry and I found a couple seats in the waiting area and plunked down. The place seemed nice enough. There were railings everywhere, and all the furniture seemed heavy. I guessed all this was to give people something to lean on as they worked on walking. I was expecting the whole place to be one mass of dull green, but it wasn't. Not that it was particularly colorful, but there were different shades of light colors on the walls and the furniture. There were a number of people walking, or rather trying to walk, with aides next to them. I could hear a few clear words from some of the patients, but a lot of what I heard seemed pretty garbled. It hit me that I was really, really nervous about seeing Grams in her new condition. Terry clutched his guitar between his knees and said nothing, staring. We didn't open books for quite a while.

Finally, Hank and his father came down the hall. "Your turn, guys. Terry, I told her you're here, and she brightened up. Expecting a master concert, I'm sure. No pressure, kid!" NT laughed and pointed down one of the hallways. "Room D 104, can't miss it."

Grams looked great. You wouldn't know she'd had a stroke if you didn't know she'd had a stroke. Until she tried to talk, of course. Her mouth moved, but all that came out were sort of low sounds. She seemed happy to see us and hugged us both. Terry and I didn't know what to say, but she filled in with her hands, she pointed to the guitar case and made playing motions.

Terry took out his guitar and tuned it. Grams looked at him expectantly, so without saying anything, Terry started playing. I recognized the first song, "Amazing Grace," even before he started to quietly sing it. He kept his voice low and sang slowly. Grams nodded her head in time to the tune and seemed to be trying to mouth the words. I had no idea what the next tune was, but Grams was pleased and again followed along. I knew Terry could play, but I had no idea he could sing as well. And, of course, old gospel songs were the last thing I would have expected to hear from him. When he finished the song, he looked at me and at the door, and I took the hint.

"Well, Grams, I better let you two enjoy this on your own. You're looking great, really great." She was smiling as she waved me out the door. Terry started another tune immediately, and I almost thought I heard her making sounds with it as I left. I pulled the door shut so the music wouldn't disturb the whole hall.

In the lounge area I plunked down next to NT, who seemed engrossed in *Huckleberry Finn*. He stopped, though, and looked at me.

"She's good, Mr. Jones. Really good. They're going at it like old pals. I left because they seemed to want to do their own thing without me." I started flipping through my English reading assignment.

"She's? Is she singing?"

"Not quite, but she was keeping time and trying to sing the words." I know he was hoping for a miracle, and so was I, but I don't think anyone really knew how it would play out.

A half hour later, NT shifted around uncomfortably. "Well, we're going to have to interrupt the songfest. I've got to get you guys home, get us all home to dinner, and I've got work tonight." He and Hank went back to the room to collect Terry and say their goodbyes.

Everyone was very quiet on the ride home. No one made any suggestions for the game. We all just looked out the windows.

Hank texted me just as dinner was ending and asked if he could come over to talk with my dad. I asked for ten minutes to finish picking up after dinner and went to work on the dishes.

By the time Hank got to my house, I had cornered Dad and filled him in on our journalistic efforts. I couldn't tell if he was more impressed with our initiative or more nervous about his possible involvement.

"So, Hank, what exactly are you asking me?"

"Well, Mr. Jonasz, it seems to me that we student writers should have as much right to publish the truth as any other newspaper. Just because we're high school students shouldn't mean that we don't have rights."

"I did some research on this a few years back when we had a client who was convicted on the basis of bad evidence, either witness perjury or a forced fake confession, I can't remember, but his daughter had started this big publicity thing that included trying to put a story about her father in her high school paper. There was a big stink since the school authorities didn't want to publish something that made the local prosecution office look bad. We got in contact with a group called the Student Press Law Center, and they kind of took over that part our case. What I remember best is that there is some case law that supports each side. There is a lot of push and pull on what constitutes disrupting the good order of the school versus students' rights. Also, for obvious reasons, the school system doesn't want to be in the position of having to defend itself in a libel suit if the student paper publishes something false. Essentially, though, if you're talking about publishing an article in a regular school student newspaper, the authorities have a fair amount of latitude about what they decide to allow."

"So, in short, do we have rights or not?"

"In short, Hank, yes and no." I think Dad was trying not to laugh. "It's complicated. Henryk said your sponsor more or less told you to get more documentation and proof?"

"Yes, but I'm not sure she would let us publish the story anyway." Hank sounded pretty angry, very unusual. "She's just going to cover for him."

I tried to step in, "I'm not so sure about that, Dad. She sounded to me like she didn't want the paper to be wrong rather than just trying to kill the story."

Hank shot me a dagger look. "Whose side are you on, Ryk?" He folded his arms. "You know, and I know, and your dad knows that the story is accurate. Slate has three fraudulent diplomas hanging on his wall. Period."

Dad jumped back in. "Yes, all that may be true. And you could certainly publish the information on your own, online, in a blog or something. And the school system might or might not come after you. If you couldn't prove everything, like your sponsor suggested, you could be in big trouble. Slate could sue you. The school system could claim you were being disruptive and harming someone and do all kinds of nasty things about it."

"But what if it's all true?"

"You're still stuck with defending yourself, hiring lawyers, all that. You'd win in the end if the story is accurate, but there'd be a lot of noise, expensive noise, along the way."

I was trying to figure out where this was going. "So, if Hank does this on his own, he's on his own?"

"Unless that student press group helps me?"

"Well, yes, Hank. That's about the size of it. And they aren't going to help you just because you publish a story and get sued. The school system would have to come after you with big guns to get the Center to see this as a rights case."

"Or," I said, "Hank could get all the proof Ms. Wells wants and get her to let the *Reporter* publish. There'd be safety in numbers. You'd have the school on your side."

Hank finally relaxed a bit. "Yes. Some of the school, anyway. And I guess either way I've got to have the story nailed down so tight no one could object."

"Ah. There's an idea." Dad was definitely grinning. "Find the facts. Prove they're facts. Let the chips fall where they may. By the way, I'd appreciate it if you would stick to Henryk's story about seeing the funny diplomas on Slate's wall himself, and leave me out of it." He had a good point. If Slate thought he could claim this was some sort of Jonasz family vendetta against him, it would just cloud the story.

"Yeah. We're not getting Mel involved, either," Hank agreed.

"Mel?"

"Long story, Dad. I'll tell you sometime. Don't worry," I saw his darkening face, "nothing nefarious. We're all good on this." I was starting to sound like Frankie, and he probably noticed.

Hank glanced at his phone, checking the time, and stood up. "Well, Mr. J, thanks a lot for listening. I guess I'll have figure out what might work best. I sure don't want you or my family dragged into some sort of war with the school system."

"But you do want the truth to get out?" I said it, but Dad's nod told me he was thinking it, too.

Hank headed out the door to his house, and I went upstairs.

I knocked on Terry's door and stuck my head in. No music. Only the clicking of computer keys. Terry had his headphones on. "What're you up to, Ter?"

He stopped and turned to me. "It's Grams." He looked like he was about to cry. "You know how I had been going over to their house for a couple weeks now, and we'd been doing her old gospel songs and talking. Well, she was carrying me, man, totally carrying me. I don't know half the stuff I was playing. I just faked it while she worked out the tune and sang the words. Now, she can't sing, not yet anyway, so I don't have the foggiest notion of what I'm doing. I got through about two, maybe three, songs at the rehab center this afternoon, and it was all downhill after that. I tried to fake my way through, but I was lost. Majorly lost. She kind of hummed along, and I could pick up some of what she wanted me to play, but it was ugly. That's u-g-l-y in caps and underlined."

"So?"

"So now I'm trying like a mother to figure out a bunch more of her songs. I don't know the exact names of these tunes, of course, so if I find one that might be right, I play a piece of it, and if it sounds like something we did together, I find the music and words. If I pick one I don't recognize, I move on. Did you know that there's about a zillion gospel songs out there? When you say gospel songs, everyone thinks of two or three well-known ones, like 'Amazing Grace' or 'Go Tell it on the Mountain' or 'Swing Low Sweet Chariot.' That's like claiming you know all about the history of African Americans because you've heard of Martin Luther King and Harriet Tubman. I've got probably a hundred here that I should learn to cover what Grams knows."

"Terence Patrick Sullivan, punk rocker and gospel musicologist."

"Don't laugh. Some of these gospel musicians are making serious money."

"And they all got their start in rehab centers."

"Whatever, cuz. When do we go to the rehab center next?"

"My guess would be tomorrow. NT will be going over after he gets up, and I'm sure he can wait until we get out of school and take us all over there."

"I'm pretty sure Grams would like that. Make that I'm positive. Can you let Hank and NT know while I'm working on my gospel repertoire?" I pulled out my telephone and started to text them. He looked at the door. "I bet you can do that in almost any room of the house, can't you." He turned back to his computer, and I took the hint.

CHAPTER 36

Hunky Dory

Wednesday morning, I met Hank on the way to the bus. "So, how's the story going?"

"Well, with what your dad said, and what Ms. Wells said, I've got a lot to do."

"Make that, WE?"

"Okay, yes. WE have a lot to do. That is, if you still want any part of this. It's kind of turning into a big mess. Actually, a lot of things are turning into a mess."

"Such as?" I got a terrible feeling in my stomach. "It's not Grams, is it? She is getting better, right? Not worse?"

"Oh nothing new with Grams, much."

"Much?"

"Yeah. You know how last night you texted my dad and me that Terry wants to play for her some more? Well, it seems that Dad thinks it's a great idea. Dad wants to pick up Terry and take him over to the rehab center right after school. He's going to talk to the doctors today, but I'm betting they'll go along with whatever Dad wants."

"Great, I'll tell Terry, and we can meet in the regular spot."

"Well, actually, the invitation is for Terry." Hank looked across the street. "That's Terry, as in, not you, not me. Terry.

Dad's already texted him, I think. Already set it up."

I was kind of surprised, "Well, this is weird, but, on balance, okay." I wasn't sure why Hank looked unhappy. "Whatever helps Grams is good, right? Probably good for Terry, too. Besides, it'll give you more time to work on the story."

"I'd rather see Grams than worry about a story."

"So would I, but I guess we'll just go with the flow, right?" The bus was coming down the street.

Hank tried to look cheerful "Go with the flow." He turned towards the bus, "and that flow includes a girl in the fourth or fifth row on this bus."

At lunch, Hank seemed to be over being left out of the visits to the rehab center. "I spent some useful time in history class."

"Paying attention, taking notes, doing all that A plus student stuff?" I asked.

"Well, making notes. This is what you need to go research first. Maybe your dad can hook you up with some online resources you can get into that will help us out. He may also have some information on those old cases you told me about." He handed me two pages of notes.

"And while I'm doing this, you're going to be hammering away at this story? Or chasing down the girl in the fourth or fifth row?"

He did an exaggerated 'who me?' gesture. "Moi? I am going to multi task. I've got plenty to do, also. You take care of finding that stuff we need, and, if you can squeeze it in, see Mel. Me, no problem, my man!" He waved a sheaf of notes at me. "Busy, busy, busy!" He headed down the hall. "See you on the bus."

As it turned out, he was pretty busy with the girl in the

fifth seat, so we didn't talk on the way home. I cornered my dad after dinner. By then I had a specific list of questions that I might have been able to pursue on the internet by myself, but I knew the legal information, cases and citations and all that, would be on data bases I had never even heard of, much less had access to, so I handed it off to my dad.

"You guys are serious about this, aren't you, Henryk?"

"Of course. In for a dime, in for the whole dollar, you always tell me. I can chase down a lot of things, but ..."

"But this takes an expert. And a lot of time."

"Well, you could excuse me from school tomorrow and take me into your office and let me do it."

"So, the good news is that you are finally getting an interest in your old man's job, but the bad news is that you want to skip school to learn it. If this were summer time, you'd be in the office, no question." He grinned, "Actually, it would take me longer to teach you how to find all this than it would be for me to do it. I'll just kiss my lunch goodbye and see what I can find." He paused a beat. "But, here's the deal. Next summer, when you really are available, you agree to come in with me and get a little education."

"Sounds fair to me, Dad." Who knows, it might be interesting, and he would probably forget all about it by then anyway.

I caught up with Mel Thursday at lunch. "Hey, Mel. How's it going?"

"Hi, Henryk, Ryk. It's going well." I waited for her to say more.

Small talk was not her "thing," so there was silence. I focused on my lunch for a minute or two. Then she surprised me. Maybe herself, too.

"How is Hank's grandmother?"

"She's doing okay, I think. She's out of the hospital and in a rehab center. She can't talk, but she seems to be able to move around pretty well, and, I guess, her brain is working the way it's supposed to. I think not being able to talk is driving her crazy. I know it would me."

"That sounds, uh, terrible. Strokes can cause so much damage. She could have developed any number of problems, but not being able to talk is…" Mel let her voice drift to a stop. She took a bite of her food. She looked at me and smiled. "So, how was that?"

"How was what?"

"My follow up to your statement about Hank's grandmother. Did it sound right? Is that what I should have said?"

I wondered if she has rehearsed it, although it didn't sound rehearsed when she said it. "Yes, Mel. That was right. It was fine. Why do you ask?"

"That was new. Asking about someone like that. My therapist thinks my next step in my quest, well my mother's and the therapist's quest, is to learn how to show an interest in someone and create a relevant response to what I hear, but not go on too long. A year ago, I would not have asked about Hank's grandmother. What do you all call her? Grams? And, if you had told me about Grams, I would have probably just have said 'That's nice' and hoped I didn't have to deal with it. Of course, a year ago, I didn't know you, and I wouldn't have talked to you, or anyone, unless forced to."

"In that case, I'm glad it's now. And I'm glad you're talking to me. And, yes, I can see how you would want to learn how to carry on little conversations with people. I guess it's automatic for a lot of people."

She actually smiled, again. "That's what they say. Not automatic for me, but I think I can learn to create the proper illusion." That was a good way to put it. I would have said, "Fake it," but I guess that's what we all do sometimes, and I suppose for Mel, it's most of the time. I never thought about having to think about how to talk in an everyday setting. I certainly think about what to say when I'm dealing with adults and/or trying to keep my version of a story under control. Probably came automatically to Frankie. And here was Mel trying to think about a simple conversation with no life-changing possibilities.

Crate sat down. "Howdy, folks. What's cookin'?"

"Cooking?"

"Crate just asked how is it going, in his own way, Mel. Trying to be different, not confusing."

"Oh. Yes, of course. It's going well, Crate. And for you?"

Crate grinned, looking mostly at me. "Hunky dory, Melantha, hunky dory." I'm pretty sure he did that on purpose. I've never heard anyone younger than my parents use that phrase outside of some dialogue in an old, old play. I knew I'd have to translate. Idiomatic expressions and clichés were going to do us in, I was sure.

She passed. "I'm glad to hear that, Crate. Things are going okay for Ryk, too." She actually had deciphered the phrase without a look of puzzlement. Amazing. I think Crate was disappointed.

"Your buddy's gone, Ryk."

"My buddy?"

"You know, the guy from the fight club. Walter."

"Oh? Not my buddy, as you say, but how do you know?"

"Heard it from someone, I don't know who. One of his crew was running his mouth in the hall."

"How is he gone? Was he arrested?"

"No. Just gone. It sounded like he took his dad's truck

and split. His buddy seemed pretty confused about the details. I don't guess he'll get too far. What? Seventeen and no money and a suspect in a murder case. Pretty easy to find him, if the cops want to. Geniuses, all of that bunch. Pure geniuses. I don't know what the criminal element is coming to these days."

"Definitely beyond help," I agreed, thinking about the help I had provided. I wondered where Walter was headed off to, wondered if he had any sort of plan or just left. I guessed that Thirsty would now be the big wheel in that crew. I didn't think he had any particular problem with me, so I would be okay. I'd stay as far as possible from that bunch in any case. Time to change the subject. "So, Crate did you connect with that outlet for your super powers?"

"Sadly, no. She has a boyfriend." He glanced around the cafeteria. "But, as they say, there's more than one starfish in the sea."

Mel looked blankly at me, then seemed about to ask a question but thought better of it.

"It's okay, Mel. Just Crate being Crate." She nodded and went back to eating. Crate and I talked about nothing, maybe football or something for a while, and then the tone ending lunch sounded. "Later, Crate. Later, Mel." She again looked like she was about to ask, but didn't.

I took the bus straight home that afternoon. Since I had talked to my dad Wednesday night, I wanted to get my homework out of the way in case he had information for me to work with. When my dad got home, he greeted me with a stack of printouts of old cases and a list of more websites that I would need to look into. Terry got dropped off by NT. At dinner we were both pretty quiet, a sure-fire way to ignite my mother's interrogative spirit.

She started on me first, "So, Henryk, how is school going?"

"Okay. Nothing exciting. Walter seems to have left town, according to rumor."

"How on earth did he do that? He's seventeen."

"I don't know, Mom. I heard he took his dad's truck and left. Someone told me that he overheard one of his crew talking. I don't know any more than that."

Satisfied, she turned her guns on Terry. "How about you, Terry, nothing exciting in your school day also?"

"Oh no, Aunt Mary. Everything was pretty normal." He looked at me and seemed to be debating whether or not to volunteer any more information than required. "I saw Hank's grandmother today. Grams."

"And?"

"And she's getting better, I think." I think he was beginning to regret even this tidbit. He should have realized that given the slightest crack in the wall, Mom would push through for more facts.

"How do you know?"

I decided to help Terry. He really wasn't into the hero thing, and what he was doing was actually pretty cool. "Terry's been playing his guitar for Grams at the rehab center. Playing her old gospel songs."

Dad jumped in on this. "And she's singing them? I thought she couldn't talk."

"Not yet," Terry said, "but she's keeping time and trying to mouth the words. I keep thinking she's going to bust loose any minute, but so far, nothing."

"But she knows the songs you're singing?"

"Playing mostly. Yes. It's like they are right there but won't quite come out."

"Wow. That's amazing, Terry. I didn't know you even knew her, and I certainly wouldn't picture you playing church music." Dad was genuinely surprised.

Terry grinned for a split second. "Well, Uncle Tomás, I guess we're all full of surprises. And, I'm a musician. Musicians play music, and gospel is the music Grams needs right now."

"He's going to get her into alternative rock when she gets better," I suggested.

"Or not," said Terry.

We finished dinner, Terry and I cleaned up, and I got to work on the material Dad brought me. I could hear Terry working out yet more gospel songs in his room as I went to mine.

CHAPTER 37

Games
People Play

By Friday, things were approaching normal. The doctors decided that Grams could recuperate at home as well as at the rehab center. I wondered if NT had talked the doctors into this, since it would mean that Terry could go to play for Grams more easily. NT brought Grams home Friday morning, and Hank got his long-postponed lesson with Carl. I was invited to come along.

Surprisingly, NT started working on the game almost as soon as the doors were shut. "Two officers, both lieutenant colonels, get busted for DUI on the army post within days of each other. One gets a written reprimand, obviously something you don't want in your permanent record. The other one is told orally not to do it again. As far as anyone could tell, these were first time offenses for both. Both of them could have been put through a low level form of court martial, very serious and career ending, so it could have been worse. The one who got written up decided that since he had his twenty years in, retirement might be a good option at that point."

I could see where this was going. "And, oddly enough, the write-up went to the black officer, and the white guy skated."

"Really, Dad? Did that happen to you? You got busted for DUI?"

"No, you idiot. I was never an officer; I worked for a living. I was a sergeant, remember." He was laughing. "And, for the record, I was never, that is NEVER, busted for DUI."

"Sorry, Dad. I should have known." Hank was laughing, too. "So, how did you find out about all this?"

"I was the arresting MP in both cases."

"Ah. I don't suppose you just happened to be in the right place at the right time?"

"Secret of good police work. Try to go where the crime is. In this case, I figured out that people were leaving the officers' club in less than pristine driving shape, so I sort of hung out along the road where I thought they might roll down. Kind of like hunters who set up their hunting blinds near a watering hole or food source."

"So what happened? Did you get in trouble?"

"No. Not really. My captain kind of looked at me funny when I brought the second guy in, the white guy, but he didn't say anything. A couple of my buddies thought it was pretty funny." Looking in the rearview mirror, I could see him frown slightly. "Some of the white MP's thought I was getting even or something, to make up for busting the first colonel, the black one. Of course, when we found out what happened to the two colonels, it wasn't so funny. And then my black buddies were pretty upset about the difference in the punishment."

Hank spoke up, "So, KK's for the army, and lose a turn for the arresting officer?"

"Something like that, I guess. I saw a lot worse raced-based things in the army, but I also saw a lot of good people trying to do the right thing. Not ready to hand out MLK's, though." He drove silently for a moment, and then said, "I've got another one, along those lines, from working at the same army base, but this has a twist. A black prisoner, a handcuffed prisoner, gets the holy stuffing beat out of him by a couple of white MP's. Broken jaw, teeth knocked out, denied him medical treatment for two days. Everyone knows it happened, but, oddly enough—"

Of course, we fell for this; Hank finished for his dad, "And the unit commander just couldn't see it in his heart to discipline his men."

"No, he couldn't. The kicker, though, is that the unit commander was black. That sorry captain covered for his boys. I guess he thought he'd have problems with the other white MP's if he did anything. Actually, what happened was almost all the MP's, white and black, were disgusted and one MP, a white one I think, mentioned it to someone, so eventually the captain got moved on to another assignment. There's another thing about that so-called officer; he would put misbehaving prisoners on a week of nothing but celery and water. You can imagine the kind of misery that would cause to a person's innards. I guess he was just old school rotten to the core. I'm not sure how you hand out KK's or MLK's on this one."

"This one won't get MLK's either," I said. "My mom's cousin lives in one of the southern states, don't remember which one, and this happened to him just last fall. He's a member of a country club, well tennis and pool club, not too big, and he invited a friend of his to play tennis with him. When they walked up to sign in and get a court, the clerk and then the manager claimed mom's cousin wasn't a regular member and couldn't bring in a"

Hank finished for me, "a guest. Who happens to be of the black persuasion. How did it turn out?"

"Like I said, no one earned an MLK here. My mom's cousin fussed with the board, and they allowed as how maybe that the manager made a mistake, just a mistake mind you. Something to do with computerizing the membership records and some confusion."

"So the computer gets the KK's?" NT was turning down Carl's street.

"Blame it on the computer!" Hank said. "That's our next try at a dynamite game: Things that get blamed on the computer that clearly are the result of human intention."

"Complicated title for a game, son." NT stopped the car in front of Carl's house. "We'll be in directly."

I had started to open my door. I quickly pulled it shut. I knew the drill. "Yes sir?"

"I told you, cut out that 'sir' stuff. And relax; you're not in trouble. Not much, I guess."

Well, that was encouraging. Not much trouble, but some? I didn't remember doing anything particularly criminal for over a week, unless you count my little raid into Slate's office.

"I have a funny story to tell you, Henryk. I was talking to detective Watson the other day. He had to swing by the jail to see some brigands. These particular rascals got caught on a camera he had set up at the Anderson house after a break-in there. The camera caught these dudes a day or two after the department went back in on that tip and cleaned out the military grade weapons." He was studying my face by way of the rearview mirror as he told me this. I worked on blank face. Where was this going? "He said that there had been an earlier break-in, just before he got the anonymous tip about the weapons. Those guys were smarter than the bunch he caught. The first bunch blinded the camera with bright lights and towels or something, so he didn't get a look at those individuals."

I was really glad that Hank wasn't there. He would have fidgeted his way into a complete confession. Actually, once I thought about it, I really wondered why NT was going at me alone. Did he already know? Had he already gotten the information out of Hank? Was this some kind of a test for me? I decided that this was a "What would Frankie do?" moment, so I played dumb and hoped for the best. "Wow, that's something. No wonder police get gray hair. Always something." I remembered that someone had noticed that when I get nervous, like when I try atrocious deception, I talk too much, so this time, for once, I clammed up.

I guess NT bought it. "Just thought you'd be interested. You think your buddy Walter might have been one of those other individuals that Watson didn't exactly catch on camera?"

"Well, he's not my buddy, but, yeah, it could be him. One of the guys in his crew seems to have half a brain. The rest are idiots, probably including Walter. Don't tell them I said so." I managed a weak laugh.

"I don't supposed you know his name? The relatively smart one." So this conversation was all about Watson chasing down Walter and witnesses and criminals in general, and not about me and my recent criminal behavior. It was about getting me to snitch on Walter's bunch without any witnesses, Hank included. I appreciated that. A lot.

"Okay. I think they call the semi-smart one Thirsty. Semi-moron might be a fairer description. I have no idea what his real name is, but when Walter disappeared, he seemed to take over. His hassled me a little in the restroom one day. Oh, nothing serious." I interrupted my explanation to reassure NT, his face starting to erupt in anger. "They just wanted to make sure I wasn't talking to anyone about anything I knew about Walter or me getting hit. I told them that I understood the health benefits for me if I kept my mouth shut, and they let me go. I just felt like Thirsty was in charge that day."

"I'll pass the name on to Watson. I'll tell him I heard it in the jail. It won't get back to you. Let's go listen to some decent trumpet. It's been a while."

On the way home, Hank picked up the game again. "This was one my teacher told me about, here in this area. Back in the early 60's, maybe '64, this high school around here was going to have its annual junior-senior prom at a local big-name hotel. A day or two before the big event, the hotel found out that the school was integrated and there would probably be Negroes, as they put it in those days, at the prom. The hotel told the students they would have to disinvite the black students. The kids in the school gave the collective finger to the hotel and moved their prom into their gym. I don't know what happened to the money they paid up front, and all that. But it made a little splash in the papers."

"That sounds like an MLK situation," I said. "I assume the hotel is long gone?"

"Nope. One of the biggest names in the industry, but, I'm sure totally reformed."

"Or not. But better," NT added. "You know, my high

school came along a while after all that. The city had to integrate before that, but there had been all kinds of battling back and forth over boundaries, and busing, and treating the schools evenly. They'd had enough of that, so eventually they just combined all the high schools into one big school; they put all the juniors and seniors into one building. You might have seen the movie about the football team when they did this. *Remember the Titans*, I believe it was called. I wasn't on the team that year, but I was a few years later."

"MLK's again, right, Dad?"

"Yeah. I'm not saying it wasn't a mess, and a lot of stuff going down that should have earned a few KK's, but in the end, it's pretty much worked out. The school has had its ups and downs, but what school doesn't these days." He turned into his driveway, and I hopped out.

"Catch you later, Hank."

Hank came over after dinner, and we started in on the article. He had brought his laptop, so we both could dig into the sources my dad had given me. We could hear Terry working away at the gospel music. I had never thought much about Terry and his music. When he told my dad he was a musician, so he makes music, I was surprised. I just assumed that it was his own personal refuge when his world got to be too much, but it was more than that. I don't think he had much, if any, formal music instruction, but he really worked at learning it. He was learning about gospel for himself as much as he was for Grams. This was do-it-yourself therapy. It seemed a lot better than "self-medicating" as they call it when someone with problems smokes pot all day or uses alcohol or some other drug to deal with the world. Come to think of it, I don't believe he had hung out with his doper friends since he got involved with Grams, even before her stroke.

It rained all weekend, which made it easier to sit inside and fuss with the Slate story. We hammered on every internet door we could find, and there were a lot. Hank had really been stung by the criticism from Ms. Wells, and he was determined to prove his story was good. We didn't have the money to pay for one of those "background" searches by a company promising to expose every secret of your search object going back to childhood, but we did a pretty good job of tracing Slate's educational and professional path. And, of course, we found information on the diplomas on his wall. So much, that we were overwhelmed at first. We became mini experts on the diploma mill business. We had copies of the state requirements for teachers and administrators. We maxed out on everything. We had way too much for a high school newspaper article, but Ms. Wells had made it clear that we had to have enough backup to fight off any threat of a lawsuit. We even studied the Student Press Law Center site so we would have some chance of defending our argument that the story should be printed. By Sunday night we thought we had everything under control. And, if Ms. Wells wouldn't let Hank's story run in the *Reporter*, we had talked ourselves into starting our own blog and leading off with the story. We weren't sure how to get proof that Slate had used the fake diplomas to get his assistant principal job, since we couldn't get into his records in the school system's personnel department, but we had a plan for that, too. Ms. Wells had steered us in the right direction when she asked if we had contacted the department. We would contact it, and then report that they wouldn't talk to us. And, of course, Hank was going to ask Mr. Slate for an interview as soon as possible on Monday. This time, the uproar we would cause would not leave us feeling like a couple of idiots. It would be Mr. Slate's turn.

CHAPTER 38

A Little Note

O n the bus Monday morning Hank was pumped. I was pumped. "Now," Hank said, "we don't say squat to anyone about this, right? I've still got to get an interview with Slate, and I've got to try to talk to the school system's personnel department. Not that they'll talk to me, but like Ms. Wells said, I've got to get that on record."

"Once you talk to Slate and call personnel, won't the cat be out of the bag?"

Hank smiled, "I'm not going to attack Slate head on. I'm just a student reporter doing a piece on educators."

"You could talk to some of the other assistant principals as a cover. Make it look like you're doing a big general story. It could be called 'The Challenge to Become a Cog in the Middle of School Management.'"

"That's certainly a catchy title. But, you're right, I'll come up with something like that. And I won't really tell personnel what I'm looking for. I'll just ask enough for them to refuse to talk to me. Do you think I should use a fake name and say I'm from another school?"

"No. If you're going to write in your story that you attempted to contact the personnel department to ask for a comment, you want a secretary or someone over there to remember turning you down, not someone else."

"Yeah. And Ms. Wells would probably say it would be unethical. I guess cops and PI's on TV shows can use fake identities to get information, but not honest reporters."

I had a sudden flash, maybe even a good idea. "I wonder if you even need to talk to personnel. Whenever a new teacher or other staff member comes to the school, there's always a little write-up in the *Reporter*. You've done a couple of those yourself already. Why not go back to the year Slate started here and see what the interview says? I bet it will mention where he went to school or something. We know from all our research over the weekend that he came here as an administrator; he wasn't a teacher here first, so somewhere buried in the old copies of the paper there should be an interview with the hot new assistant principal. I bet Ms. Wells has a closet full of the back copies going back to the dawn of creation, or at least the first year of this school."

Hank clapped his hands together so loudly other students looked at him. "Brilliant!" They were still staring, so he covered, "That's the way to beat the Xenon prince. I should have thought of it myself." I hoped there was no such thing as a Xenon prince in any video game the kids on the bus were familiar with. And I hoped that if there was such character, he needed beating. Hank lowered his voice. "Okay. So, we're getting there. All I have to do is talk my way into an interview with Slate."

"And come up with a story for the personnel department. And talk to another assistant administrator or two for cover."

"Piece of cake." Well, Hank sounded confident. But I wasn't so sure. "Just got to have that cover story worked out."

"Yeah. It would help if you could use one cover story for everyone you talk to, in case any of the people talk to each other. You know, Hank, you might, just might, consider talking to Ms. Wells this morning. Maybe she could help cover you when you run around asking a bunch of questions."

Hank glared at me, "Yeah? She's going to help me? She's trying to kill the story, remember."

My turn to glare, "No. I do not remember. What I do remember is that she didn't want you to screw up the story by being weak. She wants all the t's crossed and i's dotted. It has to be done right on the first try because there won't be a second chance. Think about it. You run around with some crazy story asking questions, and it gets back to Ms. Wells. She does talk to other teachers, I bet. At lunch, in the work room, somewhere. And then, when she has no idea what her friends are talking about, you've just made her look like an idiot. And not doing much for yourself, either. And there goes your story."

"I'll think about it," was all he would say.

When we split up at school, Hank still didn't have a good story that I knew about, but I was sure he'd come up with something. I, on the other hand, didn't have any specific job to do, other than keep my mouth shut, and, as it turned out, run into Thirsty once again. In the restroom, of course.

"Yo, Jonasz. Got a minute? Of course you do." I was on the way to Algebra class when he waylaid me and guided me into a corner. "Got a message from," he lowered his voice dramatically, "our gone guy."

"Okay?" I thought that was all over now that Walter was out of town, permanently, I hoped. "What's up?" I was keeping my voice as steady as a slight case of terror would allow me.

"Nothing, really. He just mentioned that you were a big help. He didn't say how, but he said you're a stand up dude, and the past is past, so you can chill."

Yeah, I thought, unless Walter comes back or Thirsty gets some idea of how I could help him, too. "Yeah, well, Walter knows what's up, so I guess it's all good." Lame, I know, but really, what could I say?

Surprise. I ran into Crate on the way out of the restroom. I nodded at him and kept moving.

Crate lit into me at lunch. Mel and I were already eating when he banged his tray down across the table from Mel and me.

"What the, oh, hi, Melantha, hell is going on?" His face was red and particularly ugly. "I just saw you talking to one of Walter's boys. I know you said you were okay with them, but I didn't think it meant you were playing with them. I thought you told me they were history as far as you're concerned." I don't think he took even one breath in his blast.

Mel looked as if she might just run off in mid bite. It took me a minute to figure out what Crate was wound up about. "Oh, that. Hi, Crate. How's it going? Hunky dory and all that?" This probably wasn't the best thing to say to him.

He stared at me, glared, really. "Oh it's going just fine, thank you. But what was that all about with what's-his-name in the restroom this morning?" He was leaning away from me, arms crossed, and hadn't even looked at his food.

"Nothing. Thirsty just passed on a message from Walter, telling me that everything was cool and not to worry."

"Yeah. It looked like a friendly conversation. That could lead to as much trouble as an unfriendly one."

"I understand, Crate." First Slate, and now Crate. Why did everyone seem to think I would have anything to do with Walter's bunch? "Honest, Crate. I'm not doing anything with that crew except staying away from them. Everything's good. Really. Everyone's moved on from all that mess, except I still can't do activities in PE because of my head."

Mel looked like she wanted to try out her new social small talk skills, but wasn't sure where to begin. I don't think she knew how to interrupt a conversation, so I helped. "Hey, Mel, what were you telling me about the history teacher you and Crate have?"

Mel took the cue, "Asking, actually. Crate, I was telling Ryk about how Mr. Gates insists on trying to make our class more interesting by coming in on Fridays as some famous person in history. And then we have to guess who he is. Do you think this makes any sense?"

"I don't know. It's different, but it's kind of lame sometimes."

Uh oh. "Lame? His leg?" Mel looked very puzzled.

I helped, "I think Crate means it's sort of silly."

"Juvenile, too," Crate added. "And time consuming. If you do the math, he's spending half an hour every week with this charades game. That adds up to like, fifteen or twenty hours over the year."

Mel was doing great; she came back with a relevant point, "Maybe if he tied his character to what we were studying in class it would make sense. It seems like he's choosing random famous people."

I don't think Crate had ever had or even witnessed a conversation with Mel that lasted this long without her taking off on some long diversion that lost everyone.

I remembered the conversation NT and Hank and I had had when we were talking about Phillis's government teacher. "You know, guys, there is one possibility. I heard that the state history exam is mostly just a big trivial pursuit test. You have to know all these factoids and very important people, according to some test writer. Do you think Mr. Gates is trying to get a jump start on the test by introducing all these randomly important people? Sort of hoping you all will remember them when test time rolls around in May? Is he working off a list?"

Crate nodded, "Yes. That would explain it. There's probably a master list of the fifty most important people in world history. He probably gets a bonus or something if his students get them all right on the exam."

If Hank or NT had been at the table at that moment, they would have been proud of me. "Make that the fifty most important dead white males in history."

Mel jumped on this point, and, unfortunately, went back to her old conversational style. "You are absolutely right, Ryk. My mother has a wall of books on women in history and woman's rights, or the lack thereof." And she was off to the races. She talked without stop on the mostly unrecognized role of women throughout history.

Crate grinned at me and tapped his temple. I tried to look interested, but I did get a bit lost. When the lunch tone sounded, I was happy to escape. "Catch you later, Mel. Crate." Mel looked like she wanted to say something to me, but then just waved me off as she packed up her lunch things. I liked my explanation of the weird doings in their history class and hoped I was right. I also wished my teacher would be that creative. I had the last half hour of Spanish class coming up, and then off to PE where I would sit out the activities of the day. I could always hope that Ms. Wells would get me called out of class, but I didn't have much hope.

I didn't see Hank until we got on the bus.

"I hate to admit it, but I guess you were right, Ryk." Well, that was unusual. "I went to see Ms. Wells during my second period English class. I told her what I wanted to do, and she thought it was cool. We came up with a cover story. If anyone asks, I'm working on an article called, 'It's Not Just Four Years.' I'm going to claim that I'm writing about how a lot of students will actually go to college for four years and then off to graduate school to get more training. I mean, everyone knows that doctors and lawyers and such go a bunch more, but there're a lot of careers that require a master's degree, assistant principal being one of them, of course."

It sounded good to me, "So tomorrow you start talking to a few teachers about their master's degrees, and of course, you talk to a handy administrator; Slate comes to mind."

"Precisely. He'll never know what hit him. And Ms. Wells will back me up. I've already seen Mrs. Hernandez and gotten an appointment with Slate for eight o'clock. That way I can get most of my Algebra class in, get the homework assignment, all that."

"Also, by then Slate should be through with his first round of crazy people." I was thinking about the chaos in that office in the mornings. "He'll be so glad to have a normal student in his office with no problems, he won't even notice where your questions are headed."

"Oh, I'm not going to ask him about his personal diplomas. I just want to get one more peek at those fake diplomas and get him on record saying that assistant principals like him have to have more than a bachelor's degree."

"Don't forget to schedule some appointments with other people in the school, like one of the counselors, maybe the school social worker, and a couple teachers, so it all looks good."

"For sure. Got that covered. My Spanish teacher actually has a PhD, but she told us to call her Señora Willard, not Doctor Willard, anyway. So during homework time, I talked to her for a few minutes. She obviously didn't need the PhD to be a classroom teacher, or even a master's, but she wanted to complete what she started. It was a personal satisfaction thing. And I guess she gets a higher salary, too."

"Did you see her diploma? Is it real? Do we have a school full of frauds?" I was only half joking.

"Actually, I didn't even think of that. Which is funny, considering what this all about. She seems pretty straight. I didn't even ask her where her degree was from. I just asked general questions about trying to work on an advanced degree while teaching. It was all about my cover story to get to Slate without giving away the game."

"Well, after Slate gets nailed, I bet the school system will look at everyone's degree with a magnifying glass."

CHAPTER 39

Tildy

We got off the bus and split up. I couldn't wait to see him at lunch on Tuesday, after his interview with Slate. Luckily, I had a ton of homework to do, especially since I hadn't done anything for Tuesday's classes over the weekend, so I didn't have time to dream of Slate's upcoming surprise. I never thought I'd say luckily I had homework, but there it was. And I was happy to be busy.

Frankie dropped in at dinner time, and I realized that I hadn't seen much of him for the past few days. He'd been hanging out with Tildy when he wasn't at work or school. "Hey, folks, what's up?"

After Mom made her usual fussing noises about his being gone too much, he got to his point. "You all know Tildy, right?"

"Of course, sweetie. Is she okay?"

"Not just okay, the best." He grinned at me, and I wasn't sure how to take his statement. "She's got everything straight now." Well, that was not expected. Frankie letting a cat out of the bag. He knew it, too. He looked at me for support, but I wasn't going to get into this. I didn't want my parents to know that I knew anything not straight about Tildy. I studied my food. My mother's hand went to her mouth. The longer he didn't say anything, the worse it was going to be. He realized he had to fill the silence. "She's doing great. Her student visa situation is A-Okay."

I think my mother thought he was about to announce impending grandparenthood for her, via Tildy. "Oh, my." She looked relieved. "That's nice, dear."

"Visa issues?" My dad had been studying Frankie's face, expecting worse also, I think.

Frankie got himself on track. "Yeah. Really nothing, as it turned out." He went on to explain about Tildy's class being cancelled, but she was able to take another class, online or something, so she wasn't in violation by being less than a full time student. He didn't mention that she was working part time off the books with the catering company, and my dad didn't ask about that. Real criminal behavior, both by miscreants and law enforcement, was his specialty, not bending immigration rules, visa "adjustments," as Frankie would call it.

"Terry," Dad was moving on, "how's Hank's grandmother doing? I understand you're going over there every day."

"Actually, Uncle Tomás, she's doing great."

"Can she talk yet?" I asked.

Terry actually smiled, "Oh no. Not yet, but I think she's getting closer every day. She's almost mouthing the words to the songs, keeping time for sure, and maybe about to start singing again."

"That's wonderful," Mom said. "She's actually engaged in the songs?"

"Yes. Sometimes, it's almost there, other times she looks frustrated as all get out."

"Is she getting home services?'

"Oh yes, Aunt Mary. She's gets like two hours or something every morning. Physical therapy and speech stuff."

"And then, in effect, you're giving her another dose of speech therapy every afternoon?'

"I guess you could say that. Yeah. That's what it is, sort of, I guess. Only I don't know how to tell her how to make words or anything. I just give her something she understands to practice on."

"Hank's grandmother? Talking? Singing? Have I missed something?" Frankie, I realized, was really drifting away into his own life. Our family was not the center of his attention any more.

I filled him in on the story of Grams's stroke and her amazing progress thanks, no doubt, to the heroics of Mel and Terry.

Dad needed to add his two cents' worth, "As far as I can tell, these three teens responded absolutely perfectly to a crazy situation, and the upshot is that they saved Hank's grandmother and family a world of grief. So you see, Frankie, some heroes on white horses don't have to fight to save the world." He still never missed a chance to accuse Frankie of thinking he was a knight in shining armor in his epic battles with various authorities as well as fellow students.

"Thank you, Uncle T. All we really did was what you're supposed to."

"And, Dad, it really was Mel and Terry. I was pretty much just following their instructions. But, I guess it was good that we realized what was going on and got over there fast."

"So what, exactly, are you doing Terry?" Frankie asked, "Your music is, uh?"

Terry seemed more relaxed than he had ever been at our table. "I don't know. Grams liked old gospel music before her stroke; I actually had been playing some for her. And we found out that it seems to help her now with her stroke problems, so I go over there every day and play for her. I'm not going to set the gospel music world on fire, but it works for her."

"We're not going to see an album called 'Reverend T and the punk/metal gospel singers'?"

Terry grinned, "Probably not. For now, I think I'll stick to playing for Grams, an audience of one, I should point out."

After dinner, Terry went upstairs to do homework and/or work on his new music repertoire, and Frankie stayed with me to help clean up.

"So what's up with Terry?"

"What do you mean?"

"I mean, it's like he's a different person than last time I saw him."

"He is. Before, he would fake the cool thing to keep us off his back, but now he's not forcing it. He's totally focused on Grams and getting her better. I suppose the more he fusses with her, the less he thinks about his old life. He was really quiet and down when he first got here, but now, with this Grams project, he's got a mission, and no one better get in his way."

"Cool. Definitely cool." Frankie looked at me with his head at an angle. "You didn't say much at dinner about Tildy. It looked like you were trying to disappear."

"Well, you did ask me to keep it zipped about her visa thing, and I didn't know where your little story was going."

"That's it? No worries?"

"Well, at first I thought you were going to tell us you got married to her. To keep her in the country, but I didn't think you'd tell them that, so I needed to say nothing, just in case."

"Actually, I suggested that to Tildy. She shot me down in a hurry. Never been rejected so fast in my life." He smiled broadly, "But it wasn't a total rejection. She was happy to, uh, practice like we were married, but no ring, and no kids, either. I saw Mom's look, too."

What a mess. Frankie could have set himself up for several legal problems at once. The Anderson murder, if the police circled back to him, and who knows what kind of trouble if the government thought Tildy married him to stay in the US.

I finished my homework late, but still could hardly sleep. I guess Hank couldn't either; he texted me around one. It was a dumb text, all it showed was he was thinking too much, not that I blamed him. He wasn't used to dealing with Slate like I was.

hey, bro, think u get u into my interview with slate tomorrow?

no

y?

cuz he smell a rat 4 sure he not trust any jonasz

so?

so he not know u

im black he no like black people

he no like jonaszes more

so?

so NO!! he sees me and u wont get jack it is late goodnight

And, I didn't answer his next text. He was getting all

worked up at the wrong time of night. I hadn't needed the cops at our house in the middle of the night, and I didn't need to hold his hand all night, either. I'd see him at the bus stop and get him calmed down.

CHAPTER 40

A Snitch's Note

No surprise, Hank looked terrible at the bus stop Tuesday morning. "So, Mr. Bernward, or is it Woodstein? How's the intrepid reporter? Ready to go get that Pulitzer?" Terry had been standing there humming, a gospel song I guess, and he stopped to look at us. No one was in on this, and we needed to keep it that way. "I'm not sure another lunch room exposé is going to get you any awards, Hank."

"You can't keep a good reporter down, my friend." Hank waved his phone at me, "I've got that interview with the lady in charge of lunch, or whatever it is they call that stuff the serve us, and my phone will be in my pocket and recording everything."

Terry went back to humming. Hank took one more shot at me, "You sure you don't want in on the interview?" I guess the idea of faking it was new to him. I suppose lying is an acquired art, like anything else. I knew I could have gone into Slate's office and killed it. I'm not a great liar, not in Frankie's league, but I could have pulled it off. Hank, on the other hand, was scared he'd blow it. And there wasn't much I could do. This was not the uber-confident Hank who always acted like he had the situation under control.

"Not a chance, my friend. The environment there might make me sick or something; it's probably toxic. You'll be okay. Just focus on your story, on your questions. Sell yourself on your story before you go in, and act like you believe it. You'd be surprised how well believing your story makes it easy to sell it to someone else." Terry was looking at me, listening again. "Oh you know Hank. When he gets stuck with something he doesn't want to do, he gets nervous."

"Yeah," said Hank. "I think this cafeteria story is a prank pulled by the senior editor. I bet he's laughing his butt off, thinking about me wasting all this time on a dumb story."

Terry bought this and went back to his musical world. Hank and I didn't talk any more, to be safe. The bus came, Hank flipped a switch, and his pursuit of some girl became the only concern.

I found Hank at the usual place in the lunch room. He was sitting alone. "So," I asked him, "did your pants survive the interview? Didn't have to change them, did you?"

"Of course not. Piece of cake, just like I said." Hank was definitely back to his normal self, had reclaimed his bravado.

"Didn't seem so easy this morning. I thought you were more likely to die or at least lose it." He didn't say anything. "So, seriously, how'd it go? Anything juicy?"

"Maybe a little good stuff. I did record it on my phone in my pocket, but I haven't had time to listen. I tried testing it last night, but the sound may have come through differently from in my room trying to record from a speaker in my computer."

"So what did you get?"

"I got a look at the diplomas. They're still there, big as life and just as phony. And when I asked Slate about education to be a principal, he was kind of funny. He didn't get up and point to the Master's in Administration diploma, but he nodded his head in that direction. It was the same phony one we identified. When I did follow-up questions about the kinds of classes people take to be an administrator, it seemed like he was lost. He couldn't seem to remember the actual names of the courses or tell me what was in them. I think the answers were along the lines of 'You know, administrative stuff, laws and school accounting and stuff.' He did point out that those classes were a long time ago, which is a good cover for someone who never stepped foot inside a class."

We had gone to the trouble of looking up the required courses for MA programs at several universities. We had also looked up the state requirements for an administrative endorsement. I hoped that Hank had been smart enough not to ask any questions that would demonstrate his depth on the subject. We could leave that to lawyers in court, but it felt good to have the background.

"So you pretty much have it on record that he thinks you're supposed to have an administrative master's and that there are courses involved?"

"Oh, for sure. And there are those fakes hanging in there. I'm pretty sure he used them to get his job." Hank sat back. "Next step, one more interview this afternoon, to fill out the cover story, and then, home and write the story to blow him away!"

A couple other students sat down, so we drifted into other subjects. Hank had a make-up lesson with Carl that afternoon, and I invited myself along for the ride.

On the way over Hank started up with the Indignities game again. "I got to thinking about this while I was looking at some old *Reporter* stories." I think this was when he was trying to find an interview with Mr. Slate as a new AP. "I kept seeing these articles about the sports teams, and I realized that you could almost tell the makeup of the school by its name."

"How's that?" NT glanced at Hank in the mirror. "There's tells?"

"Well, not perfect, but, if the school was named after a famous black dude, not a woman, except Harriet Tubman of course, then the school was predominantly black. How many white folks went to a Booker T. Washington or George Washington Carver school when they first opened? If the school started with a lot of white folks, then it was named after a white dude. Except for two women, Sally Ride or Christa McAuliffe, of course."

"True that," said NT. "And none of them named for Nat Turner."

"Well, Dad, he was a little rough on the white folks he came in contact with."

"You better believe it, son. Don't see a whole lot of Malcom X public schools either."

"So," I asked, "Does this show up in the game as points awarded or taken away?"

"Well, I guess you could award MLK's to any community that actually named an all-white school for a person of color." Hank continued, "Actually, I wasn't thinking about the game; I was just noticing. But I do have one for the game. Definitely an indignity. You're having a conversation with an older white dude, like in his forties or fifties, and out of the blue he says, 'You know, son, you are very well-spoken.' I mean, he didn't say, 'Gee, son, you don't sound black.' What can you say, but, 'Thanks.' And you do not add, 'For a person of the darker color, you mean.'"

NT clenched the steering wheel tightly and grimaced. "Please, please, tell me that did NOT happen to you? This is something you read about?"

Hank took the hint, "Oh, no Dad, not me. Yeah. I read about it. In the newspaper. Some politician said that about another one in a debate or something. Everyone went nuts because they were pretty sure the white politician was making a really, really back-handed insult disguised as a compliment." I could see NT looking at Hank in the mirror, but I could signal with my hands out of NT's view. I signaled by pointing at him and mouthing "Slate?" Hank nodded. Hard to say I was surprised. I wondered what else about the interview Hank neglected to tell me at lunch.

I fiddled with pieces of paper lying on the back seat while Hank and his dad discussed the penalties involved in this particular situation. I've always found myself reading things that I have no reason to read. If it's on a poster in the bus, I read it; if it's on a tee shirt, I read it, which can be embarrassing if there's a lot to read or it's on a girl's shirt. No, I'm not staring, I just … can't help reading… If it's sitting there, I pick it up and read it. That's how I ended up reading this note to NT. I saw a piece of folded paper, opened it, and started reading. It looked like one of those notes people are always passing in class.

Deer ofiser Jones. My name is Kent Jones (also). I am in the cellblock where u usully work. I see that u treet everyone pretty good, so I am taking a chanse and writing this to u. I no that my people have to hate u and u have to hate us back, but I think I can trust u. My life here is hell, plane and simpul. Sum of the black guys take turns with me when they get the chanse. Sumtimes it is just a little bit, but sumtimes I have to do a lot. It hurts and its disgusting. There are no other skinheads in this cellblock to help protect me like my frends told me when I got arrested. I terned myself in ackshully. A bunch of us jumped some ragheads and they sed that sinse I don't have a record I shud tern myself in and I wud get out real quick. But I used a bat and that got me in bigger trubel and to much bale money. I have ben her only two days and I cant take it much mor. The Mexicans don't care what happens to me, and they take care of ther own pretty good. I want u to help me get into that protetiv custodee I hear about so these guys can't keep doing me. If u can do this, I can tell u about the killing of one of our members a few weeks back. I don't want to snitch, but I cant live like this. So what can I do?

It wasn't easy reading, and I certainly didn't like to hear about what was happening to this prisoner, but I could see that this was the "Big Break" that always seems to happen just before the commercial in TV shows, except that I don't think they would talk about this on regular TV. I didn't want Hank to know what I found, and I didn't want NT to think I was snooping, so I kept my mouth shut for the rest of the ride. I read the street signs and tried to figure out if there was a logical order to them, like names of presidents, or in alphabetical order, or something. The street names were mostly one or two syllables, the bigger roads, avenues or boulevards and such, were longer words. I think some housing developers named their streets after their daughters or girlfriends or something. There were all kinds of variations on trees, probably the ones they cleared out to build the neighborhoods. I didn't find much of a pattern, but it kept me out of trouble while I thought about the letter. I was sure that NT would never have intentionally accepted anything from an inmate, so I wondered how it ended up in his possession. Maybe the guy stuck in his pocket or something?

When we got to Carl's, it was my turn to start the "drill." "I'll be up in just a few, Hank. I need to talk to your dad about something."

NT had already started to get out of the car, but he slid back in, closed his door, and looked back at me. "Well? New problems with the wannabe bad guys?"

"No sir." Oops, old habit, and I wasn't even in trouble, probably. "This is different. I didn't mean to be nosy, but I was sitting back here, and I, uh, found this." I pushed the note up to him. "It was sitting on the seat here, and I sort of opened it and read it. Sorry."

NT took the note and scanned it. Then he re-read it slowly. "Where did you say you found this?"

"Here. On the seat. Maybe it fell out of your uniform pocket or something?"

"Strange. I sure don't remember anyone giving this to me. I wonder how--? Oh well, these inmates have nothing by time to think up scams and how to accomplish them. I do know this punk, though." His face clouded up again, angry. "You sure you found this in my car, right now? This isn't some complicated thing you're involved in? You and Hank?"

My turn to be angry. "No, sir. I apologize for reading it, but it was just there. I was just looking at the junk back here and ran across it. I don't know what it's about. Or what's going on."

Christopher Wollenberg

NT relaxed a little, "Yeah. Sorry. It kind of shakes me, though. In two ways. One. That kid should not be in danger of any kind in our fine hotel. I can pretty much guarantee that he's not getting harassed on my shift, but, well, I can't be sure what happens other times. Two. I should not have that note. I would never intentionally take a note or anything else from an inmate. That's just a path to disaster, for the jail. It can lead to all kinds of problems, contraband, undue influence, favoritism. I can't figure out how that squirrelly dude got the note in my jacket. You're right, though; that's where it must have been. I usually throw my jacket down where you're sitting when I leave the jail. Oh, and then there's problem three. This sounds like something that Detective Watson needs to know about. This is probably bogus, but it could be something he needs on the Anderson case."

How is it that I keep ending up on the edge of crime scenes? Well, I guess if I purposefully sneak into a crime scene, I can't really claim innocence. But I didn't do anything on this, and here I was. "Okay, NT. What happens next?"

"Hank know about this?"

"No. I covered the paper up. He was busy talking about that idiot and his comment. I didn't think you'd want anyone else to know about this. That's why I said I wanted to stay back and talk to you alone. He probably thinks it's more on Walter's bunch."

"Good thinking. Thank you. And, I assume, you're not inclined to talk to anyone about this? Not Hank or whoever?"

Once again, I had an adult telling me to sit on something, but this made sense. "Of course not. I'll tell Hank I had heard a rumor about where Walter was, but it will be the same news that everyone already knew, that Walter just disappeared, along with his dad's truck."

"Say what?"

Oops. I assumed it was common knowledge. "Yeah, I heard it from someone at school who overheard one of Walter's bunch talking. I don't have any actual information, except that he's apparently gone." Well, of course I did have actual information about Walter's plans and where he got the money for his vacation, but I didn't see any advantage in revealing this. As long as he didn't commit any crimes, I couldn't be on the hook for aiding and abetting or accessory, or whatever. Besides, on balance, I preferred that Walter stayed as far away as possible, so I wouldn't do anything to help get him back in town. To say nothing of the stitches thing.

"Okay, then. I'm going to have to come up with a plan to hustle this kid into a single cell or even another jail where he's safe so Watson can talk to him. You go on into Carl's. I'm going to sit here and think for a minute or two. Maybe call my buddy, Watson."

CHAPTER 41

Game Over

N T came into Carl's front room about ten minutes later. He smiled and gave me a thumbs up sign but didn't say anything. I just sat there and enjoyed the concert.

NT's phone buzzed its message tone, he stared at the screen for a moment, and then snorted. His face darkened, and he looked angrily in the direction of Carl's studio.

When Carl and Hank came out, NT was still angry. Carl was his usual happy self. "Good to see you NT, how's it goin'? You know your boy here can play. For real, man."

"Good. Let's get going, boys." He nodded toward the door, and we started out.

Carl apparently hadn't noticed NT's mood. "How's Eleanor Rose doing?"

NT remembered his manners, and who he was talking to, "Pretty good, Carl. She's home now. Got some problems, but it's lookin' pretty good." We headed to the car.

Apparently, Hank hadn't noticed NT's mood either, and he started up with the game again. "You're wearing a hoodie and walking in a mostly white neighborhood. Unfortunately, you're black, and somehow, no one's quite sure how or why, when you're challenged by the white security patrol type guy, you end up shot dead. Not just a few steps back, end of game for you. KK's to the community that decides that walking while black justifies homicide."

NT's grimaced. He didn't say a word. He's usually a pretty smooth driver, amazingly smooth when you think about it, but he slammed the car around turns and charged up to stops. Hank decided not to pursue this anymore and sat quietly in the front seat while I occupied myself with wondering about the note I had found. When we got to their house, NT slammed the car into the driveway and turned to face us. We didn't open our doors.

"Game's over, fellows. Game. Set. Match. Done. O-V-E-R. It started out as looking at what makes black folks' lives so complicated, and we called it Indignities. Remember one day Hank pointed out what happened to the Irish in New York and Boston and the stuff that's happened to practically every race and religion here in the U.S., and Henryk here talked about how Jews are still on the run in the U.S. Then my mother heard about the game, and thought it was called Ironies. Still okay, pretty accurate assessment of the historical situation except that her stories are horror stories, a lot more than just indignant or ironic. But, really, the game is not a game. It's real life, and it's Injuries. I don't know what possessed me to think this could turn out good." He looked at Hank and then at me. "I know we all thought it was instructive in some perverse way, and maybe it was. Maybe I thought a bit of humor would take the strain off, but it's not funny. Funny doesn't make it hurt any less. Doesn't make it any less threatening. The more we looked at things, listened to my mother's stories, the worse it got. I just got a text message. Seems like we had another cop killing. Total mess, as far as I can tell."

"Not here?" I had to ask.

"Oh no. Down in Texas or somewhere. But, the same elements we keep getting over and over. Cop kills a black kid. Thought he had a gun; it was a cell phone; a twelve year old trying to call his mom. So then some black dude decides that killing some other cop will even the score. So then the cops kill him, and it keeps on going. And going, and going."

"Oh, Dad, did you know any of these guys?"

"Doesn't matter. Got dead kids, dead cops." He looked like he was about to cry. "And here's one for your Ironies game. The cop that killed the black kid was not white, not black either, from some other minority. The cop that got killed was black, though. But that was only because the killer missed his white partner and hit him instead. It gets harder and harder to put on the uniform every day. I'm sharing the same uniform as guys who kill twelve year olds mostly because they're black. I'm wearing a uniform that might as well be painted like a target. Heck, I'm black and that makes me a target anyway. I've got that mess at county to deal with, and all I want to do is crawl in a hole."

What could we say? Hank looked at me and mouthed "Mess at the jail?" but I just shook my head. We sat in silence while we considered the news.

We started to get out of the car when Terry interrupted with his own text, to Hank and me. It was weird, for a second. All it said was, "Amazing Grace." And it had two emojis, one was a smiley face with a wide open mouth, and one showing music notes.

"Dad, wait." Hank was grinning. "You gotta see this."

"Yeah?" Definitely not in the mood for cute.

"No really. I think it's about Grams."

"He glanced at Hank's phone. "What's all this?"

"Don't you get it, Dad? It's from Terry. He's telling us that Grams sang a gospel song. She's singing!" We both said the last part together.

NT broke into a real smile for the first time. "No stuff? For real?"

"What else could it mean?" I put in.

"Well, that doesn't solve the world's problems, but it certainly puts a little light in our corner of the world. Let's go inside and see what's up."

Terry met us at the door with the biggest smile I'd ever seen on his face. Grams was sitting in a chair behind, smiling also. Well, half her face was smiling; part of her mouth looked strange, but her eyes were shining.

"Hi, Mom! I just got the news. You're coming back!"

Grams nodded her head and tried to say something, but it seemed unintelligible to me.

"You bet your sweet, uh, something," Terry translated.

She nodded her head in agreement and said something else I couldn't understand.

NT looked a bit unsure. "Terry, can she or can she not sing?"

"She's getting there, Mr. Jones. "She sang a couple gospel songs pretty well. When I tried to talk to her, ask her a question, it came out like it just did when you talked to her. If you listen real careful, though, you can pick out what she's trying to get across to you."

NT went over to his mother and hugged her. "So, it's a start on a journey, a step or two in the right direction, right?"

She nodded and said, "Yes." Clear as a bell, but the rest I couldn't quite get.

"Wow!" I said. "This is exciting. You go, Terry. You go, Grams!" It was getting late, and dinner would be ready soon at home. "Terry, we probably better get a move on. Mom's expecting us for dinner." We headed out the door. "Call me or text me, Hank, if you want me to look at your, uh, kitchen article."

At dinner, I couldn't wait to tell everyone about the big breakthrough for Grams. "You should have seen everyone. NT's about to bust out, Hank is on the verge, Grams is thrilled."

"That's terrific, Terry. You've got Mrs. Jones actually talking?" Mom was thrilled, too.

Terry was beaming, "Well, I don't think we can say she's a hundred percent yet. But, it's a start. She was singing some of the lyrics and she did say a few things that I could understand. I think NT got some of it also."

"Are you going back over tomorrow?" asked Dad.

"Assuming they want me to, oh yes."

"You're quite the hero, young man."

Again, Terry beamed. "That might be a bit of an overstatement, but, yeah, I think I helped her some. She's got to do the hard part, though."

"I'd love to be a fly on the wall tomorrow when her speech therapist comes," I put in. "Grams is going to knock her on her rear." I looked at Terry, "You know, you probably ought to send the therapist a bill for consulting fees or something. I mean, maybe she would have started talking anyway, but I bet you made it happen a lot sooner with your Grams and Terry gospel routine."

Terry laughed, "Or she could claim I was practicing without a license. I think I'll just settle for seeing Grams get better."

Hank did not call or text that evening, so I assumed that he was buried in writing his prize-winning article. I drifted off to sleep thinking about some of the practicalities of all this. Obviously, he would bring it back to Ms. Wells. But, would she feel she had to confront Slate with it before publication? Would she need to clear it with the school principal? Would this thing ever actually come out, or would it get swept under the rug? I was sure that Hank would do the same as he did with the first go-around, and keep dated proof of his work before giving anyone a copy. We always could fall back to Plan B, put it out as some sort of blog.

CHAPTER 42

Thesaurus Rex

One of the neat things about writing on a computer is that you can use spellcheck, although obviously you have to make sure the computer is not helpfully inserting the totally wrong word. One of the not-so neat things about writing on a computer is that it has a thesaurus. Okay, if you find yourself repeating the same word too often, not okay if you decide that your article will be better if you use "big words." Some people call it using a one dollar word where a twenty-five cent one would do just fine.

Hank handed me his article when we got to the bus stop. He must have had the thesaurus on autopilot or something.

The article:

> *If you have never been summoned to the hallowed office of Assistant Principal Slate, now would be a good time to undertake this venture. It's reasonably easy: just commit a minor infraction, do something indiscreet within the bailiwick of a competent educator, with which this institution is blessed in multiple areas. Once you've been sufficiently reprimanded and issued a directive to report to*

Mr. Slate's office, you will enter the antechamber of the Slate cave. Register your presence with the ever calm and efficient Mrs. Hernandez. Seat yourself among the other miscreants and doomed souls to await your appointment with destiny. You will eventually be beckoned into the Lair of Dread by His Master Himself. Make an honest attempt not to laugh during your interrogation regarding your crimes. But, and this is most important, peruse your current environment. Observe closely the impressive array of certificates and diplomas gracing the walls. Trouble yourself with a query, "Have I ever heard of these institutions of higher learning?" Remember the names on the diplomas, and after you have "yes-sirred" your way out, documentary evidence of your crime and punishment in hand, do a little research on the noble institutions inscribed on the diplomas. You will discover, as did this reporter, that they are of dubious sources. In fact, you will find that with the exception of one diploma, from a university in our fair state, the diplomas are all engineered, faux representations of success in graduate education.

I couldn't read any more. I was laughing too hard. "This is a joke, right? You're punking me? Let me see the real one."

"What's the matter?" Hank was serious. "It's all there. Everything we found. And I go on to prove how each diploma is a phony. And I explain how Slate let me know that he regarded them as real when we talked in his office yesterday, like I told you."

"What happened to the good old news article lead paragraph rule? You know, start with the basic facts, the pyramid, all that? And who ever heard of a newspaper story written in the second person?"

"Well," he conceded, "I might have gotten a little dramatic, but I wanted to get everyone's attention."

"You don't think a simple headline and the facts wouldn't do that?"

"Well, I like it. And I bet the editor and Ms. Wells will like it, too."

"Suit yourself." I handed it back to him. "Let me know how it goes after you see them this morning."

It did not take too long to "get everyone's attention." I was called out of my second period Algebra class and told to go to see Ms. Wells. She had a class, but this was important, so we, that is Hank, the editor, and I, met with her in the hall outside her room.

"Hello, Henryk. Sorry to pull you out of class, but I keep getting the feeling that Hank here is getting a lot of help from you, so, in the interest of education, and, to be honest, controlling the story, I want you in on this."

"Hi, Ms. Wells. I'm not really doing that much." I wasn't sure where this was going.

"Well, Hank tells me that you read this article this morning. Has anyone else read it?"

"Not that I know of, ma'am. I guess this guy, the editor, has read it."

"Good. Here's the situation. There is a man's reputation, to say nothing of his entire career, on the line here, so we want to proceed cautiously." She shouldn't have paused for a breath. Hank jumped in.

"See, Ryk. I told you. She's going to kill the story, cover it up."

Ms. Wells looked completely surprised. "Whoa! Where'd that come from, Hank? No one's killing anything. I just want to make sure we do it right." She almost smiled. "And in this case, there's two steps in the process. One, Benjamin here is going to fact check your story as fast as possible. If you've got the websites and sources handy, he can move quickly. If your article says that ABC institution is a fraud, he's going to make sure that is an accurate statement. And so on. In addition to checking out the three institutions that you say are phony, he's going to go into Mr. Slate's office and verify that they are in fact represented by the diplomas you mention. He's not going to interview Mr. Slate; he's just going to verify that they are on walls as you say in your article. And, he's not going to get there by being busted for some silly infraction as you suggest in your opening paragraph. Which brings me to number two. You are going to rewrite the article so that it looks like someone who's had at least a modicum of instruction in journalism wrote it." She looked darkly at me. "It's not going to look like it was written by some literary magazine artiste!" I suppose that she thought I actually wrote the opening or at least encouraged its form. "Hank, as I said the other day, we do not do tabloids, and we are not training mini Hunter Thompsons here. If you want to do gonzo journalism, wait until you graduate from college and try getting a job in journalism. Personally, I would suggest a better route than the one Thompson took."

Benjamin, the editor, hadn't said anything, but he was smirking. Frankie would have smacked him into next week for that look, but Hank and I just stood there with our heads down. I didn't appreciate being accused of writing the lead, but I have to admit that I enjoyed Hank getting shot down. I had a little private "I told you so" moment. I didn't dare look at Hank; I was afraid I'd laugh.

Ms. Wells looked in the window of her door. "Well, gentlemen, I think everyone knows what to do. I have a class to get back to. I'll be in the newspaper office, such as it is, sixth period if anyone needs me."

"So," Hank asked me as we walked down the hall, "is she killing the story or not?"

"Not. Just being uber-careful. Remember, if she blows this, her head rolls. Nothing happens to us, maybe. But she's out of a job."

"Is that Benjamin guy going to wreck the story? Steal it or give it away?"

"I don't think so. I'm sure he's wishing he had come up with it, but Ms. Wells knows it's your story, even if she thinks it's our story. She practically accused me of writing your lead." I finally had to laugh, although it wasn't nice.

"Very funny, Ryk. Very funny, but I guess you were right this morning. I've got the story on a thumb drive. Maybe I can get out of the rest of my English class, get on a computer somewhere, and fix the story. I actually do have a draft that's kind of boring, just the straight facts. Maybe I'll pull that up and see what I can do."

"Sounds like a plan. Catch you later."

I caught up with Mel and Crate at lunch. She was already sitting at our usual table. "Good afternoon, Ms. Raptis." I said with mock formality. "How are you today?"

"Ms. Raptis? Oh, hi Ryk. Why did you say that? What am I supposed to say?"

"Oh. Sorry. I was fooling around. Hi, Mel. How are you?" I was hoping for normal at lunch but, I certainly didn't make a very good start at it.

She frowned a moment. "Well, I'm fine, thank you. And you?"

"I'm good. Everything's looking pretty good. No worries." I really wanted to tell her about the Slate story, but I couldn't. I felt kind of bad that I had conned her into helping us, but I think she was safely out of the picture now. Everyone seemed willing to believe that I figured out the diplomas almost by accident. No one was likely to connect Mel or my dad to the discovery. "So how's your small talk practice going?"

"I guess okay." She brightened a bit, "You know, I tried talking to a girl in my trigonometry class last period, I just said Hi to her, and I tried to smile. And I remembered to look at her. She smiled back and sort of said Hi also."

"And?"

Her face fell, "And I wasn't sure what to say next. So I didn't say anything." Mel looked at her lunch, concentrating on opening a container. "I don't know what people talk about, Ryk. I really don't get it. And don't tell me I'm interesting and smart and all that. My mother tells me that all the time, but it doesn't transfer to talking to people at school."

I wasn't going to say anything like that, but I could see she was getting pretty frustrated, had been frustrated for a long time, and was not in the mood for feel-good commentary. "I don't know either, Mel. I can't see you talking makeup or clothes with these kids. Maybe something about the math homework? I know it's sort of nerdy, but you are in a pretty advanced math class. Maybe girls in trig class are happy to converse about math solutions rather than makeup solutions."

Crate appeared and gave her another chance to try small talk. "Afternoon, Mel, Ryk. What's happening?"

"Pretty quiet today, Crate. How about you? Anything interesting happening with you?"

I was impressed. Maybe there was hope for Mel yet.

We never found out because Thirsty plunked down next to Mel. "Hey, Morticia! How's it goin'? Broken-face Boy, how you? Pizza Face, you good?"

My adrenalin level shot up in a hurry. I don't know what Mel was thinking; she just stared at him. Crate answered for all of us, "That's Mister Crater Face, boy."

Thirsty seemed unimpressed, "Yeah. Whatever. So, Broken-face, you know where he went? He's gone, you know."

"Who?" asked Mel.

"He who must not be named," I said. Frankie had taken me to the first Harry Potter film, and I was hooked. I read all the books, saw all the films.

"Voldemort?" Mel looked like she thought the whole world had just undergone some sort of weird transformation. Being called Morticia by someone she didn't know, and then I make my joke. Which, of course, would have completely flown over Thirsty's head.

I brought us back to reality. "No, he's talking about Walter. And, no, I have no idea where he is. Why should I?"

Crate jumped in, "Besides, if he did know, you wouldn't want him to snitch, would you? I mean, what if you were working for the cops, and he told you?"

Mel seemed happy to be back on something she understood, "What about those papers? The maps?" I didn't realize she had seen them when we got the licenses and money from Bernard's stash.

Luckily, Thirsty was in the middle of a stare down with Crate over the pizza face and snitch insults, and he didn't hear what she said. I gave her my best stink-eye look and shook my head, and she dropped it. Crate, as it turned out, had noticed. Thirsty stood up, still staring at Crate, but backing away. "See you around, boy." I wasn't sure if this was directed at me or Crate, but we both let it slide.

"So," Crate began after Thirsty was gone, "papers?"

I was afraid Mel would produce an accurate narration of the entire night, so I jumped in. "Not, sure, Crate. There was this packet of papers that one of Walter's boys passed on to me to pass on to someone else down the hall. I guess they were playing out a fake clandestine routine. Something about not being caught on the school's security cameras in the hall. The packet went from A to B to me to C to I don't know where. Or why. Don't care, either."

I glanced at Mel; she was opening and closing her mouth like she really wanted to say something but didn't know how to interrupt. Crate was looking at me intently. If he had studied Mel instead, he would have decided something wasn't right. I guess I managed my blank look pretty well because he seemed to buy my story.

"You've got weird friends, Ryk." He grinned, "Present company excluded, of course. But, seriously, man, you have got to stay away from those guys. They're dumber than rocks, but dangerous."

"My goal in life, Crate, believe me."

When Mel finally got her voice going, she seemed happy to get back to a simpler conversation. "So, Crate, before we were so rudely interrupted, I was asking, how you've been. Anything interesting?"

"Only when I hang out with you guys. Morticia?"

"Oh, that," I said, "Thirsty thinks he's cute. He calls Melantha that, and you heard his reference to me. Very cute. Or not."

Before Crate could interrogate me about the other occasions when I heard Thirsty's insults, the lunch tone chased us out to class.

Sixth period found me once again talking to Ms. Wells in her office. She called for me and Hank, so I got out of PE again. Surprisingly, it went pretty well. Hank had resurrected his "boring" version of the story and turned it into her during the day. She got to the point quickly.

"Now you've got it, Hank. If all this checks out, we should be able to put in the next paper, which comes out next Tuesday. Henryk, once again, I cannot stress to you how important it is that you breathe not one solitary word about this to anyone. Not your parents, not to other friends; don't even talk to your reflection in the mirror." She was not smiling. "I've been thinking about this ever since Hank dumped it on me. I am as much a part of this school as anyone, been here ten years now, and I do not want to make a stink that wrecks our reputation. On the other hand, assuming the facts are what they appear to be, something has to be done. I'm going to talk with the principal Thursday." She looked at Hank, "And, no, I'm not going to let him kill the story. But, he has been a decent leader here, and I can't just let a story like this catch him unawares. He deserves to know what's going on."

Hank looked unhappy. "You're not going to talk to Slate are you?"

"Mister Slate. No. I'm not his supervisor. Talking to him would be the principal's job."

"And the principal won't kill the story?"

"Well, technically, I guess he could, but –"

Hank didn't let her finish, "But, it wouldn't do him any good. I could put the story on the internet," he snapped his fingers, "just like that."

"I know. That idea crossed my mind. But you won't. And the reason is that you know that the survival of printed newspapers depends on readers knowing they get the full story by a writer who stands by the facts. Writers and editors and publishers who don't let the powers that be bully them into silence. This includes little old high school papers like ours as well as the big guns. I'm pretty sure that I can convince him to let the story ride for any number of reasons, although journalistic purity will not be the determining factor here for him."

She was right. I'm sure the principal wouldn't care about the life of the printed story, but from a practical point of view, trying to kill the story would cause a lot more trouble. Also, I doubt that he had any idea about Slate's credentials. The personnel office sent him over, and he took him on. That office might be embarrassed, but that wasn't his problem. Of course, he'd have to call his supervisor, whoever was in charge of the county high schools. I suspected that the language in that phone call would equal Bernard Anderson's at his best in Slate's office.

Ms. Wells looked directly at Hank, "I promise, you, Hank, I'll do my best. But you need to just hang tight for a day or so. I'll know by tomorrow afternoon or Friday morning at the latest if there's a problem." She turned her face to me. "And I mean, it Henryk. Not a word." She started to pick up some papers on her desk, but then she looked back up at us. "I've pulled you two out of class a lot this week, so let me give you the advice I need to give you when the story comes out. Next week will be a bit crazy, I think, and the less both of you say to anyone, the better off you'll both be. So, no bragging, no gloating. You just tell people that the story tells it all, and you have nothing to add. And, remember, reporters do not reveal their secret sources. And their sources do not talk either." Once again, I was in the position of being told by an adult to keep things quiet. Maybe the old saying was still in effect: Children (and mouthy teens) should be seen and not heard. And of course, in my case, I didn't always want to be seen, either.

Mel had some appointment with her mother after school, so I actually stayed for the literary club meeting and took the late bus home.

CHAPTER 43

Watson

Terry was home, upstairs banging away on gospel stuff, I guess, so I stuck my head in to say hi and leave him alone.

He stopped fooling with his guitar. "Oh, hi, cuz. I believe you're going to have a visit from a law enforcement type.

I'm pretty sure I saw a 5-0 car on the street when I came home. Gone now, but I bet—." He was interrupted by the sound of the doorbell. "And there we are, right on cue. Go get the door, you lucky dog. And tell the inquisitive detective that I'm fine, thank you, but don't invite him to talk to me. I believe I'll stay up here. I wouldn't want to intrude."

I went back downstairs and opened the door. Detective Watson, as Terry predicted.

"Hi. Henryk, is it?" Smooth as ever, be it the middle of the night or middle of the afternoon.

"Uh, yes sir?" What could I say?

"I need to see your brother, Francis. But I also wanted to catch you for a quick consultation. As I'm sure you know, Walter Anderson has left town." I nodded. "Now, I don't think you know a whole lot about that guy, despite what I was told at the school, but." Here he stopped and looked at me. I didn't know where this was going, but I was telling myself to zip it and not act all nervous. Fake calm was my goal for the moment. I thought he was almost smiling, or smirking, and that didn't help my nerves a bit. "But, but, it's the nature of my job to look at everything from every possible angle. Do the math in more than one way. Deputy Jones accidently let it slip that one of his son's friends saw a note that might lead us to information on the demise of dear old Mr. Anderson. And I got to thinking that we are pretty sure we got a very useful, actually life-saving, tip from a phone call that emanated from your high school. And I know, although I won't tell you how, that three figures went into the Anderson house the night before the tip was phoned in. No idea who those three were, could have been three of young Walter's besties, although I can't imagine them being smart enough to get around the surveillance system I had in there, so maybe someone else was there? That leads me to wonder if the numbers are adding up to indicate that perhaps you have been helpful on occasion. Which brings me to the whereabouts of Walter at this time."

Oops. I appeared to be busted, but I didn't see any advantage to letting him know this. I really couldn't think of anything to say that wouldn't get me in deeper, so I just looked at him like he was off his rocker. I knew that, like my dad, he would be happy to just stand there and wait for me to get nervous and talk. Well, two could play that game. I stood there and looked at him with the biggest questioning look I could produce and didn't say anything either. We stood there staring at each other for quite a while. While I stared at this nose, rather than his eyes, I had time to think about what NT had said about accessory after the fact. I didn't want to accidently cover for Walter if he was in fact a criminal, but I also thought about what my dad's warning about talking to the police when there's even the slightest possibility of trouble. I also thought about my dad's point that a good police officer usually knows the answer to the question he's asking, so he's really just looking to confirm his hunch. The problem my dad's organization has been dealing with for years is that sometimes the cops have the wrong answer but try to match the answer to their incorrect theories, and then the wrong guy goes to jail. Or, as my dad would admit, sometimes, the right guy goes to jail but for the wrong crime, one he didn't do.

In the end, though, I chickened out. I was afraid that he knew exactly what I had done, but so far wasn't letting anyone know. It would have been nice to phone in another tip, but that didn't seem too likely. "Well, Walter did say something to me about leaving town. Something about his father's friends down south somewhere. North or South Carolina, maybe?" I did a quick check of Watson's eyes to see if he was buying any of this. "It was during one of the many times that when he was basically informing me of the medical consequences of snitching."

"Why would he feel the need to do that?"

"Um. Come on, sir. I know that by now you know that Walter, or rather one of his buddies, put me in the hospital with serious facial injuries and a concussion. Walter and his friends were deeply concerned that I might identify the guy who punched me out. For a long time, I actually had no idea and couldn't have ratted on anyone if I wanted to. I've got it figured out now, but I've never said anything to anyone about it." It worked, somewhat, putting Watson on the defensive. I was accusing him of either lying or being dense.

"Oh. Sorry. I guess your dad did say something about long-standing problems with the Anderson family, but he didn't spell it out." He relaxed, or at least acted as though he was chill. "So, maybe I'll just see what kinds of friends Mr. Bernard Anderson might have had down south. Who knows, maybe they would welcome a mini Anderson in their midst."

Frankie drove up. He didn't look surprised to see Watson, so maybe he'd been called at work and agreed to this meeting. "Hi, Francis." Watson was all smiles: I'm your best friend, and you're glad to see me smiles.

"Hi, Detective. You got my guns?" Frankie was all smiles, too.

"Of course. Come on down to my vehicle. They're locked in there, and I've got some paperwork for you to sign."

"Of course. Always paperwork." Frankie frowned. He stopped walking suddenly. "This paperwork doesn't involve any kind of warrant, does it?"

"Francis, if I thought you needed arresting, do you think I'd come here by myself?

The paperwork is just documenting the return of the weapons. There's nothing nefarious going on. Honest."

That did it for me. When someone says "honest," that always seems to be the last thing on their mind. I followed them down the sidewalk, cell phone camera on the ready.

Watson handed the box over to Frankie, who made a production of looking at the guns to make sure they were his. Of course, since he didn't have his copies of the receipts with him, Watson could have switched a gun out without Frankie's knowing, but the little play went well and Frankie signed, grinning, happy to get his guns back.

"There's one thing, Francis." Ah, the honest part gets exposed, I thought. "As I was telling your brother here, I like to look every possible angle in these cases. Especially when we don't seem to have any witnesses." He looked at me standing there, phone in hand. "Say, Henryk are you recording this?"

"No sir. Do you want me to?" I wasn't being a wise guy, for once. I actually thought maybe he wanted me to record the conversation.

"Technically, Henryk, I can't tell you not to. But I would really prefer that this discussion between me and your brother be off the record." Okay, so far, so good, but then he went to his tough guy mode. "I mean, you can record me having a friendly conversation here on the public street, but what you'll get will be me asking your brother to come down to the station so we can have a more involved and private discussion." He let that sink in for a second or two. "Or, you could show me the phone is off, no camera, no recording, and stand there while I transact this little business with your brother. Your choice." Yeah, right. I put the phone way, making a show of turning it off.

"So, Francis, as I was saying, I check all the angles, and one turns out to be little bitty parts of videos on some neighbors' security cameras. We found one pretty quickly after the murder, a neighbor a couple doors down. Most people don't have those things, but one guy on the Anderson street had one. Who knows, maybe he was upset by goings on at the Anderson house. Maybe he was just concerned about someone breaking into his house while he was at work. It was aimed at his driveway and garage area, but it picked up part of what passed by on the street. Anyway, I've got some video footage for the afternoon that Anderson bought it. I got it the day Anderson died, but we didn't see anything useful the first time through. So we widened our circle and checked with everyone for several blocks around. We found only one more that hadn't been automatically erased; it showed some of the Anderson street a few blocks up, same problem, mostly front door and driveway, but revealing. I studied it this morning, frame by frame. And, this won't surprise you, Francis, your car drove down that street, probably an hour before the murder took place, but still, on that street on that day." He looked intently at Frankie. Frankie looked right back. If he was concerned, he didn't show it. "Is there something I should know about, Francis?"

One look at Frankie told me there was something there. I was sure Watson had figured this out also. Frankie, however, was not giving in easily. "No, sir. Not really. I'm on that street a lot. I was on the way home later that afternoon, when you talked to me over near the Anderson house.

"Would it surprise you to know that we found a lot of ammunition and guns at that house? Too many rounds to count and enough guns to wage a small war."

"I'm sure you did. The guy was a gun nut, along with being a Nazi. Not a good combination." Frankie was relaxing; this wasn't going anywhere.

"A gun nut Nazi with a sideline you might be aware of?"

"Sideline?" Frankie's face was no longer cool.

"As in selling ammo to people who are under 21 but old enough to own handguns?" Watson was definitely studying Frankie's face. "One of the boxes of nine millimeter ammo had your name scrawled on top. There were several boxes more stacked under it. If I were to guess, I would say that sometimes you bought ammo from him rather than ordering online and having it delivered to your house to one of your parents' names.

As a matter of fact, it was the delivery guy who found the deceased. He knocked on the door to get Anderson's signature for a delivery of ammo, all legal, of course. The door swung open, and his day went south, not as bad as Anderson's, but he lost a lot of time talking to the detectives."

"Oh. That." Frankie shifted his weight and fiddled with something in his jacket pocket.

"So, again, why were you driving down the street?" Watson seemed very relaxed, but I was moving into the shaking panic zone, and I thought Frankie would be headed that way, too. He should have been. In a sudden moment of total calm and clarity, I found myself channeling my dad. He had often told us of cases where someone got conned into telling the police things because the conversation seemed to be completely benign but slipped into dangerous areas. I tried to catch Frankie's eye, but he seemed to be trying to do one of his stare down numbers on Watson.

I coughed loudly. Frankie broke his gaze long enough to glance at me. I shook a quick "No" at him and tried to make a lips zipped motion as I covered up the coughing.

Frankie continued as if he hadn't heard Watson's question. "Oh, that would be illegal, for Anderson, not me. I can have the ammo; I just can't buy it until I'm twenty-one."

"I'm sure you know the laws, Francis. And it's pretty obvious that I can't charge Anderson with anything. So here's what I think." He was watching Frankie very carefully now, but Frankie's guard was up, so I wasn't worried. "I think that you might have swung by with the idea of picking up ammo but cruised on by for some reason. Anderson not home? Someone else there? Obviously, you didn't make a purchase; your boxes were still there when we searched the house subsequent to the murder."

Frankie didn't say anything. I was guessing he wasn't a suspect because Watson would have taken him to his office if he really wanted to intimidate him.

"We saw a vehicle, probably one of those small pickup trucks, flash by on the same video feed we saw your car. As you were cruising by not buying ammo, did you by any chance see this truck at Anderson's? By the time he was dead, Anderson's truck was there, of course, but we don't know about that truck. We know when it left the area, and that was a short while after you drove by, but we don't know if it had anything to do with this case at all. It was on the same street at about the right time to be driven by the killer."

"I didn't see it, sir. It wasn't parked at the Anderson house when I drove buy; Anderson's was there, but no one else that I saw. Like I told you before, I went to the firing range and was there all afternoon until I swung by on the way home and ran into all action at the house." I think Frankie was pretty much telling the truth; he seemed relaxed.

"Yes. I checked with the range. They confirmed that you were there all afternoon. That's why it took a couple extra days to get the guns back to you. I wanted to make sure your story was tight." Watson was back to being Mr. Nice Guy now. "Well, it's been nice although not very informative. If either one of you guys thinks of anything that might help, give me a call." He looked at me, "I'm pretty sure you know how to do that, but here's my card in case you've lost the other one."

After Watson left, I jumped Frankie. "When did you tell him about going to the range?"

"Friday. I had to, dummy. How else could I explain the gun residue on my hands?"

"And," I continued, "are you buying ammo from Bernard? Were."

"Yeah, I did sometimes. Like Watson said, it was easier than going through the ordering process. And someone has to be home who can sign for it. Big pain for Dad or Mom, and they don't like it anyway" He grinned at me. "Like my performance with Watson?"

"Oh, A plus. Of course, it helped that, for once, you told the truth." I should have known better.

"Or not."

"Not?"

"Well, I did buy ammo from Bernard that day. Otherwise I couldn't have gone shooting." He saw the look on my face. "Oh, no problem. I really didn't see anyone there. I was in and out. And Bernard was healthy and happy when I left him."

"What about the pile of boxes with your name on them?"

"He had a ton of boxes for me, ten, I think. But I didn't have a ton of money. I bought four boxes of ammo and told him I'd come back when I had more money. It would have helped if he hadn't left my name on the boxes, but I guess it doesn't matter. Of course, now I'm going to have find a new source of ammo until I turn 21."

"What about Tildy?

"Oh. Her. I didn't mention her, and I guess the range guys didn't either, or at least he figured it didn't matter since they said they had me there all afternoon."

"You don't think you should have told him about when you saw Bernard alive, so they could get a better fix on when the murder happened?"

"Not really. They had me on that video leaving the neighborhood at whatever time that was, probably around one, one-thirty, and they had that truck later on, and they've probably got a pretty good idea of when Bernard died from the autopsy. So, no, I don't want to get in any deeper." He looked at me intently. "I did not have anything to do with Bernard's death. Sure, I wanted to smack someone after what happened to you and Terry, but I wasn't going to go over there and start a big fuss, maybe get myself killed." He laughed, "Or at least lose my source of ammo. And, no, I don't want to give the cops a detailed timeline. I think they've given up on me. Sounds like Watson has some new ideas. But, remember, as they say in all the detective shows, I had the motive, lord knows I had that, the means, my own guns plus all the ones at the house, and the opportunity. But. I didn't do it. However, since it may turn out I was the last one to see him alive, it is sort of logical for the police to think I was the first person to see him dead."

"The last one other than the actual killer, you mean."

"Of course." He suddenly looked shocked. "Oh. Shoot! I did see it!"

"What?"

"The truck. I noticed it going the other way down the street after I left Anderson's house. I noticed it because it was the ugliest green I have ever seen. I remember saying something to myself about why would anyone paint their truck goat vomit green, unless they lost a bet or something."

"Did you see the driver?"

"No. There was glare on the windshield, and I wasn't really interested in seeing the driver, just laughing about that awful green."

"Maybe you better call Watson. This could actually be helpful."

"How? They've already got the truck on video with a time stamp I guess, which is more than I could provide. And I don't want to end up talking to Watson and going over everything again and getting nowhere."

"Well, I think you should call him. He knows about the truck, yes, but if he knows it's green, that might be a big help. You can just tell him what you told me, about the glare and since you were going opposite directions, you would have only had a split second to see the driver. Besides, even though it goes against your religion, it wouldn't hurt you to just one time do something that gets you on the good side of the law." I was smiling, but I was serious. I couldn't call, but he could, and should.

"For a little squirt, you make sense. Give me the card. But I'm not saying too much. I am not getting dragged into testifying when I don't know squat. Green, goat vomit green, truck. That's it. Any food around this house?"

We found a note on the table telling whoever got home first to start some of the dinner preparations, so we snacked and got the dinner things going and went about our business until our parents got home.

At dinner there was the normal "How was your day?" conversation, although oddly enough neither Frankie nor I mentioned Watson's visit. So, dinner was going fine until it took a strange turn. Everybody likes to complain about their dads and their ill-timed or otherwise off-the-wall comments, and generally speaking my dad has not been one of those dads, but he let me down big time during dinner. Maybe he and my mom had been talking. Or maybe he thought he was being funny or something.

"Henryk, a few days ago you were telling us about Terry and some girl named, Mel was it? You know, the girl who helped saved Hank's grandmother. How's she doing? Are you seeing her? You kind of put me off when I asked about her the other day."

Terry looked down at his food and suppressed a smile.

Frankie grinned and sat up. I couldn't find my invisibility cloak, or better yet, a spell to disappear, so I had to play it out. "Well, um." Good start, I thought. "Well, she's this girl I met at school. We hang out together some, but it's not like we're dating or anything." I was sure Terry would not contribute to this, but I was also just as sure that Frankie would not resist. He did not disappoint. He coughed enough to get my attention, held his right hand on top of his left parallel to the table, and slid them back and forth. I had taken a bite of food to stall, hoping that I had said enough, but Frankie's little move forced a real cough from me, and I sputtered trying not to spit my bite out.

"Are you okay, there, little bro?" Frankie was all fake caring.

I nodded and coughed some more. "I'm. Fine."

Both my parents had missed Frankie's little display, but Terry hadn't. He smiled but looked at Frankie and shook his head, no. My mom patted me on the arm, "Just ignore Dad, dear. He's not trying to pry." No, I thought, that's her job. "So, Terry, it's the Three Musketeers saving old ladies and generally setting the world right?"

"Something like that, Aunt Mary."

Dad caught on, so no more damage. He changed the subject to a case his office was working on, something about someone with diminished capacity "confessing" to enough crimes to make the local police heroes as they cleared a backlog of cases in one swoop. The trouble was that the guy couldn't have done everything they claimed, but the court was happy to let him be convicted on his own testimony that no one challenged including his own court-appointed lawyer. He, the criminal, not the lawyer, didn't have enough brains to do the crimes, and it was obvious the cops had fed him the details to boost his confession. Dinner couldn't end soon enough for me, and I was happy to leave the cleanup to Frankie as I went off to do homework, and plot my revenge.

CHAPTER 44

Terry

Thursday morning's revenge was short and sweet. I headed off to school to the old familiar song of my dad and Frankie yelling at each other, just like the old days. And I had done practically nothing to nail Frankie. "Oh," I had said, as innocently as possible, but being sure that Dad was flipping through the paper and not engrossed in a story, "Frankie, did you remember to lock up your guns last night?" I even kept my voice low, so Frankie would think I was trying to be discreet. Of course, any time you whisper in front of your parents, their ears perk up. Mission accomplished. Dad jumped all over Frankie. He started by rehashing the whole bit about letting the police search his guns without a warrant and was well into a replay of the old stuff about the need to even have guns at all. The only possible downside to my revenge would be that Frankie might not realize that I was getting him back for his gesture at dinner that was meant to suggest that I was getting horizontal with Mel.

Hank caught up with me at lunch. He was failing at suppressing a grin. I guess I was just in the mood to be mean; I started talking as soon as he sat down. "Hank. Let me tell you about how I nailed Frankie this morning." And I was off to the races; I probably sounded like Mel at her worst. I was trying to keep him from getting a word in as I went through my revenge story. Finally, he held his hand up.

"Just stop, Ryk. Shut it." He was grinning for real now. "I saw Ms. Wells. She seemed pretty happy. She'd seen the principal, and I guess it went okay. She didn't say much about her meeting except that the story would be published next week like she said. She was smiling, though."

"You know, Hank," I said, and I was smiling, too, "it's just possible that the kids here aren't the only people who want to see Slate get his. I'm sure Ms. Wells doesn't like him, and maybe the principal will be happy to see him go, too." I remembered one time when I had been walking by Slate's office and saw a teacher coming out obviously wiping away her tears and trying not to cry in public. Nice guy, no doubt. "Heck, you're going to be a hero for exposing this turkey for what he is."

"A fraud, yes. But we both know he's a lot more than that, at least from what I've hard you tell me about him."

"And none of that's coming out. He'll keep on being a hater, but no one's likely to call him on it." I was thinking about his response to the attack on Terry and what Mr. Wright told me about the gay kid who killed himself, probably because of what Slate did and did not do. And I bet he could have acted like an adult in some of the epic battles with Frankie. He could have toned things down instead of letting them escalate. And I wasn't too happy about how he treated me, either. No, not too many people would miss him, assuming the school system did something about it.

"So here's the deal," Hank continued. "The editors are organizing the paper today and tomorrow, and then Saturday we all meet at the school to put it together so Ms. Wells can take it to the printer. It comes out on Tuesday." He fiddled with his food, "And remember, what Ms. Wells said. We can't tell anyone anything. We just go about our normal business. You know, breaking into crime scenes, getting punched out by thugs, but no talking. If someone spills it ahead of Tuesday, we'll lose the scoop to the professional media."

I had a terrible thought. "What about all the people who work on the paper? Won't they know? I mean, right now it's just that senior, what's-his-name, who's the editor, and Ms. Wells, and us. But by Saturday morning, even Friday afternoon, there will be a lot of eyes on the story."

"I think Ms. Wells has that covered. She's going to have this huge blank space reserved for a story that only Benjamin knows about. She's going to tell the staff that the story needs a little more editing. Then they'll put it in after everyone's gone."

"And the printer?"

"I doubt they read anything. It's basically all done with computers, so I guess they print a proof copy, which maybe Ms. Wells or Benjamin checks, and then the copy machine does its thing. The guy boxing the papers probably won't bother to read; he'll just be thinking about finishing the job. Anyway, the headline is going to be something really innocuous that won't draw attention to the story at first. I think it's going to say 'Advanced Degrees?' so it looks like my cover story on going back to school after college. Whoever's dealing with the papers won't give it a second glance."

"Good idea. I bet when the students get around to reading it, they'll flip out. Teachers, too." I high fived Hank.

Hank met my hand and resumed eating.

I met up with Mel after school so we could ride my bus home. She said she wanted to go see how Grams was doing. I guess this was part of her efforts to get more involved with other people. We got off the bus with Terry and went to our house.

"Want a snack, Mel?" I offered as Terry and I scrounged through the fridge for food. "I think we've got some chicken left over from last night." I was a beat late with my offer. "Terry! Jeez, man, give us a break here!" Terry had grabbed the container and was scarfing down the leftovers. Mel jumped when I yelled at him. "Well, Mel, I thought there was some chicken, but apparently there isn't. Now." Terry was grinning.

"That's okay Ryk; I don't eat chicken anyway." She looked over my shoulder at a plastic red tub. "What's that?"

"Quinoa or something. My mother's on this healthy eating kick. I'm not sure what it really is, but actually it wasn't too bad. Want some?"

"Yes. Thank you. Quinoa is a grain, originally from the Andes, eaten by the indigenous people way before the Spanish got there. It's gluten free and full of nutrients, like…"

I cut her off, "Uh, Mel, TMI, remember." She stopped and looked at her feet. I spooned some quinoa into a bowl and stuck it in the microwave. "Come to think of it, I haven't seen you eat meat, have I?"

"Probably because I don't eat meat, Ryk." And then she almost cracked on me, "I suppose a really observant person would have noticed by now." Ouch. We sat at the kitchen table to eat our (healthy and not so) snacks. Mel tried her developing social conversational skills. "So, Terry, how are you? How is Grams doing?"

Terry stopped eating and looked really happy. "Actually, pretty good. She more or less sings the songs I play, and she sort of talks to me about things, but it's pretty hard to understand her most of the time." He resumed eating the chicken. I was eating some of the quinoa but eying the chicken.

"That's good, Terry. Really good." Mel looked at me. I think she was not sure how to handle the follow-up.

After a long moment of silence, I helped her out. "Yeah, Terry. Say, do you think Grams would be up to a couple visitors when you go over this afternoon?"

"Yes, that's it," Mel said. "Could we go over with you to, uh?"

I finished for her, "We'd only be a minute, Terry. Just enough to say hi. You'd still get plenty of gospel time."

"Sure. No problem. Be ready in a couple minutes."

"Just need to wash the chicken off your hands, right?" I was still bummed about missing out on the chicken.

Terry did his best imitation of a Cheshire cat grin, licked his fingers dramatically, and headed upstairs. Mel and I rinsed off the snack dishes and waited for him by the front door.

Grams seemed happy to see us. She didn't know Mel by name, of course, but she seemed to recognize her. She looked at Terry for help.

"Oh, Grams, this is Melantha. She's the girl who helped you when you had the stroke. No reason for you to remember, but she was with us that day."

Grams looked directly at Mel and said, "Thank you." Her voice sounded shaky, and she looked like she wanted to say more. Her mouth moved as if she was rehearsing, but nothing came out for a moment. Then she tried, but it seemed pretty garbled.

Terry threw in a translation, "She says that she was glad we were there for her that day, and again, thanks." Terry glanced at the door, and I took the hint.

"Well, Grams, it's been great, really great to see you up and about. We better go now so you and Terry can do your music thing."

She nodded and mouthed "Thank you." I could see a tear in the corner of her right eye.

Mel waved goodbye, and we backed out of the front door.

Mel spoke first, "That was, uh?"

"Tough, yes." We were headed back to my house to get her things. "But she's a pretty amazing old lady. She'll come back, I bet, all the way."

She was silent as we started down the street towards her house. "You, know," she finally said, "it's an interesting paradox."

"Yes?" I wasn't sure where this was going, but with no one else around, she could go on and on if she wanted to, and maybe in the end I'd know what she was talking about if I waited her out.

"Quite a paradox. I have the vocal capacity to enunciate my ideas on all kinds of subjects, but I stumble around like Grams, who doesn't have much vocal capacity at all. Right now, that is." We walked on in silence for a minute. "I know I don't handle little conversations with people very well, but I can explain almost anything I've ever read about. I don't know how much Grams knows about things, but right now she can't get the words to even come out. Not even to make small conversations with people."

"Grams knows a lot, Mel. She's got a few things confused, not because she's old but because she's been misinformed."

I was thinking about the time Hank tried to correct her on the syphilis study and the Charles Drew death. And, of course, her blame the Jews thing, which no one wanted to touch. "And yes, before this, she could really talk. Talk about all kinds of things" I got to thinking about how she handled Terry when he came home after the attack. "She can listen, too. She knows what to say and when to say it. And when not to say it. I sure hope that she hasn't lost any of that with this stroke thing. I hope her whole self comes back. It better."

"Yes." I expected more on the irony of her vocal skills and those of Grams, but she seemed to be in her own thoughts.

We walked along, and, for reasons that I couldn't possibly explain, I took her hand in mine. Not for long, a few steps, maybe ten. She didn't pull away, but I didn't think she was all that comfortable, either. I kind of gave it a squeeze and then let go.

We got to her house. "Well, it's been, uh." She stopped. I don't know if she was still mulling things over, or if my hand had thrown her off track. She stammered, "Thanks, Ryk. Bye," and crossed past all the crazy artwork in the yard and went inside.

I managed a, "Goodbye, see you tomorrow," before the door closed. My turn to think on the way home, but I didn't know what I wanted to think about.

At dinner, Dad started in on another sensitive topic, although it was a reasonable stab on his part. "So, Henryk how's the great investigation going?"

"Investigation?" Terry asked. Frankie wasn't at dinner, either working or with Tildy, I guess. "The lunch room thing? That sounds like a crock." I had almost forgotten that Hank and I had invented a lunch room story as a cover when Terry overheard us discussing his raid on Slate's office.

To his credit, Dad didn't venture a correction.

"Pretty good, Dad. Hank's making progress, but it's slow going. I guess he's having trouble getting interviews." Time to change the subject, "Saw Grams, Hank's grandmother, today."

"And?" Mom and Dad both took the bait in unison.

"And she's really amazing. Terry's got her almost talking clearly."

Terry beamed, "Well, not me really. The therapist, and Grams of course. I guess I'm helping though."

"One of those 'It takes a village things,' right, Terry?" Mom was happy. "You know, everyone pitches in to help, not just for raising children, I guess."

"Something like that, Aunt Mary. Anyway, she's making progress. Some things she says are clear, others, not so much. But it's getting better every day. And when she sings her old songs, she gets really clear."

"Speaking of the village, Terry, there's another resident of our little village that I think could use your help." Mom did not look like she really wanted to say anything, but she pushed on. "I talked to my sister Fiona, your mom, today."

"Oh yeah?" Terry's face darkened, and I could almost see him fold into himself. "She doesn't, uh--?"

"Want you to move back? Not a chance of that, Terry. You are here for the year. That was the agreement when you came down here. She's got a lot of hoops to jump through before she can even think about getting her hands on you."

"So?" Terry was probably relieved to hear Mom say this, but he didn't show it. "So?"

"So, I think she could use your help, in a little way. Nothing too bad."

"How?"

"Visit her. She's in a rehabilitation facility, and--"

"Again." Terry wasn't cutting his mother any breaks.

"Yes, again. But maybe this time." I think Mom knew how dumb this sounded. Frankie and I had been hearing stories of Aunt Fiona's substance abuse and trips to and from rehab since we were too young to understand what was going on. Nevertheless, she tried to sound optimistic, "This time, it's different. She's been in this place for a couple months, and she knows she can't get out for a few more months. So, it's not the same old con she's pulled before."

I was surprised to hear her say that. Terry and I had certainly discussed his mom's comings and goings, and I knew Terry regarded his mother as a walking bundle of lies and manipulations, but I never got the impression that Mom recognized this. I had to ask Terry's question for him, "So, what does she want Terry to do? Exactly?"

"Just a quick visit. I've been up there once already this year; last month on one of my work trips I swung up there as well. She really is doing better, the best I've ever seen. She would really like to see Terry. Needs to see Terry. We could fly up this Saturday, see her in the afternoon, and fly home Sunday."

I couldn't read Terry at all. He was doing his best empty face. But, I could see his hand trembling a little. And I think I could see some sweat on his forehead near his hairline. I expected him to just flat out refuse, and I'm sure Mom was ready for that, but he surprised us. "Okay, Aunt Mary." No argument, no questions. His voice was as flat as he could make it.

That didn't stop Mom from trying to explain anyway, trying to justify the visit, "You see, Terry, it's this idea of needing a village to help everyone, and she--"

"I've got it, Aunt Mary. Okay? Just for the sake of argument, we'll all pretend that this really is going to be different. I'll go see her; she'll tell me how sorry she is, and we'll all have a good cry, and I'll leave her sitting there drowning in her pity pool." Terry had lost the flat tone; he looked at Mom intensely, "But that's one pool I am no longer swimming in."

I guess Mom took the hint and quit while she was ahead. "Okay, then. It's settled. I'll book our flights and line up a car." Terry nodded his head but didn't say anything.

We ate silently for a few minutes, and then Dad broke in, "Henryk, if you're not too busy with Hank and his projects or that girl you're really not seeing, how about coming into the office with me this Saturday? We've got a big case coming up, and we're a bit short of help. One of the other paralegals is out on maternity leave, and I'm getting swamped."

Terry laughed out loud, "And how are you going to explain to this lady that she's been replaced by a high school freshman, Uncle Tomás?"

"Good point," I added. "What could I possibly do?"

"Document work." He saw my face, "Organization. We need to make sure we have all documents we need to support our case easily accessible to the lawyers while they're arguing in court. It's not very glamorous, but it's absolutely essential to winning a case. I've been going through these things for weeks. We have to make sure we have everything we need and know where it is."

"So what are you going to do while cuz here does all this scut work, Uncle?"

"Writing, Terry. I've got to have a brief summary for each document, and then the lawyers will go through everything again to decide what they want to use and how and when."

"You make it sound like work, Uncle Tomás."

"When you have to do it on Saturday and Sunday, it probably could be called work, but most of the time, I enjoy it. It's worthwhile and usually pretty interesting."

After dinner I gave Terry a nod towards the stairs, "I got this, Ter. Catch you later." I cleaned up the dishes and headed to his room.

Instead of the usual blast of heavy metal or his noodling around with gospel music, there was nothing playing at all. He was sitting on his bed with a large sketch pad on his knees. When I tried to look at his drawing, he pulled it back out of my line of sight. "Not ready for prime time yet, cuz."

"Okay. Maybe later. You okay?"

"Yeah. Sure. Could be worse, I guess. At least we're not going up until the weekend. I'll see Grams tomorrow afternoon and tell her I'll have to miss a couple days."

"That's not great, I guess, but she'll be okay." I tried saying nothing to see if he would say anything else, but he was on to that tactic. I'd have to ask. "So, are you okay with seeing your mom?"

"Like I said at dinner, it's going to be more of the same old same old, but what can I do?" He did not look happy.

"Why do you think it's so important that she actually sees you? Why is Mom dragging you all the way to Boston for a few hours?"

"You, my friend, have had a nice life. You haven't had a psychotic person apologizing for her craziness about once a year. My mom gets into these programs, probably because some judge gives her the choice, jail or rehab." He laughed. "She always chooses rehab. And if you stay in it long enough, don't get kicked out for drinking or drugs, you're supposed to go apologize to the people you've hurt because of your problem."

"And she's apologized to you on more than one occasion, I guess?"

"Oh yes. She's sorry, soooooo sorry, and so on. My guess is that she is at that point in her latest rehab, so, like I told your mom, time for the pity pool and tears. When I leave this time, though, I am not looking back. And I'm not going back to Boston. Once she's out, if she wants to see me, it'll be when and where I want."

Considering his mom's history, it was pretty hard to argue with that. "Well, I hope it goes better than the other times, for your sake, if not for hers." It sounded like lame optimism, but I didn't have the history he had to justify pessimism. "Well, I've got some homework. Keep on keepin' on, right?" I got a glance at his sketch as I was leaving. It looked like a large toilet with a swirl of people and words flushing away.

"Always, cuz."

CHAPTER 45

On the Side of the Law

On Friday Hank and I were able to "go about our normal business" as he insisted we needed to do. We did not break into any more crime scenes, related to murder or diploma fraud, and we did not get punched out by thugs, or even threatened, probably because many of them tended to take Fridays off. And, of course, we didn't say a thing about the upcoming story, to each other or anyone else. Lunch with Mel and Crate was as normal as any lunch with Mel could ever be. She blasted off on a soliloquy about Latin and scientific vocabulary, but it wasn't too much. Crate and I got her back to earth before any lasting damage was done. Her mother planned to take her to an appointment after school, and I told her about my dad's plans for the weekend, so we agreed to catch up with each other Monday.

As it turned out, NT had plans for me after school. Hank had a lesson with Carl, and I went along for the ride. We settled in, munching on snacks, and Hank automatically started the game. "In history class there's a general discussion about race relations in the United States, and some fool makes a crack about the crazy different shades of black even inside black families. He notes that the range might go from really dark to almost white, even among siblings. He says that's probably a good example of relations really getting down to it. The whole class starts laughing, because there's a couple of black kids whose skin is almost white." Hank was probably thinking about his own family, which has a pretty good range of skin tones with his dad and sister being considerably darker than his mother and him. "The teacher jumped on it pretty fast. He pointed out that obviously there must have been a white ancestor in the background, but that didn't mean anyone was messing around. More likely it was a rape a few generations back. I'd say the fool goes back a space, but the teacher gets an MLK for getting it right."

"And I," NT growled, "said that the game was done. Remember?" He gripped the wheel and didn't say anything for a while. Neither did we. Finally, he spoke. "We had an interesting situation in the jail the other night." He was looking in the rearview mirror at me. "We had this dude that was getting harassed, and we wanted to get him out, but we didn't want the other inmates to know that he had complained. That would have really done him in if they ever caught him on the street or further down the line in the state prison." I was pretty sure he was letting me know that he had acted on that note I found. "You've probably heard about bad cops carrying an untraceable throw-down weapon that they could use to claim someone they arrested was armed. We did sort of the same thing, only for a good reason. We rushed the dude in his cell and magically found a weapon and some pills and hustled him out to solitary. Then, we transferred him to another county's lockup, still in solitary, so he's safe, but he's close enough for the authorities and his lawyer to get to him if they need to. Win-win all around." NT smiled at me and nodded his head.

"When do I get to come see Eleanor Rose?" was Carl's greeting when we walked into his house. "I heard she's home, but nobody's invited me over for a looksee."

"Oof. My bad, Carl." NT put his arm around Carl's shoulder. "Can't take you back home tonight because I've got to go to work later tonight, but tomorrow. For sure, tomorrow. I'll let mom know you're coming. She'll be thrilled."

"Ok, NT. I'll let you slide on this one, but, hey, I'm practically family, I shouldn't have to ask." Carl's tone sounded pretty tough, but his eyes told me he was, mostly, playing with NT.

Hank broke in, "Carl, you know any gospel songs?"

"Gospel? Has your grandmother finally gotten to you? She's not going to cut me off is she? All this jazz I've been teaching you?"

"Oh no, nothing like that," and Hank gave him an update on the progress Grams was making with Terry's gospel guitar sessions.

"Well, that boy with an axe isn't the only one who can pick out a gospel tune or two. Where do you think half the jazz musicians in the world got their start? Grew up in the church and moved on to bigger and better things." He glanced at NT, "No insult intended of course, but some of us do get it on with tunes that aren't exactly what your mom approves of." He started towards his teaching studio in back, "Let's go, Hank. We've got some serious work to do. Tomorrow your dad is going to come get me, and we, you, are going to show your grandma a thing or two. I don't suppose you can give me a hint of what that boy's been playing, do you?"

Hank could, I guess, and NT and I were treated to hearing Hank and Carl working out not too jazzy versions of some of the same songs I had heard Terry working on. I was sorry that I wouldn't be at their house on Saturday when Hank and Carl let loose on Grams with her music. Terry would be disappointed also; this would just add to the pain of the Boston trip.

At dinner Terry was really quiet, almost like those first weeks when he came in August. Mom babbled on a bit about the trip, but when no one responded to her comments, she mercifully quit. I really didn't see any reason to tell Terry about Carl's plan; he was unhappy enough as it was.

"Got an interesting phone call this afternoon, just before I left work," Dad put in. "Detective Watson called me." He stopped, as if for dramatic effect. He was looking at me, trying to decide if I would react. I couldn't because I had no idea what was going on. "Seems like Detective Watson issued a warrant for young Walter's arrest. And, this is interesting as well, he found Walter hanging out in some sort of white power neo-Nazi enclave down in North Carolina. I guess he thought he could disappear into western Carolina and not get found."

"How do you think he got found so fast?" Mom asked.

"Makes you wonder what kind of intelligence operation the police have going on, doesn't it," Dad said. "I wonder if they have an undercover agent or informant in that group." I was feeling okay since it didn't sound like Watson was in any way giving me credit for his quick find. "Anyhow," Dad continued, "Watson wanted us to know that Walter was on his way back up here, in case there was any chance that his buddies would decide that Walter's arrest had anything to do with us, specifically Henryk. Without saying it directly, he was warning us to be a little more alert than maybe we've been since Walter took off."

I was still thinking that Dad had no idea of my involvement, but I wasn't happy that both he and Watson seemed to think that I might be in danger again.

Terry probably appreciated the diversion from his problems. "So, Uncle Tomás, what are the police charging Walter with? Murder?"

"No. I think they believe he is a material witness, but very uncooperative. They were probably able to get the warrant because they could show that he saw something or knows things that he should have told them when they talked to him last week, before he took off."

"Does he have a lawyer?" Mom asked.

"Not my problem, Mary. I promise. He has rights, of course, and I'm sure he'll get a public defender as soon as he gets here, if he didn't already get one in North Carolina when the locals picked him up. For all I know, he could be sitting in a jail cell right now, fighting a move to Virginia. More likely, though, he's bouncing along in the back of one of our county's cars on the way back. He'll get his lawyer tomorrow and go from there. The authorities may have a problem since he's still technically a juvenile. Of course, it could go the other way; maybe they can hold him in a juvenile facility with only nominal legal protection. Since he took off once, they won't let him loose without a court order, I'm sure. It's a mess, but not my mess."

Terry had perked up considerably with this news, "Oh, that poor orphan child. In the hands of the vicious thug po-po's. So sad." Mom and Dad grimaced at each other, but neither said anything. We all knew Terry had a right to be bitter. I was willing to jump in with my own observations along the same line but let it drop. I was a little worried about Walter's boys coming after me, but I hoped that Watson and the police had covered for me.

Mom started to say something, but cut herself off and settled for, "Don't forget, Terry, we have an early flight tomorrow." Terry and I took care of clean up. We didn't talk about his upcoming trip or the news about Walter. Keep on keepin' on was the best we could do; worrying wasn't going to change anything.

Dad's offer was actually what the doctor ordered. We were so busy that we barely stopped to eat, and I didn't have time to think about Walter, the newspaper story, or even Mel; the cliché about time flying when you're busy was pretty accurate. We worked until almost midnight Saturday and got back to the office at eight the next morning. I texted Hank a few times, but he was pretty busy, too, newspaper most of Saturday, and playing trumpet for Grams, and then some girl, I think. The case was huge, a complicated lawsuit against the entire office of prosecution in a pretty good-sized city. The point was that poor people were getting shafted by an organized system set up by the prosecutors and the city to make money. Justice and fairness were not a consideration. We had hundreds of court cases as evidence, hundreds of transcripts of what was said in court, particularly by the prosecutors and judges. Dad said that ideally they would have gotten testimony from former prosecutors, some retired judges, and all the jurors they could find, but that was impossibly difficult, so the transcripts had to do the talking. I spent the entire weekend labeling folders and making duplicate copies of everything. Dad wanted to be sure that if something important "disappeared," there was backup.

As we took a lunch break on Sunday, Dad finally got around to my interrogation. Mom would have jumped me the first time she got me alone on Saturday, but he thought he was being subtle. "So, Henryk, I've haven't heard much, nothing actually, about the big story you and Hank were working on." I concentrated on my sandwich and didn't say anything. "Thursday night at dinner, I noticed that you deflected my question. Pretty smoothly I should mention. Terry's clearly not in the loop. That's smart. What about me? Can I get a straight answer?"

He had a point; after all, he had been the one who got us started on the whole diploma thing. "Well, Dad," I said, "I suppose it depends on all kinds of things. Would there be something like attorney-client privilege here? It's kind of—"

"Complicated, I know. I've heard that one before. Usually Frankie, but you've also gone down that road, too. But, yes, I guess we could consider it confidential, not that I'm an attorney or you're a client, but we both have a stake in radio silence here."

He was right. He definitely did not want his involvement in the story out, and we didn't want the story out early. "Sounds good, Dad. Hank and I just don't want anyone to know about the story before it gets published. Obviously, all the local media would eat this up and take our story away from us."

"So all the T's are crossed and I's dotted? You got all the proof you need?"

"Short answer, yes." I grinned at him. "Long answer, everything's documented. Of course, a good journalist never reveals his sources or methods, but we're good. The newspaper sponsor has told the principal the story is coming out Tuesday, and he's not trying to stop it. I guess we'll all find out what happens to Slate together."

"Might be a win for the good guys."

"Hope so."

"Speaking of which, this case isn't going to win itself; let's get back at it. Would be nice to get out of this office and see your mom and Terry."

Terry and Mom got home Sunday afternoon, but too late for Terry to see Grams. Dad and I didn't get home until almost dinner time. Everyone was beat except Frankie, who was entirely too bouncy for the rest of us.

"Really?" he chortled at dinner, "Walter got busted?" was his response when we told him. Nobody wanted to go into any talk about the Boston trip, and there wasn't much to say about the case Dad and I worked on, so we were happy to give air to Walter's saga and let Frankie entertain us with his various theories about who killed Anderson and why.

After dinner, he chased Terry away and stayed to help clean up. "Called Watson the other day."

"And?"

"And you were right. He definitely appreciated the little bit I could give him. I guess now they can look for little green pickup trucks and narrow things down a lot quicker. Feels weird to be on the side of good for a change."

"I thought you've always claimed to be on the side of good." I laughed. "The problem, as I understood it, was that the law was not on the side of good at the same time."

"True that. Let's not tell Mom and Dad if we don't have to, okay? Bad enough to be grilled by a police detective. I don't need more from them."

"I can relate to that. Lips sealed." I was tired and ready to hit the books for a few minutes and go to bed. Who knew that working in an office all weekend cold be so tiring?

CHAPTER 46

One More Ruckus

I guess I wasn't the only one who was busy in an office over the weekend. I didn't see Slate at his usual post "welcoming" students as they entered the school, so I thought I'd swing by his office even though it was not on my regular route to my locker or first period class. I was rewarded with the sight of a couple flattened packing boxes leaning against the side of his office. Missing was the normal Monday morning chaos of students and parents waiting to see Slate about some infraction or punishment served; I guess they had been sent to some other assistant principal's office for processing. I waved to Mrs. Hernandez who smiled and waved back. It was probably her first peaceful Monday since she started working there. I couldn't get into his office, of course, but I was willing to bet money that the only thing on the walls would be the shadows of missing documents and certificates.

Ms. Wells sent for Hank and me almost as soon as we got settled into our first period classes. We had to stand outside her door since she had a class in session. She got right to the point.

"So, here's the deal, boys. The *Reporter* comes out Tuesday afternoon during sixth period. I feel bad for the teachers that period, but it's better than putting the paper in everyone's hands during the lunch periods like we usually do. The principal, and I agree with him, thinks that this could cause a fair amount of excitement, and he'd rather all the noise go out the door with the students as everyone heads to the Thanksgiving break. He'll have to answer a bunch of emails and calls, I'm sure, but he won't have a bunch of students and parents on his case all day Tuesday. He's probably already planned for a lot of questions Tuesday afternoon and Wednesday. He's undoubtedly been coached by the school system PR folks."

Hank and I looked at each other and grinned.

"Don't even think it, whatever you're thinking, guys. You do not comment on the story at all. Just say that you did a lot of research and double-checked everything. Henryk, you're probably okay, since your name's not on the byline, but Hank, you'll have to keep your mouth shut. If anyone asks, you don't know anything about what will happen to Mr. Slate."

"Well, what did happen to him, Ms. Wells? Anything?" I had told Hank about the apparently empty office.

Ms. Wells sucked a deep breath, "He's on administrative leave while they investigate, and that's all anyone needs to know. Not that it's your job to tell anyone that. All you know is that your story is tight. Let the administration handle their end." She smiled. "Naturally, when Benjamin read your story when he and I inserted it Saturday afternoon, he wanted to write a blistering editorial. Seems that he has held a very dim view of Mr. Slate for four years and was anxious to add his two bits to your story; he rattled off a long list of Mr. Slate's transgressions. He also wanted a much more dramatic headline. I didn't give an inch on either of his demands. As far as I know, he and I, and you two are the only ones who have actually seen the story. Even though Mr. Slate has left the building, at least temporarily, the principal is still in the position of being able to say he's just found out about all this Friday and that it's out of his hands."

"So, everyone's just going to cover for Slate?" Hank was still convinced that the administration would do nothing.

"No, Hank. It's called due process. You can't just fire someone based on an accusation. But, for the good of everyone involved, including Mr. Slate, he's probably going to be parked in some job in the central office until they can sort this out."

"So they believed the story, then?" I had to ask.

"Well, I assume the principal called Mr. Slate in on Friday and didn't like his explanation. At least it worried him enough to call the personnel office. I'm a teacher, remember, not an administrator. We, you, did your job, found the truth and reported it, and now it's up to the higher-ups to do their jobs."

"Did the principal tell Mr. Slate who worked on the story?"

"Couldn't have. I didn't tell him. I just told him what you guys dug up. I did give him copies of some of the pages of proof you gave me, the material that provides details about each of the fraudulent diplomas, but I did not give him any names or the story itself." She glanced at her classroom. "Well, I just wanted to make sure we're all on the same page about this. Obviously, Hank's name will come out tomorrow afternoon with the paper, but I don't think it will matter much." She scrawled times on our passes and handed them to us. "I've got a class to teach. Mouths shut and, good job, boys."

Since Hank was going upstairs to his math class, and I was in in English in the same wing, we didn't have time to talk. "Catch you at lunch, Ryk." Hank's voice was shaky. I think he was beginning to realize what a big deal this turn out to be.

At lunch, Hank was pretty quiet.

"So," I said, "any loose ends to tie up? Do we have our story straight?"

"Straight, how?"

"We're saying that we, I, noticed something funny when I was in Slate's office, and I helped you look into the diplomas. It's all on us, no one else involved, right?"

"Of course. And no one finds out what we did to double check on the diplomas. We don't want Mrs. Hernandez getting in trouble over how we got into Slate's office."

"Or Mel. Or my dad."

"Just you and I, bro. That's it. Woodstein and Bernward, all the way. We'll never reveal our Steep Goat." He looked across the room, "I might, well, could or should, be in love. Catch you later." And he grabbed his tray and headed to a table where a girl seemed to welcome him with a smile.

The rest of Monday was normal. Normal being that, of course, Walter's buddies had to say something to me. Thirsty and someone I didn't recognize caught me in the hall.

"Broken-face boy, what's up?"

"Nothing that I know of, why?"

"They got our boy. Again. Know anything about that?"

"No." My adrenaline was starting to kick in. I answered quickly before I could get nervous. "What could I know?" I wondered how they found out Walter was back in custody. I wondered how long he had been back in the county. I wondered if he was indeed still under lock and key somewhere. I wondered why I had ever tried to stop them from hassling Donnie.

"You better not know." Thirsty's friend was watching me closely but hadn't said anything. "Walter's not exactly under arrest; I mean, they haven't charged him with anything, but they've got him somewhere and won't let him loose. They let him call me last night. I don't know what happened. Naturally, I had to make sure you weren't talking to anyone."

I guess this was his idea of a gentle reminder of the consequences of snitching. I really didn't need the reminder, and I knew how much I actually had been talking. I didn't think that he or Walter had any idea, so I was okay. "Don't know anything to talk about. Don't know anyone I'd want to talk to." I had a really brilliant inspiration. "Actually, Thirsty, I would think that you and I shouldn't be seen talking. It might make someone like Slate start asking questions." If Slate was still around, he would have been interested in my conversation, and I'm sure Thirsty would be equally uninterested in attracting Slate's attention. He probably didn't know Slate was gone.

Thirsty immediately looked around, started to say something but instead scooted around a corner without another word, his buddy trailing behind looking a bit confused.

I caught up with Mel at her locker. She was holding a book, attempting to read it, while she got her stuff to go home.

"Hey, Mel, what's up?"

Nothing. She was totally focused on reading her book. "Mel?"

She looked at me. "Oh. Hi, Ryk." And she started back on the book.

"What are you reading? The book?"

"Yes. It's a book." She went back to reading it.

"What's it about? More rocket science or something?"

"Rocket? Oh, no. My Latin teacher gave it to me. It's by a lady named Temple Grandin. She's amazing. She's Aspie. She has a PhD and is brilliant. My teacher thought I should be introduced to this lady." Her head went back down into the book. "I'm surprised my mother never mentioned her to me."

"So?"

"So?" She looked back up at me. She looked down the hall towards the stairs leading to the bus exit.

I guess she thought it was obvious, but I was feeling pretty clueless. "Oh," I said. "You need to catch your bus. And read your book. Got it. Catch you tomorrow." And I was pretty sure she would read that book straight through. Maybe twice, before coming to school on Tuesday. "Have a great afternoon." I'd catch my bus and try to stay busy enough to not think about the excitement on Tuesday.

Surprisingly, I made it through Monday afternoon. I guess I'm learning to do like baseball players do. That was then, this is now, what's next? Since I couldn't do anything more about the article, and I couldn't do anything about Walter and his father's murder, there wasn't much point in worrying. Terry went over to play for Grams, and I stayed home and honed my gamer skills, such as they were (Not!).

In fact, I made it all the way through Monday night and part of Tuesday before it got exciting again. Hank had not said much on the bus, and neither had I. I think we both just wanted to get on with things, get to sixth period and the *Reporter's* release.

When I sat down with Mel at lunch, I saw that she didn't have her new book with her. Crate sat down right after I did, and she looked up. "Hi, guys. How are you two doing?" So far, so good, but then the floodgates opened, "Have you ever heard of Temple Gandin?"

"Can't say that I have, Melantha. Is she a famous actress or singer or something?" Crate could have just said hi or something basic and not started things off. But I guess he thought he was being polite. He should have known better, since he had a class with her.

"Who? What?" Mel looked startled. I started to answer, to cut her off, but it was too late. As I expected, she had read not only the book her teacher gave her, she had researched Dr. Grandin online and was ready to roll, which she did. We were treated to an extensive, and actually interesting, description of this lady's early life, education, and her current activities on behalf of autistic people. We were rescued, if that is the appropriate phrase, by One Punch.

"Hey, hey! Broken Face boy. How are you today?" He tapped me on the shoulder, making sure I was paying attention. "My boy's gone missing. You have any idea about that?" Since Thirsty had told me he talked to Walter Sunday night, I assumed he was still in some sort of police custody, so I had no idea at all.

"Um. I really don't know. I only know what Thirsty told me yesterday."

"Well, he's gone again. Thirsty tried to call him, and they tried to say they never heard of him. They made him disappear." He glared at the three of us. "Yo, Pizza Face,

Morticia, Broken Face boy, y'all better not have anything to do with this."

The three of us just stared at him. I think Mel must have done some internet snooping regarding "Morticia" and now understood the nature of the insult. I don't think she had the skill to respond, and I didn't want to add to my "broken face" description, so neither of us said anything. Crate, on the other hand, wasn't having any of this. He spoke very slowly, and in a low voice, "First of all, it's Craterface, Mr. Craterface to you, punk. Secondly, why on earth should any of us know what your fool friend is up to? So, One Inch, take your little inch long d—"

The timing on Crate's part was perfect. There happened to be a teacher monitoring the lunch room about ten steps away, and all he saw was One Punch swing at Crate, who was still sitting at the table, hands down in front of him. Crate ducked, I should learn that skill, and rolled out of his chair onto the floor. One Punch flailed at Crate, losing his balance as Crate slid sideways and stood up holding on to One Punch's leg. One Punch went over and back, hitting his head on the edge of a table. He crumpled to the floor and didn't move, blood leaking out of a gash in the back of his head. Crate looked at him for a second, grinned at me, righted his chair, and sat back down.

The teacher stared at the prone One Punch and started calling for security. Mel went right into her "emergency" patter. "You, in the red shirt, call for help. Tell them there's an unconscious boy here with a possible head injury." The teacher went over to the unmoving One Punch. "Don't move him, he may have spinal damage." I looked around for someone in a red shirt, and, of course, there wasn't one. Still, I was impressed by Mel's command.

Crate just sat there grinning. He leaned in to me and whispered, "That felt good. That was definitely cool." I wasn't so sure, but I nodded. It occurred to me that poor One Punch had not been schooled about insulting Crate since he hadn't been around in middle school with us. Even Walter would have thought twice before messing with Crate, but One Punch, poor dude, had no education, until this happened. For Crate's sake, I hoped that One Punch wasn't hurt too seriously, just educated.

When the back-to-class tone sounded, Crate and Mel and I quietly left the chaos behind us as the school nurse and various security people attended to One Punch, who was sitting up and holding a bloody pad to his head. The teacher was explaining what happened to Mr. Wright. He glanced at me as he was taking notes, and waved me over. "Could I possibly have chat with you a bit later on, Mr. Jonasz?"

"Of course, Mr. Wright. Any time."

I got about five minutes in Spanish class before I was summoned to Mr. Wright's office. Mrs. Hernandez waved me in.

"So," started Mr. Wright, "what goes around comes around, eh?"

"Um"

"What I mean to say is that the young man who sustained a dramatic, although not life threatening, injury today may have been involved in your considerably more serious injury a couple months back." He stopped and waited for me. I was being interrogated. I decided to let him ask questions, so I waited also. "The teacher who was standing practically next to our poor victim said that he swung first."

"Twice, actually, Mr. Wright. And Crate never swung at all. He was sitting there minding his own business when the kid attacked him."

"That's what the teacher seemed to think also. I don't suppose you could elaborate on that, could you. The kid who didn't hit the boy but put him on the floor, knocked him out in fact, does he have a name? You guys kind of scooted out before I could catch the names. I recognized that girl with you, but?"

"Oh. Crate. Craterface. Curtis Jordan."

"And does he have some long standing beef with this kid, One Punch, aka Robert Williams?"

So that was his name. "No, not really. Not at all. I mean, I kind of think that One--, Robert Williams, was the guy who hit me. I figured that out a couple weeks ago, but there wasn't much I could do about it. I never told Crate or anyone else." I waited.

"So why would Mr. Williams decide to come over to your table and instigate trouble with Mr. Jordan?"

"Well, you know he's part of the crew that hangs out with Walter Anderson, and he came over to ask me about where I thought Walter might be." I hoped that was enough.

"And? And do you have any idea?"

"Nope. Not a clue. I heard that he was picked up in Carolina and might be back up here in some sort of police custody, but other than that?" I shrugged my shoulders.

"So Mr. Williams was so offended by your lack of knowledge that he decided to take a swing at Mr. Jordan?" Mr. Wright had an inspiration, "Ah! He wasn't swinging at you, was he?"

I appreciated the out. "Maybe." I didn't add that since I was still alive, One Punch was clearly not swinging at me, but I thought it was a good story. I just hoped that I could get it to Crate before he was questioned by Mr. Wright. Of course, I forgot that Mel could give Mr. Wright the entire story, line by line, an audio feed of the entire discussion, and then the trading of insults would come out. As an inexperienced criminal, I always seemed to have some loose ends. I'd have to get to her also.

"Well, that explains a lot." He looked at his watch. "I have to be in court on something this afternoon, so I'll have let you go. With Mr. Slate, uh, not present, we're a little short-handed, so I guess I'll have to resume this discussion tomorrow. I'm beginning to put the finishing touches on a theory that I've been contemplating for a while now; maybe you can help me with it. Got to run. Mrs. Hernandez can give you a pass. Have a good afternoon, and try to stay away from people who want to punch you. Or punch your friends."

After sixth period, I would have to hustle to catch Crate in the industrial arts wing and also catch up with Mel. Since I was still sitting out PE, I had time to grab a couple copies of the *Reporter* that were delivered to the class and get myself down to Crate's computer design class as everyone was coming out. A few had found the article, and the buzz was starting. I quickly told Crate about Mr. Wright's conclusion, and we agreed that the story I told Mr. Wright would work. By the time I got to Mel's locker, she had left, so I ran down to her bus and jumped on. She was sitting alone, as usual.

"Hi, Mel. Glad I caught you."

"Caught? Oh, yes. Caught up to me. Yes. Well, here I am. What are you doing?"

"Riding home with you." She looked puzzled. "We didn't get to talk after that big ruckus in the cafeteria." I suddenly realized that I should also let her know about our story for the article. I didn't want her to be mad at me or, worse yet, start trying to explain what she knew about the diplomas and how we found them. "Were you okay, after that mess?"

"Yes. I guess. It was a bit confusing. I didn't understand what that boy wanted from you, and I certainly didn't understand why he tried to hit Crate. Do you know if he was okay?" She frowned. "You know, I don't think that teacher knew what to do. He was about to move the victim before I told him to stop. It states very clearly in the first aid book that you shouldn't move someone who may have a neck injury."

"The victim, as you put it, is okay. I checked. He got a nasty bump and had to get stitches where his head hit the table, but he's okay." I hoped she wouldn't ask me how I knew this. Also, I guessed that she hadn't actually heard the conversation between Crate and One Punch, so I gave her a simple story. "I think that he was mad at Crate about something from a long time ago, and became angry all over again." Close enough to the truth but far enough that she couldn't report anything useful to Mr. Wright if she was questioned.

"Good. I suppose. One Punch isn't a very nice person, and he's awfully big, but Crate seemed to know what to do to protect himself." She smiled a little, "You know, Crate is a really nice person, and I don't think he meant to hurt anyone. He must have just reacted, instinctively."

Good; that was settled. Now, the diplomas article. "Have you looked at the *Reporter* yet?"

"Not really. Why?"

I pointed to the lead article with its misleading headline. She skimmed through it quickly.

"Oh. My. Those were the diplomas and certificates you asked me to look at when we were in that man's office. And Hank wrote the story." She let that hang. I don't think she knew what to do.

"Well, um," I started out boldly (Not!). "Hank and I researched all those things and, and, well, the story covers it all. Mr. Slate had a lot of fake paperwork up there. So, and this is really important, Mel, no one knows exactly how we figured out there were fakes in that office. No one knows that I found out and, most importantly, no one knows you helped me that day. And--"

"And, we should keep it that way, right, Ryk?" She laughed. "Another secret mission. I must say that I have had more adventures with you in the past few months than I ever had in my life."

"I've had a lot more adventures than I expected also." I looked at her lap; she was holding the Grandin book. "So, we got cut off at lunch when you were explaining about the lady, tell me now, I'm all ears."

I swear she glanced at my ears, but she stifled any comment and plunged into more detail about Temple Grandin. When we got to her bus stop, I was ready for a break. I walked her to her house, and her mother met us at the door. She was wearing rubber gloves and holding a brush in her hand.

"Hi, Henryk. I'd invite you in, but the house is all fumy; I'm working on a frame, and it's too cold to work outside. My exhaust fan broke last week, and I'm waiting for a part to repair it." She restored old picture frames for a number of sales galleries in the area. It may have been her main job; she always seemed to be home.

"That's okay, Ms. Raptis. I have to run anyway. We've

got a family thing going on tonight that I have to be back for." Every year, usually the Tuesday before Thanksgiving, the Jones and Jonasz families had a get-together. Hank and I thought it was to celebrate our birthdays, which were a week apart earlier in November, but I think the adults just liked the tradition. When we were little, there were presents and all the usual birthday hoopla, but now it was just a nice thing before the big Thanksgiving push. They'd order a bunch of pizzas and no one had to work too much. We usually alternated houses, but this year would be at the Jones house for a second time in a row to make it easier on Grams.

CHAPTER 47

Celebration

This party really turned into a celebration in many ways. While we waited for the pizzas to arrive, Terry and Grams did a little showing off. I can't pretend that every word Grams sang was crystal clear, but I was able to follow all of the songs they did. I had heard the tunes coming from Terry's room, but I hadn't heard the words until Tuesday night. By the time they finished the second song, NT and Mama J had tears in their eyes, and the rest of us weren't far behind. I knew that on Saturday Hank and Carl had tried a little gospel trumpet with Grams, and I wondered if that would work in. No one wanted to upstage Terry, and Hank had his turn coming soon enough. Grams made the decision easy.

"Hank?" Her voice was shaky and scratchy. "Your, uh?" She mouthed trumpet, and then it came out on the repeat, "Trumpet? Can you get it?"

Terry looked startled, and Mama J beamed. "Great idea, Hank, go get it." She turned to Terry, "You think Hank could jam with you two for a song or two? Carl and Hank played around with gospel and Grams Saturday afternoon."

"Sure, I don't see why not."

"Could be the start of a whole new thing," NT boomed.

After Hank came in with his horn, he and Terry fiddled around for a few minutes in a corner of the room. I don't know how musicians do it, but I guess that's the point of the gift. They started jamming together like they'd been practicing it all their life. They ran through a bit of a tune together, and then nodded at Grams, and they were off. Grams sang, Hank played, and Terry played and sang softly under Grams's voice. They did a few songs, maybe four, before the pizzas arrived; they were probably at the end of Hank's repertoire anyway.

Hank and I had enough copies of the *Reporter* for everyone to read the story at the same time. Hank and I had decided to hand them out at dinner with no advance notice of what we were up to. Everyone was digging into their pizza when they got their copies. Somehow Hank had managed to convince Phillis to say nothing, since she had seen the paper already in school. Hank really wanted this to be dramatic. If he wasn't going to get a Pulitzer, at least he could go on stage for his family.

"Okay, Hank, and the reason we are all reading an article on getting advanced degrees is?" said his mother when he thrust a copy into her hands. "It's not like this is your first byline. You had plenty in your middle school paper."

Phillis couldn't resist, "Yeah, but Mom. Front page, and he's only a freshman. Pretty cool, little brother."

"More than cool, Hank." Dad had skimmed the story, knowing what to expect. "Very nicely done."

"Whoa! Cuz! This isn't a cafeteria lunch lady story!" Terry was clapping his hands. "Oh!" He got this huge grin on his face. "You dogs! You sly dogs!" He looked at me and then Hank. "You conned me with your cafeteria story the other day! Went right over my head. Well played, guys."

Hank just beamed and said nothing.

Frankie was the next to chime in, "You go, Hank! Ding dong the witch is dead! He is gone, right?"

"Yes," Terry added, "has Slate slinked? Slunk? Whatever?"

"As far as I can tell, yes," I said. "I swung buy his office today, and it was closed, and there was an empty packing box or two outside his door." I didn't add that Mr. Wright had confirmed it when he said that Slate was 'not present' in our conversation earlier in the day. I didn't want to start up on what led to that conversation if I didn't have to.

"Do you think he'll be fired?" Mom asked.

"Hard to tell," Dad said. "I would think that this would be grounds for direct dismissal, but who knows what the exact rules are. It would appear to be a case of lying on a job application and committing fraud. I'm pretty sure that some lawyers are going to get fat if he fights it."

"I can't believe it," Frankie said, "I spent four years trying to get under Slate's skin, and it turns out that I should have been getting under the sheepskins on his office wall. Bummer. Well, this calls for a toast," said Frankie, raising his bottle, (soda, of course, in a cop's house with his parents also present). "Mazel tov! Mr. Slate's finally got his."

We raised our glasses, but Dad cut in, "I'm not sure that's quite the appropriate use of that phrase, young Francis. It's not meant to cheer someone's utter hubristic stupidity and subsequent but well-deserved misfortune. It's used to convey congratulations. Although, I guess we could say mazel tov to Hank for his successful story."

Hank realized he had to add a bit, "Actually, you all, there's more to it than Hank this and Hank that. Ryk helped me a lot, including tipping me off and then getting photos of the suspect diplomas on Slate's wall." He didn't mention Mel or my dad, which was a good thing. He did make a quick nod at my dad and smile, but it was probably not noticed by anyone in the room. "Oh, Dad. One more thing. Phillis's book? What you told us last night?"

NT grinned, "Oh, yes. Small thing, but a sign my kids are growing up. Long story, but the short of it is that Phillis introduced me to a book that, well, kind of ticked me off when I first heard about it. But, I couldn't look her in the eye without looking into it on my own, not after all those years of telling her to 'look it up'. I know there's a lot of argument about *Huckleberry Finn*, and I read a little bit about it after I finished reading the book, but if I'm on the school board, it stays, no question. Just needs to be taught with a lot of background and some thoughtful discussion of the issues. Same goes for *To Kill a Mockingbird*."

NT's cell rang, and he glanced at the screen, "I've got to take this in another room. Excuse me."

He was gone for quite a while, and at first we just talked and laughed about Slate's problems and how Hank and I got the damning evidence.

"I hope nothing's wrong," my mom said glancing at the room NT had gone into.

"No worries, Mary," Mama J said. "When something's wrong in a policeman's day, the phone call is short and to the point. If there was something bad happening, he'd be in his car and on the way out by now, adrenaline pumping and nerves a-jumping." She took a long drink, "It's probably some administrative issue that came up. The head honchos are always running things by him. I've told him he should just give up and allow them to promote him into full management, but he keeps saying he likes his life now. Although at this moment, he seems to be living the bureaucrat's life without the pay."

NT returned. I couldn't read his face, so I figured Hank's mom was right; it was just bureaucratic foolishness. "Well, that was interesting, most enlightening, as you would say, Tomás."

"How's that?" my dad asked.

"That was Detective Watson." He smiled and looked around but didn't continue. He just grinned. Wait time for dramatic effect rather than interrogation, I guess.

"And?" Mom bit first.

"And we have a houseful of heroes here."

"Really?" Dad also bit. "How so?"

"Let's start with the least likely suspect, Frankie."

"Francis a hero? And the police told you this?" Mom looked at Dad, who shrugged his shoulders.

"Yep. Now, what I'm about to tell you all does not, that is N-O-T, go out of this room, you all hear? It could make a mess of things and might even get someone hurt." NT looked around and waited for each of us to nod our heads in agreement. I think the word "hurt" got our attention. "Detective Watson spent a lot of time studying videos from the houses along Anderson's street and then the surrounding area. Eventually he was able to spot a vehicle, I'm not saying which or where, but it was worth pursuing. In conversation with young Frankie here, he was able to ascertain the approximate color of this vehicle, 'goat vomit green' I believe were Frankie's exact words. Apparently Frankie drove by the area around the same time and noticed this vehicle."

"Really ugly. Sad, sad color." Frankie laughed, but he sounded nervous.

"So, as I was saying, or rather Watson told me, he was able to use the color to locate the vehicle. They didn't have the license plate, so having the color narrowed things down considerably. This led to a possible suspect, and along with some confirmatory input from another source, helped secure a search warrant."

"And?" Dad was worried, "And no one knows about this little gem?"

"Nope. No one but Watson. He never needed to tell anyone where he got the idea of a green vehicle to search the data bases for it. But knowing the color saved a lot of time. Very small detail, but pretty important as it turned out. Like I tell my fellow deputies, it's the little things that count." He smiled at Frankie. "I hate to rain on your 'I hate the police' parade, so I won't tell if you won't."

We all laughed at Frankie and started to congratulate him for being a hero, of sorts when NT interrupted. "There's more heroes that need recognition, too, you know." My stomach churned; I hoped he wasn't going to point out my various activities that helped Watson. "Let's not forget about Grams, here. Here, I should say, because Terry and Henryk and that girl, what's-her-name, did all the right things--"

"Mel," Terry interrupted.

"Mel. Did all the right things at the right time, in the right time, a terrible time. If these three youngsters weren't there, I--" He trailed off as his voice broke.

"And we are so, so appreciative that you were there and knew what to do," finished Mama J.

"Amen," said Grams quietly.

"Family," Terry said just as quietly, and we all knew what he meant; he didn't have to add any more.

Count on Frankie to keep things light, "Family, yes, but I got the last piece of pepperoni," beating Terry's reach.

"You might as well," Terry laughed. "It's worth more than the citation you're not getting from the police department for breaking the case wide open!"

NT nodded at me and then towards the other room. "I've got one unfinished piece of business to conduct with young Ryk here, so…" And we went into the next room.

"I know I don't have to tell you that this does not leave this room." NT didn't wait for me to nod, "I had a very interesting conversation with Detective Watson. We're old buddies, and lately we've been exchanging a number of interesting theories." He smiled at me, "Oh, and I want you to work very hard on your poker face when I tell you about our theories. I'm not looking for confirmation, and I'm not reporting back to Watson, so you just listen."

This was not sounding good. Was I in trouble or not? I guessed not because in that case Watson would have been there for this little conversation. "Sure, NT. I don't know what you're—"

"Yes you do, or will," he interrupted. "First of all, as you will see in a minute, you are in fact a hero, probably more than Frankie, on this Anderson thing, but no one other than me and Watson will ever know. Unless you open your mouth and blab, of course."

Okay, I thought. I'm certainly not planning to talk about anything that will get me in trouble. So where was this going?

"Someone called in a terrific tip to Watson, and he and the ATF took a whole bunch of really bad weapons, war weapons, from the Anderson house. Watson also got steered to a cache of names that may or may not have helped him locate Anderson's killer. This tip got called in from the high school the day after someone broke into the house. Watson got what he wanted, and he has no reason to identify the tipster, although he's a bit curious about why he was in the house."

I believe my poker face was doing fine so far. I had anticipated this kind of questioning at some point anyway.

"It's my belief that you know a lot more about this than you're letting on, but whatever, doesn't matter. Watson told me that you definitely gave him a useful suggestion about Walter Anderson's whereabouts. Again, not too sure how you came up with the idea that Walter went south, but it was pretty accurate. Obviously, Watson got some help from the North Carolina police, but knowing where to look was very helpful." NT tapped me on the shoulder, "Unfortunately, as you can see, it would not be good to thank you publicly, so this is all you get."

It was my turn now. "I have a question, or two, NT."

"Thought you might."

"Where is Walter now?"

"Can't say." He saw that I didn't believe him. "Really. He came up here courtesy of Detective Watson's special car service, escorted personally by Watson."

"Someone, one of his idiot crew, told me he was up here Sunday night, even talked to him, and now he's disappeared."

"Well, I can tell you this. Remember, Walter had spent a day or so in the county jail in Carolina, in an isolation cell since he was a juvenile, and the experience probably boosted his thought processes up a notch or two. I would think that sitting in a cell like that and contemplating the other detainees would encourage one to talk to get out. I'm sure he was visited by a public defender lawyer, and I'm sure he decided that he would rather waive any right to an extradition hearing once it became clear that he would be parked there until the court sorted things out. He was probably happy to be released to Detective Watson's loving care. While they were taking a leisurely drive up from North Carolina, Detective Watson must have done a fine job of illuminating the rules regarding accessory to crime. Remember when I, gently I'm sure, explained the concept of accessory to a crime?"

I nodded. I didn't like the direction this was going. Were we back to what I may or may not have done?

"And let's just say that at somewhere along the line a light went off in that dimwit's head. It may have occurred to young Walter that there's a time to be quiet and a time to squeal like a stuck pig. And when your butt's about to sit in custody for who knows how long because the cops want some minor information, maybe you just give it up."

I had to break poker face on this, "So, Walter Anderson, the king of snitches get stitches, decided to snitch?"

"Oh. I wouldn't put it quite that strongly. But Watson did have a lock on him as a material witness, so he obviously knew something despite all his denials a couple weeks back. And I guess he could see that life would be unpleasant if he kept his mouth shut."

"Won't it be just as unpleasant now? I mean, if he ratted somebody out—"

"Don't go imagining things. I don't think it was all that. I'm pretty sure he wasn't an actual witness to the murder, but whatever he told Watson led to an arrest pretty quickly." He frowned, "Damn! How'd you do that? I wasn't supposed to say anything. There'll be a press conference in the morning, so it won't matter as long as you keep quiet tonight. And, just to be sure you understand; even after tomorrow's press conference, you still don't know anything, right? Anyone asks you anything, you only know what you've heard in public. That includes don't go developing a case of diarrhea mouth with Hank or Frankie or your dad."

"No problem, NT. I have a pretty good idea about keeping quiet. Snitches and all that."

He laughed. "No problems, Henryk. I'm pretty confident in your ability not to talk. Let's get back to the party before they think you're in trouble." I still didn't know where Walter was, but I guess that was part of the plan.

Epilogue

As it turned out, the murder of Bernard Anderson was pretty mundane as murders go. And, I guess, solving it was pretty mundane too, although it seemed pretty dramatic at the time. I think Watson just went through everything he could, step by step, looking carefully at each little thing until he found what he needed. It took him something like two weeks to figure out that the killer was probably in that truck that he caught on a random private security video. I'm sure Detective Watson dealt with many much more complicated situations, obviously including any cases that he hasn't yet solved. I didn't find out these details until several months after the murderer's arrest. Some of it I pieced together from things I read in the paper, some I deduced from comments NT made, and, of course, I knew some things including more than what I told NT or Watson.

Probably what I like best about all this, well, what I find most amusing, is that it turned out that the recurring phrase, "snitches get stitches" was actually a centerpiece of the entire mess. As a threat from Walter and his buddies, it sometimes dictated what I did, such as helping Walter hide out and eventually leave town. As advice from NT, it kept me from telling all I knew to the authorities. In fact, I probably shouldn't be telling all now, but with passage of six months, and all the "bad guys" scattered either physically or just in their normal state of dimwitted idiocy, I'm pretty safe.

So, the father of the snitch rule, Bernard Anderson, got the ultimate stitches under this rule. No, he wasn't a government informant, but some of the good folks in his disjointed neo-Nazi band of thugs somehow thought he was, or at least might be. I don't know how they reached that conclusion, but it led to the confrontation that ended in his death. Green truck man apparently drove up to the house right after Frankie left with his four boxes of ammo for an afternoon shooting up targets with Tildy. Maybe if Frankie had had enough cash to buy all ten boxes, he would have taken longer loading his car and been there when green truck man, Ike, showed up.

If Bernard was in fact talking to anyone, feds or locals, it never came out. The ATF was apparently surprised; at their press conference their spokesperson seemed thrilled to find the war weapons in the secret stash in the basement. Mel and Hank and I found the stash several days after Bernard was killed, so that argues for the idea that Bernard was never in contact with authorities, and they had no idea about his little armory. But, it seems that his bunch thought he was in contact with them, snitching as it were, and he ended up dead. Apparently, the police could only charge Ike with second degree murder because it turned out that Bernard was killed with one of his own guns. Maybe Ike went to see Bernard to confront him over alleged snitching, or maybe Ike went to the house to buy ammo or even a gun, and a fight developed. The newspaper reported that guns were found in Ike's house along with boxes of ammo that had lot numbers that matched with boxes found in Bernard's house. I guess the commonwealth's attorneys didn't think they could prove he went over there with the intention of shooting Bernard. In any case, he has a pretty good lawyer because he has already pled guilty to second degree murder and theoretically could get out of prison on parole, in a zillion years or so. Frankie thinks the commonwealth's attorney cut a deal with him as a reward for the public service, removing Bernard from circulation. That's only a theory, of course and not likely to show up in any public forum

The other day NT told me, while we were on a trip to Carl's, "By the way, lest you think any less of your buddy Walter, I should tell you that Detective Watson told me that actually Walter didn't snitch at all. But, as they were driving up, Watson said something, intentionally casually of course, about a green truck, a really ugly green truck. And Walter, being tired and no longer on his A game, blurted something like, 'Oh, Ike's truck.' I don't know if Watson asked him anymore, like Ike's full name, but the damage was done. It was pretty easy to find the owner of a green truck named Ike something." NT snorted, "Like I always say, it's the little things that count."

I personally have a theory that it was Walter who first found his dead father and panicked, and started his multiple disappearing acts, leaving the poor delivery driver to find Bernard later in the day. He may have even seen Ike's truck leaving, so he knew all along who to suspect but was afraid to say. I also think that the guy who NT dramatically yanked out of his cell to protect him probably told the police that the neos were talking about Bernard as a possible snitch. If the neos thought that, they screwed up royally in sending Ike to confront him because it looks like Ike was a bit short on the skills needed to learn anything useful.

Walter may have given the police some other information; I don't know. I do know that he has completely disappeared, off the grid, as they say. I assume he was put into some sort of witness protection program for juveniles, maybe a foster home hundreds of miles away. He's got to be too scared to contact anyone around here, since the neos presumably want him erased for giving up Ike. Even if Walter didn't actually give up anything, no one will believe it, so he's in trouble no matter what. I, for one, however, do not miss him. As far as I can tell, though, he never gave me up. Watson and NT both think I provided a couple of useful tips and have never questioned me about how I figured things out. They have also never officially accused me of knowing anything, either, which I appreciate.

Although I thought Thirsty would take over that bunch, it didn't work out for them. Somehow, he didn't have whatever it was that Walter had, and they argued and fussed enough that they pretty quickly got into trouble individually and got kicked out of school.

And, speaking of criminals and people of that ilk, Slate did a pretty good disappearing act, to no one's distress, I'm sure. His story was a big item in the local news for a bit, and then he just faded away. I've never even bothered to go online to see what happened to him or where he went. Hopefully, he's in another line of work, as far from the education business as possible.

On a more positive note, Grams is doing really well. She's pretty much back to her old self. She manages to go out with Carl once in a while, and she calls Terry "My almost grandson." They don't need to jam any more, but every once in a while she calls Terry over to play for her. He always goes, but I don't think she's going to get him to play in her church, which she's hinted at more than a few times.

Terry, of course, declined the opportunity to be reunited with his mother, although he does see her when she comes for a visit. She seems to be functioning on an even keel, but Terry has too much history with her to even contemplate moving back in with her. He doesn't need the disruption in his life. He's latched on to this idea of art and music therapy and is looking for a way to try it with someone else, maybe volunteer at a nursing home or hospital or something. He's seeing a psychologist who is encouraging this, so Terry's actually talking to him.

NT finally accepted that promotion he'd been resisting. I guess he decided that having a chance to see things done right would balance out the bureaucratic foolishness that would go with the job. Of course, it may have crossed his mind that with Phillis heading off to college soon, and Hank not too far behind, a little extra income couldn't hurt.

Surprisingly enough, Frankie and Tildy are still, as they say, "an item." She's still enrolled in the community college, taking an extra class to make sure she doesn't get caught in a bureaucratic mess again. I think she's angling for a spot in a culinary school, although anyone who's eaten her cooking would swear she could teach in one. Frankie is still enrolled in the college, too. But, surprise, surprise, he finally got some direction. He's taking all these firefighting science courses and going through training to be a volunteer firefighter with the hope of getting into the academy and hired as a fire fighter.

At the beginning of the second semester in January, Crate announced that his name was Curtis. His face is still a mess, although it's probably marginally better, but I guess he wants to move on. He only glares a little at me when I forget and call him Crate. Naturally, Mel adjusted with no problem.

Hank is still waiting for the Pulitzer committee to call, I think. He's turning out interesting stories for the *Reporter*, though. He's trying to develop a story on bullying victims and their subsequent legal difficulties (the problems they end up with, not the bullies), but it's going to be hard to top his first bylined story as a freshman. He has a new girl on his arm every week or two; I balance this with my own unreasoned devotion to Mel. I don't know why, and I'm sure she doesn't either, but there it is. She is still trying to get the hang of existing in society, but, then, aren't we all, to some degree? At the end of some books and almost all movies, the "hero" usually "gets the girl." Well, I don't. I probably understand her better than most people, but I still don't get her although I'm trying. I'm still attempting to get a decent piece written for the school's literary magazine, *The Rough Rider Roundup*, but nothing's clicked yet.

You know, looking back on all this, and noticing that I seemed to lying at every step of the way when dealing with adults, I have to wonder if my story is all that accurate. I feel like it is, but then, that's probably what everyone thinks when they tell a story.

Author's Note

(A lot of real people are mentioned in this novel. As NT and Tomás would say, you could look them up.)

Aaron, Hank

Armstrong, Louis

Baldwin, James

Barbour Family

Bernstein, Carl

Carver, George Washington

Dali, Salvador

Drew, Charles

DuBois, W.E.B.

Farrakhan, Louis

Grandin, Temple

Graves, Denyce

Hughes, Langston

Johns, Barbara

King, Martin Luther, Jr.

Loving, Mildred and Richard

Malcolm X

Mark Twain

Marshall, Thurgood

McAuliffe, Christie

Morrison, Toni

Munch, Edvard

Niemoller, Martin

Obergefell v Hodges

Parks, Gordon

Parks, Rosa

Presley, Elvis Aaron

Ride, Sally

Roosevelt, Eleanor

Ruth, Babe

Thompson, Hunter

Till, Emmett

Tubman, Harriet

Turner, Nat

Walker, Madam C.J.

Washington, Booker T.

Wells, Ida B.

Wheatley, Phillis

Woodward, Bob

Made in the USA
Middletown, DE
15 November 2021